Helen Forrester was born in Hoylake, Cheshire, the eldest of seven children. For many years, until she married, her home was Liverpool – a city that features prominently in her work. For the past thirty years she has made her home in Alberta, Canada. She has travelled widely in Europe, India, the United States and Mexico.

Helen Forrester is the author of four best-selling volumes of autobiography and a number of equally successful novels. In 1988 she was awarded an honorary D.Litt. by the University of Liverpool in recognition of her achievements as an author. The University of Alberta conferred on her the same honour in 1993.

D1390652

HELEN FORRESTER

Three Women of Liverpool

Latchkey Kid

HARPER

HarperCollins*Publishers*
77–85 Fulham Palace Road,
Hammersmith, London W6 8JB

www.harpercollins.co.uk

This production 2011

Three Women of Liverpool
Copyright © Helen Forrester 1984

Latchkey Kid
Copyright © June Bhaatia 1971 and 1985

The Author asserts the moral right to
be identified as the author of these works.

ISBN 978 0 00 783487 7

Printed in Great Britain by
Clays Ltd, St Ives plc

Three Women of Liverpool

Author's Note

The author would like to thank very much the Institute of Oceanographic Sciences, Bidston Observatory, Birkenhead, the Liverpool Record Office of the Brown, Picton and Hornby Libraries, her brothers and sister, and many friends and acquaintances for supplying her with much useful information on the subject of the great May blitz on Liverpool.

It should be pointed out that this is a novel, and the sailors' canteen, the situations and the characters are imaginary. Whatever similarity there may be of name, no reference is made or intended to any person living or dead.

In the spring of 1941, Admiral Erich Raeder wrote a memo to the Führer of the German Reich, Adolf Hitler. It said:

"An early concentrated attack on Britain is necessary, on Liverpool, for example, so that the whole nation will feel the effect."

THURSDAY 1 MAY 1941

He felt better, more sure of himself, now he was back in Liverpool and had a ship again. He had a new identity card safely tucked into the old wallet his father had found for him; it was surprising how naked you felt without a piece of paper to say who you were. Robert Owen, deckhand and fiancé of Emma Thomas, once more officially existed.

The clothing the Red Cross lady had found for him, to replace his lost kit, fitted well; the brown leather jacket would keep the wind out like nothing else would. He had had his faded blond hair cut in honour of his date with Emmie and he had a present for her in the brown paper carrier he was holding. His legs had stopped shaking.

Panic had, once more, struck him when, earlier that morning, he had entered the crowded Mercantile Marine office in search of a new set of papers and a new ship. At the thought of going to sea again, he had for a moment turned to jelly. He had not really walked to the huge mahogany counter; he had been nearly lifted off his damaged feet and edged towards it by the heaving, shouting mass of drunken seamen, all trying to get attention.

The clerk on the other side of the wide counter, a pimpled youth young enough to be his son, had been unexpectedly understanding of the tall, drained-looking deckhand in front of him.

"Two days on a raft, floating around in the Channel?" he had queried incredulously. "I'd have thought there was enough shipping down there that they would have spotted you in a few minutes."

"It's a lot o' water." Robert had tried to sound nonchalant. "Corvette out of Southampton picked me up." Again, he felt the ghastly fear that his hands would lose their grip on the raft and he would slide off and drown. "I were the only survivor." Try as he would, his voice still held a quiver.

"You were lucky."

"Aye, I suppose. Anyway, t' doctor says me feet'll be all right now. He signed me off yesterday. It were the cold water that effected 'em."

"Cold can do some rotten things to you," agreed the clerk. He chewed the end of his stub of pencil and ran his finger down a list. "There's the *Marakand* loading in No. 2 Huskisson. They're short a deckhand. How about it?"

To a fisherman who, until his last disastrous voyage, had always worked in his father's smack, one ship was as good as another, so he took the clerk's proffered fountain pen and shakily applied his signature where the boy pointed with his finger. A ship was a ship, and if he were going to marry Emmie he needed the money. If he did not go to sea, he would be called up for the army – at fourteen shillings a week. Better the devil you knew than the one that you did not.

Afterwards, until he got a better grip on himself, he stood on the handsome steps of the old Customs House, his hands in his pockets, the brown carrier bag swinging from his wrist. Beside him, legs astride, hands behind his back, stood the huge policeman who kept order amongst the tough clientele of the Mercantile Marine office. The sun lit up the long row of medal ribbons on his chest, but

12

failed to soften a face with an expression that could have quelled an angry regimental sergeant-major. However, he said very cordially to Robert, "Nice mornin'. Ready for off agen?"

As Robert nodded affirmatively, the nervous twitch of his right eye was not lost on the constable and his expression returned to its usual grimness. Poor devil. Sent to sea again before he's fit, I'll bet me life. Just like the last war. He turned again to Robert and added, as if to offer some comfort, "You know, you're sometimes safer at sea than you are in Liverpool, these days, what with the air raids and all."

"Could be," Robert agreed, and then plunged down the steps, head bent to the wind, to make his way towards the gangway of the floating dock from which the ferry boats sailed across the river Mersey. There, he would meet Emmie.

With subs as numerous as cockroaches waiting for you once you'd crossed the bar, any minute could be your last. But this was also true of the hapless civilian. Air raids had been uncomfortably frequent all winter, and it worried him deeply that Emmie lived in Toxteth, within a half a mile of the much pounded dock area.

This was no way of thinking, he told himself crossly. He began to whistle firmly and winked at a very pregnant girl with a small child wrapped in her shawl. She sniffed and turned her face away from him. He grinned. Nothing like a Merseyside woman. As pretty as they come, like his Emmie with her soft voice with its Welsh inflections – and her warm body, surprisingly flexible for a middle-aged woman.

She was waiting, her face turned towards the multitude of shipping on the glittering river. A plain navy skirt flapped against thin legs and she hugged a heavy blue cardigan against her chest, while the breeze whipped at her brown curls.

"It'll ruin me set before he ever comes," she muttered despondently and tried to smooth her ruffled locks. With her long, thin face and straight, determined-looking nose made pink by the fresh air, she appeared to the casual observer to be a nondescript woman approaching middle age. But Robert Owen was certain that she was the best thing that had happened to him in his entire life.

His mother, who wholly approved of her, said that the best thing that had ever happened to Emmie was that both her parents had finally died and had thus set her free.

"Like livin' in a box all her life, poor lass," she had told her son. "Now mind you give her some freedom, share with her, like. Too many women are nought but slaveys."

He had grinned and kissed her plump rosy cheek and had promised.

While Emmie waited, she thought again of the spate of wrath which she had, that morning, suffered from her sister-in-law, Gwen Thomas; and she wondered how much longer she could endure living with her. The moment she was married she would move out and find a room on the other side of the river, a room which she could make into a little home for Robert between voyages, until the war was over and they could hope for a better place.

Gwen had been furious that Patrick, the eldest of the family which lived next door, had shot an arrow through the glass of the Thomases' back bedroom window. Then, instead of being suitably apologetic, he had calmly asked for his arrow back. Emmie had burst into laughter at the sheer nerve of the lad, and this had set Gwen off on one of her lectures about responsibility and morality, which Emmie had endured with gritted teeth. What on earth had her brother, David, ever seen in the woman? A skinny, nagging ferret, she was.

She suddenly caught sight of Robert. Gwen was immediately forgotten and she ran towards him along the gently heaving dock, her whole body aching to hold him and be held by him.

Later, when he broke it to her that he would be sailing again in a day or two, she stroked the side of his face, as if to imprint on her memory every line of it. She touched the heavy blond brows and the tobacco-stained moustache. "Dearest Robbie," she whispered, "come back safe. I can't live without you." She snuggled closer. "You know, I never had a proper sweetheart before – I never had the time or the chance."

His lips curved mischievously under his moustache. "I know," he replied. "It were the biggest shock of me life when I realised it. Did I hurt you?"

Her thin white face was suddenly scarlet. "No – well, not much." She bit her lips, and then asked shyly, "Did you mind? Me not being at all experienced, like?"

"Nay, luv." He stood up suddenly from their seat on the top deck of the ferry and pulled her to her feet. "It were the nicest thing that ever happened to me – as if you'd been waiting for me." He held her closer. "But I can tell you, my girl, you were a real fast learner, you were."

"Well, at least I'm clean – no disease, I mean." She laughed self-consciously, her lower lip between her teeth. Then she looked at him wickedly out of the corner of her eyes, a plain woman suddenly made pretty.

ii

Emmie mechanically handed twopence to the plump, untidy clippie and received her tram ticket. Now Robert was about to sail, she felt deserted, unbelievably alone. At 39, she had never expected to marry; at that age one was on the shelf. She had many times told herself that such things were not for everyone; and she had done her best to ignore her inward longings, which could make nights a sleepless misery. She had had to try to be happy that she had nursed both her parents until they died. Then, when suddenly she was free of them, she had believed that she was too old for anything but more work. Domestic work, at that.

As she sat down on the slatted wooden seat of the tram, she asked herself bewilderedly whether it was really only four months since her father had died of heart failure. He had been a regular soldier, injured in the First World War, during army manoeuvres in 1915, and subsequently confined to a wheelchair for the rest of his life. And then, within a week, her mother who had been bedridden with arthritis for twenty-three years, had followed him, as if her reason for living had gone.

With both of them to nurse, no wonder I hadn't even time to wink at the milkman or gossip with the neighbours, thought Emmie. No time – and no money, to make myself look nice enough to find a husband. She closed her eyes, as she remembered all the lifting of them, the washing for them, the repulsive tasks of caring

16

for people well-nigh helpless. And her father forever filthy-tempered and her mother so fretful and in such dire pain.

Being Mrs Forster-Harrington's daily cleaning lady and cook had been rough, too, though her grand Victorian house had been very conveniently close to Emmie's tiny row house. Every morning, since the age of thirteen, she had run backwards and forwards from it and thus earned a little to augment her father's army pension, worried all the time that while she was away her father might fall out of his chair by the window or her mother might need her chamber pot. For twenty-six years she had stoically polished and scrubbed the house, through wars and Depression, until she knew every niche in the carved newel posts, every crack between the slate kitchen tiles. She did it while kind old Mrs Forster-Harrington, dressed in black silk, sat in her drawing room like Queen Victoria and mourned the death in 1918 of General Sir Alfred Forster-Harrington.

"Gone a bit soft in the head, she had, but proper kind for all that," Emmie had confided to Robert. "When I think on it, I were real lucky to have a job — so many didn't have one. But it were all work, Robbie. I never had a minute for meself. I never been to the pictures till you took me."

"Didn't they have any friends?" asked Robert incredulously. "To visit them, while you went out?"

"Not they. Me mam always said as soldiers often don't make many friends 'cos they move so much. Years ago, one or two serving men come to see me dad for a little while — but, you know, they went away — and some of them was killed in the war." She paused,

17

and then added, "And they was both so short-tempered, they put people off, like."

After her mother's funeral, her brother, David, his wife, Gwen, and their sly, gangling 13-year-old daughter, Mari, all decorously clothed in black, had come back to Emmie's house. They had sat drinking tea in the living room, while Emmie wept out to David her fears for herself. She was panic-stricken that she did not earn enough to pay the rent and keep herself.

Gwen had sat silently sizing up the furniture in the tiny room. It's good, she had reflected. Can't buy that kind of stuff nowadays, particularly since the war began. Me best dishes would look great on the Welsh dresser. Young Mari, who had occasionally visited her grandparents in the front bedroom, had told her that there, also, the furniture was big and shiny and, therefore, probably good; David had said that the dead couple had inherited practically all of it from their parents. Now, David should inherit it, since he was the eldest; but if Emmie continued to live in her father's house, Gwen knew that David would never take the furniture from her.

While he listened to his sister's woes, David Thomas had stirred his tea with slow turns of the tin spoon. He felt tense and tired in his black Sunday suit and stiff white collar, and curiously breathless. He felt little sense of loss at his parents' death. His father had bullied him and his mother had been a nagger, though he felt sorry that she had had so much pain. Their death had, however, reawakened a strong sense of guilt regarding Emmie. He had berated himself that she had carried the whole load of his parents' invalidism, and Gwen, here, had done nothing whatever for them. He ought to have pushed Gwen harder, to take an occasional turn, so that Emmie could have gone out a bit. Emmie wasn't a bad looking woman and she had a real sweet manner with her – maybe got it from that Forster-Harrington woman. Given a chance, she might have married, and then he would not have had her on his hands now – though how any husband of hers would have put up with his parents, he could not imagine. Anyway, on his hands she was, and he knew he had to do something to get her started again.

With a slow ponderous movement, he put his spoon down in the saucer and rubbed the dark jowls of his face, while he looked out of the corner of his eye at his virago of a wife.

"Maybe I could go into service – Mrs Forster-Harrington might be glad to have me live in, now she's so old," Emmie sobbed, her pointed nose red from weeping.

"Nay. You're free now. You can do better'n that," her brother replied heavily. He was not going to see her thrown into the kind of jail that living-in domestic service could be. She'd had enough. She deserved better. "With the war on, there's a lot more work around for women now." He took a large breath and steeled himself, as he turned to Gwen. "She could have our middle bedroom for a while – till she got settled, like," he suggested.

Gwen sucked her teeth and turned a scornful glance at the dishevelled Emmie. Who wanted a plaster saint in the house? Another person to cook for?

But her husband's face reflected a stubbornness which had defeated her many a time in their married life, a woodenness which sometimes reminded her of

19

his father. She stared back at him uneasily.

David added, "She'll get work soon enough and then she can pay her shot, couldn't you, Emmie?"

Emmie gave a long shivering sigh and glanced uncertainly at Gwen. Gwen had, for the moment, put on her chapel expression, as Mari called it, a thoroughly virtuous look. It had suddenly been made clear to her how she could acquire her parents-in-law's furniture with a minimum of infighting.

"Aye," she agreed. "She can have the middle room — and there's space enough in the house, if I move our furniture round a bit, for the furniture from here."

Though very suspicious of Gwen's sudden acquiescence, Emmie said thankfully that, of course, she would pay. "And I could help you in the house," she added, as she wiped her eyes with the backs of her hands. Until she got on her feet, any company would be good company. And there was little Mari — she liked Mari.

Mari stopped munching seed-cake and unexpectedly interjected, "It would be nice if you could live with us, Auntie Emmie."

Emmie smiled waterily at her. From time to time, the child had come on her own, or with David, to see her grandparents, and Emmie had always spoiled her with a bit of cake or a sweet biscuit and a loving hug. To Mari, her aunt was easier to gossip with than her mother was. Mothers had a way of jumping on you, Mari had always thought, if you so much as said a word out of place.

With a satisfied smirk, Gwen rose, to indicate that they should leave. Once the furniture had been moved into her house, she would hold on to it; possession was nine points of the law. And if, in order to do this, she had to put up with a paying sister-in-law in the house for a while, it was cheap at the price; very different from having a couple of invalids wished on you, a fear which had haunted her all of her married life.

She sniffed. Despite the local gossips' accusations of neglect, David *had* visited his acerbic parents occasionally, and had spent good money on winter clothes and coal for them. Only Emmie had said thank you, according to David. And, she recollected bitterly, no one seemed to have ever given *her* any credit for getting by with that much less money.

iii

It proved simple to obtain work. After asking what experience she had, the employment exchange sent her to a sailors' canteen, set up in Paradise Street by a church group.

Stout, beaming Mrs Robinson, a volunteer who managed the place, was delighted to have an applicant willing to do washing up, clean lavatories and scrub floors. Furthermore, she liked the well-mannered, grey-eyed woman with a face as innocent as a nun's, yet old enough to keep young seafarers at bay.

"We have a lot of volunteers on the staff, but occasionally they don't turn up," she explained to Emmie. "Then we have to manage somehow, so we have four full-time paid people, two for each shift."

Emmie smiled and said she could cook, too. Mrs Robinson looked at the marvellous reference from the Honourable Mrs Forster-Harrington – and increased the wage offered by five shillings a week.

At seven the next morning Emmie was given a white overall and the prettiest flowered apron she had ever worn, and was sent across a small back yard to scrub two very dirty lavatories.

The yard was cobbled and was obviously much older than the buildings surrounding it; it had been adapted as a light well and was lined overhead with office windows. Little of the spring sunshine penetrated it; only a small square patch of sky far above hinted at the beauty of the day.

With her long, straight nose wrinkled in disgust, Emmie used up four pails of hot water and a whole bottle of pine disinfectant and, to the relief of the other members of the staff who had to use the ancient thrones, as well as the seamen, she had left them cleaner than they had been for half a century.

When she returned to the canteen itself, she saw that the front door was hospitably open, though round the entrance stood a wall of sandbags to protect it from blast. The two big windows facing the street had been pushed up; their panes had been criss-crossed with black tape, to minimise the danger of flying glass, and on either side big, old-fashioned shutters, their hinges well oiled, hung ready to be folded across the windows at night.

Two volunteers were wiping down the tables and chairs. They were both dressed in matching sweaters and cardigans, one in pink, the other in green. Over their tweed skirts they had tied flowered aprons similar to Emmie's. One had a string of pearls round her neck, the other a gold chain with a cross hanging from it. Though they were about the same age as Emmie, Emmie thought she had never seen two more beautiful young ladies. They greeted her cheerfully and asked her name; she did not dare to ask them their names.

Bringing with her a strong smell of sausages grilling, Mrs Robinson rushed in from the kitchen carrying a pile of clean ashtrays. "Put one of these on each table, Emmie," she ordered briskly.

"It's funny-peculiar how small things change your life," Emmie remarked to Mari later on. "All the happiness I've got came because I had to put an ashtray on a certain table. Proper queer, when you think on it."

As Emmie put down the last ashtray, two men, anxious for a late breakfast, swung themselves into chairs at the table. Both wore navy-blue turtleneck sweaters and shabby jackets over them. They grinned up at Emmie.

"Mornin', duck. What you got for brekkie?" The speaker must have been in his sixties, judging by his almost bald head fringed by tightly clipped white hair. Black eyes, like a friendly magpie's, surveyed her.

Emmie blushed slightly. "I don't know. I can smell sausages."

The other man was younger, fair-haired, with a full moustache tinged orange by tobacco smoke. He laughed, and Emmie's blush grew redder, because she felt she had given a stupid answer. Her fingers fidgeted with a corner of her flowered apron. After a second, he said to his companion, "It doesn't matter what it is, Dickie. I'm that hungry, I could eat an elephant. Had to wait hours at the bloody hospital, in spite o' being so early."

"Aye. Bring two plates of whatever's cooking," agreed his companion, taking a well-charred pipe out

23

of his pocket and then opening up an oilskin tobacco pouch from another pocket.

Emmie flashed them a shy smile and fled to the kitchen. She reported anxiously to Mrs Robinson.

Mrs Robinson paused, a half-open packet of dried eggs in her hand. Then she chuckled. "Here, take a pencil and notebook from over there, and ask them whether they want tea or coffee, bread or toast, and would they like porridge to start with."

Flustered, Emmie snatched up the notebook, while Mrs Robinson called after her, "We've got scrambled eggs, sausages and baked beans."

Emmie waited, pencil poised, until the men looked up from their conversation. Behind her, other men rolled in with the typical sailor's gait, each man's head bent slightly forward, chin tucked in, from years of living in boats' confining spaces, where heads could be easily bumped. Coughing, hawking, talking, they scraped chairs back from the tables, while the volunteers advanced purposefully, notebooks in hand.

The man with the moustache watched her curiously, as she took his friend's order; when she turned to him she found herself facing rich blue eyes, narrowed as though used to staring into sunlight. The face was weatherbeaten, lined and filled with strain. He smiled at her and she lowered her eyes modestly, as she wrote the order down. Her mother had been warning her since the First World War about being forward with men. Not that she need have worried, thought Emmie. When you're keeping house you live in a daytime world of women, children and very old men. Even the tiny shops she had patronised had been largely run by women, and her parents had never allowed her to go out at night;

when she had once or twice protested at this, her father had, in a tremendous rage, shouted her down, threatened her with his stick and told her that it was bad enough that they were left alone in the mornings while she was with Mrs Forster-Harrington and went for the groceries. Many of her neighbours were equally tied to their homes, she knew, by a horde of children, the sick or the old, and by sheer lack of a penny of their own. She submitted.

This morning, she was being rapidly surrounded by an ever increasing crowd of lively, talkative men. It felt very strange, nervously exciting.

"Tea or coffee?" she inquired of her younger customer, forcing herself to look at him. He grinned, a slow, friendly smile, which made all the sun wrinkles on his face stand out. Her heart gave an uncomfortable bounce. "Tea," he replied, and then asked, "You new here?"

"Yes," she said shyly, smiled briefly and hurried back to the safety of the kitchen. A whole lot of questions about men tumbled into her mind. Here, this very morning, she was going to meet more men than she believed she had met in the whole of her desperately narrow existence, and she really knew very little about them.

When she was a young girl and her mother was still able to move around the house a little, she had not dreamed of being tied to her parents for the rest of her life. She had hoped for a handsome sweetheart in soldier's uniform, with fine legs bound up in puttees; but her parents had kept her rigidly reined in and, very soon afterwards, the horrible battles of the First World War had taken nearly all the young men of the district, and hardly any of them returned. "Round us, there must have been three girls to every man," she guessed, as through the day she trotted patiently backwards and forwards to the tables; and once she suddenly felt sick, as she realised that the same thing was going to happen to the young girls now hoping for a husband. The young lads were again going out to die. And for what? How many men in this very room would be alive twelve months hence?

The man with the moustache came again the next morning, this time for a cup of coffee and a bun. He sat at the same table. Dickie was not with him.

Emmie snatched her notebook out of her apron pocket and scuttled across the crowded room to take his order, afraid that one of the volunteers would get there first.

"Mornin'," she greeted him shyly, wondering what had brought her to him at a run. He was sitting with his elbows on the small round table, chin resting on clasped hands. At her voice, he glanced up quickly and smiled. Despite the smile, he looked drawn and very tired.

"We got a bit o' bacon," she whispered conspiratorialy. "Would you like some?"

He had already had breakfast with his parents, out at Hoylake, but he was delighted to be specially favoured. "Ah would," he said, the smile broadening into a grin.

When he took his cup of coffee from her instead of allowing her to lay it on the table, she noticed that his hand was not too steady. The cup wobbled in the ill-fitting saucer and then tipped over. He was deluged in coffee.

She whipped a tea towel from the belt of her apron and gave it to him to wipe himself down, while they had

26

a rueful laugh together. "Lucky your trousers is navy blue," she told him. "Stain won't show."

When she brought his bill, he asked her rather diffidently if she would like to go to the cinema with him the following night.

Gwen was scandalized. "At your age!" she exclaimed. "Lettin' yourself be picked up."

Mari had giggled, and said, "It's exciting for her, Mam." Her mother's look was sufficient to freeze her into silence and, with tight lips, the 13-year-old again bent her head over her knitting.

Shaken by a series of emotions she had never expected to be able to give range to, Emmie had turned appealingly to David.

"I'm free now," she said to him, a little break in her voice. "I'm goin' to enjoy meself as much as I can."

David folded his newspaper up carefully. "And so you should," he said, regardless of his wife's grim disapproval. "Be careful who you're with, that's all."

"He's a real nice fella," responded Emmie, looking defiantly at Gwen. Inwardly, she wondered what kind of a man she had drawn out of the pack. He was certainly nothing like her father. She was trembling with nervous anticipation, as, after tea, she washed her face and did her hair. Instead of her usual bun, she rolled her long hair over a shoelace tied round her head and the result was a smooth, neat roll which framed her face; she had got the idea from a women's magazine which Gwen subscribed to. As she tucked in a few precious hairpins to make sure the roll did not slip, she wondered frantically if he were married.

Now, homeward bound on the clanging tram, she reflected fondly on the memory of that first date. There

27

had not been an air raid and they had laughed together as they stumbled round in the blacked out city. He had insisted on bringing her all the way home to her brother's house and he had actually kissed her before leaving her. With joy mixed with fear for his safety, she once more felt under her glove the small garnet-and-pearl ring which a couple of weeks back he had given her.

He had produced it shyly and had confessed when he had slipped it on to her finger, "I never thought much about getting married before – always seemed to be too much to do, fishing with me father. Prices was so bad we never made much – not enough for me to keep a wife as well. Being Methodists, me and me brothers didn't drink and we didn't dance, so we didn't meet too many womenfolk – a few neighbouring girls – but never anyone like you, Emmie. You're beautiful and I want you so bad."

They had lain in the damp April grass, amid the Meols sand-dunes, not too far from his home. Great rolls of barbed wire stretched along the beach, to protect it from possible invasion. The Home Guard, keeping their nightly watch, had left them undisturbed. Rumour had it that both the beach and the dunes were mined, but they forgot everything in their need for each other. While the sound of the waves rolling softly up the shore, and a silent sea mist drifting inland, cut them off for a little while from a world in torment, two gentle, deprived people found an ecstasy granted to few.

They lay for a long time in each other's arms, until Emmie giggled suddenly.

"I was thinkin'. Supposing I have a baby! It *could* happen, even at my age."

Robert had lifted his head and kissed her again. "Not to worry. It'll have a proper father. I wouldn't let you down, luv." He held her tightly, and then said, "If anything should happen to me before we can be married, and you're in trouble, go to me mam and dad. They'll take care of you."

"Oh, Robbie," she whispered with a sigh. "You have to come back safe."

"I'll do me best," he said, with a forced laugh. "But don't you forget. Me dad's earning enough now to keep you for a while."

She lay quiet for a moment, and then she said in a puzzled voice, "It's funny that it's taken a war to give us decent wages, isn't it?" She rolled over him until she was lying on top of him, her head on his shoulder, and then she sighed. "But I'd rather manage on poor wages and know you was safe." She felt him stir under her again and scrambled hastily to her feet. "Enough, luv, enough. I got to go to work on the morning. And you got to have the hospital check your feet again. The cold and wet you suffered on that raft must've been proper awful." She dusted down her skirt and buttoned up her blouse, looking down at him impishly. "But, you know, I wish your feet were still just a bit bad, so as we could have more time together before you have to go to sea again."

He had swung himself to his feet and caught her in his arms and kissed her long and hard. "Aye, luv, I don't want to go either."

Another time, while they sat on a bench underneath a chestnut tree in Sefton Park, she had told him about her life with her parents. He had marvelled at her patience and endurance. She had shrugged her shoulders and said, "I only did what a lot of single daughters have to

29

do – who else will look after people like that? Couldn't let them go into the workhouse. We could just manage if we all three lived together. But there wasn't nothin' left over for going to the pictures or suchlike, even if I'd had the time. We was lucky to have a low rent and something to eat each day. We'd have fair frozen to death some winters, if David hadn't bought some coal."

"It'll be easier from now on, luv," he had promised her. And she had felt indeed that a new life was unfurling for her as surely as the tiny leaves sprouting on the chestnut tree.

"Rialto Cinema," shouted the clippie, and Emmie came sharply back to the present.

iv

Gwen Thomas always averred that her life was never the same again after that young scoundrel, Patrick Donnelly from next door, had at dinnertime on Wednesday shot an arrow through the back bedroom window of their small row house.

"There was broken glass all over our Mari's bedspread. Ruined, it was," she complained angrily to Emmie and to her husband, David.

She was sick to death of her new, Irish next-door neighbours. A pack of sloths, she fumed. She had nearly choked when the 13-year-old boy had calmly knocked at her back door and had asked for his arrow back.

A small bundle of outrage, thin lips drawn back over blackened broken teeth, she had hissed back, "Arrow?

30

You ain't gettin' no arrow from me, young man. You're goin' to get a bill for seven bob for puttin' t'glass back, and I hope your dad gives you a good beatin'."

Large, calculating blue eyes, fringed with long black eyelashes, looked calmly back at her. "It were an accident, Mrs Thomas – and you could say it were blown out in the last air raid and get it mended easy." He grinned at her beguilingly, a grin that usually worked wonders with middle-aged lady teachers.

It did not work on Gwen Thomas. She wanted to strike him with the broom she was holding; but he was as tall as she was and heavily built for his age. She felt uneasily that he might hit her back. She shook a bony finger at him.

"And what good would that do me, beyond makin' a liar of meself?"

"T' city might do it for free."

She slammed the door in his face.

Bow in hand, he stood staring at the cracked black paint on the back door. All that fuss about a window, when any night the Jerries raided Liverpool hundreds of windows got broken. Old bitch.

On the way out of the tiny brick-lined yard, he gave the cages holding David Thomas's racing pigeons an angry shake. The pigeons fluttered madly round and round their prison in alarm. Next time he shot at a cat, he reckoned crossly, he should take a look at what else was in the line of flight. As his father often said, you live and learn.

"Patrick! Patrick! Coom 'ere. I want yer to go a message, afore you go back to school," he could hear his mother shouting from their kitchen. "Coom 'ere, afore I come after yez. Where are you?"

31

He dropped his bow into a corner behind the lavatory in the yard and slunk uneasily into the kitchen.

In her living room, Gwen sank on to the sofa, leaned back and flung a skinny arm across her chest. "He's started me palpitations, he has. Mari, luv, pour me another cuppa tea and bring the aspirin bottle."

Mari was just putting on her school blazer, preparatory to returning to school, but she obediently ran upstairs to her mother's bedroom to get the aspirin bottle and, on her return, poured a cup of tea from the aluminium teapot keeping warm on the hob in front of the fire.

"I don't suppose he meant to break the window, Mam," she pleaded, turning a thin, well-scrubbed face towards her mother who was lying back with her eyes closed.

Gwen ignored her plea. She shook a couple of aspirins out of the bottle, popped them into her mouth and swallowed them down with a gulp of tea. "Mind you come straight home," she told her daughter, without opening her eye. The girl slowly buttoned her blazer and, with a sour grimace towards her mother, she left for school. Palpitations! How come every time her mother fell into a fit of rage, it was called palpitations, and when she, Mari, was angry, it was called a sinful paddywack.

As she kicked a stone down the road towards school – her mother hated her to do anything so vulgar – she ruminated on the subject of Patrick. Though she was scared of him, she found him a fascinating subject for thought. Her school friends thought he was the handsomest boy in the neighbourhood and he was so excitingly wild – and a wicked Catholic, too. Only last week, at the end of the street, he had fought off three Protestant boys and left them all with bleeding noses. Cock of the walk, he was, thought Mari a trifle wistfully. But her mother's warnings about men had been drummed into her ever since she could stand, and while the other girls, Protestant and Catholic alike, giggled hopefully whenever they passed him, she held back and passed with eyes cast down, her satchel carried neatly on her back, to cover her long black plait so that boys could not pull it.

v

Emmie descended from the tram and walked briskly down a side street towards her brother's house. The wind sent bits of paper skittering before her, and a red-faced baby, which seemed to have got dust in its eyes, was wailing unhappily in a pram set outside one of the front doors. In a gutter, two small boys in brown woollen jerseys were quarrelling loudly over their coloured glass marbles.

"Evenin', Miss Thomas."

At the sound of the deep Irish voice, Emmie's lips clamped together. She half turned towards the lanky man in blue air raid warden's overalls, who had fallen into step with her. His battered old retriever, Sarge, nosed between them as if anxious not to be ignored, and she bent to stroke his dusty muzzle. "Evening, Mr Donnelly," she replied a little stiffly, uncertain how to treat him.

Patrick's father, with his shrieking wife and bevy of unwashed children, had been, according to Gwen, a no-good out-of-work until he had been made a warden. "Keeps fighting cocks, if you please. Says a bad shoulder keeps him out of the army, ha! For ever shouting at you to 'put that light out'. Never seems to miss the slightest chink in your blackout curtains. Thinks you're signalling to the Jerries if you so much as carry a candle down the yard when you got to go to the lavvie. Work? He lives the life of Riley."

For his part, Conor Donnelly regarded Gwen and David Thomas as worse than a packet of starch, with their highly polished and scrubbed house front, their ritual of Sunday clothes and chapel-going, their disapproval of little boys who sometimes got caught short and piddled on the pavement, and ate conny-onny butties while sitting on their adjacent front doorstep. Ellen Donnelly had expressed the opinion that, "Them holier-than-thou types is the worst. That Mari'll be in trouble with the boys in no time at all, at all."

Conor Donnelly could not imagine how anybody could endure such a regimented life, without even an occasional bout of drinking or fighting to break the monotony. Of course, since he had become an air raid warden he had had to mind himself a bit. He had to stay sober while on duty and be a bit careful when he was carrying stolen goods for a small group of friends who preyed on lorries serving the docks.

When he and his family had been bombed out in the previous autumn, the city had rehoused him in the empty row house next door to Mr High and Mighty David Thomas, plumber. That bombing had been a basketful, that had. Poor little Ruby, his eldest daughter, and old Sarge had been buried for nearly

34

four hours. A bloody miracle that the rest of them had been at the pictures at the time.

Miss Thomas, now she was different. She was polite to his wife and sometimes she made jokes with the kids. On Easter morning she had filled Ruby's hands with toffees – must have given her most of her ration – to share with the other kids. She was a very quiet woman, he mused, but with a bit of encouragement from the right fella she might be more lively than she appeared. His face crinkled up in a grin, as she glanced up at him. He ventured a mild joke and was rewarded by a shy laugh.

Emmie forced herself to attend to what he was saying. With his face a polished mahogany from years of inadequate washing and his long, yellow teeth, he was an oddity to her; yet his sheer bouncing gaiety was infectious and she could understand why he had been chosen as an air raid warden – he would be a real tonic if you were in trouble.

They turned towards their adjoining front doorsteps. Conor pushed open his unlocked door, while she inserted her key into her brother's carefully burnished Yale lock. Before he entered, Conor turned to point up to the sky, where a few clouds were building and a slight haze was dulling the sunshine.

"Bit o' luck and them clouds'll form a nice cover afore midnight. Should mean no raid."

"Aye. It's been over quiet lately, hasn't it? Makes you wonder what's brewing."

Conor nodded agreement. "Well, keep yer fingers crossed."

"I got to work the late shift at the canteen tonight, so I'll be up and about anyways," Emmie confided.

As usual, the slam of the Donnelly's front door caused a slight shudder to pass through the Thomases' house and rattled the wooden signboard nailed to their door. The faded board announced *David Thomas, plumber, est. 1914. Prompt attention.*

The noise immediately brought Gwen Thomas out of the back kitchen. She clucked fussily, as clearly through the dividing wall came the sound of Ellen Donnelly's strident voice above the shriek of a child. Conor's voice rumbled back.

"Really! Slammin' t' door like that! Brings all the dust down. And me just finished cleaning." Red-ringed, faded blue eyes looked impatiently up at Emmie, as Gwen licked her finger and ran it along a ledge to pick up an offending grain of dust.

Emmie hung up her coat, gas mask and handbag on the hall peg. While she nerved herself to deal with Gwen, she picked up the floppy, brown carrier bag given to her by Robert. She was always anxious not to break up her tenuous housing arrangement by letting her bitter, pent-up resentment burst forth at Gwen's never having given her the slightest help with her parents. She was grateful for David's protection and did not want to move until she was married. Though she was now paying very adequately for her lodgings and she also helped Gwen in the house, Gwen never considered it necessary to thank her and was often barely civil.

Nothing annoyed Gwen more than dust and dirt and untidiness, and her shining, neat house indicated how successfully she dealt with them. Almost invariably wrapped in a black cross-over overall dotted with blue forget-me-nots, she was a bundle of muscles. Because she kept running her fingers through her greying red hair with its tight natural curl, it tended to stand up in a wild bush. Tonight it was in particular dissarray, indicating a trying day's battle with her household gods.

"'T' glazier hasn't got no glass for Mari's bedroom window," she grumbled, as she followed Emmie into the living room, where a cheerful fire blazed in an old-fashioned cooking range gleaming with blackleading; at its side, the brass tap of the hot water tank winked in the light of the darting flames.

David Thomas was seated in his armchair beside the fire, and he looked up from his perusal of the *Liverpool Echo*. "'Allo, la," he greeted Emmie, and then he said to his wife. "I'll nail a bit o' plywood over t' window when I've had me tea. It'll be safer for Mari than glass."

"Where *is* Mari?" inquired Emmie, smiling down at her brother.

"She's away out to tea with her friend, Dorothy." Gwen clicked her tongue and reverted to her grievance. "I'll teach that lad, even if his mam won't. He'll not get his arrow back." She continued to grumble, as she went through to the back kitchen. Emmie followed her with the carrier bag.

She interrupted Gwen's tirade, by saying, "Robbie set a line while the tide was out yesterday. He caught ten whiting and he's sent you two. They feel real heavy."

"That's proper kind of him, I'm sure," replied Gwen coldly. She seized a pot of boiled potatoes and deftly drained the water from them into the sink. Through the ensuing steam, she added with a sniff, "Being engaged to a fisherman has its advantages, I suppose. T' fishmonger didn't have so much as a cod's head left today, by the time he got to me. Ever so long, the queue was."

"Well, there's the makin's of a nice dinner here," Emmie soothed.

"Humph," grunted Gwen. "Here, take the potatoes and put them on the table for me." She sighed. Provided Emmie could be prevented from taking her parents' furniture with her, she would be thankful when the woman got married and left. When the pieces had been moved into the house, nothing had been said as to the ownership; but Gwen burnished them determinedly; they were hers, because David was the eldest and should inherit.

What little Emmie said about the furniture indicated that she took it for granted that, since she had lived with it all her life, the furniture belonged to her. Besides, in the middle of a war, where else would she get furniture from for a home?

She had brought Robert home for tea one Sunday and Gwen had made it clear that she strongly disapproved of a woman of sober years suddenly marrying a man she had known less than four months. It did not occur to Emmie that Gwen had been smitten by a lingering envy of her blatant happiness, her obvious contentment.

"I must hurry," said Emmie, as they sat down to their meal. "I got to be in the canteen by seven. Mrs Robinson and the others were ever so kind about me engagement, giving me a bit of time off when Robbie was free."

Gwen responded tartly, "Well, I hope you're doing the right thing." She stirred her tea hard, in the hope of making half a teaspoonful of her sugar ration sweeten it adequately. She made a face when she sipped it. "Picking up a man like that don't seem like a good start to me."

Emmie ached to slap her.

"Now, Gwen," her husband warned. "Emmie got to know him in the canteen. That's not picking up. And he took her home to Hoylake to meet his mum and dad – quite proper. He's given her a nice ring, too."

Gwen shrugged her shoulders slightly and poured another cup of tea. Emmie kept her eyelids down and wondered if Gwen had ever been in love with poor David – or with anything except the shiny aspidistra in the front room or the bronze soldiers looking down at them from the living room mantelpiece.

To distract Gwen, David said, "I'll get me tools and do Mari's window."

That brought Gwen back to her favourite complaint – the Donnellys. "We ought to have moved from here years ago – the whole of Toxteth's gone to pot. The minute Mrs Tasker died next door I knew we'd never get decent neighbours again."

"House were empty for months. T' landlord held out for too high a rent." David gritted his teeth as he pushed away his empty plate.

"Oh, aye. And how does he pay seventeen shillings a week on an air raid warden's wages, I'd like to know. Maybe it's true that he's hand in hand with a gang o' dock thieves."

"Gwen!" David was shocked. "That's just idle gossip. Because he sometimes has lipsticks or silk stockings for sale? He could buy 'em easy from a

merchant seaman on the New York run. It don't make
'im a thief."

vii

The sharp wail of the air raid siren made David
jump. He had been washing himself in the kitchen sink,
in preparation for going to bed, and he stood in his
undervest and trousers while he dried the back of his
neck. He was numb with fatigue after a long day
working on the intricacies of the plumbing of the Royal
Infirmary, and he felt again a small, choking pain in
the middle of his chest, a pain that had been bothering
him occasionally for a couple of weeks.

"Blow them," he muttered, and hastily finished
drying himself.

He leaned over the sink to pull back the blackout
curtain and look out of the window. There was enough
moonlight to cast a shadow of the house across the
back yard. Behind the neighbouring chimneys,
searchlights suddenly sent seeking fingers across a
starry sky. It was much too light for safety. He
dropped the curtain into place, making the flame of the
candle on the drainboard dance, as Gwen came
hurrying from the living room. She carried a steaming
kettle in one hand, and the warning had obviously
flustered her.

"For goodness' sake, get your dressing-gown on and
something on your feet. We'll have tea on the cellar
steps. What a nuisance they are."

As she flung two teaspoonsful of tea into the pot,
she went on anxiously, "Our Mari's not in yet, from

40

Dorothy's. She's real late. I'll have to have a word with that young lady."

"I could go and fetch her," David offered, without much conviction.

"No. It'd just mean two of you out in the flak. You get out the blankets and cushions and take them on to the cellar steps, while I do the tea tray." She jumped suddenly, as the steady boom-boom of anti-aircraft fire made the windows rattle. Sometimes the guns sounded more menacing than the bombs did.

David would have been thankful to crawl into bed and risk being blown out of it. He did not feel, however, that he could go to bed while Mari was still not home, so he obediently arranged the cushions on the cellar steps, for them to sit on. With the slope of the staircase overhead, this spot offered good protection and the least likelihood of being crushed.

With a sigh, he sat down and arranged a blanket over his knees. While Gwen held the tea tray a little high, he tucked another blanket round her. He took the candle from the tray and set it on a small shelf above their heads. Gwen scolded, "Be careful, stupid. You'll upset the tray." She stirred the pot balanced uncertainly on the tray on her lap, while he listened for the battery to start firing in nearby Princes Park; the sound would indicate to him how close the raiders were. Beyond the rumble of more distant guns, however, all he heard was Donnelly's front door slam. Likely, Donnelly was in for a busy night.

Gwen's lips curled. "That'll be him goin' down to the wardens' post. Bangin' the door, as usual. No manners, that man."

Their own front door slammed. Quick footsteps ran

along the narrow, linoleumed passage, then stumbled through the dark living room and into the kitchen.

"That you, Mari? Come on down, quick now."

Mari was panting, as she whipped a cushion off the shelf and almost slithered down the concrete steps, her long bare legs flashing white in the candlelight.

She sat down close to her mother. Like many families seeking refuge in this safest corner of the house, they always sat very tightly together, so that if the building was hit they either died or survived together.

Gwen felt her trembling and lifted down the candle to have a closer look at her. The girl's face was blenched and her eyes stared unblinkingly at her mother from behind the candle flame.

"There, there, luv. No need to be scared. You're safe home now," she told the girl quite gently.

Her father turned towards her and added reassuringly, "It don't sound as if they're interested in the south end of the town tonight."

Above them, a number of aeroplane engines throbbed increasingly loudly.

"They'll be some of ours," David declared authoritatively. "Always know the difference by the sound o' the engines."

His words were immediately belied by a shrieking whistle passing over them. Instinctively, they ducked and flung their hands over their heads for protection. The tea tray on Gwen's lap rocked perilously. There was a moment of silence: then a deafening explosion which shook the whole house above them. They waited, like rabbits hiding in a thorn bush from a fox. A piece of plaster plopped from the ceiling on to the tray, and a cloud of thin dust enveloped them.

42

Mari buried her face against her mother's bony legs and whimpered in terror. The next bomb in the rack would hit them; she knew it. It would be a judgment on her for what she had allowed Patrick Donnelly to do to her.

He had been bothering her for weeks, touching her when she passed him, holding her against the wall of the alley one day, when she had run down it to visit Dorothy; not hurting her, just making her feel funny when he pressed himself against her. It had been most funny-peculiar, because, despite all her mother's warning about not letting a man come near her, she had wanted him to remain close. Perhaps the warning didn't apply to boys, she argued to herself.

Tonight, he had pushed her into a street air raid shelter, which nobody used except as a urinal. He had held her tightly against the wall and her silent struggles had been of no avail against his considerable weight. When in scared despair, she had stopped wriggling, he had lifted her skirt and gently stroked between her legs. And she knew now that she was on her way to hell. It had felt wonderful, incredible; and he had laughed when, not understanding the driving impulse, she had put her arms round him. He had said it was nothing to what he could do. If that was nothing, she decided without really knowing why, it was a good thing that the air raid warning had begun to shriek and that they had both run for home.

Now the bombs were falling all around her. God must be very angry with her.

"Incendiaries! Incendiaries!" Conor Donnelly could be heard, calling his firewatchers to the street.

Despite his wife's protests, David insisted on going

out in his dressing-gown to check his roof, back and front. He came back very soberly and hauled the blanket round himself again. "Looks like the whole town's alight. Hope our Emmie's all right." Then to his crouching daughter, he said, "Don't take on so, Mari. Everything's going to be all right. We're quite safe here on the steps."

You don't know what a wicked daughter you've got, thought Mari, not lifting her head from her mother's knee. God could do anything to us tonight.

viii

As the guns in Princes Park began to roar, Ellen Donnelly finished spreading the washing on her wooden airer in her living room and then heaved the heavy rack up to the ceiling again and tied the rope firmly to hold it there. The clothes began to drip depressingly onto the rag rug below and onto the otherwise bare floor. A few droplets reached baby Michael asleep in a battered easy chair. She edged the chair away from under the rack and flung her black woollen shawl over the sleeping child.

There was a quick patter of bare feet on the stairs, and her eldest daughter, Ruby, still in her clothes, dashed into the room. She was brought up short by the sight of her mother seating herself calmly on a wooden chair in front of the fire.

"Mam, shall I bring Brendy and Nora down? The guns sound awful." Her voice was tightly constricted, as she tried to control her panic. After the dreadful experience of being buried in the ruins of their former

44

home, the sound of the air raid warning always brought her close to a bout of hysterics. Her breath came in tight gasps and, from under a fringe like a Skye terrier's, eyes gleamed with tears.

"Aye, luv. Coom 'ere." Her mother held out a stout red arm to her and thankfully the skinny 12-year-old cuddled close to her heavy breast. "It ain't likely we'll be bombed again."

The guns continued to growl and, after a minute, Ellen said, "Let's have a look-see outside. Then we'll decide if we should bring t' kids down." She rose, and went to the front door, Ruby trotting closely behind her for comfort.

With a strong, red hand on either door-post, she leaned out as far as she could. The wind caught her untidy mop of shoulder-length hair and flapped her long black skirt. Metronomic searchlights flicked back and forth across the sky as if to time the drumming guns, and high in the heavens a bright flare floated gently; it silvered the slate roofs of the close-packed houses, gave a halo to a church spire and outlined the solid mass of a nearby tenement building.

"Reckon they're doin' Wallasey and Birkenhead tonight," she opined comfortingly. "Quite away from us. We'll let the kids rest for a bit. You come and sit by the fire with me and we'll have a drop of your dad's whiskey."

Ruby did not like the taste of whiskey, but since the disastrous raid which had robbed them of their home, her mother had often given her a teaspoonful of it, and it made her feel better. Now, she went to the dying fire to warm her bare feet, while her mother tried to guess where Donnelly's latest hiding-place for the bottle might be. In such an empty home there were not many places to look.

She found it on the windowsill, behind the blackout curtain, and she sat down while she eased out the cork. Ruby came to lean against her. The glow from the fire lit up their faces, as they solemnly took a sip each from the bottle. Then Ellen took a good gulp, and gasped as it caught her throat. She laughed and set down the bottle under her chair and again put her arm round Ruby.

The front door was flung open. Patrick strolled slowly in, determined to show that he was not afraid of air raids. A cool breeze followed him in.

"What you bin up to?" Ellen inquired truculently. "You're lookin' too pleased with yourself by far."

"Haven't bin doin' nothin'." The satisfied grin on his face belied his words, but she knew from experience that she would get no more out of him.

A screaming whistle overhead wiped the grin from Patrick's face, but, hands in pockets, he stood his ground, while Ruby clung shrieking to her mother. Blast swung the front door hard open and shook the old house. The blackout curtains billowed like sails in a sudden gust. A mass of soot descended the chimney, obliterated the fire and covered all of them in black dust. Little Michael, covered by his mother's thick shawl, continued to sleep, but from upstairs came frightened howls.

Ellen wiped the soot off her mouth. "God's curse upon the buggers!" she cried, and bent down to reach for the whiskey bottle.

A piece of debris landed on the roof with a sharp crump; then, for a moment, unearthly quiet.

A nerve-racking clatter in the street and the familiar

sound of her husband's running feet caused Ellen to burst out again, "Incendiaries, blast 'em!"

Patrick went to the door. The darkness was broken all along the street by sparks hissing from the small, vicious fire bombs. Dark shadows carrying sandbags ran to dowse the scary, sizzling devils, and one or two bravely tried to put them out by holding dustbin lids over them. Patrick seized one of the sandbags in the hall and ran gleefully out to help.

Opposite, a furious Bridget Mahoney flung up the empty frames of her bedroom window, sat out on the sill with her back to the street and struck out with a broom at an incendiary which had lodged in the gutter of her home. She managed, after a few wild shots, to hook it out and it fell into the street, where Patrick pounced on it happily and covered it with sand. Bridget eased herself back into her bedroom.

"Ow!" she exclaimed, as she caught her arm on a jagged piece of glass left in the window-frame. The blood gushing out looked black in the moonlight. Hastily she picked up her discarded apron from the bedroom chair and wrapped it tightly round the wound.

Early the next morning, a sympathetic Ellen Donnelly bathed off the apron stuck on the deep, ugly cut and rebandaged it tightly with a bit of an old pillowslip brought by Bridget. Afterwards, they finished the rest of Conor Donnelly's whiskey and, despite the pain, a fulminating Bridget went off to work in a large garage, where she spent her days sewing aeroplane canvas. As usual, her little boys went to school with clean hands and faces, and stomachs full of porridge.

About ten o'clock, an exhausted Conor arrived home. He was covered in dust from working on the results of a direct hit on a dairy three streets away. "Three dead – and twelve cows spattered all over," he informed his sleepy wife. He went straight to the window and flicked back the half-drawn blackout curtains. "Where's me whiskey?"

"Me and Bridget Mahoney drank it," his wife said dully. "She were hurt." She was holding Michael to her breast and he was sucking eagerly. She did not look up.

In two strides her husband reached her. He struck her hard across her plump face. Then he stumbled upstairs to their bed and flung himself on to it.

ix

To alleviate the excruciating boredom of raidless nights, the clerks and shop assistants on fire guard duty in the buildings near the sailors' canteen would take it in turns to nip into the canteen for coffee. Mrs Robinson had once remarked that they complained when nothing happened and then they complained when there was a raid. "Then they're scared stiff, poor souls," she added.

Emmie had looked up at some of the steeply sloping roofs along which a firewatcher might have to clamber to get at a fire, and had been thankful that up to now the regular canteen staff had been excused from fire-watching.

Tonight, she entered the canteen through the narrow side passage which led into the light well at the rear. The light well was already shadowing and she fingered the long hat pin she kept under her coat lapel, until she had slipped through the kitchen door. You never knew who might be lurking at night in such a gloomy place as a light well, she told herself. A hat pin was a girl's best defence.

She greeted Doris, another paid member of the staff, who was shaking up a huge basket of potato chips above a vat of fat. Near her, with a bulging sack between them sat two volunteers patiently peeling and slicing further supplies for her. One lady dropped a handful of irregularly sliced chips into a bucket of water, and moaned, "This must be the most unromantic job in the whole war."

Emmie had lost some of her awe of these well-dressed ladies, and she teased them. "Now what would the boys out there do without chips? They couldn't go on without your chips. Proper miserable they'd be."

The volunteer nodded her head in rueful agreement and picked up another potato between her beautifully manicured nails. Then she chuckled. "You're quite right – they all seem to keep going on chips."

Emmie took her new lipstick from her handbag and clumsily outlined her lips in front of the kitchen mirror. She grimaced at the uncertain result. "Painted women are the devil's children," Gwen had told her. She smiled at herself in the mirror.

After years of having only Mrs Forster-Harrington to talk to, Emmie was happy in the company of the canteen staff. The customers were usually fun, too, she thought, though she did not always understand the jokes they made; and she was sure that to many she was only a pair of chapped hands bringing plates of food.

As she closed the wooden shutters over the big kitchen window looking out at the light well and then slotted the iron bar across them, she thought wistfully of Robert in his new ship. Perhaps after the war, when he could go back to being an inshore fisherman again, he could be at home more often, depending only on the time of the tides for his trips in and out.

She went to attend to a small window on the same wall. Carefully she drew a pair of old grey velvet curtains over it. Then she lifted the telephone off the table nearby and tucked it tightly against them, so that cracks of light would not show at the curtain hem. She had never in her life used a telephone and regarded it with some deference; Mrs Forster-Harrington had felt it unnecessary to have such an intrusion upon her privacy.

Despite the wail of the air raid siren, a steady buzz of conversation came through the thick tobacco smoke. Liverpudlians are not easily stopped in mid-argument, she reflected with a little smile. The men's aplomb lessened her own fear, and she bustled round her tables as if nothing unusual was happening outside.

In the kitchen, Doris stood clutching the edge of the pig bin in which all the kitchen scraps were kept for feeding pigs. She was trembling violently, her lined face as white as the tiles on the walls. She had lost home, husband and children in the Christmas air raids the previous year and the memory was still agonisedly fresh.

Lady Mentmore, a countess, lifted her beringed hands from the washing-up water and went to comfort her. Not by even the flicker of an eyelid did she show her own nervousness.

The gunfire was heavy and the quick thump-thump of bombs hastily discharged was unnervingly close. From a table in the corner near the kitchen door came the piercing sweet sound of a mouth organ. Almost

50

immediately a strong tenor voice joined in with the words, *She'll be comin' round the mountain when she comes*. There was a general roar of voices raised to sing what she would be wearing when she came, and Emmie tut-tutted to herself, as she dried dinner plates at record speed for the countess. What would Lady Mentmore think of such naughty words, worse than anything she had heard since she left school? Proper wicked little boys' words they were. Through the open door, she glimpsed the men's faces, red from exposure or yellow from too much confinement below decks. They glowed with pure mischief as they thought up new verses, each bawdier than the last. Doris gave the countess a watery smile and the countess unexpectedly chuckled.

The canteen closed at midnight, but most people there stayed on until the All Clear sounded about one o'clock. The volunteers murmured that they hoped all the ferry boats had not been sunk. "You can't walk on water," one laughingly remarked. Doris hoped the trams out to Bootle would still be running, and Emmie, who could walk home, hoped fervently that she would not be accosted by thieves, because she had just been paid. She transferred her pay packet from her handbag to her coat pocket and checked that her hat pin was still under her lapel; too many petty thieves, either singly or in small gangs, haunted the ill-lit streets and she was always nervous.

The light of the fires in the city made the shadows of the buildings still standing look even blacker than usual. She glanced at the sky. It was flushed in several directions and the smell of burning tobacco and smouldering rubber was thick in the air. Service vehicles of various kinds, with shaded headlamps, moved like dark ghosts. Except for two drunks helping each other along, there seemed to be no pedestrians. She began to run.

FRIDAY, 2nd MAY 1941

At half-past one on Friday morning, when Emmie let
herself into her brother's house, an overwhelming smell
of soot greeted her, but when she had lit a candle in the
hallway, she was thankful to see that everything looked
much as usual. She went straight upstairs, undressed
and crept thankfully into bed.

At six o'clock the sound of Gwen's alarm jerked her
awake, and she heard Mari next door clamber out of her
creaky bed. Yawning, she crawled out herself, poured
water from her ewer into a hand-basin on the
wash-stand and splashed her face with it.

As she dried herself with a worn white towel, she
whipped back the blackout curtains and saw a cheerful
sun in a pale blue sky. Behind the houses across the
back alley, the sky was flushed, but she argued hopefully
to herself that it could be because the sun had not long
risen. She hurried into an old cotton frock.

In the living room, the curtains were already drawn
back, and David Thomas was kneeling on the hearth
rug, clearing the ashes and soot from the hearth. "'allo,
la," he greeted her amiably, between small, persistent
coughs. "Proper mess, eh? Soon get t' fire goin',
though."

Emmie agreed. Every stick of furniture was covered
with a fine film of soot. It clung to the bronze Roman
soldiers ornamenting each end of the high mantelpiece;
it had coated the net curtains at the window and the
fancywork runner across the middle of the table; even
the four precious oranges in the fruit bowl on the

sideboard were black. Gwen was going to be hard to live with today, she thought wryly.

David gave a sudden enormous sneeze and little puffs of soot rose round him.

Emmie clicked her tongue. "I'll get the floor cloth and wipe down the table and chairs, so as we can have brekkie," she said briskly. "Has the milk come?"

"I haven't looked."

Emmie went to the front door and peeped out. No milk bottle sat on the doorstep. "Well, I'm blowed," she exclaimed. "He's never missed before, not even in the Christmas blitz. I'll have to open a tin. Gwen's not going to like that."

Where the dairy once had stood, the milkman and his twelve cows lay neatly shovelled into bags, awaiting transport.

As she worked the tin-opener into a tiny tin of Nestle's milk, Emmie asked, "Did you have any incendiaries up here?"

"Aye. Had to put 'em out with sand. Woman who stores the stirrup-pump wouldn't open her door. Keeping the pump for herself, she was, in case her own house caught fire."

"That's proper awful."

"It was. I hope the warden gives her what for, today."

David, in clean overalls, was dispatched on time to the Royal Infirmary, where he was still repairing the plumbing damaged in the Christmas raids. A dreamy Mari was slapped by Gwen for not getting on with washing herself at the kitchen sink, scolded for not eating her cornflakes and was sent to school comparatively free of soot smudges.

With endless buckets of hot water and small amounts

56

of the irreplaceable, rationed soap, Emmie spent the morning washing down every nook and cranny of the living room and Gwen's bedroom, which was the only bedroom with a fireplace. The blackout curtains were taken into the back yard, put over the clothes-line and beaten, the net ones were washed and hung out to dry. The fireplaces were blackleaded and the oranges carefully scrubbed with a nail brush. Gwen herself sprinkled tea-leaves over the red, Belgian carpet in the sitting room and solicitously brushed it, remembering sadly the number of weeks it had taken her to pay for it, shilling by shilling. The china ornaments on the mantelpiece were lovingly bathed in the kitchen sink, the various messages printed on them in gilt twinkling *A present from Blackpool* or *Greetings from Llandudno* through the soapsuds. Gwen nearly cried. Lovely holidays those had been. She wondered when they would be able to go to the seaside again.

One of the whiting which Robert had caught made a consolingly large fish pie, some of which Gwen, Emmie and Mari ate at lunchtime. The rest was put away for David's tea.

Gwen reminded Emmie that she was due at Blackler's Store at one o'clock, to help in Dress Materials. She was very proud that she went to work two afternoons a week. Just before lunch, she changed into her best black dress, with its neat white lace collar, and her Sunday black stockings and shoes.

After she had left and Mari had returned to school, Emmie filled the kitchen bowl with hot water dipped from the oven tank beside the living room fire, stripped herself in the back kitchen and washed herself all over, in an effort to remove streaks of soot. Gwen did not encourage such scrubbings in the bedrooms – it made too many splashes on the polished linoleum.

ii

Next door, a sullen, resentful Ellen fried up some boiled potatoes and an egg and shoved them in front of her husband seated at the table. Conor was unusually quiet as he ate the food. When Ellen sat down by the fire, picked up 3-year-old Michael and gave him her breast, he stared past her, as if he were looking at something behind her.

The youngster suckled contentedly and Ellen enjoyed the physical pleasure of it, but finally her husband's oppressive silence became too much for her.

"What's to do with yez?" she asked sulkily.

He poked listlessly at his fried egg and sighed heavily. "It were a bad night, last night. The dairy were a shambles – blood everywhere – from the cows mostly. And them two women in Plum Street – bits of one of 'em hanging from the tree out front."

"Jesus Mary!" exclaimed Ellen. She shuddered, and Michael lost her nipple and complained fretfully. Her anger at Conor's striking her was forgotten in fascinated contemplation of this horror. She pushed her nipple back into Michael's mouth. "Maybe t' Nazis won't come again," she tried to comfort.

"There's nuthin' to stop 'em. 'specially at night. Play ducks and drakes they can." He contemplated a piece of grey potato on the end of his fork. "T' kid at the corner house 'as got a broken arm and bruises all over – part of the roof fell in on 'im. His dumb cluck of a mother left him in bed 'stead of bringing 'im down to the cellar."

"Poor little divil." She hugged her child closer and remembered, with a tremor, how close she had come to losing Ruby. What an evening that had been. The rest of the family had returned from a Christmas visit to the local cinema, to find the rescue men just hauling her out, unscratched, from under the kitchen table, which her grandfather had fashioned from oak fifty years before. She wondered idly if, when he had made it so solidly, he had had an intimation that it would save a life. Bless the sainted man. And God preserve her from another night like that.

iii

When Emmie descended from the tram, at her usual Church Street stop, on her way to work that afternoon, the traffic seemed nearly as busy as usual, though everywhere there was a strong smell of burning, and there was a general haze in the sky.

At the door of the canteen, she bumped into Doris, who promptly complained, "Me pore feet. Had to walk all the way to Bootle last night. Not a tram working. Bloody miles."

When Mrs Robinson and two volunteers arrived, they also looked tired after being up half the night, though all three were immaculately dressed. One of the volunteers, Mrs Starr, said, "I thought I was going to be late. We lost all our windows and I've been hammering old rugs over the downstairs ones ever since daybreak. First time I've ever used a hammer!"

59

Emmie listened to the lament. Did the stupid woman imagine that they had all been able to spend the morning in bed? In her opinion, complaining never did any good. You just took what life threw at you and did the best you could.

When the siren went, Emmie was busy serving a surge of men who had just come in after the closing of the public houses.

"Blow it," she exclaimed irritably, and some of the men made obscene gestures towards the ceiling. They were none of them drunk – publicans spread their meagre consignments of beer and spirits too thinly for anyone to achieve that happy state – but they were loquacious. Some of the language they used, as they consigned all Germans to Kingdom Come, made Emmie wonder innocently to Doris how Robert managed not to pick up such words.

Doris, trying to be brave, laughed shakily. "There never was a sea-going man what couldn't swear – your Robbie knows his manners, that's what it is."

While she doled out fish and chips – a little fish and a lot of chips – Emmie meditated on Doris's remark and realised that there was a side of her beloved which she did not know much about. For a minute or two, the sickening loneliness she had felt when her mother's coffin had been lowered into her grave was revived; and her new world of Robert Owen and the canteen seemed suddenly distant and alien.

As she cleared a table hastily evacuated by the buildings' firewatchers when they had fled back to their posts, there was a high-pitched swish-swish overhead.

Emmie froze. For a second all conversation stopped. The tiny silence was succeeded by a tremendous roar.

The room shook and the electric lights dipped. Everyone looked towards the ceiling.

A tumbling rumble announced the descent of the debris flung up by the explosion. Another roar, another series of rumbles.

Emmie stood terrified, the crockery rattling on her tray, as the guns began to answer the challenge of the planes.

"Put your tray down, luv, or you'll break everything." Deckie Dick, the friend of Robert's who had breakfasted with him on the morning he had first met Emmie, took the tray from her and put it back on the table. "Those two was away over ..." he began.

His voice was drowned by a crash that numbed her ears. His arms went round her and she was clamped against an old navy sweater that reeked of perspiration, as he sought to protect her face and head. In the kitchen, Doris screamed.

"Phew! That was near." Deckie Dick slowly let her go and she giggled nervously. As the guns continued their steady tattoo, a man at the next table chipped Dick, "You never misses a chance with the girls, do you?" Dick gave him a playful punch on the head, and Emmie slipped away to continue her clearing of tables.

Another crash, somewhere at the back of the building, brought Mrs Robinson running from the kitchen. "Gentlemen, there is a shelter downstairs. Take the staircase to the left of the front door. I think it would be a good idea ..." She was cut off by a series of appalling crashes, when again all faces automatically looked up at the ceiling. A crack zipped across it, but it held.

"Come on, lads. Everybody downstairs. Come on."

Deckie Dick began to move amongst the tables, touching men on their shoulders and pointing to the staircase. He turned to Mrs Robinson. "Get your ladies down, missus. It's going to be a bad night."

Without a word, she hastened back to the kitchen, where Doris was trying not to have hysterics in front of a pile of fish which she had been flouring. The fish was now covered with heavy dust.

Outside, fire engines raced pell-mell through the darkness, amid the shrill blare of burglar alarms set going in the shaken buildings opposite. Boots pounded past the front door, as rescue crews and air raid wardens ran by.

The customers no longer felt the need to look brave; the pandemonium outside was bad enough to justify a retreat, and they followed the volunteers down to the basement as fleetly as they would have abandoned a sinking vessel. Mrs Robinson, white-faced captain of her little ship, refused to descend until everyone was safely down. Then she quietly followed her crew.

At the foot of the stairs, she closed a very ancient, heavy door, bound with iron, hung there, presumably, to keep out eighteenth-century thieves and rioters. As she lowered the iron latch, she heard the upstairs front windows and shutters blow in, and the tinkle of slivers of glass sweeping across the canteen, to bury themselves in walls and tables. The blast reversed itself and blew outwards, causing a resounding crash of crockery from the tables. There was a muffled bang, when the shutters hit the empty window-frames again.

"Pooh!" she exclaimed. "Just in time." She sank down thankfully on one of the timeworn school benches which had been provided as seating.

The shelter was a windowless cellar, used for years for the storage of coal to heat the building. Its only entrance, other than the stairs, was a pavement light of heavy glass set in an iron frame. This could be swung upwards to facilitate the delivery of sacks of coal; in the construction of the shelter, it had been left as it was. A simple bolt on the inside held it down and it would form a convenient escape hatch from the basement to the street in the event of fire. Though the walls had been freshly whitewashed and the floor well swept, there was still a smell of coal. As a first line of defence against fire, a stirrup-pump with several buckets of water stood in a corner. In another corner was a small table; on it lay an electric ring and a clutter of much used tea-making apparatus. A single bulb hanging, unshaded, from the centre of the ceiling provided the only light.

Some of the men stood around smoking, while others slouched on the benches. Four of them sat cross-legged on the floor and prepared for a long wait by dealing out a pack of cards. The two volunteers sat primly together, backs straight; two middle-class women determined to be stoical.

A shivering Emmie sat by Doris with her arm round her. The bombed-out woman was sobbing quietly to herself, tears glistening on her rouged cheeks.

"Have a cigarette, me duck. It'll calm you."

A tall, thin seaman, a cigarette wobbling at the corner of his mouth, squatted down in front of Doris and generously proffered a precious packet of Player's. "You like one, luv?" he asked Emmie.

Doris smiled wanly, but made no move to take a cigarette. "Neither of us smoke," Emmie responded for both of them. "Ta, all the same."

The man turned back to Doris. "Well, you start. You're the woman that was bombed out, wasn't yez?"

Doris's eyes clenched shut. She nodded agreement.

"You should smoke. It helps. See, I'll show you how."

Her mind diverted, Doris opened her eyes. He was not a young man and bore all the marks of years of seagoing, of rotten food and working in cramped spaces. He grinned and lit a cigarette for her, drew the first breath on it and handed it to her. "There y'are, luv," he said, his sallow, hollow-cheeked face compassionate.

Emmie watched him wonderingly, captivated by his easy goodwill. Really, she thought, men *can* be kind; and she remembered, for a second, her father's unremitted bad temper. Who else, of the male sex, had she really known, other than him – and stolid, dull David? They had been no particular recommendation for their sex. She had taken Robert purely on trust; and how lucky she had been. The squatting seaman wondered why she suddenly smiled so sweetly.

While Doris cautiously puffed at her first cigarette, the barrage of noise persisted, as in steady waves the Luftwaffe swept over the doomed port. They were guided, at first, by the fires started the previous night and then by huge conflagrations which now began to flare in every direction. Far down the river, the flames' reflection danced on the water, lit up the rooms of suburban homes and warned ships at sea not to cross the bar. Forty miles away, in the Isle of Man, residents peeped between their bedroom curtains, to watch the blaze on the horizon mount higher and higher. "Liverpool's getting it again," they told each other in shocked whispers, so as not to wake the children.

In the shelter, two young deckhands who had drunk a

lot of beer decided that they must go to the lavatory. In a brief lull in the noise outside, they ran up the stairs, across the littered canteen, out through the kitchen door to the cobbled light well, where stood the ancient loos. As they relieved themselves, they look fearfully back over their shoulders through the open doors. What had once been, long ago before the offices had been built round it, the courtyard of a rich merchant's house now seemed to be a deadly funnel, down which bits of debris, shrapnel and occasional sparks travelled with unnerving rapidity. After a quick peek through the empty window facing the street, they were thankful to get back to the shelter.

"Proper shambles out front," one of them reported. "Beams and wires and stones scattered all over. Them last ones must've hit real close."

One of the card players looked up from his seat on the floor, pushed his plug of tobaco into one cheek and said, with a faint sneer, "Don't need a crystal ball to know they're close. Listen to 'em now."

"Ah, shut yer gob," retorted the returned youngster, hitching his braces up under his jacket.

"Now, gentlemen, this is no time to get upset," Mrs Robinson interjected hastily, having no illusions regarding the shortness of tempers amongst her usually overwrought, seagoing customers.

The young man made a wry face at Mrs Robinson and drifted over to the other side of the room, while the man on the floor muttered irritably, "Think they're bloody heroes every time they go to pee."

The second young man had kept his mouth shut, but now he said, with a tinge of wonderment in his voice, "There's a WVS canteen parked at the corner. T' women's doling out tea and sandwiches as if they was in their parlours at home. Feedin' the firemen, I think they are. Ordinary women just like me mam. And the flak flying round 'em like confetti."

A fast salvo of bombs nearly deafened them. Everybody crouched, hands over heads, fully expecting to be buried. When they found they had survived, they ruefully rubbed piercingly painful ears. From the ceiling, whitewash snowed gently.

Suddenly, all heads were raised; all noses sniffed. Smoke. The smell of burning wood was unmistakable. Fear jumped from one face to another. Some people rose quickly to their feet. Doris whimpered, and Emmie felt a rising panic.

"Hold it. No point in getting scared." Deckie Dick got up and put his pipe into his trouser pocket. "I'll nip upstairs and take a dekko for you. If I call, you come up orderly, mind."

The men quickly made a passage for him. Elderly, well-known and with forty years of seagoing experience spanning the First World War, he commanded respect. He ran swiftly up the stairs, the deck of cards which gave him his nickname bulging in his back trouser pocket.

The crowd relaxed slightly as, above the now more distant rumbles from outside, they could hear him working his way through the tumbled furniture of the canteen overhead. The back door slammed, indicating that it was still on its hinges.

Nothing was burning in the light well, though it was smoky. In the flickering light of fire reflected in the remaining windows of the offices across the street, he made his way to the front door with its protective sandbags. He flattened himself against the battered wall of sandbags, as a whistle sounded overhead. A huge explosion from South Castle Street sent shock waves running, and his ears rang. He listened, as intently as his hurt ears allowed. The throb of engines seemed to come from a greater distance, but in the street the smoke was thickening rapidly. Taking a big breath, he ran across the street and looked back up at the roof of the building housing the canteen. There was no sign of its being on fire, though it was outlined against a scarlet sky. The buildings on either side also showed no hint of fire.

He raced back across the road and down the steps again to the shelter. He reported, panting, "T' smoke's nothing, as far as we're concerned," and then paused to get his breath while another series of detonations drowned him out. Emmie felt her courage draining from her and she and Doris clung to each other. He continued, "There's some big fires not far away – and I could hear machine guns for a minute. Bloody Boche going for the firemen." He looked at the anxious faces surrounding him. "If we try to move, like as not we'll walk into more trouble. I'd say stay here." He sat down suddenly on a bench, aware that he was no longer as young as he had been. He looked down at his shabby boots, while men slowly resumed their seats.

When his heart had stopped racing, he said diffidently, "Think I'll walk up Lord Street and see what's to do. T' rescue squads must be hard-pressed at the back there. Anybody want to come?"

The men stopped their subdued gossiping and looked uneasily at Dick, and Dick said, "Them as has wives and kids, maybe you shouldn't. A couple of you is perhaps like me – you can please yourselves."

"My family is killed in Antwerp," said a melancholy Dutch voice from the far end of the room. "Who to rescue? This is shops and offices round here. Nobody here." He got up, a big, handsome blond man towering over most of those present.

"There's firewatchers and caretakers in every building," replied Dick simply. "Young girls, some of them watchers is."

Two men in naval uniform stood up and the four of them, without a further word, eased their way through to the staircase. Not to be outdone by the Royal Navy, two merchant seamen followed them.

Mrs Robinson said brightly, "As soon as the raid is over, we'll see if we can clean the canteen up, ready for business tomorrow."

The women nodded tired agreement. Emmie was stiff with fatigue and the enforced idleness; the worst thing about air raids was, she thought, that you couldn't hit back.

The electric light went out. Emmie gave a frightened squeak and Doris drew in her breath quickly. The glowing ends of lighted cigarettes looked like red eyes staring in the darkness. A man laughed shakily. A voice from the gloom said bitterly, "If that isn't the bottom!"

There was a jingle of keys and change, as Mrs Robinson rummaged in the depths of her shabby crocodile-skin handbag. "I've got a match somewhere. There should be some candles in the drawer of the table."

Someone lit a match and a male voice from near the floor said, "I've got a torch, Missus."

The beam seemed as brilliant as a searchlight.

"Oh, thank you," she cried, stumbling over feet as, guided by the torch, she went to the table. She snapped the drawer open. "Really!" she exclaimed. "This is too bad. Somebody has stolen both the candles and the matches. There's not even a stump here."

There was an angry murmur through the room. Petty theft was a way of life in Liverpool. Now, with everything in short supply, it could cause real problems. The owner of the torch, however, said magnanimously, "Anybody as needs to move, tell me and I put me torch on."

Batteries were harder to obtain than candles, so when a young voice said, "Thanks, friend," it expressed the feelings of everybody.

Listening to the clamour outside, while sitting in total darkness was far worse, thought Emmie. The minutes seemed longer; the noise wrapped one closer. People tended not to talk; instead they huddled together for comfort.

Gwen had told her of a woman in the next street, who had clung to a perfect stranger in the street's unlighted shelter, while they sat out the Christmas Eve raid, the year before. In their terrible fear, they had become sexually aroused, and now she was pregnant by a man she had never seen. Shocking, Gwen called it; but David, with unexpected understanding, had said that it was Mother Nature's way of seeing that people who had died in a disaster were replaced.

Gwen had responded tartly, "More likely they didn't know right from wrong."

As she hugged Doris, Emmie wondered if she herself were pregnant, or whether the change of life was making its presence felt. Though frightened, in her secret heart she hoped that she was still young enough for a bun to be in the oven, Robert's little one.

"I hope Robbie's sailed and out of this rumpus," she whispered to Doris.

"You might get a letter tomorrer," Doris suggested. Her own heart ached at the thought; even the letters her dead husband had written to her when they were courting had been lost, with him, in their burned-out home.

The racket outside seemed to be slackening, the explosions further away. "Sounds like they might be doin' Bootle or Seaforth," suggested a disembodied voice.

"God spare us," exploded Doris. "Haven't we had enough up there?"

iv

The women stood forlornly at the top of the shelter stairs. The All-Clear had sounded; the noise abated. Through the gaping front windows, the whole town seemed to glow, the shattered room lighted up as if a good coal fire was burning in the old-fashioned grate. As they moved forward, glass and china crunched beneath their feet. The counter, which normally held the tea and coffee samovars, flanked by plates of buns and sandwiches, had been swept clear. Both samovars lay on their sides on the floor, silent humps in pools of black liquid, their copper exteriors reflecting the dancing light from outside.

The light from outside did not penetrate the kitchen,

so Mrs Starr struck a match. "Ah, that's better," she cried.

Though very dusty, the kitchen was practically undisturbed. The telephone, which Emmie had put on the sill to hold down the blackout curtains of the small window, had fallen on to the table beneath the window. Emmie lifted the curtain to peer out and was surprised that, at least there, there was still glass to look through.

Mrs Starr, one of the volunteers, asked Mrs Robinson a little diffidently, "Would you mind if I phoned my son to say I am all right?"

Mrs Robinson looked up from her task of setting out candles and lighting them. "Of course not," she replied.

The phone was dead. Mrs Starr sighed, and looked at her watch. It was nearly 3 a.m.

An air raid warden paused by the open front door. "Anybody here?" he shouted. Drawn by the sudden flare of the candles, he clumped towards the kitchen. His face was gaunt, eyes burning with fatigue. A striped pyjama collar stuck out untidily from the neck of his uniform.

"Are we safe from the fires?" Mrs Robinson asked, after greeting him.

"Aye. There's a firewatcher on the roof – young Dolly – she'll tell you if fires out t' back are spreading this side."

"What's burning?" Mrs Starr asked.

"Church House. It'll be gutted. Too far gone to save. And the Corn Exchange and the White Star building – God knows how many others. Bootle's calling for fire-engines out there, but they can't spare none from here." He heaved a sigh. "Must go check next door. Ta-ra." He crunched his way back across the strewn

71

canteen floor and they heard him curse as he caught his boot against one of the recumbent samovars and it clanged like a bell.

v

While Emmie and Gwen cleaned up their home and David laid new waterpipes in the Royal Infirmary, Conor walked round his district to assess the damage of the previous night.

"Rain'll do more damage than t'bombs," he told the already very depressed families, who a few streets away from his own home had lost their roofs. "I'll get you some tarps to lay over the rafters."

He returned to the post and put in a request for tarpaulin. Then he retrieved the front and back doors of the oldest couple affected, and helped the old man hang them again.

From nearby homes still comparatively undamaged, older women, silent, hands clasped over their stomachs, drifted over to watch and then to help their stricken neighbours shovel plaster and soot out of their chaotic little homes. Children, too small for school, found jam butties thrust into their hands by strange, smiling women. Buckets of water and trays of tea were lugged from several streets away, where water was still available. Friendships which were to last a lifetime were made between tearful outbursts from women beginning to quiver from delayed shock. The acute shortage of young, strong men to help was remarked upon and an extra tear was shed for those of them fighting in Greece or on a warship somewhere in the

Mediterranean. And slowly, painfully slowly, some order was restored.

While he munched a very dry sandwich, back at the post, Conor wrote out his reports. After that, seething with rage, he went to see the bitch who had refused to produce the street's stirrup-pump, at a time when the whole road had been littered with incendiaries.

God, how he needed a drink. He seemed to be floating, rather than walking. Lightheaded, that was the word. And what a fool he had been to put at the back of the cellar of the post the half dozen bottles of whiskey he had lifted from a lorry unwise enough to park in the district a couple of days before. Now, the post was as busy as a tram terminus and he could not retrieve them without its being noticed. If he had found a better place for them, he could have had a drink right now and flogged the rest for good money.

He slammed down his fountain pen and went home.

With one side of her face still slightly swollen from the blow he had given her, Ellen was in no mood to be conciliatory. Practically the whole of the family's bacon ration piled on his plate, however, suggested that the storm might be passing. He was too tired, too overwhelmed by other people's troubles laid upon his shoulders, to make an effort to break the silence between them, and as soon as he had mopped up the last bit of grease from his plate with a piece of bread, he announced that he was going to bed.

Within minutes, he was sound asleep, and did not hear Ellen shouting exasperatedly at Patrick's back, as he went out of the front door.

"I'm not going to bed at seven o'clock, no matter how many raids there are," he had said obstinately. "I'm goin' to see a pal." And he had wandered out into the deserted street, with a lazy grin at her over his shoulder.

He slipped through the soft spring evening, to the unfinished, roofless air raid shelter where he had taken Mari and where she had reluctantly promised to meet him again. He hung around outside it for nearly an hour, but Mari did not come.

A thoroughly scared Mari was certain that the previous night's raid had been arranged by God particularly to punish her.

He walked back home, clenched fists in trouser pockets, shoulders hunched, muttering angrily under his breath. Nothing but a stuck-up Judy, that's her. Wait till he caught her again. Yet, beneath his rage, he felt no true desire to harm her; only a craven fear that she would not come again; a young Romeo who had not yet managed to persuade his Juliet to fall in love with him. Wait till he was a Spitfire pilot, he reassured himself, with embroidered wings on his tunic; then she'd come crawling, and he might just condescend to take her to a dance.

At half-past ten, he was sitting despondently on the basement steps, listening to the guns and whistling to himself, while a fearful Ruby crouched close to him, pulling nervously at her thick, black fringe. Their sleepy father had tumbled back into his overalls and gone down to the post.

vi

Dress Materials at Blackler's had, that Friday afternoon, been busy. Women were buying dress

74

lengths, in anticipation of clothes being rationed; Gwen herself had several such lengths stored away in the mahogany chest of drawers brought from Emmie's home. Out of her wages, she was also holding a little money in order to buy two pairs of silk stockings, which a girl from Hosiery had told her, during her tea break, had at last arrived.

She was surprised when her supervisor sent her over to the Dress Department to help out.

"They're rushed off their feet," she explained. "People wanting mourning clothes."

When, homeward bound, she descended from the tram at the corner of her street, her feet ached abominably. She had sold so many black dresses that she felt deeply dispirited. At one point, she had been positively thankful to be faced with a giggling 15-year-old who wanted a pale blue bridesmaid's dress.

"Me sister's boy friend's got a forty-eight-hour pass. Comin 'ome Tuesday night. Me mam's nearly out of her mind tryin' to get everything ready for a wedding on Wednesday mornin'." The girl's flippant elation had made several sad-faced women turn on her with reproving murmurs of "Really! At this time?" Unable to relate to the grief of strangers, she had gone away happy, with a fluff of blue net carefully packed in tissue paper.

"Phew!" Gwen groaned, as she tottered through the twilight. The sky was still an unnaturally bright pink, but she was too tired to care. She thought only of her clean bed, with David, solid and reliable, snoring on his side of it.

"Where's your dad?" she asked Mari, as she took off her Sunday hat, black velveteen with a bunch of feathers

75

held by a *diamanté* brooch, and laid it carefully in its box.

The girl lifted a wan face from gloomy contemplation of her arithmetic book and wiped her pen nib with a piece of blotting paper. "I don't know, Mum. I'm scared. It's late for him."

"Ach, he's probably doin' overtime. What did you do with his bit of fish pie?"

"I kept it hot for a while. Then it got so dried out in the oven, I put it back in the pantry."

"Good girl."

Good girl? Mari chewed the end of her plait nervously, and sighed, and tried to forget the extraordinary sensations within her.

About midnight, David staggered in and thankfully plunked down his heavy tool-box.

"Worked late and then I had to walk home," he told them as, regardless of the guns roaring outside, they scuttled round to get him his supper. "There's a proper raid on down town. The sound of the planes diving, as I come along, give me the willies, they did. Hope our Em's all right."

Gwen had forgotten entirely about Emmie and now she paused, tea caddy in hand, a twinge of conscience striking her.

"Anyway, we can't do anything about her," he went on practically, as he sat down to his fish pie. "We should go to bed. They're not bombing round here — too busy with the town to bother us." He turned to Mari and said with a grin, "Your room's a deal safer with the window being boarded up. Maybe young Patrick did you a good turn."

Mari stared at him for a second, her smile frozen on

76

her face. Then she said diffidently, "I suppose he did."

Gwen climbed nervously into her bed and pulled the clothes over her head, to shut out the sound of chugging aeroplane engines. Two hours of sitting on the basement steps had made her back ache and to lie down was a blessed relief. David put his head on his pillow and began to snore immediately. Mari lay quietly in the stuffy darkness of her room and wondered what had really happened to her. Could you have a baby if a boy touched you?

None of them heard Emmie's flagging footsteps, when she came in. Groaning sleepily, they got up again at six o'clock in the morning and were astonished to find her sound asleep in David's chair, a cold cup of tea beside her on the bookshelf.

SATURDAY, 3 MAY 1941

Gwen stared unbelievingly at the shattered windows of Blackler's store. She seethed with indignation. An attack on Blackler's was, she felt, an attack on her personally. It was *her* store.

She glanced along its usually immaculate frontage. Little piles of swept-up glass stood waiting to be shovelled away. The gaping holes which had once been windows filled with merchandise labelled with large, cheerful notices of special bargains, had been cleared; only one or two, where the glass, by some fluke, remained intact, still bravely displayed for the benefit of the weekend invasion of shoppers from Wales a collection of special offers.

And the Welsh were coming in in force. Dressed in their best, they came by train and bus not only to buy but to make holiday, joining shoppers from the Liverpool suburbs, in touring the damage wreaked on the city and viewing the roaring fires. People from slum and suburb alike walked into cafés and grocery shops whose fronts had been blown out, and stood around feasting on food not yet salvaged. Rowdy groups, dodging the already harassed police, calmly looted anything they fancied, laughing and joking and getting drunk on wines and spirits they found in the grocery stores. Not a few owners defended their little broken shops with cricket bats, battered symbols of integrity.

As, later on, she snipped lengths of material for a customer who spoke, with disgust, of the behaviour of a group of hooligans she had seen, Gwen said bitterly,

"You'd think we was a circus, the way they gape – and a free-for-all. Rob their own mothers, they would."

"Aye," the customer agreed heavily. "Who'd have believed it?"

ii

David usually finished work at twelve noon on Saturdays, and Gwen had left a dish of stew in the oven for his midday meal. It grew dryer and dryer and finally shrivelled up on the plate, because David had not, that morning, been pursuing the incredible intricacies of the plumbing of the Royal Infirmary. He had, instead, been pounced on by his supervisor, immediately upon his arrival, and had been sent by taxi out to Bootle, together with his mate, Arthur, a grizzled ancient, back in the work force after four years of retirement.

"Bloody chaos out there," the supervisor had told them. "No water. Gas lines flaring up in the streets. Electric's out. Report to the town hall. They'll tell you where to go."

They were joined by two electricians, who had also been impounded, and as they sat in the taxi, tool-boxes rattling in the luggage compartment by the driver, they looked out in astonishment and no little trepidation at increasing turmoil, the further north they proceeded.

The driver had to pick his way through miles of littered streets made muddy by burst water lines and, in places, lacings of fire-hoses temporarily abandoned for lack of water pressure. Timber yards crackled and smoked on both sides of the road, the draught of the flames making it hard for the driver to keep the taxi stable, for a scarifying few minutes. Occasionally, they would be redirected by police or special constables, to detour a mass of masonry spread across a street.

When they finally found the streets they were to work in, after being redirected by a series of city officials, they stood for a moment bewildered, their tools at their feet, wondering where in earth to start. Civil defence workers of every kind toiled amid the havoc, while the homeless scrambled over the debris in an effort to pick out some belongings which might still be usable. In desperate efforts to help families still entombed, some of them got into the way of rescue workers cautiously digging through piles of bricks, mortar and shattered wood, to get at victims for whom there was little hope. Others stood in forlorn groups, an occasional sob indicating some poor soul for whom it was all too much; still others were unnaturally cheerful, thankful to have survived; the true hardship of their situation would hit them later.

A hundred yards up the street, a cracked gas line gave way. A white sheet of flame roared upwards, its deadly heat threatening further damage. Rescuers and inhabitants scrambled over debris to a safer distance.

"Good God!" exclaimed Arthur, and turned to run.

David caught his arm. His breath came in frightened gasps, but he said, "It could blow the whole street up. Better find the valve. See if we can turn it off." He grabbed a tool from his box and followed by a protesting Arthur ran towards the explosion. While wardens shouted to them to come back, they searched likely spots for the valve they needed, and, within a minute or two, found it. A quick twist and the flame subsided. David stood very still for a moment, holding on to Arthur, while the pain in his chest subsided, a shivering unsung hero, like many others that day.

Soon, watched anxiously by housewives, black-shawled against the morning coolness, David and Arthur were set to work by a city hall official to reconnect a major break in a water line. The women were desperate for water to clean their damaged homes and wash the dirt off their children and themselves. The Women's Voluntary Service brought food both to workers and watchers, and they stood around in the street, their children about them, while they thankfully sipped mugs of tea. Their voices were shrill with nervous tension and they wound their shawls tightly round themselves for comfort. To David, it seemed particularly wicked that people so painfully poverty-stricken should have their tiny, crowded homes broken open like eggs. "And the men at sea – or struggling to keep the docks working," David muttered angrily to Arthur.

There was no question of going home that night; the need of them in Bootle was too grave.

As twilight approached, he and Arthur paused to stretch themselves and eat the sandwiches brought to them by the indefatigable WVS canteen staff. They both became aware of a general movement in the neighbourhood. Women, pushing perambulators or pushchairs loaded with children and bedding, were so numerous as to form a long procession in the now partially tidied up street.

"Where do you think they're goin'?" he asked Arthur.

"Walkin' out to Huyton, to sleep in t' fields, I expect. It's a deal safer'n staying here overnight."

David nodded. Except for an occasional shout to a child to mind himself, the procession was strangely quiet. There was a dull acceptance in the passing faces, framed in dusty, tousled hair. Dragging boots made a slow shuffling sound on the gritty street.

"They'll be back in t' mornin', bright and early no doubt," remarked Arthur, "to check on their homes — and sent t' kids to school – if the school's still there."

iii

Mari and her friend, Dorothy, went to the Saturday, children's programme at the cinema that afternoon and then went home to Dorothy's house for tea.

While his mother sat on the front step, nursing Michael and enjoying the sunshine, and Ruby and Nora played skipping on the pavement, Patrick sloped around the alleyways, hoping to find Mari. Unsuccessful, he irritably teased his father's fighting cocks and for his pains got a long scratch on the back of his right hand.

Conor Donnelly's area had been mercifully free from incidents on the previous night, so while he had a comparatively quiet day, he wandered down to the Hercy Dock to see if he could find an American sailor off a tanker, with nylons or lipsticks for sale. Both fetched good prices on the black market.

iv

As Gwen bustled into her home about eight o'clock that evening, she felt more energetic than she had done for some days. A few hours of good sleep, despite the noise of the raid, had restored her, and she had enjoyed at Blackler's the close feeling of unity amongst her companions, engendered by their joint dislike of the large influx of sightseers and ill-intentioned riff-raff into the town.

Mari was sitting alone, by the fire, slowly turning the heel of a sock, one of a pair she was knitting as a contribution to a parcel being made up for the men of the King's Regiment. Two of the girls in the class had fathers serving in it, stationed at Hull. Mari was a good knitter, having been taught by her mother as soon as she could hold a pair of butcher's skewers and a ball of wool.

"Yer dad not in?" Gwen inquired, as she once more returned her best hat to its box.

"No." Mari paused, needle in stitch.

Mari was feeling a little less panic-stricken about Patrick. She had stuck close to Dorothy all day, and after tea they had rearranged Dorothy's doll's house and put up new curtains in it. Mr Hale, Dorothy's father, who had to go to a chapel meeting, had kindly walked her home, since it was on his way. They walked slowly because he limped; Dorothy said he had been wounded in the First World War at a terrible place called Passchendaele, and, as had sometimes happened in her grandfather's house, Mari was reminded that the results of war stayed on and on, long after the battles were finished. Did it mean, she wondered fearfully, that her life would be different after the war? Would she, all her life, drag a foot or, much worse, be jeered at because she had been disfigured? She nearly choked, when she remembered that her grandfather had once told her that he had a friend kept permanently in hospital because he had almost no face.

She had thought about this, as she sat quietly knitting; it was all mixed up with a hodge-podge of ideas about Patrick. To her relief, her figure had not swelled up as she knew a pregnant woman's did, so she had begun to think that being caressed all over by a boy's exploring fingers did not produce a baby, and that was a relief; she had heard of girls who had committed suicide because they were pregnant and did not have a proper husband.

The explosive feelings that Patrick had aroused in her must mean something, though. She longed to ask her mother about it, but dared not. Could such an exciting feeling really be wicked? She wondered if she could ask Aunt Emmie; after all, she was engaged and must know something about it.

As Gwen put the kettle on for tea, she was not particularly worried about David; he had done a lot of overtime recently. Both mother and daughter jumped apprehensively, however, when someone thumped on the front door.

"Your dad? Hurt?" Gwen exclaimed.

As they ran along the passage, getting in each other's way in their sudden sense of urgency, they heard Conor Donnelly outside, shouting, "Mrs Thomas! Mrs Thomas!" Gwen reckoned that if the warden brought the news, it must be bad. She flung the door open, letting out a little light from the candle on the hall table.

"Get in, get in," Conor ordered testily. "Enough light to guide them from Berlin."

He hastened over the doorstep and shut the door behind him.

"What's to do?" Gwen asked anxiously, while Mari's blank little face went whiter than usual.

"Och, it's all right," he answered, seeing their frightened faces. "Yer husband rang the post, from Bootle, to say he mayn't be back till tomorrer night."

"What? Bootle? What's he doin' there?"

"It's terrible out there, missus. They need every man they can get."

"How'll he get his dinner?"

"Same as the firemen and everyone else workin' out there. From the WVS canteen, I 'spect."

"He's too old to be gallivanting round out there. He needs his sleep." Gwen's voice was angry.

Conor's deep blue eyes registered such scorn that Gwen quailed slightly. "So do we all. We're none of us youngsters, Mrs Thomas."

She was disconcerted at the snub, and her irritation at this man and his slovenly family increased. She said tightly, "Well, thank you for bringing the message. I don't know why he didn't phone earlier."

"Phones out of order, like everything else," he replied, fully aware of her distaste of him.

Gwen went slowly back to the living room and sat down on a footstool close to the fire. It was wasteful to have a fire in May, but she justified it by cooking on it, and now, suddenly, she was grateful for its comforting warmth. For the first time in her life, the idea that she might be widowed occurred to her; Conor's description of the dire straits of Bootle had struck home; accidents happened in such awful situations.

While Mari made tea and toast for their supper, the virtues of her patient lumbering husband surfaced in her mind. She remembered, with a pang, the sturdy Welsh youth who had proposed to her, as they walked soberly in Princes Park after chapel. They had had to wait seven years before they could afford to be married, and, sipping tea beside the fire, she wished they had not wasted their youth. Why, she wondered bitterly, had she been so coldly virtuous? And now it could all end in a holocaust in Bootle.

She and Mari had lain in bed a scant hour, when the air raid warning dragged them out again. "We'll get dressed in the living room," Gwen said resignedly. "It'll be safer down there."

"Poor Aunt Emmie," Mari exclaimed. "Stuck down town again."

v

Ellen Donnelly blasted furiously all them Jerries and their ilk, as she, too, that Saturday night shepherded her family down the cellar steps.

During the day, she had hauled a mattress down into the dank basement and on this she persuaded Ruby, Nora and Brendy to lie down to sleep. It was not quite so safe as sitting on the stairs, but as she remarked, "Beggars can't be choosers."

Patrick sat moodily on the top step, watching his mother nurse Michael to sleep again. The candlelight caught the white hairs amongst her brown mop and deepened the lines on her shiny red face. He felt a sudden twinge of pain that his mother was growing older. Though she was always demanding to know where he had been and what he had been doing, he loved her with a passion that frightened him sometimes. He was inordinately jealous of his father, and, when his father struck her, he boiled with inward anger that he was too small and cowardly to defend her. When I'm bigger, I will, he always told himself. He resented the succession of babies that occupied her lap, and only Ruby, eleven months younger than him, escaped being bullied by him whenever he was in a bad temper.

The noise of the anti-aircraft guns began to shake the old house.

vi

Unaware of the frantic clean-up done by candlelight after the previous night's raid, a dozen men were lounging round the tables of the sailors' canteen, gossiping amid the usual cloud of tobacco smoke.

Mrs Robinson arrived at the same time as Emmie. She was carrying two parcels and Emmie took them from her. "These are heavy," she exclaimed.

"Crockery oddments, my dear. After last night, we're dreadfully short. These are a donation from Lewis's – I went in to see them this morning."

In the kitchen, Peggie Evans, another paid member of the staff, was tidying up the last of the muddle from the lunchtime rush. "'T' fish is finished," she told Emmie and Mrs Robinson, "'T' butcher brought plenty of sausage, though, for tonight. And there's still a lot o' dried egg."

As she put on her overall, Emmie told her how the fish had been covered with dust the previous night. "At first we was goin' to throw it out. Then Mrs Robinson said what waste. So we washed it very carefully and put it in the larder. Did you have any complaints?"

"Never a word. Deep fried, there'd be nought the matter with it." She took her coat off a hook and her handbag out of a drawer. "Was I ever glad I wasn't here last night. It must've been awful."

"I were scared out of me wits," admitted Emmie. "I got a proper laugh, though, out of the note you've pinned on the sandbags round the door. 'Open for business – very open.' "

"Aye. I thought t' lads 'd believe we'd given up on 'em, with the shutters closed, like."

"You know we had the till cleaned out, during the raid?"

"No?"

"Somebody took the whole night's takings. Must've done it while we was in the shelter. We didn't stop to lock the front door."

"Stinking buggers," said Peggie forcefully, as she clapped a blue beret on her head. "Tara-well."

Doris did not arrive. She lay dead in the arms of the seaman who had taught her to smoke, under the wreckage of a shop doorway which had suddenly collapsed on them, taking both their lives while they made love.

A white-haired grocer's wife, Mrs Atkins, and the silent, elegant Lady Mentmore were redeployed to cover the work. "Perhaps she'll phone later," suggested Emmie.

"Is the phone working?" Mrs Robinson looked harried. She was bone-tired, her plump, middle-aged body refusing to run at its usual pace.

Emmie went to the table by the window and cautiously lifted the receiver and put it to her ear. "It's still dead," she announced.

"Oh, dear! What a nuisance! The crater down the street must be responsible for that. I saw the Post

91

Office Telephones van there, as I came in."

Mrs Atkins looked up from her carrot scraping. "It really was an awful night. And it could have been worse. I heard this morning that they were worried about a munition ship called the *Malakand* in Huskisson Dock. It's being loaded for the Middle East. And with the fires and that being so bad up the north end – poor Bootle – they were mortally afraid it would explode."

Emmie froze, the fork with which she was pricking sausages poised to stab. "The *Malakand*?" she exclaimed in horror. "My Robbie's on that." She turned a stricken face towards the carrot scraper. "He never told me it had munitions in it."

Mrs Atkins soothed, "Well, nothing's happened to it yet. Perhaps it will sail today."

Emmie nodded assent and slowly and heavily she pricked the neat pink rows of sausages. She tried not to weep. To sail the Med with ammunition in the hold! Even if he got out of port safely, it could be a death-warrant! She wanted to scream 'No' to God. Was He really almighty? She wanted to faint, to escape the fear which pierced her. But she could not, must not. In a war, she must not give way. Quietly, she went on with her work and missed the pitying glances of Mrs Atkins and the countess. The countess said practically, to Emmie's back, "I think we all need a cup of tea."

As she filled the four cups from the samovar, she herself was not feeling very well. The previous night, an incendiary, apparently a dud, had fallen through the thatched roof of her house, and it had taken the combined efforts of her two elderly maids and herself to lift it out of the water tank into which it had fallen. They had thrown it out of the attic window on to the lawn, where it had unexpectedly exploded. A small incident, not worth mentioning, but it had tired her. She yawned behind a heavily beringed hand, as she added lots of sugar to Emmie's tea; she understood that the lower classes enjoyed plenty of sugar.

vii

Saturday night, when you should be down at the local, sitting by the fire and telling funny stories over a pint of bitter; instead you were stuck in a sandbagged shop labelled A.R.P., listening to the pandemonium in the skies and hoping that nothing fell on you. The strain was telling on Conor Donnelly. He told himself irritably that he had had it up to here. And to add to it all, he had quarrelled with Ellen over a drop of whiskey – and she was still as sour as yesterday's milk. He went to the door and glanced up at the sky.

The brilliance of the flares had put the stars out, and the air smelled as if a million rubber tyres were burning. The shriek of bombs descending on the flaming city centre, about a mile down the hill, could hardly be heard above the concerted roar of their impact, the drone of heavy engines and the scream of night fighters as they dived. Nearer, in the park, the anti-aircraft guns kept up a steady barrage at the bellies of the bombers, which glistened like slugs, in the light of darting flames.

Inside the post, three women wardens were placidly waiting for a tin kettle of water to boil on a primus stove, their imperturbability belied by their ghostly faces. A grey-haired voluntary warden, Montagu Smith, who came in each night there was a raid, was snatching a nap on a camp-bed. In the daytime, he was the manager of the bank round the corner.

Conor had always thought that anyone who had a bank account, never mind worked in a bank, must be hopelessly stuck up. But this pot-bellied man had won his admiration the previous November. He had crawled into the shifting debris of a house, to hold the hand of a dreadfully injured old man until a doctor crawled in, too, to give the victim an injection to ease the pain while they got him out. Then they had worked the remainder of the night together, under enemy machine-gun fire.

The half-washed Irish labourer and the well-shaven polite banker supported each other. Conor never gave himself credit for the friendliness he exuded, the enthusiasm with which he would do a good turn. Montague – our Mont, to all the wardens – had a quick, orderly mind, able to size up the immediate needs in some of the horrid situations which they faced together.

"G' us a cuppa tea, Glynis, luv," Conor asked one of the women. He was hungry. In a day or two, Ellen would get over her sulks and boil up a good stew. Meanwhile, he could whistle for it. A short burst of machine-gun fire directly overhead made everyone duck instinctively. He wished suddenly he had made it up with Ellen. What was a drop of whiskey anyway, in a world where one bullet could finish him? He chewed his thumb uneasily while Glynis made the tea.

Glynis Hughes eased her tin hat further back on her head and grinned up at him. She was a small, brown-skinned woman, suggesting descent from the little people who roamed Britain before the Celts arrived. Her husband was serving in the South Lancashires and she was temporarily living nearby with her mother. She worked in a factory which made aircraft parts and she made many a lewd joke about her production of joysticks. She was used to coping with the appetite of a labourer in a steelworks and she still shamelessly bought any food she could find on the black market. Now she asked, "Like a Spam sandwich?"

"Ah would, if you can spare it."

She took out from a shopping bag a white, confectioner's paper bag and from this she carefully drew out a sandwich two inches thick with a thin slice of Spam in it. "I brought some bikkies for you girls," she told her companions, "Chocky ones."

The other two women's faces lit up. "Mm. Where did you get them from?" They, too, were housewives permanently scrounging through the shops for extra food. To earn the money for it, they worked as labourers, cleaning oil drums at a petrol installation.

Glynis giggled. "Ask no questions, you'll be told no lies."

Conor wolfed the proffered sandwich and a chocolate biscuit. He felt much better and walked outside to take another look at what was happening.

The sky was a brilliant pink, with rolling billows of smoke making rosy cushions above him. There was no one, not even a cat, in the street. He went back into the tiny shop and leaned against the wall by the telephone girl, to gossip.

He was jolted upright by a fast puffing sound, closer than the general roar, then a pause, while everyone held their breath. A heavy crump and everyone breathed out.

"Land-mine," Conor said. "Unexploded."

"Must have fallen in the park," Glynis commented, relief exuding from her.

"Here comes another," squeaked the telephonist, as she laid her head on her table and clasped her arms over her tin hat. The trainlike sound came again and Conor tensed.

An enormous explosion shook the old shop, reverberating round them in swelling waves. The telephone girl was nearly lifted off her chair, and cracks ran up the grubby walls. Mont was on his feet in a split second, clapping his helmet to his head. "My God!" he exclaimed.

A colossal growl, like that of some huge animal, indicated the fall of heavy masonry; it was followed by a rapid tattoo of smaller pieces on to the roof and into the street.

"The tenement?" breathed Glynis through chattering teeth. "The Dwellings?"

"Could be," Mont replied, as he loosened his torch from his belt. All of them dreaded a direct hit on the huge five-storey tenement nearby. It was built in a circle, round a communal yard, and was packed with young families.

Conor had already gone. He ran madly down the pink-lit street and turned left. He was brought up short by an impenetrable cloud of dust. Other than the heavy grumble from the skies, there was a weird silence.

Then, from beyond the dust cloud, came scream after scream of pain and panic. "Oh, Jesus, help us," shrieked a woman's voice.

Doors of the row houses close to the warden banged open, as shaken tenants came rushing out. Mont panted up to Conor, and said, "I'll tell Josie to phone R. and P. We're going to need a lot of help."

Conor cleared his throat and spat. "Better have a

closer look first. Could be only the houses facin', not the tenement itself."

They both took out handkerchiefs to cover their noses from the cloying dust; it was so thick that the beams of their torches were reflected back, as if they faced a wall. They turned the lights down to their feet and picked their way round huge slabs of concrete and piles of bricks, interspersed with threatening electric wires. The dust, now mixed with a strong smell of gas, made Mont cough. He tripped over a broken beam and fell, barking his shins and hands painfully, and got up again. Behind him, Conor could hear other people scrambling over the wreckage; they were shouting to each other, as they converged, and above and beyond the sound of their voices came the screams of the half-crushed.

"'Allo, la," Conor called. "I'm the warden. All men come to me." Dear God, send me some wi' a bit o' savvy, he added to himself. Judging by the curses behind him, he was not going to have to *ask* people to help tonight, which was a welcome change. He hoped Tom Massey was on duty – biggest bloody rozzer in the whole police force. He knew he could use a dozen heavyweights for this job.

A shrieking woman blundered into him. She clutched his arms and shook him. "Me lads – me lads!" she yelled into his face. She was naked, her clothing blown off her, and long, black hair flicked across his mouth, as she half turned to look back at the carnage slowly emerging from the fog.

"Hold on there, luv. Did it hit clean on The Dwellings?"

"Aye, into t' middle yard." She clawed at him. "For Jesus' sake, get me boys out."

Throughout the raid, Conor and Mont, with the Rescue Squad, sweated and cursed their way into the ruins, sickened frequently, occasionally triumphant when they brought out the living, until in the early morning, a filthy, bloodstained Conor went back to the post to write out his report. New orphans, new widows, new cripples and a band of homeless. And what for? What was it in truth all about? God's curse on them all. He rubbed his torn and dirty hands on his overalls and reached for his pencil.

viii

Arms round each other, Gwen and Mari cowered on the cellar steps, certain that each strident screech above their heads would be the last thing they would ever hear.

The petrifying crash which destroyed The Dwellings made both of them scream. Tinkling glass and a rushing draught told them that the windows had blown in.

"Me sitting room! Me aspidistra!" Gwen wailed. Her Holy of Holies would be exposed to the weather – and thieves!

Mari began to cry.

The roar of the attack on the city centre was undiminished, but locally it was as if everything held its breath, as if the explosion of the land-mine had taken everything with it. Gwen and Mari loosed their grip on each other and raised their heads.

The quiet was broken by a frantic banging on the back door. "Missus, missus! Come quick," a boy's voice cried.

Patrick! Mari scrambled to her feet.

Her mother caught her by her bare ankle. "You stay here, miss. I'll go."

In the pink light coming from between the flapping remains of the blackout curtains, it was easy to see the familiar terrain of the brick-tiled kitchen. She flung open the back door. Five shadows tumbled in together, wailing like forgotten babies.

Gwen surveyed five shocked faces, in the uncertain light. "For Heaven's sake, what's to do?"

"It's Mam. She's hurt real bad," Patrick gulped. "Coom and help her."

Gwen swallowed. "Where is she?"

"She's lyin' by t' front step. Ah can't move her. Coom quick." The usually bumptious Patrick was beside himself, his face ashen.

Crowded close to him, the other children broke into loud howls. Ruby led the hullabaloo. Her mother, her only defence against the terror of the raids, was lying inert at the door of her home; and Ruby was convinced that all the houses would collapse any minute and she would again be buried.

Despite Gwen's own nervousness and confusion, the sickly smell of the children's unwashed bodies penetrated to her. Repulsed by it, she snapped at them, "Now you be quiet. I'll get a candle and go and have a look at your mam."

As the candle was lit, the howls tailed off into small sobs. The flame showed the small, barefoot crew in more detail. They all had white rivulets down their dirty faces.

For safety's sake, Gwen decided that the children could not return to their home with her; the gunfire was too heavy. She lit another candle and handed it to

Patrick. "Sit on the cellar steps with Mari – all of you. Get a move on, now. It's not safe up here. And mind your feet on the floor – there's glass all over. I'll be back in a minute."

Ruby, dragging a protesting Michael, led the way timidly. Patrick wiped the tears from his face, put on a defiant air and stood on the top step, leaning one shoulder against the wall to stop himself shaking.

Mari half smiled at him as she looked up the steps, but he did not even glance at her. She felt unexpectedly hurt. She turned her attention to Ruby. Gosh, how she smelled.

The clangour of fire-engine bells came clearly through the roar of the blitz, as Gwen, candle in hand, hesitated in her front doorway. What would she find next door?

A string of incendiaries slithered down a short distance away. Vicious pencils of flak suddenly peppered the road in front of her. She bobbed back into the hall. The candle blew out. With it still in her hand, she crept down the two carefully whitened steps of her own front entrance, as if by making no sound she could outwit the German pilots. Then she turned into the immediately adjacent front doorway of the Donnellys and stared into their hall. In dismay, she dropped the dead candle and it rattled away on the pavement.

Just inside, Ellen half lay, half sat, against the weathered door. One hand was flung across her breast. Her eyes, wide with shock, stared at the wall opposite her.

"Oh, my goodness!" Gwen took the two steps in one stride and knelt down by the woman. "Mrs Donnelly? Are you hurt?"

There was no reply. Gwen put out a careful hand and

touched her face. She did not move. The body was surrounded by the effluvium of human excrement, and a primeval fear of death clutched at Gwen's throat. In an agony of indecision, she glanced up at the small piece of sky she could see above the roofs opposite; in the flushed torment there, the battle raged on. Her breath came in short pants and she wanted to run away, out of Liverpool, away from the dirty horde on her cellar steps, away from this scarifying hulk of a woman. But there was nowhere to run to; even the street across the doorstep was a death-trap.

She took a big breath and pulled herself together. How did one make absolutely certain that a person was dead? She might still be alive – in shock – wounded only.

A resonant bang nearby, followed immediately by a shower of bricks and mortar on the doorstep, galvanised Gwen into action. Still kneeling, she leaned forward and tried to heave Ellen further into the hall. Ellen's arms flopped and her whole body reeled towards Gwen's tiny frame. In horror, Gwen let go and scrambled to her feet. Ellen slumped to the floor.

Doing her best not to vomit, and risking the descent of further missiles, she ran a few steps to the nearest street shelter and called hopefully through the doorway, "Anybody there?" But only a faint echo came from its stinking darkness.

She ran back to her own house and scuttled through the length of it. On the cellar steps, the children were sitting as rigidly as images; one little boy was crying heartily. At the sound of her footfall they turned to look up at her, the whites of their eyes gleaming in the candlelight.

"I'm going through the alleyway to Mr Baker's next door but one," she told them quickly. "To get some help for your mum. You all stay close, now. Everything's going to be all right."

She ran through the brick-walled back yard, out of the tall, plank gate and down the alley, which, with its narrowness and high walls, seemed to offer more protection than the front street. She reckoned the Baker family, also, would be in the basement and they would hear her knock more easily if she tried the back door.

"Mr Baker," she shrieked, above the rat-tat-tat of machine-guns. Fearfully she glanced upwards and then renewed her bangs with her fists.

"Wasser marrer?" inquired a richly Liverpool voice, as the door was opened a narrow crack.

"It's Mrs Thomas. Mrs Donnelly's hurt bad and I can't lift her into the house meself. And Mr Donnelly's on duty and me husband's in Bootle." The words poured out, as she wrung her hands helplessly.

The door swung open immediately to reveal, in the light of a kerosene lamp, an elderly man who looked, thought Gwen, a bit like a tortoise wrapped in a dressing-gown.

The wide mouth in the crumpled face opened. "Step in, step in. Let me get me slippers and tell Mother." He padded away, towards the cellar door.

Gwen thankfully entered the kitchen and shut the door behind her. By some fluke of the blast, Mr Baker's kitchen window was still intact. As fear gave way to resentment, she wondered crossly why her windows should always be those to be broken. Why should she get landed with someone wounded? And have to let in five disgusting kids?

Mr Baker came panting up the cellar steps again, his dressing-gown now tightly belted, his misshapen feet encased in carpet slippers.

"Where is she?" he inquired.

"By her front door. It's open."

"Coom through then."

Seething with suppressed vexation at the unfairness of fate, she followed him through his front door, round the tiny bay windows of his home and that of the Donnellys, and up the latter's front steps. From behind the closed door of the kitchen, Sarge began to bark.

Mr Baker put the lamp down on the floor. Very gently he lifted Ellen's arm. A piece of shrapnel was deeply embedded in her side. He held her wrist for a moment, but there was no sign of a pulse.

He got laboriously to his feet. "Let's get her in and shut the door."

As a postman, he was used to lifting awkward weights and he soon pulled her along the bare wooden floor, by putting his hands under her arms from the back. Then he quietly shut the front door; it cut off a lot of the noise from outside.

He looked carefully at the wound. It had bled little and he toyed with the idea of pulling out the piece of shrapnel. Better to leave her as she was, he decided. With womanly care, he turned her on one side to look at her back. Another sliver protruded for about an inch from under one shoulder-blade.

"I reckon she were hit first in her chest and she half turned into the house, and the second piece hit her in the back," he said to a shocked Gwen. "She's dead for sure." He laid the body flat on its back and gently closed the staring eyes. Then he glanced round him, puzzled. "Where's all the kids?"

Gwen licked her white lips. "All in my house, with our Mari."

"That's proper kind of you, Mrs Thomas." He took a crumpled handkerchief out of his dressing-gown pocket and, with a grimace of distaste, wiped Ellen's life-blood from his hands. Gwen stood uncertainly before him, her hands clasped tightly together. Her irritation had faded and she felt numb, unable to make herself think.

"It's more'n anybody's life's worth to go up to the post in this," Baker went on heavily. "As soon as the All-Clear sounds, I'll get up there and tell him – and get some help to move her." He rubbed his almost non-existent chin, grey with a day's beard, and then smelled the dried blood still on his hands. Sickened, he dropped them to his sides. "The kids'll do fine with you." He looked down kindly at the small wraith in front of him. "Five of them, isn't there? Poor little buggers – excuse the language."

At the remembrance of the repellent collection sitting on her well-scrubbed steps, Gwen felt nauseated again. But she could not, in all conscience, send them back home, while their dead mother lay where she did. "Donnelly'll have to get a relation to come in and look after them," she said.

"Aye," he agreed. "I'll leave it to you how you tell them."

Gwen stared up at him, aghast. How could *she* tell them? Surely it was not her responsibility? But Mr Baker's mind had gone on to other things, and he said, "I'll let the dog out in the morning, if Donnelly isn't back."

In her own house, she faced the children, as they rose

expectantly from their uncomfortable seats on the steps. Ruby held a sleeping Michael; she looked as if she might faint.

Mari was in the kitchen, calmly making cups of cocoa for their guests, while the early morning breeze fluttered her long white nightgown and made the gas jet dance.

The sounds from outside indicated that the attack had shifted slightly to another part of the town, though the rhythmic beat of engines overhead continued.

Gwen looked resentfully at the little crew and cleared her throat uneasily, while the children waited like marble statues in a cemetery. She said carefully, "Your ma's hurt rather bad. Mr Baker next door but one is looking after her. He'll send her to the hospital." She cleared her throat again, some pity for them seeping into her. "You're not to worry. Everything's goin' to be all right."

Relief dawned on Ruby's face. She said to Nora and Brendy, aged 7 and 6 respectively, "See, I told yer so. We're all goin' to have a nice cup o' cocoa, and when the raid's over, we'll go home to bed." She turned to Gwen. "I could go to Mam now – the kids'll be all right with you and Mari."

"No. No," Gwen responded hastily. "Your mam wants you to stay to comfort them."

When she turned to fuss round the cocoa maker, Patrick followed her and stood squarely in front of her. His face was grim and the fine, blue eyes looked at her fearlessly. "I *know*," he said scornfully.

"Well, don't you say nothin' for the minute," Gwen murmured out of the side of her mouth, like a convict. Then, feeling ashamed, she added, "I'm real sorry, lad." She felt like adding, I'm sorry for me, too.

Mari glanced up from her stirring, surprise and fear

mingled in her expression. Patrick's face crumbled, tears welled up again.

He's only about 13, Gwen thought, for all he's so big. Instinctively she moved towards him and put her hand on his shoulder. She tried to reassure him. "It'll be all right when your dad comes," she said.

Mari bit her lips to restrain her own desire to cry. She put four cups on a brightly printed tray, filled them and took them to the children on the steps. She said with forced cheerfulness, "Here you are, ducks."

When she turned back to pour out cocoa for her mother and Patrick, she saw with a pang of jealousy that her cold, fastidious parent was holding Patrick's head against her skimpy chest and crooning, "Never mind, luv, never mind." And Patrick, tough cruel Patrick, was actually crying as if his heart would break. Her own lips quivered, as she took down some more cups from their hooks.

Gwen herself was in torment. The children must stay with her until their mother's body was removed. That meant they would probably have to sleep the rest of the night in her house; and they probably had nits in their hair – she would have to burn the pillows afterwards, which would make David thoroughly angry because of the cost of new ones. But what else could she do?

She was personally revolted by their dirtiness; even this beautiful boy smelled as if he had never had a bath since he was born. With a sigh, she urged, "Have a cup o' cocoa, luv. Make you feel better." She took a cup from Mari and handed it to him. "What was your mam doin' at the door on a night like this?"

He took a small gulp of the scalding liquid. "There were a terrible bang – and then it were dead quiet, like.

106

So she run up to see if it were the houses opposite what were hit – 'cos they'd need our help, if they were." He faltered, and then went on, "I heard her cry out and I run up meself – and there she was on the floor – and she never said nothin' – and I knew." His cup rattled against his teeth, as he took another sip.

"God rest her." Gwen put her empty cup down on the drainboard. "We'd better get down the steps. You, too, Mari. We'll wash up tomorrow."

SUNDAY, 4 MAY 1941

Ruby's arms were stiff from holding the dead weight of young Michael. Every so often in his sleep, he would nuzzle into her non-existent breasts, looking for the comfort of his mother's milk. Then, frustrated, he would whimper and sleep again.

Patrick sat with eyes closed and fists clenched. He was tortured by the idea of his mother lying alone in the house next door. He wanted to go to her, look at her, try to wake her from her long sleep. But he was afraid of the demons in the sky, afraid of facing alone the fact of her death. After a while, his head fell forward, his mouth opened and he, too, slept.

Just before five o'clock, they all awoke with a jerk to a profound silence, except for Gwen who continued to snore.

Mari shook her mother's arm. "Ma, it's stopped. They've gone."

"Who? What?" Gwen jerked her head from against the cellar wall and blinked. She had been having a nightmare, a nightmare in which the whole house crawled away as a result of the infestation brought in by the Donnelly children. Through her fogged brain, she heard the long, thin cry of the All Clear.

"Phew!" she exclaimed. Then she gazed blearily down at the appalling weight of responsibility sitting on the inhospitable stone steps below her.

Brendy, aged 5, struggled awake and stood up on wobbling legs. He stared round the alien staircase and then roared tearfully, "Where's me mam?" He started to struggle past the knees of the other children, to get to the top of the steps, howling like a miserable dog. Nora, a year older, turned to follow him. She began to whimper. As she threatened to teeter backwards down the steps, Ruby grabbed her wrist.

"Leave me go," the child yelled savagely. She began to beat her big sister in the face with a small clenched fist.

Patrick got up slowly. With frightened, bloodshot eyes, he glanced down at his hostess and then at the other children. A curling spiral of unvented rage ran through him. "Brendy! You shut up or I'll clobber yez. Mam's been hurt and can't come to yez."

Brendy's howls came down a full octave, and Nora stopped trying to get a hold on Ruby's hair to tear it out; when Patrick decided to hit someone, he often distributed the favour throughout the family. Nora's white-lashed eyes narrowed and she made an obscene gesture at Ruby.

Patrick addressed his snivelling siblings again, his voice suddenly placating. "Mrs Thomas is going to let us stay here, aren't you, Mrs Thomas?" His eyes were on Gwen now, pleading, defeated.

Gwen was dizzy with lack of sleep and could not bring her mind into focus. She rubbed her face and then ran her fingers through her frizzy hair. She nodded. Even if Ellen Donnelly's body had been removed, the children would feel the absence of their mother more keenly in their own home and would ask more questions – and she did not want to have to break the news to them that they would never see her again. Better by far to keep them in her own home and let Donnelly do the job in the morning.

She stood up. Her whole body ached. And where was David in all this? He should be at home taking charge of everything. It was unfair that she should carry the whole burden. She began to simmer with resentment. And Emmie hadn't turned up either, to give her a hand.

"I want to pee," wailed Brendy, clutching at himself.

"For heaven's sake, take him down the yard," she ordered Patrick, as she yawned mightily. "Tut, he hasn't got any shoes on – lift him over the glass in the kitchen – and no socks neither – 'is poor little feet is purple."

It was as if Brendy's sad straits forced her awake. She turned to her drooping, equally sleepy daughter. "Mari, get the dustpan and brush, and get the glass off the kitchen floor, so the little boy – and the little girl – you ain't got no shoes neither, luv? – don't cut their feet."

Nora was not to be wooed by a kindly tone. She stuck her finger in her mouth and looked sulky. Gwen turned to Ruby. "And you, what's your name?"

"Ruby, missus." From beneath her shaggy fringe two sad eyes gleamed dully.

"Well, you got shoes on. You bring the baby upstairs with me, and we'll put him on a potty and then into bed. The little girl can wait in the living room a minute, till Patrick comes back with the little lad." She lifted a stiff, unyielding Nora up the stairs and deposited her on the living room hearthrug, which seemed to be clear of broken glass. The child ignored her and stared around the strange room.

Thankful that someone seemed to know what to do, Ruby trailed upstairs, a fretful, complaining Michael in her arms. She looked with awe at Emmie's bedroom into which she was ushered. Though its pretty, rose-covered curtains, which normally masked the blackout curtains, had been torn by glass, to Ruby it looked like a film star's bedroom. A matching curtain hung from a corner shelf, to make a wardrobe, and Ruby eyed its cascade of printed flowers wonderingly. The window glass had fallen in a rough heap beneath the sill, and Gwen leaned over it to slip the ripped blackout curtains across the casement.

Ruby shivered in the draught. She felt as if she had expended every scrap of energy she had, and she was sick with apprehension about her mother; she was silently counting the minutes until morning, when she could ask her father how she was and whether she could go to the hospital to see her.

Gwen pulled out a rose-wreathed chamber pot from under the bed. Michael objected violently to being held over it, and kicked and screamed. Gwen persisted until he made water – she was not going to have her beds soaked. A puddle was left on the heavily patterned linoleum. With the enraged child under one arm, she pulled back the bedclothes, to expose the whitest sheets Ruby had ever seen, and then shoved the little boy into bed.

"Now you be quiet," she ordered sharply. "Your Ruby's going to come and lie by you and make you warm, aren't you Ruby?" Ruby assented and started to climb into bed, shoes, dress and all, but Gwen looked at her in such a scandalised fashion, that she hastily reversed herself and pulled off her faded cotton dress and hooked it on to the bed knob. Then she kicked her worn lace-up shoes under the bed.

"That's better," Gwen approved.

Emboldened by the approbation, Ruby inquired, "Me mam? Which hospital did they take her to?"

Gwen looked at the whey-faced, skinny child nearly as tall as herself, the bony chest half-covered by a grubby vest. She knew nothing of the silent terror with which Ruby had faced the night; she saw only that the girl was swaying on her feet. She replied carefully, "Mr Baker was going to see about her being taken to hospital. I don't know which one, though. But you don't have to worry. Mr Baker is proper kind, and Mrs Baker will have gone in to comfort her, until the ambulance arrived." The latter statement made her realise what an accomplished liar she could be, but she cringed at telling the brutal truth. "Now you get into bed, and in no time your Dad'll be here and tell you all about it. Mr Baker was going to send a message up to the post as soon as the All Clear went."

Ruby smiled weakly and climbed into the wonderful bed. Two pillows and real white sheets – and blankets. Gwen tucked her and the complaining child into the bed and left them, taking the candle with her. As soon as she had left the room, Ruby got out again and felt around for the chamber pot.

"Our Emmie is going to have to make do on the sitting room sofa, when she comes in," Gwen told Patrick, who was waiting by the cold fireplace in the living room. He was still holding Brendy. Brendy's head had sunk on to his brother's shoulder and he was sound asleep. Patrick had managed to light the gaslight which hung from the middle of the ceiling, and a bright shaft lit up the back yard. Gwen tushed, and ran to the window to close the dusty blackout curtains over the flushed dawn sky. The breeze blew them up into the room, so she hastily picked up her work-basket and balanced it on the sill, to hold them down. A clatter of glass dropped into the kitchen rubbish-bin told her that Mari had done what she had been ordered to do. Gwen sighed, and turned to survey her remaining unwanted guests. "Now, what to do with you?"

"Dunno," responded Patrick mechanically. Round and round inside his head, went the picture of his mother as he had last seen her; nothing else touched him.

"I know. I'll put the girl here ..." She paused, and then asked, "What's your name?"

A malevolent, pinched face was turned up towards her. "I'm Nora," the tight lips spat out.

Gwen recoiled slightly. What a horrid, wizened-faced brat. "I'll put you and the little lad here – Brendy, isn't it? – in our Mari's bed. Mari can sleep with me." Not for all the wealth in China could she bring herself to put any of the children in her own huge double bed; she would never sleep comfortable in it again, she told herself. "And you, Patrick, can kip down on the sofa here. I'll get a blanket out for you. But first bring the kids upstairs."

She preceded him, the candle flame streaming a thin line of smoke behind her. "The whole place smells of smoke," she remarked over her shoulder, "but it's all from outside. Nothin' to worry about."

Patrick did not care what the place smelled of, as long as he could lie down, curl up and try to obliterate the fact that his maddening, bossy, beloved mam was dead.

Nora's stony expression relaxed and she followed Gwen up the carpeted staircase, sidling along like a stray dog in search of something to eat, sniffing, touching everything. She went straight to the dressing

116

table and, standing on tiptoe, reached over to pick up Mari's most prized possession, a china lady in a crinoline.

"You put that down!" Gwen's face was dark with immediate anger. "You don't touch nothin' in this house, young lady."

Nora glanced up at her with pale, expressionless eyes. Slowly she opened her hand and let the china figure drop. It broke into three pieces.

"You naughty little vixen," Gwen shrieked at her. She caught the child by the shoulder and gave her a sound slap on her bottom. "Our Mari'll be broken-hearted, she will, you little devil. Get your frock off and get into bed afore I mairder you."

With a look of complete satisfaction on her face, Nora removed her dress, to show only a pair of tattered knickers.

Gwen pulled a chamber pot from under the bed, this one with a pattern of violets to match the mauve curtains. "You pull them panties down and pay a call," she ordered a bridling Nora. Nora did not seem to hear, so Gwen took her by the shoulder and shoved her down on to it.

Patrick had stood with Brendy in his arms, waiting for Gwen to finish with Nora. He was used to loud voices and slaps and to Nora being a trial to his mother; it was nothing out of the ordinary.

Boiling with rage, Gwen whipped back the bedclothes and he thankfully put Brendy, fully-clothed, into the bed. "And you get in, miss, and let's have no more trouble," she ordered Nora. Nora, knowing the precise breaking point of most adults, felt it was wise to comply.

Outside the bedroom, Gwen and Patrick came face to

face with a bewildered, sulky Mari; she did not like her room being taken over by two dirty kids. "You get into our bed, Mari – on your father's side. I don't know what we do when he comes home. And I don't know what he's going to say."

She opened a drawer of a fine oak chest on the landing, one of the pieces of furniture appropriated from Emmie's home, and took out two thin, but clean, blankets. "You go make yourself comfy on the sofa in the living room," she told Patrick.

She had to repeat her command before Patrick took any notice. As Mari passed, she had caught his hand and squeezed it. "I'm sorry," she had whispered, and he realised with a gleam of comfort that she understood how he felt. He wanted to cry on her shoulder. To Gwen he said, "Yes, missus."

While Gwen lay, rigid and awake, beside Mari, Mari suddenly remarked, "You know, mam, it's over half an hour since the All-Clear went, and Auntie Emmie isn't in yet."

"Your aunt's big enough to take care of herself. She'll be in just now – probably gossiping somewhere." Gwen could not take any more; she had been tried beyond endurance, and the very thought of Emmie and her Robert added to her grumpiness. The sly bitch and her greediness about the furniture.

Though Emmie went through the motions of being a good sister-in-law, her bitter resentment against Gwen's refusal to help with her sick parents was all too apparent. Mari's reminder that Emmie had not yet returned made Gwen feel that she did not care if the woman never came back; yet, underneath it all, her Methodist conscience smote her hard – Emmie had carried a terrible load which Gwen could have eased. Angrily, she turned over in her bed. If Emmie were dead, she would be free of the remainder of her own sins of omission. Savagely, she *wished* her dead, as she lay seething with frustration at her current predicaments.

Suddenly, as a new horror occurred to her, she sat up in bed beside the sleeping Mari. She had never looked to see what had happened to her precious sitting-room – the aspidistra in its big, green pottery bowl, set on a table in the bay window, the settee and two easy chairs which she had recently recovered herself in bright orange-flowered cretonne, and the piano, still not quite paid for, which Mari was learning to play, taught at a shilling a lesson by Mrs Cooper down the road. Was it all ruined by the blast?

She could not bear it, if it were all spoiled. She started to turn back the bedclothes, to go down and look, and then flung them back over herself. She could not endure to know now, and she turned her face into her pillow and quietly wept herself to sleep.

Patrick, too, cried – into the patchwork cushion on the sagging horsehair sofa. The pain was so great that it was as if the shrapnel in his mother's body had pierced him.

A light tread descending the staircase made him lift his head abruptly. Was Mari coming down?

"Pat, where are you?"

"Here, Rube." He let his head fall back on to the cushion.

"I were so scared, Pat." She crept towards him through the darkened room and knelt down by the sofa. He sat up and her seeking arms went round him.

"It were the worst raid." Patrick's voice was more gentle.

"I'm worried about our mam. Mrs Thomas don't say much."

Patrick ran his tongue round his lips. Then he said very softly, "She's dead, Rube. Didn't you realise it?"

"Oh," she gasped, putting her hand against her mouth to control an involuntary shriek. "No, Pat. I thought she'd fainted."

She put her head down on his blanketed lap and he could feel her shivering. Then she began to sob. He sat stiffly under her weight. "Don't, Rube," he muttered. "Don't."

"I can't help it. What are we goin' to do without Mam?"

"Dunno," he replied thickly. But he did know. It happened all the time when mothers died. Ruby would take her mother's place. Like many another motherless girl, she would learn to wash and cook for the family and tend little Michael. He was glad he wasn't a girl. He lived for the day when he would be big enough, hefty enough, to go down to the docks and stand in the pen, to be picked again and again for work, because he was the biggest and best. And he would bring home real wages and take a pretty girl, like Mari, to the pictures. Ruby would slave most of her life for nothing, because her mother was dead.

No wonder Ruby wept.

ii

During this terrifying Saturday night and Sunday

120

morning, while Gwen coped with her unwelcome visitors, five hundred German bombers converged on the already stricken city, with orders to wipe it out, make it unusable by the convoys of ships from the United States.

They were met by Defiant fighter planes darting bravely in and out of the searchlight beams, in an effort to confuse and harass them. But the Defiants were too slow and their guns were wrongly placed, and not all the gallantry and skill of their crews could compensate for the planes' deficiencies.

There were not many seamen in the canteen that night, nor had the firewatchers come in for their accustomed snacks. Deckie Dick was seated in his usual place at the centre table, from which vantage point he could look out of the window to watch the passing scene and also observe all that was going on in the canteen itself. He idly shuffled the deck of cards, from which he derived his nickname, from one hand to the other, as he regaled a bored younger merchant seaman with the story of the rescue work he had participated in the night before.

When the first bombs whistled down, neither staff nor customers sought the shelter of the basement, but when suddenly the attack seemed particularly near and intense, everybody dropped what they were doing and fled for the stairs. As they tumbled down the curving flight, the window shutters flew open with an angry rattle; the front door was blown off its hinges and shot across the canteen, followed by a torrent of sand from burst sandbags. As the blast receded, the door flew out again, to crash against the lamp post on the pavement.

Miss Piggot, one of the volunteers, had tripped on the

bottom step and fallen, taking a swearing, flailing Scot down with her. Now, they both picked themselves up off the stone floor and ruefully rubbed their knees. "My poor stockings," wailed Miss Piggot, lifting her skirts to look at the tears. Mrs Robinson pushed her to one side and quickly closed the stout door which guarded the foot of the staircase. She sat down on one of the benches and smiled at a thin, pimpled Royal Naval rating already perched there. He was rolling himself a cigarette, with trembling fingers. "Soon be over," she told him comfortingly. He replied wryly, "I'd rather be at sea." And her plump face creased with laughter.

"Phew!" exclaimed Emmie, as she sat down by Deckie Dick. "That were close." She shivered and rubbed her bare forearms, as if she were cold.

"Aye. Looks as if we're in for a bad night." He looked tired beneath the grey stubble of two days' beard. As a night watchman, he was not used to heavy physical labour and he had spent the previous night heaving beams and chunks of stone out of the way of rescue squads. As he glanced down at Emmie's anxious face, he was thinking he would be thankful to be back at work on Monday night, when he could, between his rounds, kip down in a warm corner of the warehouse which he watched. He leaned his bald head, with its fringe of white hair, against the whitewashed wall and closed his eyes against the glare of the single electric light bulb hanging from the ceiling. Pity the lodging house in which he lived was so noisy; otherwise he could have slept in a bit longer that morning.

As the raid progressed, the electric light began to flicker, so Mrs Robinson opened her capacious handbag and took out a candle and some matches. She lit it and then glued it down on to the corner table, by drips of its own wax. Then she blew it out.

The uproar outside became intense. "Good thing they're bringing in mining engineers, to help out," remarked Dick, his eyes still closed. "They can advise the heavy-rescue men."

Emmie nodded and leaned forward to rest her face on her hands, to stop herself shaking.

Mrs Robinson turned to the taciturn countess, who was seated stiffly opposite her, her ankles crossed neatly, her skirts precisely arranged around her. "I wish I had shut the canteen at ten o'clock," she remarked. "I had an uneasy feeling this morning that there would be another raid tonight."

The countess looked down her Norman nose and sniffed delicately. "On no account should you have closed. It would show that we are intimidated." Her wonderful diamond rings flashed, as she dismssed the Luftwaffe with an impatient gesture.

The naval rating drew on his cigarette and stared at her. Proper rum old dame, she was. If he were as rich as she looked, he would be thirty miles away from any place like Liverpool.

A gaunt and hunched ship's stoker, sitting cross-legged on the floor playing cards with three others, suddenly looked up. "Can yer smell smoke?" he inquired nervously of the company.

"Be funny if we couldn't, after last night's effort," grunted one of his fellow players. He shuffled his cards secretly, close to his face.

"I mean in here," the stoker responded irritably. Holding his cards to his chest, he got up, went to the door and opened it. Conversation ceased. He crept up a couple of steps and peered around, then bolted down again, as a huge swish followed by a roar and the sound of tumbling masonry indicated a hit nearby.

"Shut the door, you bloody fool," shouted a highly alarmed voice.

"Had to take a look-see," grumbled the equally shaken stoker. "T' canteen might've bin bairnin' over our heads."

Emmie fidgeted unhappily beside Deckie Dick. Why planners never put lavatories in air raid shelters was beyond her. It was certain that they must live far away from air raids; otherwise they would have known that the banshee wail of the warning was like a switch turning on your waterworks. She wondered if some of the fellows felt as she did, and she giggled shakily.

Deckie Dick opened his eyes. "What's ticklin' yer, luv?"

She blushed and whispered into his ear. He laughed, and replied, "I'm in the same boat."

The card players had been murmuring together. Now the owner of the pack knocked them together and put them in his back pocket. They got up and stretched. "Got to get back to the ship," they informed Mrs Robinson, "raid or no raid."

Mrs Robinson, alarmed, half rose from her bench. "You can't go out in this, Mr Petersen. No one would expect you to." But she read the panic in their eyes, and she sank down again. A ship out in the river might seem a safer place than the bedlam surrounding them.

Their opening of the door let in a dull roar, punctuated by occasional shouts and the sound of lorries from the docks being driven in low gear, as drivers tried to get themselves and their loads to safety.

They scurried up the steps, only to throw themselves flat on the littered floor at the top, as another deafening detonation made the old building shudder and sent bits of plaster flying from the ceiling. The subsequent rumble of falling masonry confirmed their opinion that, if they *could* get away, they preferred to be aboard ship. Who wanted to be buried under eight floors of eighteenth-century stone blocks?

As they scrambled over the remains of the sandbag wall, they were shaken to see that the street was as light as day.

"Get under cover," shouted an irate auxiliary policeman, running towards them half sideways, like a crab, to gain the greatest protection from the office walls.

The men took no notice of him and sped past him, bent on reaching the overhead railway which might well still be running and would take them south, away from what appeared to be the raid's main targets. In so doing, they saved their lives.   With her face buried in her lap and her arms clasped over her head for maximum protection, Emmie prayed that Robert was safely out of the port. She jabbed Deckie Dick with her elbow, and shouted above the noise, "Do you think Robbie will've sailed yet?"

Dick paused before answering. He knew that the *Malakand* had not yet left dock and he knew what she was being loaded with. But why add to the girl's worries? He answered her quite cheerfully, "She may have got away this mornin'."

Relieved, Emmir returned to worrying about the need to go to the lavatory.

In No. 2 Huskisson, Robbie heaved the last of a series

of spitting incendiaries off the foredeck and into the water.

"Watch it!" shrieked one of his mates, and pointed upwards.

Robbie whipped round.

A barrage balloon, half deflated, loosed from its moorings, was settling into the rigging.

Someone shrieked to Robbie, "Get away. It'll explode."

Robbie scrambled aft and with the rest of the crew watched helplessly as the grey monster was pulled and pushed by the breeze. A particularly strong gust loosened it and it flopped on to the for'ard deck.

Several men started towards it, but they were grabbed and held back by more cautious seamen.

A second later, the grey, silky mass burst into flames, a huge, scarifying ball of fire.

Regardless of the deadly cargo beneath their feet, the officers ordered hoses out and for fifteen agonised minutes the crew deluged the roaring fire with water, while more incendiaries were scattered down on to the hapless freighter.

A Nazi bomber swooped along the nearby dock sheds dropping a further load of incendiaries. Orange flowers of flame burst from the roofs, and in minutes a mighty conflagration stretched from Huskisson to Seaforth, like a brilliant multicoloured curtain. The wind generated by the fire sent huge fingers of flame out to the boat, and the crew found themselves surrounded by fire licking along the ship from stem to stern. Robbie could see the raw terror which struck him, reflected in the eyes of the others; yet they and the auxiliary firemen sent to help them held on to their hoses until, through the noise of the blaze, came the firm voice of the shore relief master, "Abandon ship."

Black, singed and panting, they regrouped on the dockside and were immediately put to work jetting water into the holds, while a special tender was sent for, to bring oxy-acetylene apparatus to the boat.

"Goin' to try scuttlin' her – cut a hole in her side," a fireman said to Robbie, as they sought to hold a wriggling hose towards the ship.

"Aye, they'd better be quick," Robbie gasped, "or we're all for Kingdom Come, and half of Liverpool as well."

iii

There was a fumbling at the door of the canteen shelter. Mrs Robinson hastened to open it, and an air raid warden entered in a puff of smoke. His tin hat was askew and he was swaying with fatigue. "Just checkin' who's here," he assured them, and, pointing to each person, he counted the number present.

"What's happening up there?" asked Mrs Robinson. Her face was wan and her lipstick smudged, giving her a clownlike appearance.

The warden flopped down on the end of a bench and the weary shelterers turned towards him. He took off his tin hat to rub his bald head. Emmie noticed that his trousers were thick with dust and there were holes in the knees.

"Lewis's store is a raging inferno," he said to Mrs Robinson, in answer to her query. "Must've lost most of their firewatchers. T' firemen is stuck for water." His dispirited voice lifted a little, and he grinned, "'T' fire brigade has pumped all the water out of the Adelphi's swimming bath into Lewis's. That'll larn that snobs' paradise."

A ripple of laughter at the expense of the city's finest hotel went through the company.

Too bad about the firewatchers, thought Emmie, but if you didn't laugh at what was funny you'd soon go mad.

"Our telephone at the post is out," he went on more soberly. "Bloody havoc without it. Seen a couple of post office engineers just now, slinging lines every which way, to get us connected up again. And there's another two of them sittin' in a crater right in the street here, splicin' telephone lines as calm as if they was havin' afternoon tea at Lyons'." He stood up and stretched. "It's a bloody miracle they're not dead."

"Should we try to move out of here?" asked Mrs Robinson.

"Nay. You're safer here than anywhere. South Castle Street, at the back here, is a shambles, what with fire and direct hits. I'll come back and tell you, if the firemen think you should move."

"Do they need men up there?" inquired a lanky individual in battered beige denim trousers, as he got up clumsily from the floor.

"Not now, they don't. They will when the All Clear goes, though."

"Not tonight, Josephine. Sit down again," cracked a wit.

The warden clapped his helmet back on to his head, grinned in a friendly way and clumped back up the steps.

A collective sigh went through the company and they settled back to wait again.

The light went out. Mrs Robinson quietly lit the candle. Its flame seemed to emphasize the lined faces of the men and women, picking out a drooping eyelid, a blackened tooth, the sole of a shoe with a hole in it, the glitter of a cheap ring on a chapped hand.

From the gloom, a forlorn young voice informed its neighbour, "Me leave's up at eight o'clock tomorrer mornin'. Got to be back in camp by then. I were on me way to the station when this lot started. Ah coom in 'ere, thinkin' it'd all blow over in an hour."

"You got a bleedin' hope, mate. You live around here?" Deckie Dick inquired.

"Aye, wi' me gran. Lives in Pitt Street. She were scared enough last night, without this on top."

Emmie remembered that a heavily built youth in battledress had scuttled into the canteen when the first bomb fell. Poor lad. No more'n eighteen, he must be.

The young voice continued, a little muffled from the owner's face being buried in his lap, his tin hat perched atop the back of his head. "Dunno whether to go back home or go t' station and show up late at camp anyways."

"Report back to camp," rumbled several voices, and Deckie Dick added, "Aye, you'll be in real trouble if you don't – absent without leave, they'll jump you for. There's people as'll look after your gran." He raised his head from his lap, to look at the crouching boy. "I'll go meself, if you like. You give me your address and her address. I'll go and see her tomorrer – and I'll write to you straight away. You'll get it the next day."

The boy glanced up quickly at Dick's ruddy,

good-natured visage, faintly lit by the candle. "She'd be proper pleased. She's real lonely," he said somewhat more cheerfully.

With Mrs Robinson's fountain pen, he clumsily printed the addresses on the back of a café receipt and passed the paper to Dick.

Dick folded it up carefully, put it into a shabby wallet and returned the wallet to his back pocket. Above the wallet he pushed in a grubby comb; he always said that a comb was the best defence against pickpockets or even plain losing your wallet. Now he thought that it would not hurt him to go and sit with some old Irish biddy for an hour, to help a youngster. It would be something to do. He had been lonely ever since his wife's death a year earlier.

The noise outside gradually lessened, as if the main target of the raid had been shifted. Ears pricked and heads were cautiously raised.

Emmie thought for a second that she heard women's voices outside. Women's Voluntary Service van, she guessed, feeding the firemen and the wardens. My, she could use a cup of tea herself.

"I'm goin' upstairs," announced Deckie Dick heavily. He winked down at Emmie.

Emmie promptly jumped up. "I'll come, too."

It was evident from a lewd gesture on the part of Deckie Dick where he was going, and Mrs Robinson said apprehensively, "Emmie, you should not go upstairs yet; it's too dangerous."

Emmie was immediately defensive. Nobody was going to tell her any more what she should or should not do; she'd had a bowlful of that from her parents. Besides, if she didn't go soon, she'd wet her knickers.

Emmie smoothed her skirts and tossed her head. "I'll be all right, Mrs Robinson. Dickie'll look after me." She glanced teasingly at Dick, as if single-handedly he could force the Luftwaffe into retreat.

Left to himself, Dickie would have run up the stairs and urinated just outside the front door, and then returned as fast as his tired legs would have carried him. But Emmie would be counting on his going through to the backyard privies.

The man sitting next to Dick yawned and glanced at Emmie. "You lucky bastard," he muttered to Dick.

Dick laughed. He felt that at his age it was a compliment.

In the middle of the wrecked canteen, they paused to look through the gaping hole where the window had been, at the dancing shadows on the wall of the building opposite.

"Good Heavens!" Emmie exclaimed fearfully. "There must be an awful fire behind our building."

"T' warden said as we were OK. Come on now, quick." His words were nearly drowned in the rumble of a series of bomb explosions, as the Luftwaffe took a run at the centre of the fire they had started alongside No.2 Huskisson.

Except for glassless windows, all the buildings round the light well seemed undamaged, though the sky glowed red above them. They ran across the cobbled yard, glass crunching under their feet, and with sighs of relief paid the long-delayed calls.

Close to hand, the tumbling roar of a wall collapsing brought them both out at a run, Emmie still pulling up her knickers. It buried the warden beneath its shattered stone, as he ran along the street. Another bomb exploded in the fire at the back of them, sending a shower of sparks into the air. Emmie screamed.

A further swish and crash made Dick hurl her to the ground, his plump body on top of her.

"Jesus, save us!" she shrieked, as she hit the unfriendly cobblestones. She clung to him.

"Keep yer head down. God, that was …"

With a deafening crash, the whole of the canteen was blown out.

An agonised blow on the forehead made her yell again, as she and Dick were lifted by the blast. Then, clinging to Dick, she was rolling and falling. She saw the ground beneath them crack and open in a tremendous yawn, as if in some unearthly dream. Dick seemed to slip from her, as she hit sliding rubble and then half fell, half slid, down and down on to a shuddering floorspace, mercilessly bumped and bruised as she went. She was aware, in a split second, of the earth closing over her as if a great door had been slammed, of a dreadful weight on the lower part of her body and of an ear-rending storm of noise. Then silence, except, from nearby, thin horrifying screams like souls crying out in Dante's *Inferno*, as she sank into oblivion.

iv

In smothering dust, Emmie fought for breath. As she coughed and choked and spat, the pain in her head was all-encompassing. She endeavoured to raise a hand to clear her face of rubble, but both hands were pinned against her stomach by a huge, warm solid mass; she shuddered as she realised what it might be.

132

She tried shaking her head and then moaned when the movement not only added to the pain in her head, but pulled her hair as well; its longer strands appeared to be caught under some unyielding weight.

Suddenly she sneezed enormously, her nose ran and she could breathe a little more easily. Small anonymous pieces of rubble, dislodged by the sneeze, slipped down the sides of her face.

As greater consciousness seeped back into her and she laboured for air amid the cloying dust, the dawning knowledge that she was buried made her tremble violently.

She became aware of stinging pain all over her face, in addition to the throbbing in her head. Cautiously, fearfully, she opened her eyes a slit. She could see nothing.

She was blind! She was sure of it. The trickles she could feel from her eyes must be blood, not tears. She screamed in horror, a howl of pure terror. Dust again entered her throat and the screams became strangled coughs. Then the pain in her head overwhelmed her and she faded into unconsciousness again.

She came round slowly, aware now of being surrounded by reverberating, booming noise. The ground under her, if it were ground and not a floor of some kind, vibrated continuously, adding to her own shuddering. The sagging weight on her body also moved slightly. At first her fogged mind believed the movement was also caused by the noise; then a large breath was exhaled, followed by a series of coughs.

In sudden joy, she croaked, "Is that you, Dick?"

Though she got no reply because of the paroxysm of coughing, she felt a hand run down the side of her and heard a faint rattle of what sounded like pebbles falling as the same hand apparently explored a little further. Then, with a satisfied grunt as the coughs eased, the body carefully rolled over until it was positioned tightly beside her. A series of muffled curses in a man's voice came from close to her ear. Thankfully she took a larger breath, to ease her constricted lungs, only to set off a further desperate coughing which threatened to cause her to vomit, as powdered plaster cloyed her throat again.

Above her, there was a series of ominous creaks, and in the distance the sound of water trickling. The surrounding uproar seemed to have decreased.

"Hold it, luv. Hold it," came a frantic whisper. "Yer noise'll bring the whole issue down on us. Breath shallow, if you can."

She did her best to control the coughing, lifting a hand, tingling with pins and needles, to cover her mouth. Between efforts to clear her throat, she giggled hysterically, "Oh, Dickie, I'm so glad you're here."

"*I'm* not," came the dry response. The body packed tightly beside her fidgeted slightly. "God spare us!"

She began to laugh wildly at this, only to choke again and to have her hair pulled painfully as she moved.

"Hold your hush, luv," he cajoled softly and caught one of her hands as if to comfort her.

She sobered as best she could. "Are you hurt, Dick?" she inquired hoarsely.

"Not much, I don't think. Wind kicked out o' me." His breath came laboriously. "Feel like I did after a fight once, in a bar in New York. Got beat up." He squeezed her hand. "How about you?"

134

He could feel her trembling increase. Carefully, he lifted an arm round her, as she whimpered, "Dickie, I think I'm blinded. I can't see anything. Me hair is caught under something – and me face is all wet and sticky. I'm afraid to touch it."

He did not reply for a moment and then he assured her, "Well nobody could see in this dark. Are you sure? Open and close yer eyelids. Do they work? You're lying on your back, aren't you?"

"I can move me lids. They're awful sore."

"Humph. Well, try touching round them, very lightly, to see if the eyes is still in their sockets."

Sickened by the implication, she nevertheless moved her fingers cautiously round her cheeks and over her closed lids. She moved her eyes from right to left and then blinked. "They seem all right," she announced with marked relief. "They're running like mad."

"Aye, you probably got dust in them; but it's my bet you'll be all right, when there's light to see by. I were lucky – I had me face against you when we fell. Can you move your legs?"

Diverted, her trembling lessened, and she obediently bent her legs slightly and wiggled her feet. He felt the movement, when she arched her back. "All of me seems to work," she announced with a tremulous laugh. "I can't turn me head, though, 'cos me hair's caught under summat."

They lay quiet for a minute, while the dust thinned. Then she asked pitifully, "How long will it take 'em to get us out, Dickie?"

He sighed – carefully, so that he did not commence to cough again. He had been thinking about this and was privately convinced that it would be a miracle if they

135

were ever found. While Emmie had been unconscious, he had lain over her, dazed by the fall, his mind trying to grapple with the mystery of where they were.

They had been in the light well, lying on the ground, against the wall of the canteen under the little kitchen window. They must, he argued, have fallen straight through a fissure opened up by the bomb explosion. Yet, could they fall though a solid yard? He had definitely fallen through open space – he would remember the sensation until the end of his days.

The answer seemed to be that they lay in some old cellar under the cobbled yard. And who would dream of looking for them there? Only the people in the shelter knew that he and Emmie had gone into the yard, and judging by the fearful groans and shrieks with which his ears had been tortured for a moment or two after the bomb fell, those in the shelter were either dead or dying.

If all the buildings had come down, there could be sixty feet or more of debris above them. This had to be the end. And yet in him, bruised and scared as he was, lay a tremendous passion to live.

"How long, Dickie?"

"Dunno." The dust was settling now and it was much easier to breath, but delayed shock caught up with him and he fainted. Emmie felt the body stuffed in beside her relax and she thought he had died. She poked him with her elbow. He did not respond. "Dick! Oh, Dickie!"

Total fear engulfed her again and she began to scream helplessly, rendered almost insane with fright. She gibbered at him, as she tried to reach his face and finally succeeded in running one hand over it. Then she felt his chest heave slightly. She quietened and it seemed as if he were sleeping, and indeed he did pass into a light slumber.

She lay sobbing softly and between the sobs prayers tumbled from her lips. Promises to lead an immaculate life if only God would get her out of the tomb in which she lay came almost incoherently forth, as she tried to make a pact with the Almighty.

"I'll never hate Gwen no more. I'll help her all I can. She can have the bloody furniture. Oh, Jesus, hear me. What will Robbie do if I die? He's been so lonely for lack of a wife, oh, God. Have pity on him, if not on me. I know I'm as wicked a piece as ever was made, but I'll never miss chapel again, I won't. God have pity on me."

Deckie Dick became gradually aware of this litany, as he awoke and his mind began to clear. He was himself afraid of death, particularly a painful death. How would the Grim Reaper strike? Would the debris shift, to slide down and crush them? Would they die of thirst? Or starve like rats? Or, worse still, be eaten by rats before they had a chance to starve?

There was an increasing smell of escaping gas, faint but distinct. Deckie Dick also addressed his prayers to whatever Gods might be to let the gas thicken and engulf them. It would be a comparatively quick death; he had thought of sticking his head in the gas oven after his wife had died. With one son, Georgie, killed at Dunkirk and the other one, Billie, long since emigrated to the States, there was no one left to care about him. Now he wished, prayed, that this quick death might be granted to him and to the sweet woman lying next to him. Selflessly, he begged that there be at least sufficient concentration of gas to render her unconscious, so that she never knew what hit her, even if it

137

was not sufficient to snuff out a tough old devil like himself.

V

Conor staggered into his crowded post, and Glynis Hughes looked up from tending a stout woman with a knifelike pain in her chest. The woman was nearly purple in the face and Glynis had been trying to keep her from going into hysterics, until one of the First Aid men, who had been called from the Dwellings, arrived with some more nitro-glycerine. The man followed Conor in, pushed him aside and plunged through the crowded room. Glynis snatched a spoon from a used teacup and handed it to him. She held the struggling woman, while he forced the life-saving liquid down her throat. In seconds, the pain abated, and Glynis thankfully left her to the care of the new arrival, while she pushed her way over to Conor, who stood like a zombie amid the crowd, his eyes half closed with fatigue. He was covered with grey-white dust, except across his knees and stomach, where his unform and the dust were stained dark red. Around him, the room hummed with voices, through which cut the sound of the telephonist relaying details of casualties and damage as they were brought to her. The line had been broken during the night and, despite a quick repair, the telephonist was having difficulty, as she laboured in a high-pitched voice to overcome the crackling of the line.

"Got a cup o' tea, Glynis?" his voice grated, as she reached him.

She eased her little buttocks past the back of the

138

telephonist's chair and laid a hand on his arm. "Sure. I'll get you one. But – but first I got to tell you somethin'. Come out in the street a mo'; it's quieter."

How am I going to do it? she worried. He always teased about his old woman, but he was fond of her for certain. And she was a kind woman, me mam always said. Dumbly, Conor allowed himself to be ushered into the street and a little away from the gossips by the door. Glynis turned and looked up at him compassionately. "Conor," she whispered.

"Is it one of the kids?" he asked, suddenly alert.

"No, Conor. It's Ellen." She grasped one of his hands hanging limply by his side. "She's gone, Conor. Mr Baker came earlier. Said she got a piece of shrapnel straight to her heart. 'Twas instant. She didn't suffer. I'm so sorry, Conor." She was trying not to cry, as he stared unbelievingly down at her. "The kids are all right. Your next-door neighbour – Mrs Thomas, isn't it – she's got them all and is taking care of them. The house is OK, too."

Conor licked his dry lips. "Where's Ellen?"

"She's laid out in the church hall – along with the others from The Dwellings. Monty got her picked up from the house real quick, in case your kids went in there. He's still here, if you want to pop over and see her."

His hand clenched hers tightly and the weary eyes closed. "I'm accursed," he said bitterly. "Accursed."

Glynis shivered. "Don't say that."

"First we lose everything we got, and nearly little Rube as well. And now Ellen."

"Go and see her," urged Glynis, a little desperately. "Father O'Dwyer'll be there, no doubt, to talk to."

"And what good will that do, to me or to him? And what good can I do for Ellen — Ellen!" He almost shouted and then his voice broke.

"You have to arrange her funeral — I'm sorry to say it."

He looked round him, like an animal trying to escape when cornered, then back at the tearful woman still holding his hand. "Glynis, down behind the filing cabinet in the post there's some whiskey — there's half a dozen bottles and more in the cellar. But don't say nothin'. Just get one out for me."

She smiled through her tears. So he did indeed smuggle whiskey. "To be sure," she said. "Trust me. We'll have a hot cup of tea with a good swig in it. You come back in, lad, and sit down a minute."

When she returned to him with a steaming cup of tea smelling strongly of whiskey, he was seated on a wooden chair, his face in his hands, and was weeping. Opposite him a middle-aged man, wrapped in a blanket, his bare feet sticking out from under it, sniffed and caught the odour of the spirit. Out of the corner of her eyes, Glynis saw the tired eyes light up. "I'll bring you a cup — exactly the same," she promised. "In a minute."

She put the cup and saucer into Conor's hand and then put an arm over his shoulder. He turned to her and hid his face against her breast. The tea slopped into the saucer. "I'm damned, Glynis," he mumbled. "Why Ellen? She never done anything wicked in her life!"

"I don't know," she replied sadly, and patted and stroked him, as if she were comforting one of her children.

When Gwen heard the knock on the front door, she thought it was David returning and that he had mislaid his key. She flew down the stairs clad only in her long, white nightgown and thankfully swung open the door.

She did not recognise for a moment the anguished man on the door step. Then a familiar Irish voice, with an unaccustomed wheeze in it, greeted her politely. "Mornin', Mrs Thomas. I'm told you kindly took me kids in?"

In the interests of modesty, she wrapped the cotton folds of her nightgown more tightly round her. Then she said, "Yes, indeed, Mr Donnelly. They're here. I think they're still asleep."

Without being invited, he stepped into the highly polished hall. Gwen's lips tightened, when he failed to wipe his feet on the doormat, a new one with the word *Welcome* knotted into it. He brought with him a strong smell of whiskey – and raw meat, was it? She shivered as she shut the door quickly behind him.

He looked uneasily round the hall and then sighed. "Do they know?" he asked her bluntly.

"No. Come in here for a minute." She ushered him into the small sitting room, and nearly cried out at the sight of her biggest aspidistra lying smashed in a pile of earth on her new red, imitation Belgian carpet, a carpet which had only two more payments to be made on it before it was entirely hers. Despite the breeze coming through the glassless windows, the room smelled cold and dank from disuse. Both the cretonne curtains and the blackout were in shreds. Gwen felt, in sudden rage, that she could happily strangle a German with her bare hands.

"What happened?" Conor almost snapped at her, as he turned to her.

A little frightened of the tight, frozen look of the filthy, tear-stained face in front of her, she stuttered an explanation. "Patrick knows," she finished up. "He's asleep on the sofa in the other room."

"I'll have to tell 'em, Mrs Thomas." He looked at her imploringly, hoping she would do it. But she was on the defensive now. There was a limit, she told herself. Enough that she had had these dreadful children thrust upon her. She couldn't.

"What if I get Patrick in here, and you talk to him?" she suggested.

He nodded, and turned to look out of the devastated window, while she gathered her nightgown even more tightly round her and went to get the boy.

"No!" she exclaimed in genuine horror, as she looked down at Ruby and Patrick tightly intertwined under the blankets on the sofa. She bent down and tapped Ruby on the shoulder. The girl woke with a jump. "Your father's here," she announced frigidly. "He wants to see Patrick in the sitting room. You stay here, miss." She would deal with their shocking indecency afterwards. Brother and sister sleeping together! She was scandalized.

Hardly comprehending what she had said, the two children looked up at their outraged hostess. Patrick yawned and then, without a word, he swung himself off the sofa and lurched unsteadily out of the room. Mrs Thomas pursed her lips and stared down at Ruby. Ruby slowly laid her head back down on the cushion she had shared with Patrick. She began to cry helplessly.

Gwen turned towards the fireplace and rolled back the hearthrug, preparatory to making the fire. "I should think so, too," she muttered angrily. "Such behaviour I never did see."

Yesterday, Patrick would have sworn that he hated his father. But now the object of his jealousy was dead and his father suddenly seemed a pillar of strength. He stumbled towards him and Conor held him, while they both wept heartily. Finally, Patrick snuffled, "Rube knows."

In the living room, Gwen put down her poker. She was suddenly cold. without a word to the weeping girl, she ran quickly upstairs to get her dressing-gown.

Immediately she vanished, Ruby sat up, untangled herself from the blankets and ran, barefoot, into the sitting room and flung herself into her father's arms.

With an arm round each of his children and tears smudging his dusty face, Conor asked them not to tell the little ones that their mother was dead. "Tell 'em she's in hospital being mended," he suggested. "Better they know when your gran comes down from Walton. I tried to phone the post there, so as to get hold of her quick – it were dead – so I wrote to her, but with it being Sunday today, she won't get it till tomorrer." Gran was his own mother. Ellen's mother lived in Dublin – and he realised suddenly that he must write to her as well.

"You all stay with Mrs Thomas, till I can get home. And you help her, Rube."

Ruby agreed sulkily that she would help her. "Pat, you feed me cocks – and beg a few scraps from Mrs Thomas for Sarge." The boy sniffed lachrymosely and nodded agreement. He could hear Gwen in the next room raking out the fireplace. Even the sound of the poker seemed angry.

Gwen was just putting a match to the paper of the newly laid fire, when Conor entered, Ruby hanging on to his arm. Patrick followed, his face stony.

Conor loosed himself from his daughter and bent down to seize one of Gwen's coal-blackened hands and shake it hard. His breath stank of whiskey; still kneeling, she recoiled from him.

"It's proper kind of you to take in me kids, Mrs Thomas. I'll not forget it. Mr Baker said you would keep them for a while. By the looks of things, I won't be home until tomorrer – at least. It's terrible up at The Dwellings. You never saw anything like it. Keep the kids away – it's no sight for them. I've written to their gran, but with everything being upset in the town she probably won't get the letter till tomorrer afternoon at earliest." He paused for breath and looked at her anxiously.

"I – but – I …" she began, a fearful sinking feeling in her stomach.

He burst into speech again. "I tried to get the wardens' post up there on the phone. Can't get through to anybody." He seemed to take it for granted that she would keep the children with her, and went on, "We won't tell the little ones their mam is gone, till their granny comes to comfort 'em." He took a turn about the room, while Gwen watched him, speechless for once. "You can say she's in hospital, doing fine, soon be home, like."

She opened her mouth, to make an excuse for not keeping the children, but he deflected her by asking, "Where's your hubby?"

"Still workin' out at Bootle. And our Emma isn't in yet."

Overwhelmed by his own troubles, Conor failed to realise that Emmie must have been in the thick of the air raid. He said mechanically, as he hugged Ruby again and turned towards the door, "She'll probably be in just now."

While the children saw their father out, Gwen leaned forward and mechanically struck another match to light the fire, which had failed to kindle. She sat on her heels, watching the flames creep through the newspaper and wondered what to do. There was not enough food in the house to feed everybody and little money in her purse to buy more. David would be furious if she exceeded her housekeeping money. Mechanically she gave the fireplace a quick whisk with a brass-handled hearth brush, and then continued to sit listening to the wood crackle, feeling exhausted, defeated.

Ruby watching her, hesitated in the doorway and then advanced diffidently. She put her arm shyly round Gwen and said, "Don't cry, Mrs Thomas. I'll help yez."

Startled, she turned in the curve of the child's arm. A little stiffly, she put her own arm round Ruby. "Well, thank you, Ruby." The girl smelled to high heaven. Hadn't her mother taught her to wash herself? Perhaps she hadn't been taught not to sleep with her brother, either, she meditated grimly. She scrambled to her feet. She *must* do something.

While Mari still slept, Ruby and Patrick were set to work, she to sweep up the remaining glass in the living room and he to tack some pieces of old lino culled from the cellar, over the gaping windows. The table was laid and a small helping of cornflakes put out for each child.

"And after breakfast, if you're going to be here overnight, everybody had better have a bath."

Both Ruby and Patrick were taken aback. They had never had a bath; only an occasional wash all over in the kitchen bowl; they were saved from having to reply by Nora and Brendy rushing down the stairs in a panic, having forgotten where they were. They surveyed the living room with popping eyes, broke into roars of tears and demanded to go home to Mam. Ruby mothered them both and soon they were shovelling cornflakes into their mouths, while they watched very suspiciously the preparation of the tin bath set in front of the fire.

Michael shrieked from upstairs and Ruby ran up to him. He had soaked the bed and was standing on it, holding the brass head rail. In the half darkness of the room, Ruby held him to her and told him Mam would be coming soon to fetch him. No amount of soft talk, however, would persuade him to eat cornflakes or even drink milk from a glass. He wanted his mother's breast.

Gwen surveyed him in harassed silence for a moment, as he sat on Ruby's knee kicking out in a furious paddywack. Finally she said wearily, "He'll eat when he's real hungry. Let him be for now. We might as well bath him first." She moved the dish of cornflakes away from Michael's flailing arms. "Do you have any clean nappies or pants for him at home? And any clean clothes for the other kids?"

"There's some," Ruby answered her doubtfully. "Me mam washed Thursday." She dreaded that Gwen might command her to go to fetch them. Her stomach churned at the idea of finding her mother lying so still in the hall.

Patrick came in from the kitchen, carrying a steaming bucket of water to tip into the tin bath. "I'll go and get 'em," he said heavily. "I got to feed the birds – and Sarge. They'll have taken Mam to hospital by now – won't they, Mrs Thomas?"

Gwen had forgotten about Ellen. She hesitated, and then said, "I think so, lad."

Mr Baker had remembered to let the dog out into the tiny back yard, and Sarge greeted Patrick ecstatically. He padded into the house behind the boy.

Patrick went straight to the front hall, almost hoping that his mother would be lying there, made comfortable by nurses, and that she would open her eyes and say she was fine, just waiting for the ambulance. But there was only the quilt from Ruby and Nora's bed piled against the wall. Slowly an all-consuming rage spread through him, that strangers had taken away his mother without his seeing her again. He kicked angrily at the quilt, and Sarge, who had been nosing round it, slunk back, tail between legs. He stamped his feet and then banged his fists against the wall, bent his head and hit that too against the hollow plaster. "Yer pack of sewer rats," he screamed at the anonymous ghosts who had come in the night to carry away his mother. He forgot about the clothing he was supposed to collect and ran through the house, up the stairs and down again, kicking open doors, screaming obscenities which echoed through the house, yelling what he would do to a German if he ever met one. He picked up some used cups from the kitchen table and slammed them on to the floor and crunched the broken pieces under his boots, until the fury of frustration waned and he stood sobbing helplessly in the deserted kitchen.

There an anxious Ruby found him. She put down on the floor an extraordinarily clean Michael, clad only in his jersey. The child was sucking his thumb, tears still wet on his face. He glanced round the kitchen, looking for his mother. Small sobs shook him from time to time and he stared in a dazed fashion at his big brother.

Ruby put her arms round Patrick. "It's no good, Pat. She's gone."

The boy pushed her away and turned his back on her. He mopped his eyes with the end of the woolly tie of his jersey.

"We have to find some clothes for Mrs Thomas."

"Damn her."

"Don't knock her, Pat. She's trying to help. We'd be in a right muddle without her – and no Dad either."

He turned a dark, passionate face on his sister. "I can't stand her. I'm not having no bath. I'm going to see what Dad's doin'."

With a huge sniff, he swung past her, opened the front door and slammed it after him.

Ruby stared after him, her whole body trembling with fear of the responsibility left to her, fear of offending Gwen, fear of not being able to cope with Michael, Nora and Brendy, fear of being terribly alone to face everything – perhaps yet another air raid that night.

vii

"It's quietened," Emmie pointed out. "It must be Sunday morning by now. We've been here ages, Dickie, and I'm so parched. Are you thirsty?" The voice was thin and quivery.

148

"Aye, I am. 'Could use a pint." He cleared his throat. "Yer know, there's a bit o' water here, somewhere. I can hear it trickling – faint, like."

"I know. It's not very far, but I can't move 'cos of me hair." Emmie's voice quavered and threatened hysterics again.

"There's a straight wall on t' other side of you, isn't there?"

"Yeah." She raised her arm up as far as she could reach, and winced with pain from bruises acquired in her fall. "There's enough space above me – I think – for me to sit up. She ran her fingers along the obstruction above her. "It feels as if there's a very big rough stone over us. It slopes down towards you, till it must touch you. If I could turn on me side, I could give you more room."

"Sardines in a bloody tin," he snorted. "Can you reach over your head to your hair where it's caught?"

"Mm. I've bin tryin' to pull some of it loose."

"I've got a penknife in me pocket. I doubt I can get it out, though. I've hurt me wrists, and me hands is as sore as hell."

"Oh, Dick! You never said you was hurt?"

"It's nought terrible. Could you reach in me right-hand keck pocket?" She felt him wriggle himself slightly upward, so that he was more level with her.

With her long, bony Lancashire fingers, she hunted feverishly down his side, stretching as far as she could. She touched his belt. "Lower," he instructed her. "Look, I'm goin' to ease meself a bit across you." She felt his head move across her shoulder till it lay against hers. He tried to ease the dead weight of his body over her arm. He grunted. "That's it. See if you can reach now."

149

The long fingers ran down his thigh, paused and then scrabbled at the pocket opening. "If you truly can't get it, I'll put me own hand in – but it's that tender, I don't want to."

"Hold still," she advised him. "I'll winch the pocket lining out." She giggled nervously. "You've got all sorts in here. I got your hanky out."

"Well, don't lose it. Put it where you can find it. We'll wipe our faces with it."

She obediently hauled it out and stuffed it down her chest.

Again the long, exploring fingers. He gritted his teeth; not with pain, but to control the sudden arousal which her warm nearness and her gentle fingers was exciting. The tendrils of hair against his cheek were having their effect, too. Many times, when he had seen Robert and Emmie walk out of the canteen with arms around each other, he had been pierced with envy and wondered what she would be like to bed. Now, however, crammed in a hell-hole which was likely to be their coffin, his desire for her was so strong that he longed passionately to roll back on top of her and have her.

She was his best friend's girl, he reminded himself forcefully, and with eyes screwed tight he kept himself rigidly still, until she almost shouted, "I got it. I got it."

"Good," he muttered, and took a large sighing breath and promptly sneezed.

She was panting with the effort she had made and began to cough again. When the paroxysm had passed, she cleared her throat, and said, "Afore I start sawing at me hair, I'm going to wipe your face with the hanky." She paused, and then added with a tremor in her voice, "Me own old dial is too sore. I'm bleeding a bit, I think."

150

"Ta." Poor kid, he thought. If her face is ruined, how'll she endure life, even if we are rescued?

She could feel his breath on her cheek. "Is *your* face hurtin' at all, afore I touch you?"

"No, Em. I think I were pressed against you when we fell."

His face was carefully wiped. She spat on a corner of the hanky and ran it clumsily around his eyelids. God, how he wanted her. She was surprised, yet pleased, when a kiss was planted on her cheek. She pushed the hanky back down the front of her blouse. "Now," she said almost cheerfully. "I'm goin' to start chopping. Proper sight I'll be when I'm finished." It was comforting to feel the man's warmth against her, especially when a particularly loud crash made the whole structure above them vibrate, and small rushes of debris slithered down on them.

The smell of gas had gone, Dick realised. The firemen must have managed to turn off the main. So much for that. He did not know whether to feel relief or disappointment. Willy-nilly, as shock had receded and been replaced by more mundane yearnings, a faint hope crept into him, that maybe the bomb that hit the canteen was not engraved with his and Emmie's names, that they might, by some miracle, be found.

Whimpers came from the girl next to him, as she tugged and cut hair by hair. She sighed and stopped work, to rest herself for a moment. Then she said without preamble, "We must have fallen into somebody's cellar – right under the yard, 'cos we was still outside – and I fell and slid quite a ways." Her voice was mournful. "I ache all over from it. Who'd build a cellar under a yard?"

"Plenty o' people, not too many years ago – about a coupla hundred, maybe. For keeping smuggled goods in – or privateers hiding their loot."

"They would? How'd they bring the stuff in?"

"A hidden door from the cellar under the building – where the shelter was, like."

"There weren't no back door out of that shelter."

"Could've been bricked up when they built the present building."

She sighed, and recommenced the cutting of her hair. If she could get her head free, perhaps she could move enough to find the water that trickled so maddeningly close to her. As they lay at present, Dick could not move much either.

viii

Though the raid was over, and to Emmie, deep in her prison, the din seemed less, the noise outside from the roaring fires was sufficient to make everyone converse in shouts.

With shoulders hunched and bodies bent close to their jetting hoses, firemen had managed to advance a little into the raging inferno of South Castle Street, at the back of Paradise Street. Then the water pressure fell to a trickle and they had to beat a hasty retreat. Petrol in a pump caught fire and it blew apart. Dispirited men watched helplessly as, fanned by a light breeze, the flames began to eat their way towards Paradise Street. Wandering wisps of smoke worked their way through the wreckage. Neither Emmie nor Dick said anything, as they lay rigid with fear in the face of this new menace.

The building in which the canteen had been housed had blown outwards across the street. It effectively blocked the movement of traffic, already in difficulties because of the bomb hole further down, in which Post Office engineers struggled to restore some kind of telephone service for the authorities.

A gang of Army Pioneers, aided by volunteers, both civilians and servicemen, inched their way down the centre of Paradise Street, shovelling smaller rubble into wicker skips; larger pieces were hauled to one side. "For Christ's sake, why don't they bring in some cranes?" groaned a man in blue mechanic's overalls, as he heaved and shoved in company with a German Jewish pioneer. They turned to move a huge metal desk which had lain upside down under the girder they had just shifted. "Jesus!" the mechanic exclaimed, as he stooped to get a grip on it. With all his strength he heaved and rolled it on to its side – and looked down in horror at what had once been little Dolly, the firewatcher.

Her uniform had been blown off her. Terribly crushed, her entrails spread out, only the long gleaming hair indicated that there lay someone who had been soft and pretty.

The Pioneer looked down at her in silent pity, while the less hardened civilian shouted, "Curse them, curse them!" beside himself with horror. He bent down and gathered the frail, sticky remains up as best he could and took them to the pavement. There was nothing to cover her with. Soon, he knew, somebody would come along with a bag to put her in. Weeping, savage with rage, he went back to work.

Help *was* coming. Through moonlit lanes and narrow streets snaked a stream of fire engines and ambulances, water tankers, kitchen lorries, mobile canteens and vans of food. Rescue parties, including miners and demolition experts, spent an uncomfortable night crammed into trains as they converged on Liverpool. Through broken roads, spanking clean American soldiers manoeuvred bulldozers and dump trucks, and great shovels, also mounted on caterpillar tractors, bigger than anything most Britons had seen before. They would eat into the choked thoroughfares and make a path for other vehicles.

The looters came gaily from the suburbs and the countryside, to rob those who had already lost so much.

ix

An unexploded land-mine, sitting quietly at the back of a deserted insurance office, suddenly blew up and the ear-splitting bang shook Emmie's and Dick's tiny refuge. It shook not only the debris above them, but the ground on which they lay, like some huge earthquake. In terror, they clutched each other, their heads buried into each other's shoulders, to avoid the dust which rose once more around them. Bits and pieces rattled and fell above them. The great stone over their heads held, however, though the beam which was holding down Emmie's hair shifted slightly and the remaining strands of her hair were freed.

"My God!" Dickie's teeth were chattering helplessly, as the bang was followed by a series of rumbles, gradually dying away into quiet.

Ears pricked, they waited for the next onslaught, but there was only the creaking and shifting of the ruins and the occasional splash of water. Very dimly, they also could hear what might have been slow traffic and, at times, felt the faint vibration of it.

As the dust settled again, Dickie muttered to a whimpering Emmie, "It *has* to be morning – that bang were too big for a bomb – it were something special. Come on, luv. Now's the time to feel around for a stone and bang on that wall by you, so a rescuer knows where to look."

Emmie stirred and half sat up. Dickie exclaimed at her sudden movement.

"Me hair came free in the last shake-up." She laughed tremulously and felt round for a likely stone.

For nearly half an hour, they banged steadily, to no purpose. During that time they had both, shamefacedly, to urinate and now lay in wet clothes.

As they rested, feeling surprisingly weak, Emmie said, "David – me brother – 'll be out lookin' for me. What about your folks?"

Dickie explained that he had nobody and that this was his weekend off from his duties as night-watchman at a seed warehouse. "They'll wonder where I am come Monday, though, when I don't turn up for work."

"Gwen – that's Dave's wife – she won't bother. She hates my guts. Be glad to see me dead, I truly think. All she cares about is her house. If you breathe out, she'll dust all round you."

Dick laughed. "She can't be that bad."

"She is," insisted Emmie. "Dave's proper patient with her. It'll be him as comes to find us."

"The wardens and the Rescue Squads is good at finding buried victims," Dick replied, to reinforce her hope of help.

David was, however, sound asleep on a bunk made of chicken wire in a street shelter in Bootle. He had worked until the siren went, on repairing water pipes in narrow, badly damaged streets, while housewives and children hung round him, waiting for the taps, or at least the fire hydrants, to start gushing again. They also had no gas with which to cook, and often torn chimneys made it impossible to build a fire in a grate. Once water was restored, a good many kettles got boiled in the back yard on a fire made from splintered beams. In most cases their tiny stores of food were ruined, tins laced by slivers of glass, the contents of cupboard blown into pieces and lost in the general mess of broken plaster.

On Sunday morning, fed by a grateful housewife, David and his mate, Arthur, continued to work, laying new water pipes. Two streets away, another gas main sent a scarifying sheet of flame into the sky, threatening to engulf the slums around them in fire.

A little soothed by the thought that David would be seeking her, Emmie said to Dick, "You'd better have your knife back afore I lose it in the dark."

He fumbled round until he found her hand and the knife. As he slipped it into his shirt pocket, he felt her begin to sit up again.

"My God! Me poor back," she groaned, as the stiffened muscles were stretched.

"Now watch it," Dick warned. His voice sounded muffled, the words coming reluctantly from a parched throat. "Move carefully. If you touch something solid, don't push it or we'll have an avalanche down on us."

"OK." If she could stop shivering, she thought, she would be less clumsy. The shivering would not stop, however. As she sat up, it became a wild shaking, her teeth chattering uncontrollably.

Dick heard her wincing, and the shuffle of her skirts against the loosened earth, as she finally got herself seated upright. Instinctively, she turned towards him, to bend forward and touch him. "Ow!" she squeaked, as she hit her head on the sloping stonework over him. When she rubbed her scraped forehead, it hurt much more than she had expected; there was a trickle, which might have been blood, down over one eyelid, and she whimpered slightly as she carefully wiped it away with a shaky finger.

"Steady on, girl."

"Suppose I move too far away and I can't find you again?" she croaked.

"Na," he assured her. "We're like a pair o' mackerels in a tin – waitin' for the tin-opener."

Her shaky laugh was close to being a sob.

She heard Dickie sigh with relief as the pressure of her body on him was eased when she moved. Very carefully she tucked her feet under herself and then kneeled up. She promptly hit her head again and sat back dizzily until the throbbing stopped. In a wild hope that there might be an aperture through which they might creep to greater safety, she rapidly ran her hands up and down and along the wall beside her. Her spirits fell, when she found that the huge rough-hewn stones of the wall met tightly with the sloping slab which roofed them over. There was enough height on the wall side for them to sit up, if they kept their heads bent, and she reported this to Dick.

"That'll be a relief," he replied. "I'll stay put till you've felt right round."

157

She crawled with difficulty a foot or two along the wall, until, where her feet had rested, her exploring fingers found what felt like a metal girder sloping the opposite way to the stone above her. She tried to reach over it, but the way was blocked with rubble; she managed, however, to slip her hand under it and work her fingers through a pile of cobblestones and plaster. As she eased her hand carefully in, there was a loud creak and dust began to rise.

"For God's sake!" Dick's voice held panic.

She snatched her hand back under their sheltering slab. "I'm doing my best," she said crossly, and then sneezed. The sound was answered by another small rattle of debris from the same direction. She stayed frozen until the last small piece seemed to have dropped. Then she voiced the need of both of them. "I wonder where the water's running?"

"Let's listen hard."

The sound indubitably came from somewhere beyond the iron girder.

She burst into tears.

"I'm comin' up beside you, Em. Just sit still. Steady as you go, there's a girl."

He wriggled out of his narrow niche, his shoulders aching sharply, the rest of his bruised body complaining bitterly. Guided by her whimpering, he hauled himself alongside her. He sat, panting and dizzy half leaning against her, and then he straightened up. "Phew, that's better." He listened again, and then said, "There's water there all right. May be from the pipes leading to the canteen taps."

Emmie sniffed. "Doesn't matter where it's from. It's on the other side of a bloody great girder, and the girder's too big to either climb under or over. Even if you could, there's a lot o' smallish bits very loose there." she tried to still her chattering teeth, and then quavered, "I don't know what we did to deserve this. We're not wicked."

Dick gave a rattling laugh. In the pitch-darkness, he tried to visualise the tiny space in which they found themselves. Then he said ruefully, "War's like the weather; it falls on the good and the bad alike. Only them what starts it takes care to be well away from it." Then, with determined cheerfulness, he went on, "Never mind that. First, I'm going to move forward a bit, so you can lie along this big wall. You lie on your stummick, and very, very slowly slip your hand under the girder again and work your fingers into whatever's there. See if you can feel wet. It'll be easier for you to do than me – 'cos o' me weight, like. I'm plain fat."

"Right." Her voice was a little firmer. After a tight squeezing past each other, she managed to do as he had suggested, and she worked her arm further and further under the girder until part of her shoulder lay under the unyielding metal. It was all bone dry.

With her arm still stretched into the rubble, she lay and listened carefully. "It's no more'n a foot beyond, I'm sure," she wailed in despair.

"Not to worry," Dick wheezed. "It might make a puddle in time and we'll be able to reach it. Have you still got me hanky?"

"Yes. Down me chest."

"Good. If it makes a puddle we can reach, we'll get at it by soaking the hanky in it."

She remained prone for a moment, while she mentally savoured the joy of cold water. Then she cautiously withdrew her arm and heaved herself round until she could sit up.

"Eh, I'm that sore, and you must be, too," her tremulous voice came out of the darkness. "Why don't they come? It's been pretty quiet for a while now. It has to be morning. Surely they'll be lookin' for us?"

"As soon as you hear anything that sounds like them coming, we'll shout as hard as we can, so they know we're here. And we'll bang with the stones again."

"T' warden what come to the canteen counted us all. He'll tell the rescue men how many people to look for."

"Aye, he will."

Outside in the street, the Pioneers carefully consigned the warden to the mortuary and, with him, the remains of the police constable, who would at least have known there were people sheltering in the canteen basement.

Further down the street, in a bomb crater, a newly bathed and clean-overalled Post Office Telephones engineer relieved his exhausted colleague. Elsewhere, linesmen continued to string wires from anything they could hang them on, in an effort to re-establish communications within the city.

As less fatigued aid arrived from other towns, a mood of ebullience spread amongst the toilers. This was the end of this run of raids, they told each other. Everybody would be able to go to bed tonight and sleep it off, ready for work on Monday.

Emmie found Dick's hand and held it, as she dozed. Sometimes a very distant rumble shook their tiny lair; it sounded like big lorries moving, a promise of rescue, and they were comforted.

Without warning, there was an enormous roar, a detonation greater than any previous one, and the whole ruin in which they lay shivered and groaned. Loud cracks overhead made Emmie scream. She flung herself against Dick; in equal terror, he turned and clung to her. Again, a tremendous dust enveloped them. Instinctively, they ducked their faces into each other's shoulder, cowering together as they nearly choked.

The pandemonium died away to a rumble, only to be followed immediately by a whole series of explosions which shook their precarious shelter. Almost directly overhead they could hear the fall of masonry followed by the lesser sound of smaller debris slithering like a hundred snakes down through the wreckage. The great piece of stonework above them shuddered.

A terrified rat scuttled across Emmie's lap, sending her into hysterics.

Despite the desperate efforts of its crew and the fire brigade, fire had finally reached the main hold of the *Marakand*. Surrounded by flames, dive bombed all night, firemen and crew had been unable to scuttle her, and now, under whatever cover they could find, they crouched defeated. A four-ton anchor, blasted into the air, fell into the engine-room of a hopper and sank it as well. Acres of dock and warehouse were mowed down by the tremendous blasts and the ever-encroaching fire. Only after seventy-four hours of almost continuous racket did a weird silence descend on the embers of a whole district.

"I never want to see anything like it again," Robbie muttered fervently to his deckhand friend, as their captain checked his sooty, worn-out crew. "I'll be thankful to go to sea again."

Fogged by fear, unable to produce even one more scream, Dick and Emmie lay tightly together, both

161

breathing shallowly. Each time the torn building over them lurched, a fresh poof of dust would surround them and they would cough and splutter.

Outside, the late spring morning was made horrible by a blizzard of burned paper which blew about the city, getting into people's eyes, clinging to clothes and faces like black snowflakes. The burned records of innumerable enterprises flattened during the night had been caught by the wind and whirled out of every broken building. Up and up they went into the smoke haze, to descend again in a supernatural storm. Through the smoke, flames still licked greedily.

By noon the road outside the canteen was passable to a single line of traffic driving very carefully, and further efforts were being made to find the remainder of the firewatchers assumed to have been on duty with Dolly. The air raid warden on day shift and new police, all looking wondrously spruce, had come on duty, and a heated altercation broke out between a demolition squad foreman puttering along the edge of the debris, and the new warden.

"How was I supposed to know there was a canteen there? There weren't no warden around, nor a cop for that matter, on this street. Thought it was all offices – and as for firewatchers, I've only got one unaccounted for now."

"Well, there *was* a canteen here and it'd be open," replied the warden irritably, "and we'd better get weaving on it." By his accent the demolition foreman must be from Manchester, presumably one of the over three thousand men which the warden had heard were being sent to Liverpool. No wonder the man didn't know where anything was.

"How many people, do you reckon?" inquired the foreman resignedly.

"Could be as many as forty."

"Good God! Somebody should've told me." He scratched his crew-cut hair and put his helmet more comfortably on his head. "They didn't say nothin' in the command post."

The warden raised a gloomy face from contemplation of the anonymous piles of wreckage round him. "The command post lost nearly the whole shift."

As he strode towards them, the police constable in charge of the area, looked bleary-eyed, despite a clean and tidy uniform. He had just arrived, to commence his shift, only to find a new command post being assembled and nobody very sure of what the situation was. "Looks as if Constable Wilson got it last night. We can't find him," he was told. Heavy-hearted, he had taken the first telephone call on the re-established line. Now he shouted towards the warden, "There's a phone inquiry about a Miss Piggott – serving in the Sailors' Canteen – do you know if that's bin tackled yet?"

"I only just coom on duty," replied the warden defensively. "And t' command post's only just bin replaced – pack of strangers. There weren't nobody in a fit state to tell nobody nothin'. Joe, here, he just coom from Manchester." He cocked a thumb towards the lugubrious foreman, who looked even more glum.

The constable's face went red with suppressed rage. Bloody fool, why didn't he use his common sense and show the new foreman? Poor Wilson and the command post couldn't help being dead.

"Get a bearing on where the entrance was," he ordered the warden through gritted teeth, "and explain to the foreman how it were laid out. I'll get you more help, and alert ambulance people. The entrance to the shelter underneath the canteen was to the left of the entrance from the street." He ran back to the newly reconstituted command post.

While the warden, like a questing terrier, trotted up and down the partially cleared street, the foreman assembled his squad and checked that they were equipped with shovels and crowbars – and skips to hold the rubbish they would have to remove.

The warmth of the fires, further over, was born towards them, making them sweat. The hiss of water hitting flame and the drum of pumps bewildered the warden. If it were only quiet enough to climb the rubble and listen; then they would stand a chance of hearing survivors tapping. There were other noises to add to the confusion: explosions from No. 2 Huskisson dock; detonations, as Lancashire mining engineers showed another demolition squad how to break a way through mountains of wreckage, without bringing an avalanche down on themselves; the lives of men with demolition experience were to be preserved at all costs – their peculiar skills were all too rare. In a nearby street, a huge bulldozer manned by American soldiers was slowly crunching its way through a blockage, and that also added to the racket.

"I've got it," shouted the warden triumphantly, as he rubbed one eye watering with a mot in it. "Opposite the stump of this lamp-post."

Huge and ponderous as the foreman was, he immediately began to climb the fall opposite the broken lamp standard, walking with surprising lightness, probing gently with his crowbar, before committing his team to the search. When he was satisfied that he understood the lay of the pile, he set his men to work. "Come on, lads. Quick – but careful – mind." His melancholy expression fell still further. "Doubt anybody's alive under that."

A portly gentleman in a business suit and bowler hat accosted the watching warden, "Excuse me. Can you tell me where the Sailors' Canteen is? My wife was on duty there last night, and she has not come home this morning. When I tried to telephone, I could not get through."

The warden looked up sharply and then bit his lip with tobacco-stained teeth. "Aye," he said slowly, with a sigh. "It were here. They're workin' on it now, as you can see."

The gentleman's ruddy complexion went glistening white. His grey, military moustache quivered; words would not come. Finally, he breathed, "I was afraid of that."

The warden caught his arm, concerned that he might collapse. "Sir! They could be safe in the shelter – it were a good stout cellar." The warden had not an iota of hope. But then, he told himself, you never knew what quirk of fate could save the life of someone. "What was – is – her name, sir?"

"Clara Robinson, Mrs Clara Robinson." The man was already out of his black jacket and folding it neatly. He laid it down by the lamp-post stump and placed his bowler hat on top of it. "Thank you," he said fairly steadily, as he got a grip on himself. Then he turned and picked his way over to a labourer clearing a path from the edge of the fall inwards. "Give me a shovel. I'll help you," he said between tight lips.

"Best stay back, sor," a middle-aged Irish navvy, working ahead of the other labourer, advised him. "It's dangerous." He lifted his pick again and swung it down on the obstruction before him.

"I *have* to do something," Alec Robinson said firmly. He undid his gold cufflinks and rolled up his shirt sleeves.

The foreman came carefully down the slope of the pile, placing each foot precisely so that he did not fall into the debris.

The warden shouted up to him, "T' cellar had a pavement light what led right into it."

"That'll save a lot." The foreman's face lifted slightly, as he redirected his men, to facilitate the unearthing of this narrow window of heavy glass framed in iron and set directly into the pavement to give some light to the cellar. If it had not been pounded into the ground, it could give the rescuers immediate access. Then he turned and sized up the blenched business man who was working his way towards him.

"You could clear some space at the edge of the pavement," he told him kindly. "Make a way through to where the road has been cleared. We'll need a bit of space to lay 'em down, maybe, when we bring 'em out." He saw Alec Robinson's eyes widen with horror, and added hastily, "They could be hurt." He turned to the labourer. "Find 'im a shovel."

Alec Robinson thankfully took the proffered shovel and bent to the task, his heart heavy. An ambulance was already nosing its way cautiously along the street, followed closely by a fire pump. A wobbly stream of water was directed at the ruins further back, to damp them down and possibly contain the fire raging behind them, until the rescuers had finished their work. The stream was weak because of fractured mains, and the turbulence in the air caused by the fires themselves blew much of the water back on to the firemen and the rescuers. Still, they persisted.

While the workmen picked their way in with meticulous care, para-medical personnel, black bags in hand, came at a shambling run along the littered pavement opposite.

They were too early, so, with tin hats pushed to the back of their heads, they lit cigarettes and stood gossiping about a new film one of them had seen.

In what seemed to have become their own private bomb crater, the clay-bespattered telephone engineers continued their patient splicing of lines.

When Alec Robinson paused to mop his forehead, he was approached by a tall cadaverous man dressed in the grey uniform of a chauffeur. The man took off his peaked cap, revealing a bald head across which a few wisps of white hair had been carefully plastered. "Sir, I'm looking for the Sailors' Canteen. I'm Higgins, sir. The mistress has not come home, and we – that is, Mrs. Fleming, the housekeeper, and me – thought I should come down on the bus, to see if she's all right – the car being mothballed for the duration, sir." He turned and surveyed the appalling wreckage. "I trust I'm not looking at the canteen?"

Alec Robinson replied gruffly, "You are. Who is your mistress?"

"The Dowager Countess Mentmore. She's a volunteer."

A minute later, a chauffeur's cap and jacket were carefully laid by Mr Robinson's bowler hat and black jacket, and the demolition foreman had to find work for another volunteer.

The rescuers worked like moles, shifting obstructing masonry, splintered woodwork, pieces of filing cabinets and desks, a slippery cascade of law books, a huge Victorian lavatory, all interlaced with electric wires which might still be live, and miles of water pipes and gas pipes. A lot of this was passed back and piled on the pavement. Stout pieces of timber, desk drawers, finely panelled oak doors, all were used by the labouring men as props in the twisting passageway they were making. Every time there was a further explosion from No. 2 Huskisson this perilous little entry was shaken by the blast, but still the men perservered.

x

That dreadful Sunday, as Emmie lay in Dick's arms, her mind wandered. Both of them were drained by fear, thirsty beyond words and very hungry. It seemed to her that she was lying in Robbie's arms on the sandhills, behind the great sea wall at Meols, and they were talking of building a small cottage not too far from there, with a good slate roof and a parlour for best occasions.

She woke suddenly, not sure what had alerted her. Instead of the sunlight on the waving, coarse grasses of the sand hills, she faced a midnight blackness. She touched Dick's face with her hand, and he stirred and muttered hoarsely, "OK, luv?"

"Mm," she replied. She shivered; the wall felt cold against her back.

It felt wet! Her cotton blouse and petticoat were

sticking to her back. She must have sweated heavily or wet herself again. But there it was once more – a cold drop, a trickle down a strand of her torn hair and across her neck.

"Dickie," she gasped. "Wake up. There's water running down the wall behind me back. I can feel it."

Water? He swallowed and tried to answer her, but his dried lips would barely move. He felt clammily cold and he shivered.

"Sit up, Dick. I'm goin' to turn meself over."

"Can't sit up, 'cos of the slope over me," he managed to reply thickly. She was right, though. He could smell the odour of water on dust – and he could also smell an increased amount of smoke. His heart leapt with fresh apprehension. He eased himself away from Emmie, to help her turn.

Emmie was as excited as if they had already been rescued. Her mind cleared as, wild with hope, she knelt up and ran her hand along the wall. There *was* a steady dribble down it at one point. She put her sore cheek against it and then turned to lick it. Her tongue was promptly covered with grit, but it was moistened, none the less. She tried again and spat out the grit. "There's only a bit," she announced in a fractionally clearer voice. "I'm going to try and soak your hanky, though."

The water flowed faster, forming a small pool round her knees. The handkerchief was soon quite wet and she passed it to Dick to suck. He thankfully wiped his lips and put a corner in his mouth. He too had to spit out grit, but the relief was tremendous. He managed to move a little out of his niche and curve himself round Emmie as she knelt, to dip the hanky again into the wondrous little pool.

Emmie undid her skirt button and awkwardly hauled off her blouse, cursing roundly when she caught her elbow on the rough wall. She pressed the garment into the tiny stream. As it became wetter, she struggled to get out of her cotton petticoat in order to soak that also. "It'll make a little store of water," she puffed.

"I'm sorry I can't see you."

She blushed, and managed a small giggle. In the dark, she had not considered her nakedness. Thankfully, she pressed the sopping blouse to her throbbing face. She tried to wipe it gently but it hurt too much.

All around the great slab that protected them water began to drip, to a point where, no matter how they lay, they became wet, and they again huddled in each other's arms, to keep warmer, while they speculated on the source.

"Could be a leak from a pool which built up somewhere above us," offered Dick. "And now it's sifting down to us."

Their little lair shuddered, as a quick series of explosions from the *Marakand* shook it; a heavier splatter of droplets fell round them. Dick felt Emmie begin to tremble and he held her closer. Again he was tempted to take her, now that the air felt cleaner and he could breath properly. She wriggled more tightly to him and he knew that she wanted him. She turned on her back and he moved on top of her, so that there was space above them.

Despite the limited space, it was a wild lovemaking, as if both of them were young and filled with the frantic desire of youth. Every terrifying shift of the broken buildings above them; every great blast that numbed their ears as the deadly cargo of the *Marakand* wreaked havoc, though adding to their fear, also intensified their passion, until finally they lay exhausted and almost unbelievably at peace. They continued to caress each other, Emmie with a strange wonder that some one other than Robbie could make her feel so good. As she stroked him, she murmured incoherent endearments and he chuckled. "Not bad for an old man, eh?" he joked, and fell asleep.

He was awakened by her hoarse voice saying, "Dickie, I thought I heard something scrabbling about then."

"Eh, what?"

"Listen? Is that a voice?"

They held their breath; then without a further word felt round for the stones they had used to bang the wall with.

Frantic with hope, they both banged, and shrieked, "Help! Help! Help!"

Emmie's voice was much weaker than she realised, her throat swollen from her earlier screams, and Dick's was not much better; he realised ruefully that he had exhausted himself with Emmie; it was hard to get breath enough into his lungs to yell.

They paused to listen again. They could hear only the groans of the pile above them, as it slowly settled. Emmie began to cry.

xi

Gwen felt, that Sunday, that her life had been broken into, just like burglars broke into houses, that her house was as good as doorless and anybody could plunge in and out of it without so much as a by-your-leave. Never before had she had to extend a hand to anybody; she prided herself on minding her own business, on having the whitest doorstep in the street, the best-dressed daughter and the cleanest-looking husband – and, of course, getting her washing out on the line before any of her neighbours, on a Monday morning. Sunday was a day to meet one's friends at chapel and show off the hat one had retrimmed, and to anticipate with pleasure eating one's meat ration, slowly braised in the oven while one was at service.

And instead, she was surrounded by the most awful bunch of little horrors anybody could have wished on her. She surveyed them grimly, as they sat round the table at midday, eating like starving dogs. It was a pure miracle, she thought, that she had managed to provide a dinner at all; just like the story of the loaves and fishes. The Thomases' meat ration had been extended into a stew with the aid of a bag of potatoes, culled from Mrs Donnelly's kitchen, and three pennyworth of fades – discarded, shrivelled vegetables – from the corner shop. Nora, who had been entrusted with the message to the corner shop, had also brought two loaves of yesterday's bread and some milk – on credit. "The first time in me life I ever arst for anythin' on tick," moaned Gwen.

Patrick had been soundly clouted over the head by his father, for coming to view the ravaged Dwellings, and he now sat sulkily shovelling stew into his mouth, while Gwen slapped a couple of spoonfuls of it on to her own plate. She picked up her knife and fork and began to cut the tiny cube of meat, when suddenly she remembered.

"Emma!" she exclaimed, and put down her fork.

Ruby looked up from her task of feeding an unwilling

Michael with bits of bread sopped in a saucer of gravy. Mari who had got up only in time for the meal, asked with a small yawn, "Isn't she in bed?" She smiled across at Patrick, but he dropped his eyes and did not smile back.

"It were such a hectic morning, I clean forgot her. She never come home."

Mari stared at her incredulously, while Ruby stuttered, "Do you think she caught it last night?"

Mari licked her lips. "What about Daddy?"

"He'll be all right." Gwen's reply was automatic. Her husband was always all right, as dependable as the Liverpool one o'clock gun, which, before the war, had marked the time for the city. No one had told her of the carnage in Bootle – or, indeed, in the city itself; the wireless had merely reported a raid on a north-west town.

She sighed, as she looked round the table. Only Ruby and Mari were interested in Emma; the others continued to eat, Brendy happily pushing bits of vegetable into his mouth with his hand. "Really, Brendy," Gwen expostulated. "Use your spoon, you naughty boy." He took no notice and she leaned across the table and gave his hand a small slap; then she stuffed a spoon into it. He tried shovelling.

She turned to Patrick, as being the only older male present, and said agitatedly, "I'll save her some dinner, anyway. And you, when you've finished, run over and tell your dad she's missing. He'll know what to do. He'll ask about her for us."

Patrick nodded agreement. If he had a real message to deliver, surely he would be able to stay to watch the men at work on The Dwellings. He quickly ate the last

173

mouthful on his plate and half rose from the table.

"Have your pudding first," Gwen ordered. "A few more minutes ain't goin' to make no difference."

Pudding as well. For the first time that day, Patrick's spirits rose a little, and he ate eagerly the large helping of bread-and-butter pudding she put in front of him.

"Where did Miss Emmie go?" he inquired.

Gwen explained about her job in the Sailors' Canteen in Paradise Street and that she was on the evening shift. She ran her fingers through her greying red curls. She had been too busy to comb it and had not even washed her face.

"I'll take me dad's bike and tell 'im first; then I'll ride down to Paradise Street and see what's to do there." He looked excited at the prospect and gave Gwen the same beguiling, conspiratorial grin that had mesmerised Mari in the air raid shelter. Mari, seeing it, felt again the extraordinary sensation which his exploring fingers had introduced her to. She flushed and went slowly on with her dinner.

"I hope she's all right," Gwen said mechanically. "She might've gone over to see Robert Owen's mother." In her heart she felt that Emmie was a deliberate nuisance in not turning up for either breakfast or dinner. Serve her right if she'd got killed. Decent girls came straight home. And then there were all those merchant seamen hanging around the canteen – a lot of no-goods with only two ideas in their heads, drink and women.

Patrick could not find his father at The Dwellings because he had taken half an hour off to go to see the local undertaker about his wife's funeral. He reluctantly approached the constable in charge of the incident, who promised to put an inquiry about Emmie in motion immediately, and to let Mrs Thomas know as soon as he had news. The constable refused to allow him to go close to the ruins, so Patrick again mounted his father's rusty bike and sped away to join the sightseers in the town. At the top of Duke Street, he was stopped by a soldier with a rifle on his back, who wanted to know his business and promptly turned him back.

Patrick knew the town like a rabbit knows its warren. He gravely cycled round the corner out of sight, then dived down an alley and proceeded along back ways. He did not return for tea.

xii

Gwen gave the children a tea of bread and margarine and home made gooseberry jam and sent them out to play in the street. It was the first day in her married life that she had given barely a thought to the condition of her little house, except nearly to weep over the bed which Michael had wetted; it was now being dried out with the aid of three hot-water bottles. She sat with eyes closed, wishing passionately that David would return. He would know what to do about the Donnelly children – and Emma and the windows – and the fact that she was going to be over her housekeeping money.

She was sound asleep in the chair, mouth open, gently snoring, when Conor Donnelly, followed by Ruby, walked in through the open front door.

She awoke, startled to see an awful apparition standing before her on her rag rug. It was white with dust from head to foot, the face caked. Two red eyes glared out at her from under a battered tin hat; ominous brown stains marked the front of him. There was a faint smell about him as if of a butcher's shop, mixed with old sweat. A gap in the face was mouthing something about Emma.

Frightened, she jumped to her feet so quickly that she nearly knocked him down.

"It's me dad," explained Ruby simply.

Gwen forced herself into wakefulness. "Did you say Emma?" she asked. Then, without thinking of the effect on her fireside chair, immaculate in faded cretonne, she said, "My, Mr Donnelly, you look dreadful! Sit down. Would you like a cuppa tea? Have you had your tea?"

Conor flopped thankfully into the little chair and tried to smile. "Ta, I could use a drop."

"No trouble." To offer a cup of tea was a strict convention, but she surveyed him with dismay. Never in her life had she seen anyone look so dreadful. Even the chimney sweep at the end of a day's work – or the coalman – never looked as bad as that. For once her Methodist training surfaced, and she asked impetuously, "I got a bit o' dinner left. Why don't you wash your hands and face under the kitchen tap, while I make it hot for you?"

He had eaten nothing hot for forty-eight hours and he accepted eagerly.

It was amazing what a bit of hot food would do for a person, thought Gwen in gratified surprise, as she watched Conor polish off the dinner intended for Emma. Scuttling round to make the food ready, she had forgotten again about Emma, but now as he slurped at a cup of tea, she remembered and inquired if he had news.

He sighed. "Aye, I have, Mrs Thomas. The canteen's flat. They're digging into the shelter under it now."

"And Emma's in it?" Her heart bounced uncomfortably. It was one thing to wish a person dead or gone; quite another to probably have the wish granted so promptly.

"I suppose she's there. They're trying to finish the job afore it's dark – same as we bin doin' at The Dwellings."

"Do you know how things are in Bootle?"

Anxious not to scare her unnecessarily, since her husband was out there, he played down the shocking fate of Bootle.

"Me hubby didn't even come home for his dinner," Gwen remarked quite crossly. "Don't they know men have families to look after?"

Conor ignored the remark and pursued the question of Emmie. "Miss Thomas were engaged, weren't she?"

"Yes." Gwen was surprised that he knew. She had forgotten that the engagement of a woman of mature years would have been an interesting piece of gossip to be mulled over by the fire in the local public house.

"Is he at sea?"

"I doubt it – yet. They were loading at No. 2 Huskisson, according to Emma."

"What?"

Gwen jumped. "At Huskisson. Why?"

Conor told her the news, received over the post telephone, of the fearsome destruction wreaked by the exploding *Marakand*. "Most of the bangs you've been hearing today is from her," he finished up.

"Well, I can't say as I think much of him, to be truthful – but I wouldn't wish that on him." She had a sudden picture in her mind of the tall, well-built man, ruddy-faced and blue-eyed, and knew in her heart that she was deeply jealous of Emmie. Emmie was so content, so satisfied, as if part of the time she was moving in a dream. David had never made her glow like that. She felt a surge of longing go through her thin frame and she examined her nails carefully so that Conor would not read her feelings in her face.

Conor said heavily, as he got up from his chair, "I'll see if we can trace him. Robert Owen, deckhand, on the *Marakand*, wasn't it?"

She nodded absently.

MONDAY, 5 MAY 1941

Neither Emmie nor Dick admitted to each other an increasing hunger; hunger was something which had been with them, on and off, all their lives. At her brother's house, Emmie had for the first time enjoyed adequate meals, though Gwen was by no means generous in the portions she gave her. Now, however, she endured a clemming misery.

As they became wetter, the water which had been such a Godsend became a trial. Dick shivered constantly, teeth chattering, from the cold as well as from nervous strain.

Not only did they lie in puddles of water, but in their own urine and ordure, and the odour vied with the smell of smoke and wet plaster; the wisps of smoke saved them, however, from attacks by rats, the contemplation of which made both of them heave at times; the vermin with which Liverpool was infested retreated as the fires advanced.

At one point they thought they heard the scrape of metal on stone and then a distant shout. In response, they banged the wall with a stone and cried out again and again. The wall was as thick as a castle keep and if there was anyone there, the frantic cries went unheard.

In a sudden burst of fury, Emmie had said venomously, "If I ever get out of this fix, I'll go into munitions. I'll send them something to make *them* smart, I will."

"You can make good money at it," Dickie replied practically. "A lot more'n you could servin' in a cafe."

This idea had set her off on a laboured, barely audible description of what she would like to do after the war, if she had some savings. "I'd buy a nice little sweet and tobacconist's," she confided to Dick. "It'd give me some real independence – and summat to do while Robbie's at sea."

"He might like to swallow the anchor and help you."

"Nay," she insisted, with unexpected woodenness. "He can have 'is own job. This is for me. I never ever thought o' planning for meself afore this." She contemplated a hopeful future for a little while. Then she said, her voice cracked and broken, "You know, a lot of women get tired of being bossed all the time, but unless you got money you got to put up with it. I'm tired of it. I want to be free – and Robbie will benefit. We'll have more money for both of us. Go on holidays and suchlike."

Sporadically, they planned holidays and dreamed of sunny beaches, until an ache in Dickie's back became a piercing pain; his temperature started to rise and finally his speech to wander, until he was talking to Emmie as if she were one of his sons.

Emmie, too, began to feel light-headed, and the unbroken darkness robbed her of any knowledge of the passage of time. Unaware of the frantic battle being waged in No. 2 Huskisson, in which her beloved Robbie fought as hard as anyone, she concluded from the intermittent booms which shook the ground beneath her that it was night and a raid was taking place at a little distance from the town centre.

Just before midnight, and continuing well into Monday morning, enemy aircraft swept over the east coast, like a cloud of disturbed hornets, curved round over Liverpool Bay and followed the shining Mersey to their target.

The anti-aircraft guns had been reorganised during the day, to good effect, and a heavy barrage greeted the raiders, making it difficult to bomb accurately. Nevertheless, incendiary bombs deluged the city, and the haphazard scattering of high explosives brought out of bed at a run all those citizens brave enough to retire in the first place. People sleeping on the platforms of the underground railway forgot the hardness of their sleeping place and turned over thankfully, and those in air raid shelters or out in the fields beyond the city congratulated themselves on their forethought, miserable as they might be. The stunned victims of the earlier raids, now herded into schools and church halls, faced this further threat to their safety, and more than one such shelter became a bloody grave before morning.

Though night fighting was a new art, the pilots in their slow Defiants used all their ingenuity to defend the port. "Learnin' on t' job, like us," one auxiliary fireman remarked cynically, as he gazed upwards for a moment at the fireworks in the sky. A thin cheer went up from his battered brigade, when a Nazi airman was spotted bailing out and floating downwards, his parachute spread above him. "Hope he gets lynched," cried several savagely tired Liverpudlians; but he was picked up from the river the next morning, drowned, like so many of Liverpool's own men.

Ignoring the pandemonium and the danger, Rescue Squads still picked their way delicately through great heaps of what had once been a city. With the aid of shaded lamps or, infrequently, a floodlight, they peered and called and probed, with occasional success, while searchlights flicked like mad pendulums back and forth across the sky and malevolent pieces of flak flashed like javelins amid the rescuers.

Panting, trying to keep calm, Emmie held the head of a babbling Dick to her naked breast, clasping her arms tightly over him as she sought to protect him. As the hubbub continued, furious sexual desire engulfed her again. It boiled in her, an urgent, primitive need, and she murmured incoherently to him. Dick himself was aware only of a warm, comforting presence in a world of nightmare, as pneumonia took hold of him. His breath came in harsh rasps.

"Don't let him die, oh, God. Don't let him die," she implored, as she realised there would be no response from him. While the ear-splitting din round her increased, she began to believe that he was indeed dying; her self-control deserted her, her mind gave way and she shrieked like a rabbit in a snare.

ii

As she saw Conor out of the front door, on Sunday evening, Gwen managed to insert into his monologue the suggestion that the children might now return to their own home, since it was fairly certain, from experience in other raids, that the Germans had finished this onslaught. Shocked, Conor had turned back and vehemently begged her to keep them with her for one more night.

"Their nan should be here by tomorrer night," he assured her. "She'll stay a few days, though she's still got me dad to care for at home. Then Rube will have to manage for us – we'll hope the raids'll be finished by then."

When Gwen still demurred, he insisted, "I *can't* stay home with them tonight. They need every man they can get at The Dwellings. What would people say if I stayed home, I ask you?"

Because of what people might also say about her, Gwen reluctantly agreed to keep the youngsters.

She went slowly back indoors. In the yard, Conor's dog started to bark and then to whine. "Blast him," she muttered viciously. The kitchen door to the yard opened, and Patrick entered, the dog sidling after him. He looked white and strained and glanced at her uncertainly before dropping his eyes to the importuning dog and patting it.

He's scared, Gwen sensed. Frightened to death of something.

"What's up, lad?"

"I don't think anybody's alive down there," he burst out, his breath coming quickly, as if he had been running.

"Where?"

"Down Paradise – where your Emma was."

Gwen felt herself go cold. So the worst had happened. She had wished it and she was responsible. She wanted to be sick.

"It's somethin' terrible down there, missus. You should see the fires." His lips trembled. He had seen what he feared even grownups could not cope with and he was frightened, humbled. Dreadful Mrs Thomas looked suddenly like a pillar of strength; her basement steps a safe stronghold.

The gates of hell yawned before Gwen. If you wished

a person dead – and it happened as you wished – it was as good as murder. She gaped at the beaten child whose grubby hands clutched for support at the back of the chair. Then she said very slowly, "What you and I need is a cuppa tea." She tried to pull herself together, and added, "And I'll make you gooseberry jam butties to go with it." She walked unsteadily past him to the kitchen and he and the dog followed her forlornly.

Faintly from the street floated the voices of Ruby and some neighbouring little girls singing a skipping song. The thud of the rope stopped and a quarrel broke out, in which Nora's strident shrieks predominated. A few moment later, a flustered Ruby dragging a recalcitrant small sister interrupted the tea making, and from the staircase another voice chimed in, as Brendy, clad only in his vest, howled, "I want me mam. Where's Mam?" He came pattering into the kitchen, pushing his way past his sisters.

Gwen gulped and half closed her eyes. "Be quiet!" she cried exasperatedly. "Shut up, Nora." She bent down to catch Brendy, who threatened to exit through the back door in search of his mam. "Hey, you're supposed to be in bed, now."

Nora stopped her battle with Ruby and joined in with Brendy. She looked up resentfully at Ruby and cried, "Aye, where's me mam?" She pouted, and rubbed her arm where Ruby had slapped her.

Gwen snatched up Brendy and tried to soothe him. "Your mam'll be back soon," she told him, patting his back gently. "You know she's gone to hospital to be mended."

Though she heard both Patrick and Ruby catch their breath behind her, this was sufficient to reduce Brendy's howl to a sob. "Where's she broken?" he asked with a trace of interest.

Gwen sighed. "She's got a cut — just there." She touched Brendy's protruding ribs. "The doctor'll sew it up — and then she'll get better and come home, I hope."

"Get away," Nora exclaimed in disbelief, her pout wiped off her face. "With a bloody needle?"

"Don't you use language like that round this house, miss," Gwen scolded. "Or I'll wash yer mouth out with soap." Nora bridled, her sly eyes peeping defiantly between the almost white lashes. Gwen went on, "For sure, they stitch cuts up with a needle — and white cotton."

"Well, I'll be buggered!" Nora's eyes opened wide with amazement. "They couldn't?"

Gwen put down Brendy, picked up Nora's hand and smacked it on the back. "I told you to mind your language, you little vixen."

Nora scowled and was silent.

Brendy pulled at Gwen's apron. "When'll she come?" he asked piteously.

"Soon, luvvie, soon. Now you come up to bed. You'll get cold down here."

After Gwen, Ruby and Patrick had shared a pot of tea and he had told them some of the details of the shambles in the town, including the information that the rescue squads were still digging for survivors, Gwen sat white and silent for a moment. Then she said heavily, "You'd better go and feed your dad's cockerels."

He went grudgingly into his own back yard and stood watching the birds in their separate cages pecking at the black market corn, as he sprinkled it in front of them. When he unthinkingly put his fingers on to the chicken wire which held them in, one bird pecked him. He swore at it. The burst of anger brought him out of the lethargy into which he had sunk, and as he sucked his finger, he watched with interest a plane high in the sky. It climbed in the pearly atmosphere until he could hardly hear its engine, and slowly a great ambition rose in him, to fly himself, to be a bomber pilot and give the Germans what for. He looked at the closed back door, where his mother had been fond of leaning, her latest baby in her arms, to catch the sun and wait for him to come back from school. Tears welled up and with them a murderous desire for revenge, a boiling tide of feeling which stayed with him for years. "I'll teach 'em!" he cried, as tears of grief ran down his face.

iii

Gwen crawled into bed beside Mari. In the next bedroom Michael whimpered fretfully.

"I wish Ruby could shut that kid up," she fumed uselessly.

Mari stirred uneasily. "He's hungry, Ruby says. He wants his mam. She used to feed him from her breast. I seen her."

"Good Heavens! That's not decent. He's far too old for that."

"Ruby says that's why he wants his mam so bad."

Gwen cleared her throat, a little embarrassed. "Well, a little girl like you shouldn't be talkin' about such things." She turned over, and buried her head in her big feather pillow. Mari thought she had gone to sleep, but she said abruptly, "I'd better get him a titty-bottle from the chemist tomorrow." She sighed, and then went on, "Till I can teach him how to drink from a cup."

A resounding crash, an hour later, took the corner grocery shop, and the sunken-cheeked woman who kept, it straight into oblivion. Mother and daughter flew out of bed. Nora, Brendy and Michael were howling in unhappy unison with the air raid siren.

Ruby met them on the landing, with a bawling Michael in her arms. She was panting with terror, her big grey eyes nearly popping out of her head. Nora and Brendy crowded behind her.

"Downstairs, quick," ordered Gwen, as she struggled into her dressing-gown. "And you, Mari, take the candle – and don't drop grease on the stair carpet."

Patrick had opened the front door and was watching the Defiants darting in and out amid the searchlight beams. "For goodness' sake, come in," yelped Gwen in nervous concern. "That's how your mother caught it."

He shut the door reluctantly as the other children scampered through the living room to the kitchen and the cellar steps. Inspired, Gwen snatched her sweet ration out of the sideboard drawer as she went past, and what had threatened to be a weary, noisy gathering became suddenly happily quiet when she distributed toffees all round.

At half-past four on Monday morning, they went gratefully back to their beds.

At five o'clock, David was dropped at his door by a car intended to carry the walking wounded.

He staggered into his home and sank thankfully into the familiar depths of his easy chair. He leaned his head back and the pain in his chest surged again. To hunt for the matches and light the gas jet was out of the question;

he concentrated instead on trying to breathe. Finally, the spasm passed and he sat absolutely still, beads of perspiration coating his forehead, until he heard Gwen running down the stairs. She hurried in, tying her plaid dressing-gown round her, as she pattered across the linoleum. Patrick stirred but did not wake.

"Dave!" she exclaimed. "Am I ever glad to see you." She peered at him in the half light. "Golly, you look dirty. Have you had any tea?"

David felt as if he were floating along in a mist, everything distorted, nothing close to him. He breathed with effort, afraid to move much, lest the pain recommence. The staircase up to bed loomed as an impassable barrier. "I'd like a cuppa tea," he managed to reply. He closed his eyes, and the faintest smile broke the exhaustion of his face, as he envisaged the whole of Liverpool afloat on pots of tea.

Gwen quickly folded back the little hearthrug. "Aye, David, what a time I've had. I've got all the kids from next door here. Patrick's there." She gestured towards the sofa, half hidden in the gloom. "Poor Mrs Donnelly – struck down in her prime."

"Dead?"

Gwen was kneeling in front of the fireplace, quickly raking out the ashes and then stuffing balls of newspaper and pieces of firewood into the grate. She paused and turned a pinched, weary face towards him. "Saturday night."

As best he could, David tried to pay attention to the story of the children, the windows, the broken aspidistra bowl, the dog in the back yard and Emmie's absence. Finally, she said, "And last night the gas went off. I put a whole shillin' in the meter and nothin' happened."

David sat with his eyes closed. Emma! "What did you do about Emmie?"

"Told Mr Donnelly and he's inquiring."

He knew he could not go out himself to look for her, so he simply nodded and said, "You can draw a couple of quid from the Post Office Savings. Aye, I hope she's all right." After these garbled instructions, he allowed himself to rest.

He was hazily aware of her feeding a horde of children, correcting them sharply and dispatching them to school. He woke sufficiently to return a hearty kiss and a hug from his daughter, doing his best to appear merely tired. Gwen had handed him a cup of tea, but he sat with it on a little table beside him until it went cold.

When Ruby left him, Michael yelled and had to be held back from following her. As the front door slammed, he threw himself on to the floor and kicked and screamed, arms flailing.

David was thankful when the piercing howls became sobs and then the sobs were separated by silences, as the little boy discovered David staring at him. The blazing blue eyes closed and, thumb in mouth, he went to sleep on the hearthrug at David's feet.

Gwen had run upstairs to put on her clothes, and now she came down and said, "Thank goodness, that's over. He won't eat, 'cos his mother used to feed him herself. I'll get him a titty-bottle from the chemist when I go down the road." She turned to survey David. "Would you like some cornflakes for your brekkie? Or do you want to get washed first?"

"Nay," he replied slowly. "See if you can get the doctor to come. I keep getting a pain in me chest."

"Pain? Why didn't you tell me? You don't look well, that's for sure."

The detail of the cramp in his chest was laboriously explained to her, as she flung her coat over her flowered overall and crammed her beret over her errant curls. She half ran the quarter-mile to the doctor's house.

According to his troubled wife, the doctor had been out all night. She would send him over as soon as he returned.

Breathless, Gwen returned more slowly. She was sick with fear. Was it a heart attack? Or warning of a stroke? She must keep him quiet – and that meant keeping Michael quiet, as well. She'd pick up a bottle and teat from the chemist when she passed his shop, if he were open.

As she went to turn into the chemist's doorway – she could see him inside, though the "Closed" sign still hung on his door – she bumped into Mrs Hanlon, a big, florid woman, the wife of a docker who lived a few doors away. Mrs Hanlon was bubbling with the exciting news of the demise of the corner shop and its owner, which lay in the opposite direction to the doctor's house and had consequently not been seen by Gwen.

"And what you goin' to do, now Blackler's is burned down?" the woman asked, wrapping her black shawl more tightly round her and leaning forward to breath into Gwen's harassed face.

The news was a real shock to Gwen, and Mrs Hanlon seemed to expand and contract, like a balloon in process of being blown up. Blackler's gone – and with it, presumably, her wages. Gwen's heart sank.

"And Lewis's," went on Mrs Hanlon ruthlessly. "T' firewatchers must've been roasted alive."

Gwen felt as if the whole universe was crushing down on her. "I got to go to the chemist," she intervened desperately. "Mr Thomas is sick."

Mrs Hanlon ignored the interjection and prattled on happily about The Dwellings and the pile of bodies there.

Suddenly, with overwhelming passion, Gwen hated her. Was it really a Roman holiday to her? Didn't she realise that every bomb that fell was like a huge stone in a pool; the effect grew and grew, like ripples in a pool. Not only did it destroy homes; it upset completely the lives of everybody near. And for what? For what?

As the remorseless voice went on and she tried unsuccessfully to ease herself behind Mrs Hanlon in order to rattle on the chemist's door latch, she thought of Michael screaming for his lost mam, and she wanted to run home and take him in her arms and tell him everything would be all right – in a while, when the ripples ceased – and to put a hot poultice on David's chest and tell him the same.

The chemist opened his door and at his polite "Excuse me" Mrs Hanlon moved out of the entranceway. Gwen whirled behind her and left the woman standing open-mouthed.

iv

A frantic Monday for every city official, with one hospital out of commission and several others badly damaged; in Webster Road mortuary over half the bodies nameless; water in short supply; wavering sheets of flame still flaring upwards from burst gas mains; dangerous electric cables snaking over many a road and in and out of wrecked buildings; hordes of hungry and homeless people; and the centre of the city a mighty funeral pyre.

To those Liverpool housewives who still had a home, however, the main problem was that they could not do their washing. Monday was national washing day and on Tuesdays one did the ironing.

As Gwen hurried through her back yard, on her return from the chemist, she realised that even if the trickling kitchen tap provided enough water, she could not hang the washing out in the yard to dry. The air was filled with tiny bits of grit and burned paper – she had a piece in one eye and it was watering miserably. A sandlike film had formed on all her brightly polished window sills, and when she ran her finger along the clothes line as she passed, she found it thick with dust.

She paused for a second, her hand on the doorknob, to get her breath before entering the house, and looked down at the neat sealing-waxed parcel the chemist had made of a feeding-bottle and comforter. Then with shoulders bowed like an old woman, she opened the back door and went slowly in.

David lay on the sofa, asleep. His usually ruddy face was ashen and Gwen noticed with a pang that his two days' growth of beard was grey, not black. He was still in his overalls.

Michael snuffled gently on the hearthrug. He was awake, sucking his thumb as usual. He held the little, brass-handled hearth brush in his arms as if it were a teddy bear.

She ran upstairs to get a woollen shawl with which to

cover David and was immediately thrown into a towering rage when she discovered, in passing, that the drawers of the chest in Nora's and Brendy's room had been opened and the contents were scattered all over the floor, amid feathers from a burst pillow. "Blast them!" she cursed, nearly crying.

She had just tucked the shawl over David, who did not stir, when there was a polite knock at the front door. Expecting the doctor, she hastily took off her overall and smoothed down her skirt, before answering. She was still shaking with suppressed anger.

On the unwashed doorstep stood a nun. Gwen glared at the tiny elderly figure in a spotless white wimple and a shabby, but perfectly pressed, black dress. Little highly polished black boots peeped out from under the heavy skirt and a large rosary hung from her waist. Her hands were tucked into her big sleeves. The face in the stiffly starched frame was paper-white and lined like crumpled tissue. Two gentle grey eyes surveyed Gwen and showed faint amusement, as Gwen stepped hastily backwards as if to avoid contamination.

Assuming that the nun was begging, she asked rudely, "What do you want? We're Methodists. We don't give to Catholics." She started to close the door.

"I have come with regard to the Donnelly children. I am from their school." The voice was soft but authoritative and Gwen opened the door slightly again. "I wanted to inquire if you need help with them."

With a long sigh Gwen said, "Well, I'm managing." She bit her lower lip and, remembering her manners, asked, "Will you step in for a minute? The parlour is wrecked, but come in anyways."

The nun floated in after Gwen and surveyed the dying

195

aspidistra lying amid its earth and the broken shards of its pot in the middle of the red Belgian carpet, the linoleum nailed roughly across the windows, and the soot in the hearth.

Gwen hastily brushed broken plaster off a straight chair brought from her mother-in-law's house. "Sit down," she invited cautiously.

"Are *all* the children with you?" asked the visitor, seating herself.

"Yes." The word came in a little gasp, and suddenly Gwen was pouring out to another woman, a woman, not a nun, all her worries about Michael, her fears that she could not keep Patrick under control, about Ruby's little shoulders having to carry such a terrible load in the future, and about foul-mouthed Nora and Brendy. "Their gran's supposed to come today," she finished, pushing back her wild hair from the eye that was still watering. "And me husband come back this morning with a pain in his chest. He's asleep back there. We're waiting for the doctor now."

"I understand. I can quite understand your concern." Gwen had been standing in front of her, and now the sister caught her hand and patted it. "I'll have some additional clothing sent over to you – and a box of groceries – you could pass them on to their grandmother – if she arrives safely."

Afterwards, Gwen warmed some milk and put it into the new feeding-bottle. How strange it was. Under all that black cloth lay the kindest of human beings. She said to Michael, who was sitting on the rug, rubbing his eyes and whimpering, "I won't be a minute, luv. Auntie's coming with a nice bottle – and an old lady's goin' to send you some little pants – specially for you."

196

She picked the child up and held him in the crook of her arm, his drooping head against her flat chest, and put the teat into his mouth. After a moment's experimentation, he began to suck eagerly.

v

The shops which had survived were closed. The black-clad assistants were hurrying home, after a frantic Monday of dusting and sweeping and the resorting of stock blown off the shelves. The foreman of the rescue squad wriggled out of the zigzag tunnel he and his gang had moled into the ruins of the air raid shelter under the canteen. He took off his breathing apparatus.

"We're into it," he announced to the anxious little crowd hanging about outside. "But there don't seem to be nobody alive."

Mr Robinson's mouth tightened and Higgins threw away his cigarette end angrily. They climbed as close to the tunnel entrance as the foreman would allow them. There, they leaned on their shovels and waited. Both were covered with dust, their blackened shirts clinging to their backs with perspiration. Not by so much as a quiver did either show their agony of mind; yet Alec Robinson thought that if it were not for the support of the shovel, he would collapse. The tall, thin chauffeur took a cigarette packet out of his shirt pocket and offered a smoke to his companion. Without taking his eyes off the tunnel entry, Alec Robinson nodded refusal.

He was able to identify his wife of thirty years by the modest engagement ring on her crushed hand. The chauffeur, faced with the naked, torn body of his

197

beloved mistress, peered in the gathering gloom at her contorted face and then at the three magnificent rings on her hands, and muttered, "Yes, it's Her Ladyship," before quietly fainting. He had to be carried across to the other side of the street by two exhausted labourers and revived by the First Aid contingent. When the body of Her Ladyship was turned over to her family's undertaker, the rings were missing.

The police reported to the constable in Toxteth that no one answering to Emmie's description had been found.

vi

It was as if the whole population was swaying on its feet. One more blow and it would, if from nothing else, collapse from fatigue. By Monday evening Gwen had decided that the Sunday night raid must be the last one; the Germans had never before raided four nights in succession; she reckoned they would not come a fifth time. If it wasn't the last of the series, she felt she would drop dead; she could not take any more.

Conor Donnelly had not helped this feeling of despair. He had slapped the children's and his ration cards on the kitchen table, as if they had come to stay another week at least. Then the doctor had arrived, taken one look at David and hurried home to his telephone, to order an ambulance; Gwen had hardly had time to wash her husband's face and hands and help him out of his dirty overalls, before the vehicle arrived and whisked him off to Walton Hospital.

"They would choose the hospital furthest away," she

198

grumbled to Mari, Patrick and Ruby, at lunch-time. "How'm I goin' to get out there to visit him, I'd like to know. This mornin' I'd no one to leave Michael with, so as I could go with him, to see him settled in, like."

Mari ignored her mother's whining complaints. "He's not going to die, is he, Mam?"

"Of course not," snapped Gwen peevishly. "If they can't cure a heart attack we're in a proper bad way." Her panic regarding Dave must not be conveyed to Mari.

In the afternoon, she announced to Michael, who was having a great game on the heathrug with a collection of saucepans and lids, "Now we got to go and do the ration books – yours as well – 'cos Annie's corner shop's gone with the wind. Got to find a new grocer. And all that beastly red tape, to register again."

As she trudged back home up her own familiar street, carrying a very tired and fretful Michael, she passed the pile of rubble which had been Annie's shop and she stopped to sigh sadly in front of it. The pillar box still stood amid the rubble, and Mr Marsh, the neatly uniformed postman, was just unlocking it to collect the letters from it. "Nice day," he said mechanically, and she laughed almost hysterically, "Aye, I suppose it is."

A few yards further on, she met Bridget Mahoney, her neighbour from across the road. Bridget was looking red-faced and sullen, but she listened as Gwen told her about the Donnelly invasion of her home, something she knew about already. "And to crown all," Gwen finished up, "our Emma is missing down town somewhere, and I'm worried to death about her."

Bridget regarded her dully, as she nursed her bandaged arm, cut when she had removed the incendiary bomb from the gutter of her house. Her body trembled and she could not answer Gwen at first. Then she muttered, "So's me husband – in Greece. Got a telegram just now."

Gwen was aghast, stuck for words, knowing that she should say something optimistic and comforting.

Bridget swallowed. "I don't know how to tell me boys."

vii

Conor received with some anxiety the information that Emma had not been found in the canteen's air raid shelter. The constable on duty, who had given him the news, added heavily, "Either she were struck down on her way home – or she took shelter somewhere else and got buried there."

"We could try checking amongst the unidentified." Conor sighed. "Could start with the living. I'm off duty now – I'll see what I can do on the phone."

Four unidentified women between the ages of 25 and 35 lay in three different hospitals, their names unknown, though only one had been found in a street Emmie was likely to have traversed on her way home. The voice at the other end of the telephone added laconically, "Of course, there's several hundred unidentified bodies, a goodly number unidentifiable, at Webster Road mortuary."

Patiently, Conor hitched lifts to the various hospitals; looking at the women was the only way to be certain.

One woman had recovered consciousness and had identified herself. Another had been claimed by a frantic

200

husband. The third one had just died and Conor was allowed to view the body before it was wheeled away to the mortuary.

To see the fourth one, he followed hopefully a young probationer through a packed women's ward, filled with lively chatter. Behind a screen, a person lay on her back, arms neatly arranged at her sides under tightly tucked-in bedding. Her breath fluttered uneasily from blanched lips. Her eyes and head were sheathed in bandages, as if a white turban had slipped half way over her face. Her head was supported on either side by what Conor supposed were sandbags. An angular, elderly nurse raised an eyebrow, as Conor intruded softly.

He whispered, "I've come to see if she's Emma Thomas." The nurse nodded and stepped back, while Conor peered down at the end of a nose, prettily curved white lips and a rounded chin with an unexpected dimple in it, totally unlike Emmie's long narrow face.

The nurse's face softened, as he nodded negatively. "Poor little lass," she murmured. "It's her eyes, you know."

With a dreary ache in his heart for Ellen, mixed with sorrow for the pretty young woman he had just seen, he decided that he would try the dead.

A delivery van driver gave him a lift to within a couple of streets of his destination. He had to wait, while a calm, slender woman in a white coat dealt with a sailor in a tight-fitting Royal Navy uniform, who could not have been more than nineteen. The sailor stood timidly at the counter, his round white cap clutched in both hands in front of his chest. The acne spots stood out on his face and neck against an unnaturally pale skin. Together, he and the woman went through a series of large brown envelopes holding the effects found on or near the bodies in the mortuary. Time and again he nodded affirmatively, as he recognised the pitiful possessions. Sometimes he hesitated uncertainly and the woman put those envelopes on one side.

Conor felt himself reeling at the strong smell of disinfectant mixed with the ghastly odour of disintegrating bodies. He lit a cigarette and drew on it heavily, as he watched the pile of envelopes in front of the hapless sailor grow and grow. Finally, the woman drew the shaking boy further into the building. Conor began to whistle softly to keep his courage up; he had seen enough at the shambles of The Dwellings to understand what the youngster was going through. Thanks be to the Holy Mother that his Ellen was decently wrapped in a winding sheet in a proper coffin, and tomorrow, when his mother had arrived, they would see her respectfully committed to her own grave.

The sailor suddenly bolted past him and out of the front door. When the woman turned inquiringly to Conor, tears were streaming down her face. "He's from Seaforth," she burst out, as if she must share her agony of mind with someone. "He had fourteen bodies to identify, and some of them were a mess."

She had no trace of anyone who could be Emmie; the only likely corpse, picked up in Whitechapel, which was the continuation of Paradise Street, had been identified.

She rubbed her damp eyes with the back of her hand. "I'm sorry, Mr Donnelly. Try the temporary mortuary near the scene." She paused and tapped the table with the end of her pencil. "If I were you, I would talk to the men on the spot."

Between the mortuary and Paradise Street lay

Emmie's home. He thought he should drop in *en route* and assure Gwen that the fact that he had no news of Emmie was probably good news.

He was surprised to find the front door open and, after a perfunctory knock, he walked in.

He was immediately engulfed by his children, their faces smeared with jam, as they rushed from the tea table. They were followed by Gwen holding a feeding-bottle. Behind her, a man half rose from his chair by the fire. Robert Owen had duly received the information through the police that his fiancée was missing, and, since not much more could be done regarding the still exploding cargo of the *Marakand*, he had been given a few hours' leave. He had come just as he was, blackened and reeking of fire, his eyebrows and hair singed. When, at last, he had found a tram blundering along in the right direction, he had endured with suppressed fury the stares, and occasional giggles, of the other passengers, at his outlandish appearance.

Gwen looked inquiringly at Conor above the children's heads. He nodded negatively and she sucked in her lips as her sense of guilt returned to her. She shouted suddenly, irritably, at the children, "Now, Patrick – you kids – get back to the table and finish your tea. Now, Mike, you come to Auntie and I'll put you on the sofa, and you can show your dad how you can hold your bottle."

When the child had been propped up on the sofa cushions, he put the teat in his mouth and looked triumphantly at his father out of the corner of his eye. His father had, however, other things on his mind.

"You must be Emmie Thomas's intended," he said to Robert. "I been lookin' for her just now."

The air raid siren interrupted Conor's and Robert's conversation with the police constable they found on duty at the corner of Paradise Street.

"Oh, blast 'em," rumbled the constable exasperatedly.

Robert's heart sank, as he looked out over the enormous, smoking pyre facing him. He thought he'd seen the worst in Seaforth, but here was just such another scene of devastation – and possibly his Emmie was under it. He wanted to run across the road and start tearing it aside single-handed, to find her, but instead he had to listen to the doubts expressed by the constable that there were any more bodies there; certainly nobody alive.

High in the sky anti-aircraft fire flashed white. There were few clouds. Despite the smoke haze, it was much too clear for comfort.

From the south, where Toxteth lay, the guns spat forth. Conor, so tired that he was becoming a little incoherent, prayed in the back of his mind that his children would be spared. With a quivering match he lit a cigarette handed to him by Robert; one more flash of light was not going to help the Germans; the fires still burning would guide them beautifully.

The constable glanced uneasily at the firemen, rescue teams and a demolition squad still at work amid the destruction, and the women of the WVS mobile canteen nearby. The blue flash of the men's lanterns made them look like ghosts. Nobody ran for cover as the gunfire increased. He began to herd the chattering crowd of sightseers into a nearby underground shelter. It beat him where all the onlookers came from. He'd have thought that every man and woman in the city had enough to do at present; and if they didn't, that they would be thankful to sleep. But here they were, come to gloat. Ruddy vultures, the whole bloody lot of 'em. He blew his whistle impatiently, to summon one or two stragglers, and to draw the attention of the solitary telephone engineer, still toiling in the nearby crater.

The engineer took no notice. The whole job was almost completed and he continued to check the lines which he and his colleague had been sedulously splicing together all day. In cooperation with the exchange operators, the reconnected phones were rung in nearby offices. Sometimes the line was still dead, the telephone shattered under the debris. Occasionally, a late-working clerk or a firewatcher or cleaning lady would lift the receiver and assure him that *everyone* had gone home, which never failed to make him smile. Now, with the increasing noise overhead, he was frightened and was glad of these nasal Liverpool voices responding to him. George, he told himself wearily, you're getting a bit old for this game. When a piece of flak whizzed down and buried itself in the clay side of the hole, he clapped his tin hat on to his bald head, clenched his teeth over his cold pipe and went on working.

The constable returned to Robert and Conor and they all stared skyward. Beneath the hissing of water from the firehoses and the rhythm of the pumps, they could hear the steady chug of engines from the east, and they moved to the shelter of the sandbags surrounding the entrance while they discussed what could have happened to Emmie. The sandbags had been pierced by flak and were slowly bleeding their contents on to the pavement. Conor absently poked a bigger hole with his finger, while the constable assured him, "They cleared the shelter, the rescue squad did – they were proper tired – and then they went home to get some sleep." He turned, to rebuke someone trying to leave the shelter, and then, in answer to an impatient query from Robert, he said, "Well, you could talk to the new incident officer – the other one was killed last night."

A series of thuds not very far away announced the arrival of the Luftwaffe, and George nervously collected his tools into his tool box and said to himself, "Me lad, this is where you beat it."

He hastily had the line he had been working on rung by the operator. It failed to ring, and he cursed his wasted effort. The exchange operator said sharply, "Mind your language, if you please," and transferred her plug to another call. He made a face and was just about to remove his instrument from his ear, when distantly down the line came a hoarse female voice singing falteringly *Men of Harlech*. He grinned. The receiver must be off the hook and some cleaning woman probably dusting round it. He listened for a second; the sky directly over-head was quiet, though more distant sounds of combat warned him not to linger. The song became a series of harsh sobs. It seemed to him that very faintly he heard also the rumble of a male voice, and then, a little more strongly, the tune again sung in Welsh. He gave a small laugh. Welsh miners sang it a lot better, probably because they were always singing; he had been told that they sang even when they were entombed in a mine accident.

Entombed! My God!

"Can you hear me?" he shouted, in incredulous apprehension. There was no reply, only the weak, cracked voice carrying the tune.

He called the telephone operator. Could she heard it? But the voice had stopped and the operator told him loftily not to be so daft. Lips pursed, he put a clamp to mark the line and scrambled out of the hole. Like a lumbering bear with a tin hat on its head, he ran down the newly cleared pavement, looking madly for the constable.

The WVS volunteer, a mug of tea in each hand, directed him to the entrance to the shelter.

"Get away," exclaimed the constable, when he poured out his suspicions to him.

"I'm not joking," spluttered George furiously. "I tell you I heard it. It's possible, I tell you. And buried miners always sing – and this woman was singing in Welsh. Me grandmother was Welsh – I know Welsh when I hear it. Damn it."

"It's her," Robert interjected with conviction. He caught at the constable's arm. "Come on. Who do we have to see to start 'em digging?"

The constable swallowed, while Conor said simply, "Emmie Thomas is Welsh."

George looked a little bewildered at this exchange and they hastened to explain to him about the missing woman. "And you think this is technically possible, that the telephone fell somewhere near her and still managed to remain connected?" the constable asked the engineer.

"You've just said the canteen was on the ground floor. It wouldn't have far to fall, if it wasn't blasted out; if it were protected by a wall that didn't give, like. Anyways, I heard her."

"Let's try the line again," Conor suggested impetuously. He started to move out of the sheltered doorway, but the constable held him back and pointed to the bit of sky they could see above the sandbag wall. It was filled with flashing light, and a series of reverberating booms came from the direction of the docks. "You're chancing your own lives," warned the constable. "What number was it?"

"I've forgotten. I can find out. I marked the line."

"For God's sake, let's try it," Conor urged. "Come on," he called to George and Robert. He started to run across the road, George skittering unhappily behind him, followed closely by Robert. A shrill shriek overhead sent the three of them into the gutter, hands clasped over heads, noses in the dirt.

The missile passed over them, to fall into a fire slightly closer to the river. Its explosion sent a mass of burning debris flying into the air, to start fires in buildings hitherto untouched. Firemen dropped their hoses and ducked for cover wherever they could find it, only to regroup a few minutes later and continue their tasks. Conor, George and Robert stayed firmly in the gutter until the remainder of the stick of bombs had been deposited in a neat line across the city, and had sent to Kingdom Come one ambulance driver and her assistant, twenty-two homeless people in a rest centre, two pedestrians never identified, one firewatcher and one special constable; the thin red line was becoming frighteningly thinner.

A series of bombers sweeping the length of the fan-shaped city, now dived one after the other to loose their deadly loads, and sent up fountains of rubble as their bombs scored hits. The three men cowered in the gutter, hearts racing, as all kinds of lethal odds and ends pinged and plonked on the road and pavement round them. A group of soldiers and rescue men, their hooded lanterns bobbing, chanced running for the air raid shelter. Robert heard a muffled cry, as one was hit. He crammed himself further into the littered gutter.

During a moment of lessened hubbub, Robert cautiously turned his face to peep upward. The gun flashes were like an enormous storm of sheet lightning. Tracer bullets and flares added to the scarifying display. A further beat of heavy engines made him push his face tightly against the pavement's friendly curb. George, his head near Conor's feet, stretched out a careful hand to touch the warden's boots for comfort. He could feel panic rising in him, but he was haunted by the sound of the quavering voice and he tried to concentrate on the technical arguments why he should be right. He'd *prove* he was right, he would, even if he had to dig for her himself.

In Paradise Street, a big Victorian chimney, balanced by a piece of side wall from the building in which the canteen had been, shivered and fell, its stonework rattling over the wreckage at its foot. The usual cloud of dust spumed upwards. Through chattering teeth, Conor prayed for his life to his patron saint, who had not heard from him for some years. Conor had said bitterly that he was accursed; yet even so, life seemed unexpectedly precious when it looked like coming to an end.

The Defiants succeeded in disorganising the raiders and the bombing moved further north. Robert was so stunned with noise and fright that it was a moment or two before he could make himself scramble to his feet, to find the constable bending over George, as he got to his feet, and shouting through the noise, "Come on, get back in t' shelter."

Though terrified out of his wits, George was determined. "I'm goin' to try that line again. Won't take a mo'."

"You're clean out of your mind," the constable bellowed. But he ran with them to the cavity in the street.

They crouched together in the clay hollow. George found the wire with a clamp on it. He clipped on his headphones.

"No." He found also that he could no longer contact the telephone operator.

"It could've been one of the WVS women at the corner singing," suggested the constable.

George boiled with frustration. He checked his splicing again.

Conor leaned closer to him and shouted into his ear, "I believe you."

Robert thought he would lose his reason if one of them didn't do something constructive soon. "It must've been the chimney what fell just now — broke whatever connection there was." He turned to the constable and asked, "Who do we go to — to ask for rescue men?"

"The incident officer, like I said." The constable was feeling most unhappy and cursed his indecision. He was, in principle, the ultimate authority, but he did not want to pressure the incident officer into a wild-goose chase; yet the engineer presumably knew his business. As they crawled over the gummy clay and out of the hole, he said finally, "Let's talk to the incident officer."

210

A curious chug-chug-chug, like a train coming rapidly into a station, made them all slide back into their refuge and hug the side of it. Not too far away, something crashed into the wasteland. Tensely they waited for the explosion.

Nothing happened.

Cautiously they lifted their heads. Again the sound of a train. Again they pressed themselves into the clay. A tremendous detonation in the direction of Exchange Station drew a string of vivid swear-words from the constable. "Now I know what we got – a bloody land-mine – unexploded. Now isn't that nice?" His sarcasm was bitter. "Blow us all into next week, it could, while we're lookin' for this woman."

TUESDAY, 6 MAY 1941

"I've never heard of such a thing before." The hard-pressed incident officer sounded kind, but he was used to survivors clutching at all sorts of straws to assure themselves that a loved one was still alive. "I think you *must* have misheard," he added to George. "It's easy enough."

"We can trace the number," George informed him coldly. "Look in your telephone book and see what the canteen's number was, and I'll trace if the line is the same."

It took a little while and the close co-operation of the telephone exchange supervisor to establish fairly certainly that it was indeed the canteen telephone line. Then, with his nose in the air, George climbed into his van and went home to bed. Let the high-and-mighty incident officer work out *where* she was.

The incident officer wasted no time. He sent for a heavy-rescue foreman, recently off a train from London, and to his surprise the man said calmly, his Cockney accent sounding strange to the men around him, "There was a case like this in London."

The plans of the buildings in the Paradise Street area, carefully prepared at the beginning of the war, had been burned with the command post the previous night, but an off-duty warden, who might know the canteen, was traced with commendable speed, through the warden of his home district; and he tumbled out of the Anderson shelter in his garden and came down on his bicycle while the raid still raged.

He could not suggest where Emmie could be, but, when asked to draw a plan of the canteen, he included the cobbled back-yard.

"Where was the phone?" asked Robert.

"It were in the kitchen at the back."

"Exactly where?"

"On a little table by the window, as I remember – though I can't be sure." He stubbed out his cigarette. "'T' window faced the yard."

"She must be in the yard, or in the wreckage of the kitchen," interjected Conor between a series of yawns. His legs felt like lead and he told himself that once they started to dig, he would go home and kip down for a while.

To Robert Owen, the dark small hours were a nightmare, while with infinite care the heavy-rescue foreman from London and a group of miners from nearby St Helen's, with other experienced people, plotted Emmie's possible position. They decided to explore whatever might remain of the light well.

Robert was sick with fatigue from the battle in No. 2 Huskisson; burns on his hands were a throbbing misery. Conor tried to persuade him to go home for a few hours, but he refused. Someone thrust a mug of coffee into his hand and he drank it gratefully. Then he insisted on going down to Paradise Street to help the rescue squad. Shoulder to shoulder with the miners, he helped to pass debris back to the road, as painstakingly slowly a new tunnel was made, to pass over the huge stone wall which had formed the back of the canteen shelter. Pieces of office equipment, beams, furniture and some precious pit-props were carefully eased into place, to hold the tunnel open. He worked like an automaton, the fear he

216

had felt when he went to the Mercantile Marine office to obtain another ship long since forgotten, lost under greater and more immediate terrors. Nothing seemed to matter now, except that Emmie be found alive.

When the All Clear howled across slateless rooftops, to be followed shortly by the first rays of the rising sun, the pace of work increased. A rotund WVS woman, a flowered wrapover pinafore covering her uniform, brought mugs of tea and a basket of fresh scones with a scraping of margarine on them. "Made them myself before I set out," she told them proudly. "We've still got gas on our side of the water."

Her face showed the same weariness as that of the rescue team, but she was so fresh and clean that Robert felt as if his mother had come all the way from Hoylake to help. "Have you heard her yet?" the woman asked.

"Nay. T' foreman's goin' to go in a bit further, now he's got a block and tackle rigged. Then he's goin' to ask the fire engines and everything to be quiet, while he listens – afore the streets get busy, like. Couldn't do it while the raid was on – no point in it, with guns and all."

She touched his arm and said comfortingly, as the weary group munched and slurped thankfully. "Och, you'll find her if she's there. You're all great lads."

Robert lifted his mug to her, his eyes twinkling suddenly. "You're great ladies," he said.

It was only when the new police constable on duty managed to organise a short period of quiet that Robert realised what a shambles of noise they had been working in. In the stillness, he was surpised to hear a seagull squawk, as it came to rest on top of the broken roof of the building behind him. Not very far away, burning wood crackled, and from the direction of the river a ferry boat hooted cheerily.

The squad waited, tense as Olympic runners, while a miner as small as a jockey eased his way along the tunnel they had made. Apart from his torch, he carried a piece of piping to use as a listening device.

To Robert, it seemed a lifetime before a soft rustle and a tumbling pebble heralded the man's careful emergence. Once clear, he stood up and removed his mask; he coughed helplessly to rid his lungs of dust. His watering eyes made little rivulets through the dust on his cheeks. He nodded negatively.

Robert's teeth began to chatter. He clutched the foreman's arm. "Let me go down," he pleaded.

"No, son. You're too big."

ii

During Tuesday morning, Gwen, with Michael on one arm, squeezed into the stuffy privacy of the nearest public telephone box. It was still functioning, so she telephoned Walton Hospital.

A tired, uninterested voice assured her that Mr Thomas was resting comfortably.

Gwen determined that on Wednesday morning, she would keep Ruby home from school to care for Michael while she attempted the journey across the town to visit the hospital. She fully expected, however, that keeping Ruby home would not be necessary. Grandma Donnelly would surely arrive in time for her daughter-in-law's funeral that very afternoon, and would remain to care for her grandchildren. After lunch she must see that Ruby and Patrick were clean and tidy, ready to accompany their father to the funeral.

She had had a sharp spat with Patrick that morning about the necessity of going to school. The broken nights had taken their toll and he wanted to remain in bed. It had ended with her slapping him hard across the head and threatening to complain to the headmaster, if he did not go. At first she had thought he would slap her back, but he had got up and gone sulkily to school with the other children.

At lunch-time, as she handed him a bowl of soup and a cob of bread, she said to him, "You're a bright lad, Patrick. If you learn to read and write as good as Mari, you'll never be hungry or out of work. And I would like that for you, scamp that you are."

He had nodded agreement and lost some of his sulky look. He dreaded the afternoon. He was afraid he would cry at the funeral.

Ruby sat silent, steadily drinking her soup. She knew *her* reading and writing days were over. She looked down at the soup bowl, spoon poised, and wondered what happened at funerals. Her thin lips quivered.

A box of groceries, some children's clothing and a parcel of nappies were delivered immediately after lunch by a cheeky youth on an errand boy's bicycle. Gwen smiled. The nun had not forgotten.

A worried Conor, looking incredibly neat in a clean blue overall, washed and ironed for him by Glynis Hughes, collected Patrick and Ruby. "Their gran and me brothers' wives haven't come from Walton yet," he told a very sober-looking Gwen. "Here's a slip of paper telling 'em which church. Will you give it to them, if

219

they come late?"

"Where you goin'?" asked Nora, held back firmly by Gwen, while Brendy sucked his thumb and stared at the funeral-goers.

"Never you mind," Patrick told her savagely. "You and Brendy go to school." Ruby began to cry.

"You stay with me, and after school we'll go down the street and buy a sweetie ration." Gwen shepherded the youngsters back into the house, where Michael was trying to feed Mari's long discarded wooden bricks to a patient Sarge.

Grandma did not arrive that day, nor did any other relation, and an extremely hurt Conor went straight back to his post after returning Patrick and Ruby to Gwen's house. "I'll try to get through on t' telephone to the warden up there and ask him to send a message. They may've got t' lines restored by now."

Once more a resigned Gwen saw her charges scrubbed from head to foot and put into bed, Michael soothed with a bottle of milk and Brendy happily sucking his brother's dummy.

"What about me mam?" asked Nora, sitting up suddenly in her white bed. "A girl at school says she's dead. What's dead? Is it like when the cat was run over?"

Gwen gulped, while Ruby shivered by her in one of Gwen's own nightgowns. Ruby's eyes were huge and imploring. Gwen said coolly, "They're still mending your mam. You don't have to worry about her. And soon your gran'll come to take care of you."

"Well, what *is* dead?" Nora insisted, as she unhurriedly pulled the blanket over herself, and Gwen tucked the sheet round her chin.

"It's when you go to Heaven," replied Gwen, and added almost wistfully, "It's proper peaceful, like, and you're with God."

"Oh, aye," replied the child, just as if they were talking about lollipops, "Sister Theresa talks about it sometimes. Do you get lots to eat there?"

Gwen laughed, for the first time for a week. "To be sure," she replied promptly. "No shortages at all."

She waited for Ruby to climb into her bed beside Michael. The girl looked drained and as hagridden as Bridget Mahoney from across the road had looked that afternoon. Impulsively Gwen bent and kissed her on the cheek. "Now you cuddle down and sleep and don't worry about nothin'. You'll feel better in the morning."

When she went into her own bedroom to see Mari, the girl was sitting on the edge of her bed, pulling off her socks. She, too, looked older than her age, her eyes black-rimmed. "I wish we had news of Auntie Emmie," she greeted her mother.

Gwen sighed. "They'll find her. Don't worry. Now hurry up and get into bed and get some sleep."

She went slowly down the darkened staircase, automatically holding a corner of her apron under the candlestick, to catch any wax before it fell on to the stair carpet.

In the living room Patrick was sitting on the black, horsehair sofa. He had his head in his hands and was crying.

She put the candlestick down on the table and held him against her apron. "Now, don't take on so, luv. She's at peace now."

She took her handkerchief from her pocket and bent and wiped his tears. He took it from her and blew his nose hard.

Gwen felt as if she herself had hardly got into bed before the air raid siren went, followed almost immediately by a tremendous run of explosions. Once more, she gathered her frightened brood and hastened to the cellar steps, where, for four hours, she tried to cope with tears and quarrels, while outside a thundering tumult raged.

WEDNESDAY, 7 MAY 1941

As clerks and typists struggled over the debris to report for work in non-existent buildings, the incident officer offered to send a relief crew, to replace the men hunting for Emmie. The men refused to be relieved.

The incident officer did not argue with them. Amongst the motley gangs of workmen there was a stiff pride that they did not stop work until they had themselves carried the victims out.

An intact corner of the light well had been reached. The searchers tried listening there, but heard nothing. They did, however, find a woman's shoe and this gave them new incentive to continue.

Robert could hardly stand, but he continued mechanically to pile rubbish into skips and to lend a hand where he could. He could not identify the shoe as Emmie's.

Gathered as close as the police would allow was a large crowd of sightseers, clerks in well-pressed business suits, their female counterparts in neat black dresses with white collars and white summer hats, housewives in spring suits, with pretty baskets on their arms, and the male flotsam and jetsam of a port, who, despite two years of war, seemed to have nothing particular to do.

An untidy little office girl came out of a building still standing behind the crowd and pushed her way into the middle of the partially cleared street. She held a saucer of milk. "Kitty, kitty, kitty," she called, and, as a thin black cat sidled up to her, she put the saucer down, and explained to a young woman standing watching, "It's

225

the offices' pussies. They got no home now." Another cat approached tentatively, and she renewed her call.

Young typists and clerks were searching the edges of the ruins for filing cabinets, account books, any records which would help to re-establish their companies, when it was agreed that a miner particularly experienced in mine rescues should go down the tunnel and decide how they should proceed further. In a moment he was gone, flicking himself along the tortuous zigzags and ups and downs, like an eel through rock-patterned water. Though the smell of this disaster was different from that of a mining accident, the dust was the same, and when he felt cobblestones under him, he paused to readjust his mask. It was surprisingly quiet, as he flashed his torch along the lines of what cracks he could see. It was clear from their angle that, further on, the yard had collapsed. This puzzled him. He turned the torch upward, to examine the fearsome mass above him. To move further in, he decided, could be dicey.

"'Allo," he called tentatively, not too loudly – it wouldn't take much to start a fall, he reckoned. "'Allo, there."

Dead silence, except for an uneasy movement overhead. Blast it. He drew his piece of piping from inside the front of his singlet and this time put it to the cobbles – afterwards he could give no real reason why he did so. He bent his ear to it and listened intently.

It seemed to him that he did hear something, a movement, other than the rustles in the wreckage bearing down round him. But it was from underneath him.

He laid his head, ear down, against the unfriendly

cobblestones and held his breath. Very carefully he tapped on the stones with the end of his torch.

The girl couldn't be under him? Or could she? He tapped and listened again. There was a small, strangled cry. And it *was* from underneath, but a good distance further to his right, he guessed. Taking a chance, he cupped his hands round his mouth and put his face to the stones. At the top of his voice, he shouted, "We're coming. Hold on there."

She heard him, a muffled echo. With overwhelming joy, she tried to shout back, but she had screamed so much, was so exhausted by fright, hunger and thirst that the noise was not enough for him to hear. Beside her, Dick muttered incoherently in a high fever, as if he had pneumonia.

Perplexed, the miner ran his torch again along any cracks he could find, to see their direction. He tapped the surface in several directions as far as space would allow, but there was no echo, and no further cry. He backed down the tunnel as fast as he dared, trying to imagine, as he retreated, how parts of the light well might have fallen, and into what kind of space. It had to be a cellar, he decided.

As he emerged, panting, scratched and mystified, Robert ran lightly up the debris to meet him, followed by a protesting foreman. "You shouldn't run over it like that, you fool," he bellowed. "Bring the whole mess down!" He forgot his complaints, however, when the miner said there was indeed someone there. "Under you?" he exclaimed in disbelief. "But it's a yard – a light well. Cobbled. Seen it meself when I went down a bit back."

"Well, get down there and get her out." Robert was

nearly beside himself.

"Hold on, lad." The foreman was aggrieved. "These buildings've bin blasted several times from different directions. It's not that simple." He turned to the miner again. "You're sure you heard her?"

The man smiled, his teeth flashing white in his filthy face. "I heard somebody, all right."

"Thank God!" exclaimed Robert in relief. But anguished dread then filled him. What horrifying hurt might Emmie have suffered? He fought down a wave of nausea.

The returned miner was talking again. "She must be lying in a hole under that yard. But most of the yard must be supported by solid earth – otherwise the cobbles would have caved in years ago. They'd be a dead weight."

"Some kind of arches might be supporting 'em," another man suggested. "Arches can hold up cathedrals."

"Aye, but we *could* be digging down through solid rock, if we go down through the cobbles."

"How far into the yard, measuring, like, from where you was lyin', do you think she was?" The foreman rubbed his heavy-muscled arms which ached intolerably. He was bent on pinpointing as accurately as possible where they must penetrate.

"A way," the miner said immediately. "I went over the stone foundation wall what you told me about – back o' where the canteen shelter must've been – and all me body was on cobbles. She must've been at least twenty feet from me, bearing half right; and I tell you, the voice came from below – not level with me."

Robert caught the foreman's arm. "I know!" he broke

in eagerly. "Me grandad told me often enough. Privateers – and smugglers – used to have hiding-places for contraband – and you said the cellar of the canteen was much older than the building above it. Could be there's some merchant's old cellar under that light well."

The foreman sighed and pursed his lips, and then said rather condescendingly, "It's an idea. But God knows how she fell into it."

"This fella here said it would be hard to go down through the light well itself. Could you still get into the shelter?" asked Robert, fatigue forgotten, and the plan of the building he had seen the warden draw clear in his mind.

"Oh, yes. It was all well nigh cleared out by the time we'd finished. Have to go down carefully, because of the of the big chimney collapsing over there, last night."

"Did you see any doors in the walls?"

"No, lad. We'd 've gone through 'em if we had – to make sure nobody was there." The tone was scornful now.

"Look again," Robert persisted. "If they had a secret cellar under the light well, then they had a place to get into it. Maybe it were bricked up when they built the offices. Round here they've bin building and rebuilding for centuries – even the offices were real old. There must be all kinds of little places built over – even small rivers have been."

The men stood round arguing amongst themselves, while the foreman thought this over. The ultimate responsibility was his and he was not going to put his men at risk unnecessarily.

Finally, when Robert had begun to think he could not bear another moment of suspense, he said, "OK. I'll go down meself and look." He turned to a young miner who was particularly small-made. "You, Evans, you can come with me."

They had been squeezing slowly round the shelter's walls for nearly five minutes, before Evans said triumphantly, "I've got it. See, this is brick, not stone."

The foreman flashed his torch along the wall. Once pointed out, it was possible to see a line under the whitewash where the texture of the wall changed. He crawled closer to the younger man and then carefully tapped on the brick and listened. No response.

ii

Some of the rescue crew, who could do nothing for the moment, went down to the WVS van to get some lunch, while, amid the smell of wet plaster mixed with that of a charnel house, the foreman dug out the first bricks with the care of a surgeon. The wall would be weaker at this point and the old brickwork could crumble suddenly under the weight of the wreckage above.

The wall proved to be four bricks thick, and when the fourth one suddenly gave and fell out on the other side, a poof of surprisingly cold, damp air blew out at them.

Evans broke into excited Welsh; then remembered his English. "The lad up there was right. There's space here." He put his face close to the hole they had made, and shouted, "Anybody there?"

In the light of the foreman's torch, his face fell. "Try again," the foreman urged.

"Anybody there?"

Very faintly came a croaking sound that could have been a human voice.

The wall was broken as fast as human hands could do it without causing a fall. As soon as the hole was big enough, young Evans wriggled through feet first. He felt around with the toes of his boots, to make sure he was not dangling over a hole. Cautiously, he stood upright.

"Lend us the torch." The foreman passed it to him and he flashed it round. "It's like a blinking castle dungeon," he reported. And then he called, "'Allo! 'Allo!"

From beyond a massive blockage facing him came a faint response, a distant sob.

"We're coming. Hold on. Are you by yourself?"

The reply was unintelligible.

Evans tried again. "Are you badly hurt?"

There was a pause and then Evans clearly heard an effort at a throat being cleared. "No," came the answer.

Meanwhile, in preparation, other men worked feverishly, pushing pit-props and tools down the tunnel and through the hole in the wall. They whistled when they saw, by the light of a powerful lantern, parts of hefty stone arches. There was room to stand against the wall through which Evans had clambered; but the rest seemed to be an almost solid mass of wreckage.

"She's on the other side of that," said Evans, his young face gloomy in the light of the lantern, as he gestured to his right.

The foreman, who had followed Evans through the hole in the wall, glanced quickly round. He said, with more optimism than he felt, "We'll find her. God, it must be five hundred years old, this place. They knew how to build in those days – and that's what's saved her, though there's more'n one fall here." He rubbed the end of his nose and then went on, "Reckon she's tucked up not far from the wall we've come through, but it's goin' to take a while afore we get through that lot."

The floor of the cellar was earthen, which at times was a help to them, in that they could loosen large pieces of debris by digging for a little way under them. Miners can almost sink into the earth when they dig, but a bucket brigade had to be formed, to move earth and debris out of the way as it was dug, and these men had difficulty in keeping up with the moling miners.

"At this rate, we'll be home in time for tea," one of them joked.

The moles themselves, though fast, moved with the greatest care, with the minimum of noise, with the least disturbance of the dense mass poised above them. A faint smell of burning made Evans shiver; occasionally small runnels of water would cascade down on them. "From the fire-hoses," the foreman told them firmly. "Water and gas is turned off. You're not goin' to drown."

Every so often the gasped curses would cease and the leading man would call to Emmie, partly to reassure her, but partly to keep them on course.

She would answer them with a faint croak. Every tired nerve alert, she had listened through an eternity of time to the muffled sounds indicating that help was coming. Sometimes the men had paused, to consider how to deal with an obstruction facing them; there was no sound, and at such times her spirits would sink. They had given up, deserted Dick and her. Dreadful, agonised fear went through her parched, starved body. She tried to shout but little noise came. She felt around the sick man beside her, to find her petticoat with which she had earlier wiped Dick's burning face. It was half under her, and she laboriously hauled it out, to suck it and dampen her mouth. Though they were lying on wet ground, it seemed impossible to do more than moisten their lips and tongues.

She found the stone with which she had tapped earlier and hit the wall unsteadily with it.

"That's good," said a voice surprisingly close to her. "Every time I call, you tap, eh?"

She tapped once in acknowledgment and prayed she would not pass out.

Outside, Robert Owen stood hunched in his Red Cross, brown jacket, nearly out of his mind with the frustration of the long wait. As he mechanically emptied buckets or handed in pieces of wood, his mind would hardly function, and suddenly he heeled over and fell face down on to a pile of debris. The watching crowd murmured and shuffled.

A First Aid man who had been checking his canisters of milk and water, and the tube which he could poke through a small hole in the obstruction between himself and a victim, and thus feed the sufferer until he was freed, dropped his satchel and ran to Robert. He went down on one knee and gently turned the exhausted man over. The doctor and driver from the ambulance also hastened across the street and together they lifted the limp figure and laid him down on the pavement, which had earlier been so sedulously cleared by Alec Robinson and Lady Mentmore's chauffeur. The lady doctor knelt to wipe gravel from his bruised face and half turned him on his side, so that he was less likely to choke if he vomited. She checked that he had no false teeth in his mouth and then lifted one of his eyelids. She smiled and took his pulse. Still amused, she got up slowly, dusted down her slacks and said laconically, "Gone to sleep on his feet."

She turned to the warden, who had come from helping the constable keep back the crowd. "Better find out who he is," she suggested, "and send him home."

"He'll be right mad if I do. It's his girl what's bein' dug out." He ran his tongue round broken teeth. "I'll get a couple of blankets and we'll lay 'im in the hallway of the office opposite."

The First Aid man returned to digging through his satchel. For the third time, he checked its contents: hypodermic syringe, pain-killers, sterilised pads, sticking plaster. A stretcher had already been carried as close to the tunnel entrance as possible. There was nothing he could do but wait. He envied Robert, sound asleep in the hallway. It was thirty-six hours since he had been to bed himself.

Far below the horrifying ruins, the miners burrowed like ferrets, thin sinewy arms flashing in the lantern light, flat-stomached bodies swinging in rhythm, as they passed buckets of earth back to a space near the broken entry to the old cellar.

Jimmy, the foreman, moved his helpers around as if he were playing a complicated game of chess, his seamed face a picture of intense concentration, as he improvised the steps of the rescue. No two rescues were ever the same; no two buildings ever fell in exactly the same way – their stresses and strains had each to be weighed up anew, and their constant tiny shifts watched with feline intensity. Not only had he to rescue those buried; he must at all costs ensure the safety of his team, and as he sometimes remarked, "Me old woman would be proper put out if I buried meself and she was done out of a good funeral."

They came up within two feet of her, to a tight tangle of splintered wooden beams and what might have been part of an iron girder, the same obstruction Emmie had felt in her first search for the dripping water. Now she squeaked with shock when her foot was grasped by a warm hand slipped under it.

They were stalled.

"Sufferin' Christ!" The foreman's disappointment was as bitter as if his own daughter lay beyond the girder. "Get First Aid to bring some water and a shot for her, while we decide what to do."

The nervous young man crawled down the tunnel and fed both Emmie and Dick with water and then a little milk through the tube he thrust over the girder. She refused any sedation. Without a hint of his inward horror of the tight confinement of the suffocating tunnel, he whispered encouragement and told her that her fiancé was waiting outside.

"He's there?" Her voice was suddenly comparatively clear. "Thank God, thank God." She began to weep, soft, helpless crying in which was mingled a tremendous joy. He was there, he was safe.

When the miners were ready to start again, he backed down and told the surprised foreman that he had two living victims to get out.

Like dogs getting at a bone buried under a tree root, Evans hollowed out a space in the earthen floor under the girder. He then grasped her ankles firmly and told her he would help her wriggle down and under, on her back. When her knees were through, he grasped her bent legs and heaved her upwards. She cried out at the scratches she received, but she was through, her eyes dazzled excruciatingly by the blaze of the torch held by a second man behind Evans.

After calling Dick and getting no response, Evans turned himself on his back and squeezed himself into the space Emmie had occupied. He flashed his torch quickly round the tiny refuge, sickened by the stench. Near Dick's head, neatly wedged between a piece of stone and what looked like the remains of a table, was a telephone. So the engineer had been right. With a grin, he turned to the job of easing the barely conscious Dick out.

With difficulty, the warden managed to wake Robert. "They're bringin' her out," he said, a smug satisfaction in his expression, "and she's not badly hurt."

Without a word, Robert stumbled to his feet. Across the road he saw her being carefully carried down the slope of the debris. She was wrapped in a white sheet and strapped to a stretcher.

He pushed his way through the crowd of excited onlookers and ran across the road. Emmie was alive — and absolutely nothing else in the world mattered.

iii

On its way to Walton Hospital, the ambulance carrying Emmie, Dick and Robert, passed the bus in which a very subdued Gwen was travelling back home from her visit to David in the selfsame hospital.

Regardless of the thirty-odd other men in the ward, she had put her head down on the white coverlet of David's bed and cried. Too ill to do more than hold her hand, he had been staggered when she had laid her cheek on his work-scarred palm and told him he must get better, because she could not face life without him. She had paused to give a weepy sigh, and added, "Half the time I dunno what to do for the best."

"I'll be all right," he had whispered with an effort, and closed his eyes. It was nice to be wanted and not to be regarded as merely a walking pay-packet.

When she got home, Nora and Brendy were rolling round on the kitchen floor like a pair of angry young wolves. Patrick was kicking them none too gently in an effort to separate them, while Mari watched him from the living room, where she was seated at the table, trying to do her arithmetic homework. Ruby sat near her with Michael in her arms, feeding him from his new bottle. She was shouting, "Leave them be, Pat. They'll stop of themselves in a minute."

Gwen took one look at the fighting youngsters and total exasperation seized her. She strode through the crowded living room and squeezed quickly behind Mari's chair and into the kitchen. "Stop kicking 'em," she ordered Patrick, and he slunk back, muttering, "I were only tryin' to stop 'em."

Nora rolled triumphantly on top of a beleaguered Brendy, and Gwen bent down and administered the heaviest slap she could on the girl's small cotton-covered bottom. As quick as a cat, the child loosed Brendy and jumped to her feet. A stream of invective poured from her, as she rubbed her stinging bottom.

"Any more of that and you get no jam for tea," threatened Gwen, as she picked up the kettle to fill it from the kitchen tap. Nora made a face at her, and

Ruby hastily called the little girl to her. "You coom 'ere afore you get into more trouble, our Nora."

Brendy lay on his back and laughed, as he watched her go.

Patrick had a tin bowl of grain in his hand, some of which had spilled on to the kitchen floor in the mêlée. He squatted down and began to scoop the precious seeds together. "I were goin' to feed the micks," he told Gwen defensively.

"Aye, feed the pigeons – and you'd better do your dad's cocks, too."

After he had fed the cockerels, Patrick stood, empty bowl in hand, and looked round the familiar muddle of the Donnelly backyard. He burst into tears. Where *was* his mother? Where had she gone after death? Her body had been in the coffin the day before, but that wasn't her – not really her. Would he never again come through the back yard, to see her leaning against the doorpost, waiting for them all to come home from school? He did not know how to bear the pain within him.

An hour later, Gwen surveyed her troublesome brood across the littered tea table and prayed that their grandmother would turn up soon.

Patrick looked as if he had been crying. Deep compassion for him and for Ruby welled up in her; they must both be feeling terrible despair. Yet they were being very brave. Impulsively she leaned forward and pressed Patrick's grubby fist lying on the tablecloth. He looked up at her, startled, and saw the pity mirrored in her faded blue eyes. Quickly, he withdrew his hand and picked up his piece of bread and margarine. "Everything's going to turn out all right," she assured him, feeling a little shy herself.

He nodded.

She turned to Ruby. The girl looked crushed. She was staring vacantly at her empty plate. "Would you like another butties, luv? I can soon cut you one."

"No. I'm all right."

"Coom 'ere."

The girl rose and went to stand by Gwen's chair, like a schoolgirl called before the headmistress. Gwen put an arm round the thin body and gave her a hug and a smile. "Come on, now. Cheer up. Your gran's goin' to come soon – and I'm goin' to be next door all the time, and you can ask me." The girl smiled faintly, and unexpectedly put her arms round Gwen's neck, as she had so often done with her mother. She did not cry.

Mari watched in jealous shock. Her mother never hugged her. All she ever got was a peck on the cheek and an admonition to be a good girl. She had endured the invasion from next door, because of the strange magic of Patrick's presence. Now she wished crossly that they would all go back to their own house and that her father was home to give her a smacking kiss and call her his pretty young lady.

At midnight, she was sitting on the cellar steps, reading *Gone With the Wind* aloud to Patrick and Ruby, while one of the worst raids Liverpool had ever experienced raged outside.

On a mattress dragged down to the bottom of the steps lay Nora, Brendy and Michael, mercifully sleeping the sleep of the totally exhausted.

Gwen nodded over a cold cup of tea, while her mind went round and round in weary confusion. What if Emmie is injured – not killed? Do I have to nurse her as well as Dave? It would, she felt be a fit judgment on her, for not helping Emmie with her parents; the pain-filled face of her acid-tongued mother-in-law haunted her for the duration of the raid.

THURSDAY, 8 MAY 1941

Constable Doyle consulted his notebook and then knocked on Gwen's front door. At least for this family he had good news – as far as it went.

He made himself smile as the door opened, to reveal Gwen in her dressing-gown, followed by five children in differing states of readiness for school.

"Me husband?" Gwen faltered, at the sight of the uniform.

"No, missus. Miss Emma Thomas live here?"

Relieved, Gwen replied that she did normally, but she was missing.

"Well, missus, you'll be pleased to know she's resting comfortable in Walton Hospital. Be out in a few days."

"Thank you kindly for stopping by to tell me," she began to close the door.

The constable cleared his throat. "I should tell you, missus, that we've heard as the hospital was bombed last night. We don't know the extent of the damage yet. I'll know in an hour or ..."

Through white lips, Gwen murmured, "Dave!" and fainted on her neglected doorstep.

Though the constable was resigned to carrying news that had this kind of result, Gwen's collapse was unexpected. He helped to carry her in and lay her on the living room sofa. She came round within a minute or two and, through chattering teeth, asked if he or Mr Donnelly would let her know when they had more news of the hospital. "Me husband's in there, as well as Emma. I'll go over meself as soon as I've got the children away to school."

"The north end's a shambles," Constable Doyle warned. "I doubt you'd get through. I'll come as soon as I've any news." He turned to Ruby and Mari – never had he seen two sisters so totally unalike – and told them to make a strong cup of tea for their mam. "Lots of sugar in it – and see she rests a while."

ii

On the previous Wednesday, the day before the raids began, Mrs Owen, Robert's mother, had said a thankful farewell to the evacuated mother and children who had occupied her spare room for some months. "I can't stand the quiet out here a day longer," the mother had told her. "I'm goin' home to Great Homer Street."

Now, on this perfect spring morning, she asked Mr Burnett, the chemist in Hoylake village, for something she might sprinkle round the newly scoured bedroom, to kill off any vermin that her unwelcome guests might have left there. "Me daughter-in-law elect is coming out to live with me. She's in Walton Hospital at present, recovering from being buried under the canteen she worked in. Poor girl. She's real nice. I'll be happy to have her."

Mr Burnett looked over his gold spectacles. He swallowed. "Do you know Walton was bombed last night?"

Mrs Owen's hand flew to her throat. "Oh, no! Poor lass, poor lass – and poor Robbie."

She had trouble waking Robert from the sleep of the absolutely worn out. He would have to go into

Liverpool, anyway, she told herself, to be signed off from the *Marakand* and then find himself another berth. She sighed at the thought.

When he heard the news, he was wide awake in a moment and jumped out of bed. He seized his trousers and struggled into them.

"The phone to the hospital's dead. I tried it – or rather, Mr Burnett did."

"I can go over."

"Well, you have some tea first. The kettle's boiling." Dear Lord, what a mess he was in, too. A black eye, hardly any eyebrows or eyelashes – all singed off – likewise his front hair. And both hands bandaged by the hospital, because of the burns on them.

iii

Conor had not been home since before his wife's funeral on Tuesday. Now, on Thursday morning, after what Glynis Hughes described as a lively night but not in the usual sense, he hesitantly opened his front door. He had snatched an occasional nap at the post, but now he knew he must really sleep; otherwise, he would collapse.

On the floor of the passage inside, lay his letter to his mother, returned through the dead-letter office. A wobbly hand had scrawled in pencil on it, "Address Unknown. Return to sender". Then in brackets the writer had added, "Whole street bombed. Tried to trace in Rest Centre without success."

He stood in the narrow hall, paralysed. He could not believe it. He had been so harassed himself that he had not thought about his parents' danger.

If they were hurt or killed, why hadn't his married sister, who lived in the same street, let him know?

A slow coldness crept through him. From bitter experience, he could visualise the scene so well. A dozen houses down, a whole series of families related to each other carried out dead or dying; no one surviving long enough to give names to the authorities. Those same authorities, hopelessly overloaded by the sheer magnitude of the raids, would in time name most of the victims – but not yet.

He leaned his head against his paintless front door, and cried aloud, "Holy Mother have pity on me!" He beat his fist against the unresponding wood. "I'm damned! Accursed!"

Nearly demented, he fled back to his post – and the telephone.

With some difficulty, he got through, on the newly restored line, to the wardens' post nearest to his parents' house. Then he came slowly back to his own street. Instinctively, he sought the only people left to him, his children; he turned the rapidly tarnishing brass knob of Gwen's front door and walked in.

Michael was asleep on the sofa, an empty feeding-bottle lolling by his cheek. From the kitchen came the splash of dishes being washed.

"Are you there, Mrs Thomas?"

The splashing stopped immediately and Ruby came running in, wiping her hands on a dish towel. "Dad," she cried eagerly.

He held out his arms to her. She ran into them and with his head bowed over her he began to sob helplessly. She drew back. "Dad, what's up?" she

246

whispered, frightened by such a lament.

While she sat on his knee in the muddled room, he told her. He wept unrestrainedly, unable to hold in his despair and grief any more.

Half girl, half woman, she listened quietly, arm around his neck. Then she started to comfort. "Don't cry, Dadda. We'll manage," she said hoarsely. "Mrs Thomas'll help me – while I get started, like." She clung to him while he tried to control himself.

"I'm sorry, luv," he said, and wept on.

She was frightened to see her hot-tempered father cry, but it also put him on a level with Patrick, and she said, "Aye, everybody cries sometimes, Dadda," and gritted her teeth and hugged him closer.

When her father's weeping ceased, she said quite eagerly, "Let's go and buy a bit o' food, Dad, so as we can move back home."

That afternoon, Gwen and Mari sat and looked at each other over their teatime toast and dripping. The house was extraordinarily quiet and seemed to exude the misery of its damage and neglect. Gwen thought her heart had never been so heavy. By dint of taking three trams in a circular route and walking quite a distance, she had managed to reach Walton Hospital. The fright engendered by the bombs on the hospital had given David another heart attack. He had, however, survived, though he would need much nursing and would probably never be able to return to work. She had also briefly visited Emmie, who was heavily sedated and an alarming bundle of bandages and sticking plaster. There she had met Robert, sitting by her bed. He had told her that when Emmie was discharged from hospital, his mother would take care of her at his home in Hoylake, until they were married. It was the only good news of the day. Confound her – and her furniture – she could have the lot of it.

Mari broke into her gloomy contemplation by saying brightly, between sips of cocoa, "Tomorrow's your day for Blackler's."

Gwen nodded. "It's burned down. I'm out o' work – like plenty of others."

"They might start up again," Mari replied. "You could go and see. There's probably a notice set up in the ruins, to tell the staff what to do."

"Aye. I'd be glad of a full-time job, now your dad's so poorly." Her face brightened. "I'll go this evening. People's got to buy clothes and bedding from *somewhere*."

"I'll walk down with you, if you like."

"Would you, dear? I'd enjoy your company."

iv

One of the loneliest people in Liverpool lay unvisited, except by Robert Owen, in a huge, overcrowded men's ward at Walton Hospital. Identified by the pay slip in his wallet, still in his back pocket, Deckie Dick opened his eyes on Thursday evening, to the long glinting rays of a setting sun reflected on a shiny, white ceiling. He was in a bed and shivering; yet at the same time feeling dreadfully hot. He had been vaguely aware of being bundled about, of being sponged and feeling chilled.

A face loomed over him. It was topped by a little white cap above a wrinkled brow. A pair of sharp blue eyes, red-rimmed, peered at him. His wrist was clasped by cold, bony fingers.

A misty mouth said, "He'll be all right now."

Another blanket was tucked over him. He fell asleep, only to be awakened by more fumbling hands. The air raid warning was wailing its devil's notes, and two giggling young women were lifting him out of bed. They stuffed him underneath it. "Safest place," they assured him, and wrapped his blankets round him.

"Where am I?" he asked.

"Walton Hospital," they told him, and he breathed, "Thanks be," and slept contentedly on the floor through the rest of the night.

The entire population of Liverpool had been waiting tensely for the warning to go. Some of those who still had a bed had climbed into it, feeling that they *must* sleep, no matter what happened to them. Now they raised their heads to listen. But the raid was small, short and scattered; many of the townsfolk slept through it. London became the main target, though German squadrons were beginning to regroup in preparation for an attack on Russia. In the days following, mass funerals were held, and people who thought they could not cry another tear, wept some more.

One morning, a curiously shrunken and shaky Deckie Dick, dressed in clothing supplied by a charitable organisation, tottered out of Walton Hospital and went back to the room he rented in Pitt Street. The landlady had relet it. "Ah thought you must be dead," she told him. She had, however, stored his few belongings, in case he had a relative to claim them.

Weak and bewildered, he went into a tiny café, sat down at a greasy table and ordered a cup of coffee.

From his wallet he took out a small piece of paper with an address written on it and he smoothed it between thumb and finger. The granny of the young conscript he had met in the shelter also lived in Pitt Street. Robert Owen had told him that everyone in the shelter had been killed. She must be feeling bad, he ruminated, as he slowly stirred his tasteless coffee. It wouldn't hurt him to go up and see her; the old biddy might even know of a room to let.

Ten minutes later, he was climbing the bare, littered stairs of a lodging house similar to the one he had lived in, though this one seemed to smell even worse.

He did not have to knock at the door of the first-floor front room. The occupant had heard his footsteps and had opened it a crack.

"Mrs Pickles?" he inquired of the one grey eye peeping at him.

The crack widened. In the dim light he could make out only a female form draped in a black shawl. "What d'yer want?" The voice was full of suspicion.

"Ah come about your nephew, Wilf."

A sharp intake of breath. "Well, what about 'im?"

"Mrs Pickles, can I come in and sit down? I bin ill or I'd have come before. I met your lad in an air raid shelter and promised to look you up."

A pause. "Come in."

Inside the bare, clean room, he turned to the woman. She was very small, with a pinched, thin face out of which large steel-grey eyes regarded him with sudden compassion. Her skin looked pale from poor nourishment and lack of sunshine, and was a mass of fine lines. She had no teeth. About 55 years old, he reckoned.

She said, "Aye, you are ill, I can see that. Sit down on the sofa bed. I was just goin' to make a pot o' tea and a bite of toast." She picked up a kettle from off the small fire and poured boiling water into a teapot, much blackened from being kept hot too near the fire.

Dickie sank thankfully on to the edge of the sofa; the springs complained bitterly.

"What about Wilf?" she asked. "You know he were killed? He were all I got – a real nice lad."

As gently as he knew how, he told her about the scene in the air raid shelter and of his promise.

White cup and saucer in one hand, she looked down at him, her mouth quivering. He thought she was going to cry, but she did not. She simply sighed and sat down abruptly. She took the lid off the aluminium teapot and stirred the tea vigorously.

As she handed a cup to him, she asked, "What was you ill with?"

He told her about being buried with Emmie and his subsequent pneumonia, and as he talked some of the stress went out of him.

She listened patiently, and at the end she said, "I don't think any of us will ever be the same again after all this. It's as if all our lives was overturned in the course of a week, isn't it?"

"Aye." He smiled wryly, and stirred his tea. He wondered if he still had a job. Then he burst out suddenly, "Being buried like that – it taught me life was worth having. Funny, isn't it?"

She smiled and her eyes crinkled up with a promise of laughter, when she felt better. "Have another piece of toast," she invited.

Through two pots of tea and a pile of toast, they sat

251

knee to knee, two lonely people tossed together by a war they did not understand.

He stayed with her for the rest of his life.

SUNDAY, 29 JUNE 1941

"It feels proper queer – to be married at last," remarked Emmie. "I thought we'd never make it."

"You mean when you was buried?"

They were wandering along Hoylake Promenade, idly pausing from time to time to watch children digging in the sand, while their elders snoozed beneath copies of the Sunday newspapers, and dogs ran yapping after balls tossed by strolling owners. It was hard to believe that, not too far from them, out to sea, men stalked each other mercilessly and that, in Europe, the art of murder was reaching new heights, while in England itself cities burned.

"Not so much being buried," Emmie replied uneasily, "Though that were bad enough. But you havin' to go back to sea afore I were out of hospital – and bein' so long in the hospital, with me nerves, and lookin' like a piece of red raddle when they took the bandages off me face; I were fit to die when I saw meself in the mirror. I thought you wouldn't want me no more."

"Tush, luv. I'd always want you. There's more to a woman than a face. Anyways, there's nothin' that time and a spot o' warpaint won't cover." He bent and kissed the top of her newly permed hair. No need to tell her that he had been nearly shocked out of his kecks when he had first seen her. But the doctors had been right. She was healing and they'd done some neat stitching on her, which they swore would fade, and the bruises on her poor body were going, too. The doctors had said it was a pure miracle that she had no broken bones and she wasn't blinded.

He tightened his arm around her waist and he saw her

wince and immediately loosened it again. Bugger the Nazis. Just wait till he got a chance at one, he promised himself bitterly. He'd never felt such boiling hatred in his life before. It bubbled in him, awaiting only the opportunity to explode.

She turned her face towards him. "I love you so," she said unexpectedly, and he was diverted immediately by a fresh surge of longing.

"Look, duck. Let's nip 'ome. Me mam and dad allus goes over to see me brother on Sunday afternoon. Let's go 'ome and have a little matinee. What say?"

She bit her lip and then grinned quite cheerfully. Why say that so much of you still ached that you could hardly bear to be touched. He'd be gone on the eight o'clock train, back to his boat and the god-damned Atlantic. She'd have weeks of nothing before he returned – always supposing he got back safe. Time enough to get herself well again – and try for a job in munitions, so she could send a bit back to the Jerries with her best compliments.

The Latchkey Kid

CHAPTER ONE

The ladies of Tollemarche, Alberta, were always wonderfully clever at disposing of their menfolk; so that these gentlemen, if not already in their graves, were encouraged by their wives to depart northwards in search of business, or, to escape from constant nagging, to conferences in Ontario or hunting trips in British Columbia. And it was surprising how frequently they found it necessary to motor down to Edmonton or Calgary.

The ladies' sighs of relief, as the sound of their partners' cars disappeared with distance, indicated that the gentlemen would certainly not be missed, as long as the flood of money engendered by the discovery of oil in Alberta continued to flow so gratifyingly into their joint bank accounts during the boom years of the 1950s.

Unhampered by demanding males, the ladies were free to control the city's social life, which burgeoned forth as a result of the suddenly acquired wealth of the inhabitants. The big oil strike near Tollemarche had been responsible for an upheaval in the existing order; and the fight for social status, before a fixed pecking order could be re-established, was a ruthless one, waged in every drawing-room, church hall and charitable institution.

In this war amongst the teacups, the worst sufferers were the children.

The ladies were not quite so successful in disposing of their offspring as they were of their husbands, though they did their best. It was difficult to do without children, because they were a necessary status symbol and a subject for conversation. The ladies, therefore, had four or five babies as quickly after marriage as nature would permit, and thus provided themselves with an indefinite number of conversational gambits.

The trouble was that after they were born, children had

5

to wait for six years before they could be sent to school and forgotten for most of the day. The ladies had several methods of dealing with this problem, or 'making them independent and self-reliant' as they called it. The easiest and most commonly used method was to ignore them as far as possible.

It is startling how quickly children discover that they are not wanted. Once a child could walk and had, through dire necessity, learned how to shed a wet pair of training pants and put on his snow suit, he would vanish into the street, not to be seen again until lunch time; once he was tall enough to reach the refrigerator door handle, the problem of lunch was also solved – he could get it himself.

Another method was called 'having activities'. This consisted of enrolling one's child in a private playschool, which sent a car to pick him up in the morning and deposit him back on his own doorstep in the late afternoon. After this, he could be hastily driven to a music lesson, followed by a painting or a dancing lesson. This type of day was guaranteed to exhaust even the most energetic youngster, and he would thankfully walk home, to watch television, eat his supper and put himself to bed.

Some people had baby-sitters of varying degrees of unreliability, mostly young girls in their teens, who were themselves expecting illegitimate babies and needed a temporary home, or elderly women lacking much strength to deal with children. All of them seemed to have in common a cold dislike of children and a determination to do as little as possible for their inadequate wages.

In these circumstances, a determined mother could be free to groom herself, hold office in this or that community activity, or find a job, in order to fulfil herself; though none of them seemed to be able to explain why acting as a bank teller or the secretary of a charity, for example, was more fulfilling than looking after their own children.

The perfectly kept living-rooms of Tollemarche homes were for visitors; the basements, despite their fire hazards, were good enough for the children; there they often slept and there, if the temperature went much below zero, they also played.

Conscientious parents, and there were some, viewed the situation with dismay. Public pressure was against them, and they often fought a bitter battle to maintain the kind of home life in which they believed.

It was into this world that Captain Peter Dawson, a Canadian army officer, brought his young Welsh wife, Isobel. She was the daughter of an old friend of his, who had married a Welsh lady and settled in Caernarvon. Both Isobel's parents had been killed in a motor accident, and Peter Dawson had obtained leave from his unit in France to attend their funeral in Wales. There he had met a distraught Isobel and her broken-hearted schoolgirl sister, Dorothy. He had helped Isobel sort out her father's tangled financial affairs and had fallen in love with her quiet, fragile beauty. He had pressed her to marrry him, though he was considerably older than she was, and she had accepted him at a time of great emotional exhaustion. Leaving Dorothy in the care of a great-aunt to finish her education, Peter had, at the first opportunity, brought Isobel back to his native city of Tollemarche. Isobel soon realized that she had not made, from her point of view, the wisest of marriages, but Peter was very kind to her and she did her best to make him happy.

She had been married only four years when her husband was murdered while serving as a member of the Canadian peacekeeping mission in Cyprus. He had had only one more year to serve before he could have retired into civilian life, and both he and Isobel had been looking forward to this. Her grief at his death was deep and sincere.

She had, as yet, no child to console her, and she had cabled her sister Dorothy to come from Wales to spend the winter with her. Captain Dawson's parents, themselves stricken, had no idea how to deal with their weeping daughter-in-law, and were thankful to leave her to Dorothy.

Sociable Dorothy, although only seventeen years old,

7

managed to infuse some sort of order into Isobel's shattered life, hoping that soon Isobel would decide what she would do in the future, so that she herself could go back home to Wales, which, from the vantage point of Tollemarche, seemed infinitely cosy and desirable.

One cool September Saturday, as the first snowflakes drifted quietly across the picture window, a white-faced, rather exhausted Isobel sat sewing in her living-room. On the following Monday she proposed to go back to the job she had taken to make it financially possible for Peter and her to buy their little home. She had told Dorothy that she felt that the steady routine of her secretarial work would, for the moment, be most helpful to her. She found it impossible to admit, even to herself, the relief which flooded her whole being at the idea that she was no longer bound to live out her life in Tollemarche.

She put her needle and thread neatly away in her sewing box, brushed stray cotton threads from her skirt and went to the window to draw the curtains, before preparing supper.

Across the road, two little girls who frequently came in to visit Isobel, eat toffees and gossip, were teetering uncertainly on the edge of the sidewalk. They had apparently exhausted all the games that a four-year-old could invent, and they were shivering in the wind as they considered exploring the world on the other side of the road.

'Sheila and Penny's parents must still be out,' Isobel remarked. 'I can't see Mrs Brent's car yet – I suppose she is still at the Lady Queen Bees' tea, and Mr Brent must be still at his curling club.'

Dorothy stopped laying the table for supper and stared at her sister, her blue eyes wide with disbelief. 'You mean those kids have been by themselves all the afternoon – just for the sake of a tea – or curling?'

'Certainly. Probably they couldn't get a baby sitter. Anyway, Sheila always has a latchkey tied round her neck, so they can get into the house.'

8

'There ought to be a law against it,' replied Dorothy emphatically, as she banged knives and forks down on to the table.

'There is – but it doesn't seem to be enforced.' Isobel sighed, remembering many an argument on child care which she had lost, being invariably defeated by the rejoinder that she had no children and, therefore, knew nothing about them. Her tone changed, and she said decisively: 'I'm going to come home with you, as soon as Pete's affairs are cleared up. Tollemarche was livable with Pete, but without him it will be intolerable. These empty women make me sick and their neglected kids break my heart.'

Dorothy tossed her head to clear her long black hair from her eyes, and grinned elfishly at Isobel. 'We could live together and paint London pale pink,' she said hopefully. 'Or Wales!'

Isobel smiled at the tall, rangy girl. 'Pink it shall be,' she said.

Dorothy went on with her work for a minute and then asked: 'Isobel, what happens to these kids, supposing they don't drop themselves over the railway bridge in sheer despair?'

'Well, some of them are chronically in and out of courts – they become pretty unscrupulous. Some, as you know, seek revenge – they riot, they take drugs and generally make damned nuisances of themselves. Some nothing can spoil, and they grow up into the nicest young people you can imagine.'

'Like Hank Stych, who rents your garage?' asked Dorothy, a hint of mischief in her eyes. She had already met this young man, when he had last come to pay his rent, and found him startlingly different from the Welsh boys of her acquaintance – a big, silent boy with disillusioned, almond-shaped eyes sunk above high cheek bones, a boy who had stared unblinkingly at her until she had begun to blush with embarrassment, so that she had felt stripped, not only physically but mentally as well. Finally, he had

9

held out a bunch of one-dollar bills to her, said 'Rent,' and without another word had vaulted over the veranda balustrade and loped down the path to the garage. Very odd, she had decided, and yet nice. 'Does he wear a latchkey round his neck?' she inquired.

'Hank?' Isobel looked thoughtful. 'Yes, Hank's all right – brought himself up like Sheila and Penny are doing.' She laughed. 'He's probably been promoted to a key ring by this time.'

'I like him,' said Dorothy, determined to show she could like the unusual.

Isobel's eyes were still merry. 'Better watch your step with him. Nobody ever told him where to draw the line, and he's not as innocent as he looks – he's got quite a reputation for wildness.'

Dorothy opened the oven to see how the dinner was coming along, and her voice was muffled as she tried to avoid the steam from the casserole she was peeking at. 'You were saying that he has written a wonderful book – and that it's going to be published?'

'Yes,' Isobel sounded anxious, 'and I am really worried about it. You know, Pete and I encouraged him like anything in his writing. What we didn't know for a long time was that this book is his revenge on his parents.

'Doll, you know that this province is known as the Bible Belt?'

Dorothy nodded as she closed the oven door.

'Well, by Bible Belt standards it's the filthiest book imaginable. What this town is going to say when it reaches here isn't hard to imagine. Olga and Boyd Stych are going to be blamed, because everyone will think they were agreeable to its publication. It will ruin Olga socially.'

Mrs Stych and her arch-rival Mrs Frizzell had both called to express their condolences to Tollemarche's most interesting widow. Dorothy had dealt with both of them, aided by Isobel's giddy young sister-in-law, who had explained the social nuances of it all by saying: 'That pair of grasping alley cats would tear the eyes out of anyone who managed to make the social pages of the *Tollemarche Advent* on a day when they should have been featured. They just want to be seen calling at the house.'

'I don't think Hank realizes how devastating it may be to his mother when his book comes out,' Isobel went on.

'Do her good,' said Dorothy laconically.

'Well, I feel guilty,' Isobel responded.

'Maybe people will be more careful of their children after they've read it,' suggested Dorothy hopefully, and then added: 'She's nothing but a social climber, anyway.'

'She's a coming lady in Tollemarche.'

'That ghastly, fat Humpty Dumpty of a woman?' exclaimed Dorothy scornfully.

Isobel nodded, her lips compressed, and then said: 'Yes, that ghastly, fat Humpty Dumpty is heading for a great fall, poor thing. And it is partly my fault.'

11

CHAPTER TWO

Mrs Theresa Murphy, the Mayor's wife, had, by dint of playing first violin in the local amateur orchestra, established herself as one of the cultural leaders of Tollemarche. On four Thursday evenings during the winter she could be seen, dressed in spotty black and glittering with rhinestones, sawing happily away on her violin through four public concerts, under the baton of Mr Dixon, the elderly English master from Tollemarche public school, who tried gamely to keep the rest of the orchestra in time with her, since he had long ago given up trying to keep her in time with the orchestra.

As the wife of the civic leader, Mrs Murphy had to do considerable entertaining in generous western style, but in this field she made no attempt to keep pace with Olga Stych or Donna Frizzell; she knew when she was beaten.

Since culture did not hammer quite so hard on Mrs Frizzell's door, she had more time to plan parties. Her annual garden party, for buyers of fleets of cars and trucks who dealt with her husband, was always a memorable occasion, reported upon in detail by the queen of the social columns of the *Tollemarche Advent*, a lady who could make or break a local hostess. Mrs Frizzell found it impossible to forgive Mrs Dawson's becoming a widow the same week as her party; a history of Mrs Dawson one night, and the remarks the following night of the lady secretary of the United Nations' Society on the role of the Canadian peacekeeping force in Cyprus, had meant that for the first time in years no report of Mrs Frizzell's party appeared, though room had been found for a report on one of Mrs Murphy's receptions.

Mr Frizzell's business did not seem to suffer from the omission. He did an ever expanding trade in cars and trucks under his big red neon sign, which proclaimed on one side

FRIZZELL'S GARAGE – YOU CAN TRUST MAXIE, and on the other FRIZZELL'S GARAGE – I GREW WITH ALBERTA. His critics agreed that he had sure grown with Alberta – just fatter and fatter!

Mrs Frizzell was the ruthless driving force behind his business. She nagged him northwards to the Peace River district, to establish garages there, and even as far as Fort McMurray, with instructions to buy land for future service stations. Then she went on with the lovely task of making herself the most important lady in Tollemarche.

Mrs Olga Stych, the wife of a consulting geologist, her next-door neighbour, dared to challenge her on this; and their homes, which had, until the commencement of building in Vanier Heights, been two of the nicer houses in the best district of Tollemarche, echoed their ambitions. They were filled with wall-to-wall broadloom and the finest imitation French Provincial furniture. Their L-shaped living rooms were graced by open fireplaces, with the latest shapes in petrified wood adorning the mantelpieces. Each owned a weird splotch of colour in a white and silver frame, painted and framed by a local artist. One had only to buy a Wedgewood coffee service or a piece of Bohemian crystal and the other would have the same the following week.

Through the six months of Alberta's bitter winter each lady tried to outdo the other in the number of coffee parties given and the number of charitable offices each managed to obtain. Through the summer, as the skyscrapers grew on Tollemarche Avenue, they boasted of the glories of their country cottages and the important people from Edmonton or Calgary who had spent a weekend with them at these summer homes. Theresa Murphy persuaded her husband to buy an entire lake and news of this purchase spoiled both Mrs Frizzell's and Mrs Stych's summer.

Each week the ladies spent anxious hours in Andrew's Beauty Salon having their hair tinted and set, still more anxious hours in Dawn's Dresse Shoppe or the Hudson's Bay Company store, adding more dresses and hats to their already over-extended charge accounts. Olga Stych's

13

generous figure would be a nightmare to any dress shop, and her dresses were consequently always more expensive than Donna Frizzell's were. In despair, one day, of finding a well-fitting winter coat, she hastily counted up the amount of land around Tollemarche which her husband had bought up and decided he was worth at least a Persian lamb coat. This error proved to be nearly the last straw needed to break his credit, since he had raised every cent he could in order to invest in land for building. He protested to her hotly about this extravagance, but was quickly sent back to his rocks, cowering from her wrath.

. The third fall after the oil strike in Alberta came slowly in, while Isobel mourned her husband, quite unaware that she had mortally offended Mrs Frizzell by crowding her August garden party off the social page of the *Tollemarche Advent*. The glory of the Indian summer crept across the land with pale sunshine, golden leaves, deep-blue skies and treacherously cold winds. The publication day of Hank Stych's book went unremarked in Tollemarche, mainly because the only bookseller in the town had not had time to unpack his new stock, and book reviews were featured only once a month in the *Tollemarche Advent* and then only in an obscure corner of an inner page. The leaves fell thickly in the more established portions of the city, to the envy of residents in the bare new suburbs who were still awaiting paved roads and street lights, never mind trees.

Mrs Donna Frizzell looked despondently out of her picture window. The unfenced oblong of grass in front of the house and the narrow path to the sidewalk were full of leaves twirling in the wind. Mr Stych, during his last visit home, had already cleared the adjoining garden, and the Frizzells' leaves were gaily invading his once tidy lawn. Mrs Frizzell's lips tightened as she guessed what Olga Stych's remarks would be when she saw them.

That intolerable woman, she thought bitterly, had managed to become president of the Tollemarche Downtown Community Centre by a majority of a single vote, and Mrs Frizzell had had to be content with the vice-

14

presidency, which office she declared gave her all the work and none of the authority. (She gave no credit to Olga Stych for her undoubted talents as an organizer.) To make matters worse, Olga was also the secretary of the Noble Order of Lady Queen Bees – a pack of overdressed snobs, groaned Mrs Frizzell, whose members set the standard for every social event in the city. Maybe, if she could squeeze a mink coat out of Maxie, it would help her towards the membership which always seemed to elude her by a vote or two, a vote strongly influenced, she feared, by Olga Stych. One day, she promised herself, if ever she got the chance, she would give Olga Stych her comeuppance.

In the meantime, since no amount of nagging would persuade Maxie to rake up the leaves or to allow her to employ a man to do it, she would have to do the job herself.

Mixed with the need to tidy up the garden was a desire to show her neighbours her new purple, slim pants and striped purple and yellow jacket. She therefore eased her thin shanks into these all too revealing pants, put a pair of gilt oriental sandals on her feet and hastily touched up the mauve polish on her toenails and fingernails. She peered anxiously into her six-foot-wide dressing-table mirror to see if any white hair showed after her last auburn tint, and found to her satisfaction that all her hair was the same improbable shade.

She went through the house door leading into the garage, seized a rake and plunged into the cold wind. She began to rake from the front of the house towards the road, then realized she had nothing in which to put the leaves. With an irritability caused as much by her slimming diet as by the lack of a box, she almost stamped down the stairs into the basement, which was comfortingly warm, and found a couple of cardboard boxes.

Working with feverish haste, for the wind was piercing through her elegant jacket and Gentle Curve bra underneath, she filled the boxes, staggered with them to a row of garbage cans in the back lane and dumped their contents into the bins. Her feet were icy cold in their open sandals when, on the fifth trip back to the front lawn, her patience was rewarded.

Mrs Stych drew up at the kerb in her new European car, bought, needless to say, from Maxie's arch-rival down in Edmonton. She heaved herself out and opened the trunk to display several large paper bags full of groceries. Mrs Frizzell hastily drew in her stomach, tucked in her tail, and posed with her rake, just as she had seen the Hudson's Bay Company model do when showing pants. A pair of University students passing by hastily averted their faces to hide their giggles.

Mrs Stych, however, did not avert her gaze. She peered over the bag of groceries clasped to her bosom and was almost consumed by envy. Five feet high and weighing one hundred and seventy pounds, a veritable Humpty Dumpty of a woman, Mrs Stych had no hope of ever being able to wear pants gracefully.

Mrs Stych ate with all the avidity of one who has known starvation. Her father, an immigrant from the Ukraine, had carved his pig farm out of raw bush. Her pregnant mother had pulled the plough when they broke a part of their holding for wheat and vegetables, and Olga's first memories were of carrying away stones from the furrows. They had known such hunger that even now Olga could not bring herself to throw away a single crumb and always ate whatever was left after a meal.

Looking now at her plump, well-kept hands, two heavy diamond rings worn above her unexpectedly old-fashioned wedding band it was hard to believe that her mother was a work-bent Ukrainian peasant who still wore a black kerchief over her hair and spoke little English.

Mrs Stych fixed her button eyes upon the elegant figure of Mrs Frizzell and bowled purposefully across the lawn. Her high, grating voice was caught by the wind and carried half a block, as she asked: 'Aren't Maxie able to do the leaves?'

'He's up at Grande Prairie, seeing to his new garage and car lot.' She smiled, showing an excellent set of artificial teeth, as she rallied her forces. 'Enterprising, that's Maxie,' she added, her eyes agleam with malice.

While she spoke, she remembered Maxie's grumble from behind his newspaper, the last time he had been home, when she had told him to do the leaves.

'Do 'em yourself,' he had said. 'You ain't got nuttin' to do while I'm away up the Peace, not now Joanne and Betty is married.' His pursed-up, babylike lips had quivered. 'I got no time, you know that.'

In the tirade which immediately followed, Mrs Frizzell had reminded him that she was a pillar of the community, all for the sake of his business. She was secretary of the Tollemarche United Church Willing Workers' Group, vice-president (not president!) of the Tollemarche Downtown Community Centre, a driver for Cripples' Transport, a member of the Car Dealers' Wives Society and, she would remind him, a member of the Committee for the Preservation of Morals. And, she would like him to know the Morals Committee had just succeeded in having D.H. Lawrence's books banned from the cigar stores.

Mr Maxmilian Frizzell had never read a book since leaving school and did not know who Lawrence was, so he put down the newspaper and took up the *Car Dealer and Garageman* with what dignity he could muster. The next morning he departed, thankfully, for the North, to see his new garage and a silent, obliging Métis woman of his acquaintance.

The leaves remained on the lawn.

The high heels of Mrs Stych's new, mink-trimmed bootees were now sinking into the Frizzell lawn and threatening to snap at any moment, so she knew she must be quick. She therefore ignored Maxie's undoubted enterprise, and asked: 'Any news from Betty yet?'

Mrs Frizzell brightened. She fell right into the trap, as she said: 'Yeah, she got a daughter in Vancouver General yesterday. Don't want me to go over yet. Her husband Barry's taking care of the other two kids – he's a real capable boy.'

'It must make yer feel old, being a grandmother for the sixth time,' promptly replied Mrs Stych, her face carefully arranged to indicate that it was a disaster.

Mrs Frizzell was not, however, so easily crushed. Scottish ancestors, one of whom had married a Cree, (who was, of course, never mentioned by any member of the family), had given her a physical and mental toughness which enabled her to fight methodically for anything she wanted badly. Now she wanted to squelch Olga. It had to be done, however, without giving too much offence – Mrs Stych was, after all, a Lady Queen Bee. Old at fifty, indeed!

She smiled sweetly.

'At forty-five, I don't mind. I married young and so did Joanne and Betty.' She lifted her lance. 'I'm just so glad they're settled with good, respectable boys for husbands.'

Mrs Stych winced. Mrs Frizzell had no need to remind her that her neat, conforming sons-in-law were far more popular in their home town of Tollemarche than Mrs Stych's own son, Hank.

Hank, when Mrs Stych thought of him at all, always gave her a headache. Consequently, she had done her best to ignore his existence. But Donna Frizzell never failed to remind her of his dragging progress through school, compared to Betty and Joanne's smart performances. Now, at nearly twenty, he was still struggling to pass his Grade 12 examinations in high school, having been assured by his father, the school, and society at large that the world held no place for a boy without his Grade 12. Mrs Stych could many times have wept with humiliation when Donna hastened to tell her of yet another minor car accident in which his ancient jalopy had been involved, yet another girl with whom he had once been seen who was 'in trouble'. For a boy who only worked part-time in a supermarket he had too much money, and this was another source of innuendo from Mrs Frizzell. Olga herself was far too busy to worry about what Hank was doing, but she wished Donna would mind her own business. And now she had pierced her again in this sore spot.

18

Mrs Stych clutched her groceries more tightly to her bosom and tried to heave her high heels out of the roots of the Frizzell grass. One day she would get even with Donna for this. Hank might be wild, but nobody had pinned anything serious on him yet. The Frizzell sons-in-law might wear halos, but when it came to financial success they were nowhere.

'Yeah,' agreed Mrs Stych, at the same time disinterring her high heels. 'They sure need to be good boys, being so hard up. Betty and Joanne must have a hard time managing.'

Mrs Frizzell had been feeling that victory in this verbal exchange was hers and had been preparing to leave the garden. Now, bent over a box, she nearly choked at this reference to her daughters' poverty. She jerked herself upright, just in time to intercept a charming smile from Mrs Stych, as she looked back over her shoulder on her way to her own front door.

Mrs Frizzell, in a red glare of rage, for a moment imagined Mrs Stych as a neatly wrapped bundle of well minced beef.

CHAPTER THREE

Mrs Stych had just set down the last of her bags of groceries on the kitchen counter and begun to unpack them, when there was the sound of a heavy truck drawing up outside her house.

'Mother!' almost wailed Mrs Stych. 'And the girls coming for bridge!'

She trotted into the living-room, where three bridge tables had already been set out, and peeped through the picture window.

Her mother was already clambering laboriously down from the seat beside the driver, displaying a lumpy mass of grey woollen stocking and woollen knickers in the process. Her brother was already changing gear, and as soon as the old lady was safely on the sidewalk the vehicle ground noisily forward, with its protesting load of smelly pigs, towards the market.

Mrs Stych felt a little relieved. At least that humiliating old truck would not be parked outside her door when the girls arrived. She could just imagine the scathing looks with which Mrs Josephine MacDonald, the president of the Noble Order of Lady Queen Bees, would have regarded it. Perhaps, she hoped guiltily, Joe would return to pick up her mother and take her home before any of the guests arrived.

The old lady's footsteps could be heard, ponderous and threatening, on the front steps. Mrs Stych vanished immediately into the kitchen and continued to put away groceries, as if unaware of her mother's arrival.

The porch door clicked as her mother slowly entered. There was the sound of feet being carefully wiped on the doormat, as once sharply requested by Mrs Stych soon after her marriage had taken her into polite circles. Two heavy farm boots were then heaved off. The door into the living-room was opened.

20

'Olga, where are you?' called her mother in Ruthenian, her brown, wrinkled face beaming. 'I have come for three hours while Joe is selling the pigs.'

Mrs Stych, untying her apron, bustled out of the kitchen and tried not to show her despair.

'Why, Mother!' she exclaimed, embracing the stout shoulders and implanting a kiss on her mother's cheek. Is it really necessary for Mother to smell eternally of hens? she wondered, and ushered her into the kitchen so that the unmistakable odour should not permeate her carefully prepared living-room.

Mrs Palichuk sank onto a scarlet kitchen chair and eased off her drab grey winter coat so that it draped over the back, retaining, however, the black kerchief which modestly veiled her hair. She was dressed in a clumsy black skirt and a heavy grey cardigan, and, in honour of the occasion, had put on her best apron, which was white and had been exquisitely embroidered by herself. It always astonished Olga Stych that her mother's horribly distorted hands, with their thick, horny nails, could produce such delicate embroidery and could paint with such skill the traditional patterns on eggshells at Eastertide.

Mrs Palichuk planted her stockinged feet squarely on the white and beige tiles of the kitchen floor, and looked around her. She enjoyed exploring the intricacies of her daughter's kitchen. The electric toaster which turned itself off when the toast was done and the electric beater enthralled her. She was happy enough, however, to return to her own frame house, built by her husband after their first five bitter years spent living in a sod hut. It was heated by a Quebec stove in the kitchen and she cooked with wood on another iron stove, and no cajoling by her widowed son, Joe, was going to make her alter her ways now.

'Expecting visitors?' Mrs Palichuk asked, speaking again in Ruthenian.

As usual, Olga answered her in English. 'Yeah,' she said, setting the coffee pot on the stove. She took out the electric beater and arranged it to beat cream, while Mrs Palichuk watched, fascinated.

'Eleven for lunch and bridge.'

In her heart Olga Stych hoped her mother would take the hint and depart. Then she realized that the older woman could not go without Joe to transport her, and she wondered what in earth she was to do.

Dimly, Mrs Palichuk perceived that she was in the way, and it hurt her.

'I won't disturb you,' she said. 'I've brought my embroidery – I'll sit quiet while you play.'

Mrs Stych rallied herself. 'It's all right, Mother. You're very welcome. It's just you don't play bridge.'

'Oh,' said her mother with a sniff, 'I'll be entertained enough, watching your fine friends.'

Mrs Stych cringed at this remark. It was bad enough to have to produce a mother who smelled of hens, worse to have all one's guests disconcerted by the beady eyes of an old countrywoman. She said nothing, however, but continued her rapid preparations for her guests.

The back screen door slammed and a second later her son Hank padded silently into the kitchen. He was a tall youth with very broad shoulders and deep chest, a trifle plump like most North American boys, but giving an impression of great physical strength. His skin had a yellowy tinge and he had the same deepset black eyes as his mother and grandmother.

He unzipped his black jacket and flung it on a chair.

'Hi, Ma,' he said mechanically and then realized that his grandmother was also present. His face lit up. 'Hi, Gran,' he said with more enthusiasm, went across to her and embraced her with a bearlike hug.

Laughing and fighting him ineffectually, his grandmother roared pleasantries at him in a mixture of Ruthenian and broken English. At last he let her go, and, puffing happily, she straightened her kerchief and skirt. 'How's school?' she asked in Ruthenian.

Hank spoke no Ruthenian but he could understand the

simple sentences his grandmother used – more easily, in fact, than her garbled attempts at English.

He made a wry face and shook his head, his eyes holding, at that moment, the same merry twinkle as his grand-mother's, a gaiety missing from his mother's expression.

'He don't work,' said his mother disapprovingly. 'Always out somewhere. Did you do your homework last night, Hank?' she asked in a voice devoid of real inquiry.

He was very hungry and answered her query absently. 'Yeah, I did.' Then he asked: 'What's cooking, Ma?'

'Got the girls coming for lunch and bridge. Make yourself a sandwich.'

Obediently Hank got a plate, took two slices of bread from the breadbox, and, after rummaging about in the refrigerator, found some luncheon meat, a glass of milk and a cardboard cup of ice cream. His grandmother watched, her toothless mouth agape.

In all the desperate, toiling years she had been in Canada, neither her husband nor her son had ever made themselves a meal, except on one or two occasions when illness had confined her to bed. Yet here was her grandson fending for himself, leaning amiably against a kitchen cupboard and eating a self-made sandwich, while his mother gave infinite attention to food for women who should have been at home attending to their own children. It was with difficulty that she refrained from making a sharp remark.

After a moment, she managed to say through tight lips: 'Come out and visit us on Sunday.'

Hank looked uneasily at her. 'I can't,' he said. 'Got a date.' Then, feeling that the reply was too abrupt, he added: 'I'll sure come out and help with any work Uncle Joe wants doing on the next weekend.'

Mrs Palichuk smiled. 'I know you will. Come then, work or no work.'

He agreed, and lounged away to his room, from whence the sound of his portable typewriter could soon be heard.

'He don't really work,' said his mother crossly. 'That

23

typewriter used to go half the night. Now he don't bring it home from school half the time.'

Mrs Palichuk came to Hank's defence.

'He seems to be keeping up his piano playing,' she said. 'He was trying out the new one that Joe bought for his little Beth to learn on, and even I knew he was playing well.'

Olga grunted, and then admitted grudgingly: 'Yeah, he practises on our old piano in the basement. Does some at school, too, I suppose. But he won't try competing in the Festival – he's too lazy.'

'You don't give him enough time, you and Boyd,' said Mrs Palichuk. 'You never did encourage him. Always out gallivanting, and him home with a sitter or maybe nobody at all, for all I know.' She sniffed and wiped her nose with the back of her hand. 'You didn't even give him one of those fancy cookies just now,' she added in an aggrieved tone.

Mrs Stych glared at the exquisite collection of cookies she was arranging on a tray. 'He's too fat,' she snapped. Her voice became defiant: 'And what time did you and Dad ever spare for us?'

Indignation welled up in Mrs Palichuk. She closed her tired, bloodshot eyes and saw herself again as a young woman, buxom and pregnant, set down in wild bush country, her only asset a husband as young and as strong as herself. She remembered how, side by side, they had hacked and burned the underbrush, borrowed a plough and pulled it themselves, working feverishly to get a little harvest to last them through the first arctic-cold winter. In those hungry, freezing years she had borne and lost two children in the small sod hut in which they lived, before Olga, coming in slightly easier times, had survived. She had fed the precious child herself and carried it with her into the fields, watching it as she wielded a hoe or sickle, tears of weakness and fatigue often coursing down her dusty cheeks. A year later Joe had arrived, and the first doctor in the district had attended her in the first room of what was now a complete frame house. She remembered the doctor telling her, as gently as he could, that it was unlikely that she would have more children, and the shocked look on her husband's face when he heard the news. They would need children to work the land when they became old. Her husband had been kind, however, had kissed her and said the Lord would provide.

And the Lord had provided, reflected Mrs Palichuk. The farm was well equipped with machinery and did not need the hand labour of earlier years. Olga and Joe had been able to go to school, though they had plenty of farm chores as well. Olga, the brighter of the two, had clamoured to be allowed to go to college in Tollemarche, and both parents had encouraged her in this, hoping she would become a school-teacher; but she had met Boyd Stych and got married instead. It was not fair to say that her parents had had no time for her or for Joe; all four of the family had worked together, and, as the settlement grew, they had enjoyed churchgoing and Easters and Christmasses with their neighbours.

Her exasperation, added to her feeling of being unwanted, burst out of her, and she almost shouted at her daughter: 'Your father and I were always with you, teaching you to be decent and to work. Joe always makes time to play with his kids – he's got to be both mother and father to them – in spite of having to run the farm alone since your father died. You're just too big for your shoes!'

Mrs Stych was unloading savoury rolls and a bowl of chicken salad from the refrigerator and she kicked the door savagely, so that it slammed shut with a protesting boom. When she turned on her mother, her face was scarlet and her double chin wobbled as she sought for words.

When the words came, they arrived as a spurt of Ruthenian, the language of her childhood.

'I'm not too big for my shoes!' she cried. 'You just don't know what it's like living in a town – it's different.'

Mrs Palichuk wagged an accusing finger at Olga.

'Excuses! Excuses!' her voice rose. 'You were always good at them. Anything to avoid staying home and looking after Hank. How he ever grew up as decent as he is, I don't know.'

Arms akimbo, Olga swayed towards her mother.

'Let me tell you,' she yelled, 'Boyd and I are somebodies in this town, and mostly because I was smart enough to set to and cultivate the right people.'

'Rubbish!'

'It's not rubbish – it's true.'

Mrs Palichuk heaved her formidable bulk off the frail chair and thrust her face close to Olga's.

'And what good will it do for Hank, if it is true?'

Olga drew herself up proudly.

'His name will be in the Social Register,' she announced.

Mrs Palichuk was reduced to stunned silence for a moment. Then she roared, like a Montreal trucker stuck in a lane: 'You'll be lucky if his name's not on a tombstone – like his friend who killed himself.'

Olga's voice was as tremendous as her mother's as she screamed: 'Don't be ridiculous!'

Hank materialized silently at the kitchen door, some school books under his arm. He surveyed the two women, who were oblivious of his presence as they tore verbally at each other. With a shrug, he retrieved his black jacket, pinched a couple of cookies from the carefully arranged plate and drifted quietly away through the front door.

When he stopped to look back along the road, he saw two cars draw up in front of his home, one after the other. A sleepy grin spread over his face. The bridge-playing girls had arrived, a collection of overdressed, overpainted forty-year-olds. As the sound of their giggling chatter reached him on the wind, his amusement faded and gave way to loathing. There was Mrs Moore, the dentist's wife, mother of his friend who had committed suicide because life did not seem worth living; and there was Mary Johnson's mother looking as prim as a prune, not knowing that her daughter was no better than a streetwalker. Hank made a vulgar sound of distaste, shoved his hands in his pockets and continued on his way.

26

He remembered how, as a child, by dozens of small acts of perversity, he had brought his mother's wrath down upon himself, so that she did at least notice his existence. His father, being a geologist, was away from home most of the time, so that Hank could, to a degree, forgive his neglect. But his mother had nothing to do except care for him, and this she had blatantly failed to do. Instead, she had toadied to these ghastly, grasping women in glittering hats, women who themselves seemed to have forgotten that they had husbands and families.

As he had grown older, his anger had turned to cold bitterness, and creeping into his mind had come the idea of revenge, something subtle enough to humble his mother, make her realize that he lived, without killing her.

After long consideration, he had decided that he would try to write a book so outrageous that the Presbyterian élite of Tollemarche would ostracize the whole Stych family and thus put an end to his mother's inane social life. He had worked at the idea with all the intensity of youth, and now it was about to bear fruit. The book was, apparently, the kind of tale for which all young people had been waiting and its heavy sales in the United States had amazed him; the first hardcover edition had sold fast enough to surprise even his capable publisher.

He tried now to think with savage pleasure of the dismay likely to afflict his mother, once her female companions heard of it. He found, however, as he loped along, ostensibly to school, that he could not feel the same bitterness that he had done when he first started to write. Instead, he was glowing with hope of a future which, until recently, had seemed to him to consist solely of repeating Grade 12 over and over again in a remorseless, inescapable cycle of misery. Hank Stych, he told himself smugly, was a success.

CHAPTER FOUR

Mr Maxmilian Frizzell owned the biggest garage and car salesroom in Tollemarche. It took up half a block of Tollemarche Avenue and was gaily painted in red and white. Above its well-polished showroom windows an electric sign proclaimed to the world his slogan, YOU CAN TRUST MAXIE.

At the back of his premises he owned a used-car lot which faced on a less fashionable avenue, and here he sold second-hand cars, trucks and motorboats. His salesmen in the front showroom were sleek as well-fed cats, immaculately dressed in dark suits and ties, while the ones on the back car lot were chosen deliberately for their comfortably seedy looks; they leaned more towards coloured shirts and zippered jackets, and their haircuts were longer.

One Saturday morning, some two weeks after Mrs Frizzell's encounter with Mrs Stych, Mr Frizzell was seated at his office desk in a glassed-in area above the garage proper, from whence he could see all that was going on at both back and front of his property. He was going over his books and noting complacently that he was doing remarkably well.

He got up slowly from his chair to stretch himself and went to the window, overlooking the back car lot. It was busy, and all the salesmen were occupied. The autumn sun glinted softly on the pastel-coloured vehicles, most of which Mr Frizzell expected to sell before winter paralyzed the second-hand car business for four months. To one side of the lot was a collection of European cars and leaning over a snow-white Triumph was Hank Stych, talking to one of the salesmen. The salesman was just closing the hood, and Hank walked round to the back of the car and bounced it firmly up and down with his hands.

28

'Why does Van want to waste his time showing a car as expensive as that to a kid like Hank?' wondered Mr Frizzell irritably. Surely the man had enough sense to take him over to the other corner, where aged Chevrolets lay wearily beside battered Valiants, motorbikes and scooters.

The salesman and Hank, however, seemed to have reached some agreement and strolled towards the office, where fat old Josh presided over the financing section with the careful rapacity of a born moneylender.

Mr Frizzell shrugged his shoulders. Josh would soon cut Hank down to size. He dismissed the subject from his mind and decided to go down to the tiny lunchroom he ran for his employees, to get a cup of coffee.

His appearance caused a rapid scattering of employees who had outstayed their coffee break, and he sat down contentedly to munch a doughnut with his coffee. A few minutes later, Van entered, looking very pleased with himself.

'Sold that Triumph,' he called to Mr Frizzell.

Mr Frizzell stopped munching.

'Who to?'

'Hank Stych.'

'You're crazy!'

'Nope. He bought it all right.'

Mr Frizzell swallowed a piece of doughnut whole.

'How's he going to pay for it?' he asked, trying not to appear over-anxious.

'Traded in his jalopy, put a thousand down and the rest over six months.'

'Now I know you're crazy,' exploded Mr Frizzell. 'What the hell – '

'It's O.K., Boss. It's O.K., I tell yer. He wrote a cheque and Josh okayed it with the bank – phoned Hnatiuk, the manager, at home.'

Mr Frizzell slowly dunked the remains of his doughnut into his coffee. 'You're kidding?' he said without much conviction.

'No, I'm not. Ask Josh. Hnatiuk at the bank said he's

29

always had quite a good balance in his savings account – for a kid – and he's deposited quite a bit of money recently. He's got the money, all right.'

'Well, I'll be damned,' said Mr Frizzell, forgetting for a moment his Presbyterian upbringing. 'Where's he get it from?'

'Dunno. Ain't our headache.'

Van swallowed down a scalding coffee and got up. 'It's my lucky day,' he said cheerfully. 'Go see what else is cooking.'

'Sure,' said Mr Frizzell bewilderedly, 'sure.'

Hank drove the gleaming little Triumph out of the lot. She was a peach, he thought lovingly, a perfect peach, and all his, provided he was satisfied after giving her a run on the highway. He drove her carefully in and out of the busy Saturday morning traffic and wondered idly how he was going to explain about her to his mother, without saying where he got the money from. She was going to learn the hard way about the book, he was determined about that. His father wouldn't even notice the car, he thought, without much bitterness – too busy with his oil hunting. Probably wouldn't be home for weeks anyway.

Well, his book, his beautiful, shocking book, was published at last, and being bought by every kid in the States, so the balloon was bound to go up one of these days. Judging by the latest letter he had received from New York, care of Isobel Dawson, it was going to go up with a bang – there had been sufficient talk of banning it to make sure that everybody bought it, without any real danger that it would be banned from the bookstores. Maybe it might just make his mother realize he was alive. At any rate, everybody would think she had condoned his writing it and that should raise a fine storm for her. He clenched the steering wheel so hard that the car wobbled, and he hastily righted it. It would serve her right.

He had given up his Saturday job in the supermarket some time back, so today he would just drive and drive, drifting along the miles of highway toward Edmonton.

He stopped for a red light, prepared to make a right-hand turn as soon as the arrow flicked green. He knew the change would be slow, so he took out and lit a cigarette while he waited. He whistled mechanically at the back view of a girl waiting to cross the intersection, though of late girls seemed to have lacked their usual charm for him. The girl turned her head and half smiled at him behind her glasses. He knew her. Her name was Gail Danski, a prim-looking chick, but not so prim when you got her into a dark corner, as he had once discovered when taking her home after a school dance.

'Hi,' he shouted. 'Like a ride?'

She hesitated, and was lost.

She cuddled in close to him as they tore along the highway. Hank was fun, even if it did look as if he would never make Grade 12 and never earn much. He knew how to give a girl a good time.

'Where we going? Mother will be looking for me.'

'Let her look.'

She rubbed her leg against his.

Since it was obviously expected of him, he took his right hand off the wheel and put his arm around her shoulders. She laughed and took off her glasses, then gently slid her hand into his pocket.

'I haven't had any lunch,' she complained.

'We'll stop at a drive-in, and then what say about a nice, quiet park?' He might as well make hay while the sun shone, he told himself.

She giggled and looked sly. 'O.K.'

It was just too easy, he ruminated, as he bit into a huge hamburger at the drive-in. All you had to do was write about it afterwards, and you could make a real fast buck. Then he remembered the long, toilsome months when he had worked to perfect a style of writing, giving hours to his literature and language assignments, more hours to dissecting other people's novels. No, it was not that easy, he decided, smiling a little ruefully to himself, and there was a lot more hard work ahead.

31

His friend regarded him curiously over her hamburger. It was strange how Hank had a way of withdrawing from one's company at times, just as if he had forgotten one was there. Still, he looked fine when he smiled like that, almost handsome, with his wide mouth and perfect teeth.

'Wotcha laughin' at, Hank?' she asked.

'It wouldn't interest you, hon.'

It was midnight when he finally eased the Triumph to a stop in front of his parents' house and swayed gently up the steps. He could not, at first, unlock the door, though the porch light was on; the keyhole kept moving. He should not have had that last drink or that last kiss. That girl was unbelievable. Who would imagine that a thin, stuck-up-looking type like that could know so much? And yet, unaccountably, he had not been happy with her. Finally, he had felt sick at his behaviour and had dropped her off at her home with a feeling of relief that she was not the clinging type and perhaps he could avoid her in future. Girls like that were toys, and he was fed up with toys.

He found the keyhole, opened the door quietly, and crept into the living-room. His mother must have gone to bed. He went along the passage as silently as he could, and, safely in his room, flung himself on his bed without undressing. He felt dirty and his head ached.

He hauled a pillow out from under the bedspread and arranged it to ease his throbbing temples. He had had enough of this kind of game, he decided. Maybe he could settle down a bit now, quit high school, travel – and write. It would be good to get out of Tollemarche, out of Alberta, and see the world a bit. Suddenly, he was asleep.

He woke up only when his mother slammed the front door as she went out to church. He lay quietly, with a comfortable feeling of pleasant anticipation of the day before him, imagining his mother in her pale blue Sunday outfit getting her European car out of the garage and manoeuvring it down to the United church. Time was, he remembered, when she had attended the Greek Orthodox

Church, where he also had gone when small, but its splendour had palled when she had realized that more fashionable people belonged to the United Church. Hank chuckled, and then winced when he moved his head suddenly. Even God could be fashionable.

He got up, took a shower, combed his hair with care and put on a new black T-shirt. He ate a dish of cornflakes while wandering around the kitchen and then went out to look at the Triumph, still parked in front of the house. His mother would imagine some stranger had parked his car there. But the car was his and it was beautiful. He loved her like a woman and he ran his hands lightly over her as if she would respond to his touch. She was silent and acquiescent, however, so he climbed in and drove her round several blocks, just for the joy of it, taking the sharp corners so fast that her tyres shrieked in protest. Then he went slowly back to within two blocks of home, drove up the back lane and stopped before the old wooden garage which he had rented for so many years from Isobel Dawson.

As he entered the garden through the back gate, Isobel got up from in front of a flower bed where she had been planting bulbs. He was pleased to see her looking less pale than when he had last seen her, and she grinned at him with something of her old cheerfulness. She wore a shabby, tweed skirt and a turtleneck sweater which had shrunk slightly, making her look even smaller than usual. She had no makeup on and her long fair hair was twisted into a knot on top of her head. Hank could not imagine how she managed to look so elegant in such an outfit; the concepts of breeding and natural grace were unknown to him, and the quiet air of command she had scared him slightly. All he knew was that compared with the trollop he had been with the day before, she was like a princess, a very untouchable snow princess seven years older than he, who had recently lost her husband.

Fear of hurting her in any way made him abrupt. 'Got something to show you,' he announced without preamble.

'Oh?' she queried in her soft, clipped English voice.

Dorothy's voice held a distinct Welsh singsong, but years in London had worn away any trace of it from Isobel's speech.

'Yeah, come on outside.'

Still holding a trowel in one dirty hand, she followed his huge, droopy figure into the lane.

'My goodness!' she exclaimed. 'What a lovely car!'

She walked all round his precious beauty and admired its finer points. Finally, she came to stop beside him and looked up at him with a serious, troubled air.

'You know, Hank, the car is very nice indeed, but is it wise to buy it just at present?'

He was immediately defiant, his black eyes narrowed and his mouth hard.

'Why not? It's my money, isn't it? I can do what I like.'

She answered him gently, pushing a loose lock back into her bun as she did so.

'Yes, my dear, it is your money, and you really earned it. The car is lovely – but do you think you should flash money around yet – I mean, before the town knows how you came by it?' She stopped, then said: 'Look, come and have some tea with me before you start work. Have you seen any American papers?'

The endearment caught him by surprise and his face softened. He did not know of the English habit of using such affectionate epithets rather haphazardly, and he was impressed that she should consider him her dear.

'O.K.,' he said, considerably mollified, and followed her obediently up the garden path and into the kitchen.

The two women students who rented rooms from her had gone to church, and the remains of their breakfast lay on the table in the breakfast nook. Isobel looked at the muddle with distaste, then quickly washed her hands, put a kettle of water on the gas stove and assembled cups and saucers on a tray, while Hank ambled curiously around the old-fashioned kitchen. It had none of the clinical efficiency of his mother's, but it did remind him of his grandmother's kitchen out on the farm, with its prosaic line of battered saucepans which shared a shelf with a large bowl for making bread and a hopeful looking collection of cake tins.

There was cake, satisfying and fruity, and he sat on the edge of the chesterfield in Isobel's sitting-room and ate it appreciatively between gulps of strong, sweet tea from one of her best bone china teacups.

He liked this room, he decided. A man could put his feet up here without fear of being rebuked, and maybe he could even leave things about. Her desk looked untidy and a basket by the fireplace was filled with old magazines and newspapers. On a little table by the piano was a pile of much thumbed music.

He got up and went to the piano, sat on the stool and found that it revolved. He did a slow twist on it, laughing at her as he did so, then played a chord. She did not object, so he broke into a piece by Debussy and she listened attentively. After a few minutes, he became aware of Peter Dawson's portrait staring down at him from the top of the piano, and he stopped.

'I didn't know you could play,' she said. 'You are quite good.'

'Always got an A in music,' he replied, still contemplating the portrait. 'Paid for lessons out of my newspaper money.' He nodded towards the photograph. 'Sorry about Peter.'

She was suddenly tense and her voice came stiffly: 'Thank you.'

Seeing her quivering lips, he wished he had not mentioned Peter. What a clumsy lout he was! Desperately he wanted to comfort her, but how does a man comfort a girl crying for someone else, he wondered anxiously. 'You'll feel better later on,' he floundered. 'Lousy job – the army.'

She controlled herself with an effort. 'Yes, but I think he felt the peacekeeping mission was very worthwhile.'

He tried to change the subject. 'Funny to think you're a Canadian.'

She realized he was trying to lead the conversation away from her husband, to be kind and make up for his blunder. 'I suppose I am,' she said. She picked up a New York paper from the pile on the coffee table. 'I wanted to show you this.'

He felt a little snubbed and was angry with himself. He took the paper from her, however, and after a quick glance at her set face, read the column she indicated which was headed 'Book Reviews'. He whistled under his breath.

' *"The Cheaper Sex* . . . a disgusting book . . . vulgar pornography . . . shocking," ' he read in a mutter, and looked at her sheepishly.

She had recovered herself and tiny humorous lines were gathering round her eyes.

'Now read this one,' she commanded.

He read aloud: ' "Delicate delineation of a boy's sensations on discovering physical love . . . powerful and evocative description of adolescent suffering in an unsympathetic society . . . the best to come out of Canada for years . . . " Aw, hell!' He slammed the paper down, his face going pink in spite of his efforts to appear blasé. 'Do you think it was a sick book?'

Isobel smiled and said: 'No, I told you it was a good book, and I was right. A lot of things which are thought rather wicked in North America are regarded as normal in Europe. The thing is that, in a day or two, the *Tollemarche Advent* will wake up to the fact that you wrote it. There will be headlines – and I don't think your parents are going to like them much.'

Hank's voice was sulky as he replied: 'What do I care? I started to write it so as to shake them. They never cared about me, did they?'

'They are going to care now.'

'They're about twenty years too late. Anyway, I did finally send it under a pen name – Ben MacLean – mostly to please you,' he said defensively. Then he added, with a sudden burst of frankness, 'I reckoned the news would seep out anyway in time and cause them to lose plenty of sleep.'

'I think in a place as small as Tollemarche it will come out,' she agreed.

'Waal,' he drawled defiantly, 'let it come out. That's

what I originally intended. Now, I don't care either way, Isobel.'

The use of her first name did not imply familiarity, as it would have done in England, though she had never really got used to being on first-name basis with everyone; she was invariably disconcerted by this custom.

She leaned forward to pick up a cigarette box. When she opened the lid, it commenced to play a tinkling version of 'The Bluebells of Scotland'. She offered him a cigarette from it.

He was charmed by the tune and took the whole box from her while he listened; his face reflected an almost childlike absorption. This was the first time that he had been past the big covered back porch of her house, and everything was new and interesting.

'Say, where did you get that?'

'It belonged to my Welsh grandmother – she bought it in Edinburgh while she was on her honeymoon.' She enjoyed his obvious fascination with it and it reminded her of another suggestion she wanted to make to him.

'You know, Hank, if you really want to write for a living you should go to London and Edinburgh, go to Europe, too – perhaps try working for a newspaper or magazine. See something of life.'

'I've seen plenty already,' he snapped, his face suddenly hardening, though basically he appreciated the personal interest which prompted her suggestion.

She ignored his tone of voice and agreed with him.

'You have in a way – but you know, there are other places than the Prairies and Jasper and Banff – and, by and large, the world isn't very interested in books about Canada. You will need to branch out and – '

She stopped, anxious not to offend him. His presence kept at bay the pictures that danced through her mind, of Peter lying in the dust, her Peter who had, she realized suddenly, always had the same slightly defensive outlook that Hank had, of trying to forestall criticism.

'The Bluebells of Scotland' had also stopped, and he put

the box down slowly, his eyes turned thoughtfully towards her.

'Branch out and . . . ?' he asked.

'Acquire a veneer of civilization,' she said unexpectedly, with a brutal honesty possible only with someone she regarded as an old friend.

Impulsively she put her hand over his and said with passion: 'You are going to have to deal with a smart, slick world, quick to ridicule those who do not understand its manners – a world where you want friends, not enemies. You can't defy the world as you can your parents; you have to work with it a little – and be polite to it.'

The hand under hers clenched on the settee cushion, his face went red, and his eyes flashed such vindictive rage for a moment that she thought he would hit her, then he controlled himself, sitting silently by her on the settee, until she felt his hand gradually relax.

'Hank,' she said rather hopelessly, 'I didn't mean to hurt you.'

He slowly lifted the hand which had been clutching his, opened it and very gently implanted a kiss on its palm, and laughed when she gasped at the caress. She was too innocent, he thought.

'I kiss the hand which beats me,' he said melodramatically, and put it down firmly in her lap before he had any further ideas. 'Yeah, I know I'm a savage compared to your itsy-bitsy English world.'

She was still shaken that anyone should calmly kiss her when she had not been long widowed, but his remark stung her into retort.

'It's a very tough world,' she said defensively. 'English people are generally very well qualified and if you are not good at your work you'll soon go under, there.'

He had quite recovered his good humour, and said: 'O.K., O.K., what do I do now, ma'am?'

'It depends on whether you have any money left.'

' 'Bout five hundred bucks – from working in the store and from the articles you helped me to place.' He paused, and then said, 'I used the advance payment for the book to get the car.'

His eyes twinkled when she told him he was rich.

'When does High School finish?' she asked.

'In June next – but I'm quitting right now – I've had enough.'

She was still telling herself she should not be put out by a kiss from a youngster who did not realize what he was doing, and she tried to nod her golden head with an appropriate display of adult wisdom, as she said: 'Yes, you're wasting your time. Has your publisher asked you to go to New York?'

'Yeah, he has. Next week. Mostly about the film – and they want to talk about another book.' He pulled a crumpled letter out of his shirt pocket, opened it and handed it to her to read.

'Sent me a cheque for expenses, too.'

She was immediately businesslike and succeeded in putting some suggestions to him in her crisp English way, which banished from her mind again any other thoughts.

'What about asking Albert's to set you up with a really quiet-looking business outfit for New York? Take the clothes you have on with you, so that if he wants you dressed up as a teenager you have the proper clothes for that, too.' She paused, looking at him reflectively, and then asked: 'Don't you think you had better speak to your father about all this?'

Hank chuckled. 'I'd have a job. He's away up the Mackenzie in a canoe – with a prospecting party.'

'Oh, dear. Well, what about your mother?' She looked imploring, and he realized that her eyelashes were golden, too. She was a true blonde. 'Hank, you really ought to tell her.'

He withdrew his mind from contemplation of her eyelashes, and asked heavily: 'You kidding?'

'No.'

'I just hope the shock rocks her to her Playtex foundations.' He sounded malicious, and then, as Isobel made mild noises of protest, he went on in more conciliatory tones: 'Aw, I'll just tell her I'm going on a trip right now – an' don't you tell her.'

'I don't really know her. I've met her twice on formal occasions, but I am at work all day, so I don't often see my neighbours. And I don't intend to meddle in your family life – if you can't talk to each other, it's none of my business.' She smiled at him. 'You have always been a careful tenant in the garage. If you have a table and a typewriter in there, I don't mind. I've known you for years. I know you write under the pseudonym of Ben MacLean and wish to keep your literary activities secret, so I have never seen anything wrong in taking in your mail.' She leaned back against the settee, her eyes regarding him quizzically, and said: 'There. I've done my best to square my conscience for your sake. How's that?'

'And what about all the times I've asked your advice while you were doing your yard work?' he teased.

'Well – um – the students who live with me sometimes ask advice, too.'

'Oh, brother!' he exclaimed, looking suddenly troubled. 'They'll be coming back from church soon – and Dorothy, too – and I don't want you embarrassed.'

'Embarrassed?' She was surprised.

'Yeah. You know. Neighbours talkin' and that kinda thing.'

'Good heavens! One can be friends with men without that sort of gossip. What do they think I am – a baby snatcher?'

He was hurt to the quick.

'Not here you can't,' he almost snarled. 'And I'm no baby.'

She looked up at the six solid feet of him, at the huge, deep chest under his black shirt, at his bulging arm muscles. Then she raised her eyes to his cross, slightly plump face, its high Ukrainian cheekbones and sallow skin, now flushed with anger, and finally at the intelligent, black eyes, almost pleading to be told that he was a man.

40

She pitied him, and said, smiling gently: 'No, you have grown up in the years you've had my old garage, and you are very much a young man.' She hesitated, and then said very sweetly to comfort him: 'And it was nice of you to think of my reputation.'

He did not tell her that hers was the only female reputation he had ever given any thought to and that he did not know why he bothered. He just stood looking down at her for a moment, his eyes still pleading, and then abruptly he turned and picked up the tray and carried it into the kitchen for her.

'I guess I'll go and do some work,' he said heavily. 'I got the rough outline of another novel in my head.'

She forced herself to be cheerful. 'That's the spirit. You'll go from strength to strength, I know it.'

He felt happier. She could surely be real sweet when she tried, he ruminated. He saluted her, went through the screen door, vaulted the balustrade protecting the steps, and swaggered down the garden.

The Triumph was soon garaged, with its nose almost touching the back of his chair. He sat down at the old table by the window and put a new sheet of paper into the typewriter.

'*Mother and Son*', he typed, 'By Ben MacLean'.

41

CHAPTER FIVE

On Sundays Maxie Frizzell caught up with the various jobs his wife Donna required him to do. He sometimes thought it would be pleasant to lie in bed with his wife on Sunday mornings, now that there were no children to interrupt them, but Donna reckoned they should be through with all that kind of stupidity, so he was resigned to the sporadic consolation of his Métis up north.

Donna's latest demand was that he should extend the patio and then roof it over.

'I helped you by clearing all the leaves in the yard,' she told him half a dozen times, 'and I got a cold while I was doing it. Now just you get busy on that patio.'

Maxie made himself some coffee and took it out to the patio, where he surveyed the work to be done. He had already prepared the ground for the extension of the concrete flooring, and, since this was likely to be the last Sunday of the year when it would not freeze, the next job was to prepare the concrete mixture, which lay against the wall in a large bag.

He worked slowly but efficiently for nearly two hours, fearing that, if he did not finish the work quickly, frost would make it impossible for him to continue; then, tired and sweating, he went and sat on the front doorstep to rest.

Next door but one, new neighbours had recently moved in and a man was at work in the garden, slowly digging a flower bed, while a small boy pottered about trying to help him. They were both very fair complexioned, and they chatted sporadically to each other in a language foreign to Mr Frizzell, who imagined that they must be Dutch or German. He remembered his wife mentioning to him that some immigrants had moved into the street, and, because he knew that neither Donna nor Mrs Stych would bother to call on immigrants, he felt vaguely sorry for the newcomers' isolation. When the man looked up from his digging Frizzell lifted a tired hand in salute and the man gravely acknowledged it.

Closer to hand, the white Triumph was standing outside the Styches' house, and Mr Frizzell gazed at it uneasily. Though he did not like Stych much – too stuck up by far with his university degree and his oilmen friends – he hoped that Hank had not stolen the money for the car.

He saw Olga Stych go off to church an hour early and deduced that she must be helping with some small church chore before the service. Then Hank came out and drove off, and he cursed him quietly. That young so-and-so might easily have got his Betty into trouble, if he had not caught them in time. Children, he muttered fervently, were just a curse sent by God.

This reminded him that it was nearly time for church, so he heaved himself to his feet and went to make some more coffee, this time for Mrs Frizzell as well.

She was sitting up in bed, her glasses already adorning her gaunt face and her hair curled up tightly on rollers. She accepted the coffee with a grunt and told Maxie not to sit on the bed, because he had cement on his jeans.

He lowered himself gingerly to a gilt chair and stirred his coffee, the spoon circulating slowly until it finally stopped and he sat staring at it.

Mrs Frizzell drank her coffee quickly, then scrambled out of bed and proceeded a little unsteadily to the kitchen, her cotton nightgown drooping despondently round her. She took a roast from the refrigerator, put it into a baking tin, wrapped two potatoes in tinfoil and put both meat and vegetables into the gas oven. Having adjusted the heat and thus satisfactorily disposed of the problem of lunch, she went to the bathroom for a shower and then returned to the bedroom.

Maxie was still staring at a half cup of coffee.

'You sick?' she asked, as she struggled into her best foundation garment. Her body was still damp and the garment was too tight, so she was pink with exertion by

43

the time she had managed to zip it up.

'No.'

'You'd better shower or we'll be late.'

'Yeah.'

He got up reluctantly, put the cup down on the dressing table and walked slowly towards the bathroom. At the bedroom door he stopped. His wife was painting her eyelids green.

'You know Hank next door.' He made it a statement rather than a question.

Mrs Frizzell turned. She looked weird with one green eyelid and one veined pink. 'Sure,' she said.

'Has he been left any money by somebody?'

'Not as far as I know. She'd surely have told me if a rich relative had left him somethin' – I'm sure she would. Why?' she inquired, as, tongue clenched between teeth, she carefully finished her second eyelid.

'Nothin'. I just wondered.'

Mrs Frizzell stopped half-way into a bone-coloured skirt – bone had been last year's fashionable colour, according to the *Tollemarche Advent*.

'Maxie Frizzell! What do you know that I don't?'

He was sorry that he had brought up the subject and hastily departed for his shower, shouting that he would tell her while he was dressing.

By the time he came back she was ready, looking like a spangled Christmas doll, her bone suit augmented by a scintillating green, three-tier necklace and bracelet, a startlingly flowered green hat, tight, incredibly high-heeled shoes of shiny green, and her fox stole.

She was sitting tensely on the gilt chair.

'Well?' she demanded.

'Say, you do look nice.' He went over to her, holding a towel round his middle, and gave her a smacking kiss on the cheek.

She pushed him off irritably.

'What's this about Hank?'

44

He let the towel drop and dug around in a drawer for some underwear.

'Maxie, cover yourself! You're not decent!'

He ignored this and leisurely got into his undershirt.

'Hank,' she reminded him, her anxiety to know apparent in her rapt attention.

'Well, he bought a Triumph off us yesterday.'

'So what?' She was disappointed.

'You don't get a Triumph one year old for cents.'

Mrs Frizzell digested this truth, and the import of it slowly became clear to her.

'That's right,' she said thoughtfully. 'Mebbe his father got worried about him driving that old jalopy – it weren't safe. He might have helped Hank buy a new one – he's making enough money.'

'His father don't hardly know he's born yet,' said Maxie scornfully.

'How's he payin' for it?'

'A thousand down and the rest over six months – plus his old wreck, of course.'

'Cash?'

'No, cheque – but it's good – Josh checked with the bank, called Hnatiuk at his home. Hnatiuk says his savings account has been in good shape for a boy this past two years.'

Mrs Frizzell licked her finger and smoothed down her eyebrows with it. This was truly a mystery. She pondered silently and then was suddenly alert. Hank must have done a robbery to have so much money – he must have – there had been one or two bad ones recently – a Chinese grocer had been shot to death, in one instance.

She was filled with excitement. She would get hold of Mrs Hnatiuk after church and see if she knew anything about it. No good asking Olga Stych; she'd just stick her nose in the air and say that Boyd was doing very well.

'Hurry up,' she said, as if the church service would be over all the quicker if Maxie got a move on. And then she said: 'Mebbe he's one of that gang that has been holding up grocery stores.'

'Mebbe,' said her husband. 'I don't care what he's done. None of my business. The finance company will pay us and they'll soon squeeze the balance out of him.'

'For heaven's sake!' Such a scandalous-sounding mystery, and he didn't care. He didn't care about anything, except cars and trucks. A fat lot he even cared about being late for church and she trying to keep up a good style.

'For goodness' sakes, hurry up,' she exclaimed, standing up and folding her stole around her. 'I'll go get the car out.'

The Reverend Bruce Mackay, the patient and acquiescent minister, went on to 'fifthly' in his sermon, and Mrs Frizzell was sure he would never end. Mrs Hnatiuk, who was wearing a fast-looking white jockey cap, was only two rows in front of her and Mrs Frizzell did not know how to bear the suspense. The final hymn had eight verses, not to speak of a chorus of Hallelujahs at the end of each one; Mr Frizzell enjoyed this and sang in a pleasant tenor voice.

Across the aisle, Mrs Stych expanded her tremendous bosom to shout to the Lord in a wobbly soprano. Borne along by the music and the comforting sermon, she was happy.

It was over at last. The minister stood at the door and shook the hand of each member of his congregation, with a kindly word for each boy and girl. The children viewed him with wary respect, since, in spite of his air of benignity, he frequently exploded when faced with old chewing-gum stuck under the pews, the choir guardedly shooting craps during the sermon, and similar juvenile straying from the path of righteousness.

Mrs Frizzell eased herself – it could not be said that she exactly pushed – through the crowd so that she was next to Mrs Hnatiuk, while Maxie stopped to talk to clients.

Out on the pathway, Mrs Hnatiuk was surprised to find her hand gripped enthusiastically by Mrs Frizzell, who was normally so condescending, and her health solicitously inquired after. Mr Hnatiuk had taken one look at the approaching Mrs Frizzell and had dived for cover into a knot of other businessmen. Mrs Hnatiuk was cornered.

Mrs Frizzell circulated painstakingly through all the usual conversational openings, the weather, the forthcoming Edwardian Days Carnival Week, the coming winter and what winter did to the car trade, wondering how to get round to Hank's Triumph. She was unexpectedly helped along by Mrs Hnatiuk, who said: 'Ah, there's Mrs Stych. I just love her little car.'

'Yeah,' said Mrs Frizzell, with satisfaction. 'Maxie just sold her Hank another nice one, a Triumph.'

'My! They must be doing well,' said Mrs Hnatiuk. 'Three good cars in the family, counting Boyd's Dodge.'

'Maxie said Hank paid for it himself,' dangled Mrs Frizzell hopefully.

The fish failed to rise.

'Did he?' exclaimed Mrs Hnatiuk. 'He must be working at something good.'

'He's still in high school. Doing Grade 12 again.'

Mrs Hnatiuk's five little girls were still in elementary school and, consequently, she did not come into frequent contact with high school students. She was, therefore, unaware of Hank's reputation for being rather irresponsible. She said maddeningly: 'Say, that's a nice stole you've got. Mrs MacDonald's got a blue mink, but that one of yours is nice, too.'

Mrs Frizzell nearly screamed. Either Mrs Hnatiuk really did not know much about Hank or she was just being perverse.

'Where do you think he got the money from?' she queried.

'Who?'

'Hank Stych.'

Mrs Hnatiuk's pale blue eyes opened wide. 'From his father, I suppose. Where else?'

'He might have stolen it.'

Mrs Hnatiuk's eyes nearly popped out of her head. 'Do you think so?'

It was obvious that Mrs Hnatiuk was not telling. Mrs Frizzell mentally crossed her off her list of guests – she'd never really be anybody anyway – and abruptly made her farewells.

She moved down to the kerbside, smiling graciously as she elbowed her way through the crowd. Mrs Stych was having difficulty starting her little car, so Mrs Frizzell bobbed her flower-decked head down until her hawklike nose was level with the half-open window.

'How does Hank like his new Triumph?' she asked.

Mrs Stych ceased her frantic turning of the ignition key for a moment, and looked perplexed.

'Triumph?'

'Yeah. His new car.'

Mrs Stych pursed her heavily painted lips and looked at Mrs Frizzell as if she feared for Mrs Frizzell's mental health.

'He hasn't got a new one. You know he's not working yet.'

She gave the ignition key another desperate turn and the engine burst into song.

'But,' Mrs Frizzell began, 'he – '

Her words were lost in the sound of grinding gears, and the car leaped away from the sidewalk, knocking Mrs Frizzell's hat askew and leaving her mouthing furiously at nobody.

CHAPTER SIX

Hank was not in when Mrs Stych returned home from church. She made a cold lunch for herself and then left to visit her mother-in-law. Every Sunday afternoon she meticulously visited either her mother or her mother-in-law, these indications of filial affection being indispensable to anyone of her aspirations, with a public image to maintain. She never bothered to write to her husband while he was away, husbands being regarded as of very little importance, except as sources of money.

While Hank was, in his grandparents' opinion, too small to be left alone, the two grandmothers had insisted that he accompany his mother, and he had enjoyed wandering round the Palichuk pig farm with his grandfather or playing in a corner of the lounge of his Grandmother Stych's more fashionable home. He was the youngest grandchild, however, and as he grew to be a hulking, noisy ten-year-old, his aging relatives found him very tiring. After the death of Grandfather Palichuk, the custom arose of frequently leaving him at home. Even now, he remembered with a shudder the appalling loneliness of Sunday afternoon, spent trailing noisily around the streets with a group of equally neglected youths, returning to the empty home to eat his supper while the television set bawled commercials at him to fill the silence, until he heard the scrape of his mother's key in the lock.

Occasionally, his father was at home during the weekend. But he also felt that he should visit his mother. He had, too, a lot of paper work to deal with while in Tollemarche, and only rarely shared his Sunday supper with his son. He was a taciturn man who found it difficult to talk to a boy; but he did sometimes spare time to tell him of his travels in the wilder parts of Alberta, of encounters with grizzly bears, white water rushing through narrow gorges, being lost in unexpected snowstorms, in an unconquered wilderness totally alien to his suburb-bred son.

When Hank was fifteen, his best friend, Tommy Moore, committed suicide by quietly dropping himself off the railway bridge into the icy waters of the North Saskatchewan. He had threatened to do it for some time, but only Hank had taken him seriously and tried to dissuade him. Hank felt stripped of the only person in whom he could confide, and, for a while, considered following his example. Perhaps it was fortunate that at that time he discovered girls, and a year later met the Dawsons, who always seemed to have time to stop and gossip with him. He had by now forgotten the faces of many of the girls he had run around with, and Peter Dawson was dead, but there was still Isobel, the one steadying influence in his life.

From watching Isobel and her husband he had discovered that there was much more to sex than just taking a girl to bed or being uneasily married to a frigid, grasping woman.

Peter Dawson had been considerably older than Isobel and since he had only a few more years to serve in the army, had decided to establish a permanent home in his native town. It had taken their combined savings to make the down payment on a house in overcrowded Tollemarche and Isobel had declared that she could manage without a car. She therefore advertised the garage as being for rent, and at the same time got herself a job as a secretary to an insurance broker, to fill in the time until Peter should be at home permanently or a family should arrive.

When a younger and less sophisticated Hank had come quietly through the back gate in search of the garage, the couple had been busy planting a lilac tree. He had watched them silently as they lowered the little bush into the prepared hole, with considerable argument as to how the roots should be spread. It was a different kind of argument from any he had heard before; it was friendly and joking. When the earth had been finally pressed down round the tree roots, Peter Dawson had put his arm round his wife's tiny waist and they had surveyed their handiwork with obvious satisfaction. He had kissed her on the nose, and they had strolled around their small domain, debating what else they should do to the garden.

Hank had hastily retreated round the side of the garage, while they decided where to put a sand box for the child as yet unconceived, and then he had re-entered the gate, giving it a diplomatic slam behind him.

He had not had much hope that they would rent the garage to a teenager, since teenagers were regarded generally as being as reliable as something out of the zoo. Peter Dawson had, however, asked who his father was, and had then inquired if the family was any relation to Mr Heinrich Stych, who used to teach in Tollemarche Public School.

'Yeah – sure,' replied Hank. 'He was my grandfather.'

Captain Dawson was immediately more friendly.

'Well, that's great! He taught me when I was a boy. Of course you can have the garage. I don't think we will be needing it for a while.'

He asked what kind of a car Hank had and was very encouraging when Hank told him that he and his friend Ian were going to rebuild one.

Hank paid five dollars from his paper money as the first month's rent, and, later that day, he and several of his friends pushed a dowager of a car round from his back lane, where it had been dumped by a tow truck, into the Dawsons' garage. The Dawsons themselves had enthusiastically helped to heave it over a rut and up the slope to the garage.

Ian MacDonald and he had stripped down the old wreck and searched junk yards for spare parts. Mr Frizzell, before the unfortunate episode with Betty, had been prevailed upon to donate four old, though still serviceable, tyres; and finally the great day arrived when he backed it slowly out of the garage and drove it round to his own home in the vague hope that his mother might like to see it.

'I won't have that thing standing in front of the house,' she had said forcibly. 'Take it away.'

Crestfallen, he and Ian had driven to Ian's house, but Mrs MacDonald had gone to an art exhibition and Mr MacDonald to a service club meeting. Ian's kid sister, who was playing mothers and fathers with her friends in the crawl space under the porch, said it was marvellous, so they had to be content with this infant praise and with taking her and her mud-covered friends for a ride round the block.

Wrathfully indignant at his mother's lack of appreciation of his efforts as a mechanic, an idea which had long been in his mind, that of writing a novel, had crystallized. He would write a book which would cause a sufficient furore to upset both his parents thoroughly and make them realize that he was a person to be reckoned with. To do it, he had to have more privacy than his room allowed, and he had tentatively approached Captain Dawson, who was home on leave and was painting the porch, for permission to put a table and chair in the garage, so that he could work there.

Captain Dawson sensed that there was more behind the request than was readily apparent. He was used to handling a great variety of young men, and his piercing stare, as he considered the request, made Hank quail; he had a suspicion that Peter Dawson could make his wife quail at times, and in this he was right.

'Why can't you work at home?'

Hank decided that, in this instance, honesty was the only policy possible and had said frankly that he wanted to try to write a book. He did not feel he could write freely if the typescript was readily accessible to his mother.

The Captain wiped the paint off his hands and carefully avoided showing his amusement. He agreed that a mother's censorship would be very limiting, and, after consulting Isobel, who was enchanted with the idea, he said that the furniture could be brought in.

'You had better change the lock on the door,' she had teased, 'because I might be tempted to peep at the manuscript.'

He had gravely changed the lock and kept both keys. She had, however, through the months of work, taken a real

52

interest in what he was doing, and he found himself confiding in her more and more. It was she who, when the manuscript was ready, had given him an introduction to Alistair MacFee, a professor of English at the university. Professor MacFee had read it had been startled by its undoubted merit, and had carefully discussed it chapter by chapter with him, suggesting how to improve it. Glowing with hope, Hank had gone back to the garage and pruned and polished. Then the professor and Isobel, both young and enthusiastic, had helped him to choose a likely publisher to whom to send it. The English firm which they first suggested returned the typescript. Undaunted, Hank sent it to a New York firm and they accepted it. He was so excited that he forgot about the revenge the book was supposed to wreak on his parents.

Now, *The Cheaper Sex* had been out in the States for some weeks, and it seemed as if everyone under the age of twenty-one wanted a copy. On the day of its publication, Hank had gone jubilantly to Isobel's back door, armed with an autographed copy for her and her husband.

He had found an ashen-faced Isobel, showing none of her usual gaiety or cordiality. She had written a receipt for the month's rent for the garage, which he had proffered at the same time, and had received the book with a watery smile. She had then wished him good luck with the sale of his book and had quietly shut the door in his face.

Bewildered and hurt at her lack of interest, too shy to ask what the trouble was, he had gone back to the garage completely mystified, and had spent the rest of the evening painting his jalopy electric blue.

When he finally went home, he saw the *Tollemarche Advent*. It informed him in letters an inch high that Captain Peter Dawson had been murdered in Cyprus.

His first instinct was to rush back to Isobel. Then he told himself that he was a nut who had written a book in her garage, and that he had no right to intrude.

As a way of showing sympathy, however, he had the following Saturday morning put on his best suit, which was

53

far too tight for him, and gone to the memorial service for Captain Dawson in the nearby Anglican church. In total misery, he watched, from the back of the church, the stony-faced widow, flanked by her husband's mother, a surprisingly elegant woman in smart black, and his father, a retired Royal Canadian Mounted Police officer looking tired and grey, as they went through the formalities of the service. Absorbed as he was by the sight of a family in grief, a new phenomenon for him, he could not help observing, with some awe, the large number of military men present to testify to their friendship with the dead man. They sure looked smart, he thought, and from that moment he began to cultivate the straight, dignified bearing which was to be his hallmark in later life; only occasionally did he forget and relapse into his old North American droop.

His quick eye also registered with some interest that not one of the ladies present, as far as he could judge, belonged to his mother's circle. This quiet group of people looked so simple and unassuming that at first he could not think what made them interesting to him, and then he realized that they gave every appearance of complete sincerity. Like Isobel, they were what they looked, quiet people doing very necessary jobs and a that moment grieving for one of their number who had left them.

He thought that he left the church unnoticed, but Isobel saw him as she stepped out of her pew, and, as far as anything could penetrate to her at such a time, she was touched by his solicitude.

It had been apparent to Hank for some time that, in spite of repeating Grade 12 at school, he was likely to fail his exams again. French and Ukrainian, mathematics and chemistry bored him to the point of insanity; only in music and English could he hope to get decent marks. On December 28 he would be twenty years old, and he wondered bitterly when he might be allowed to grow up. He decided to consult Mr Dixon, his English teacher, who was also his counsellor and, therefore, knew more about him than did the other teachers.

Mr Dixon, friend of Mrs Murphy and conductor, in his spare time, of the amateur orchestra, had accidentally launched Hank on his writing career a few years earlier by encouraging him to enter an essay competition sponsored by a service club. The essay, on 'The Dangers of Smoking', had cost Hank a number of Sundays of hard work, and he estimated that he must have smoked at least eight packs of cigarettes while writing it, but to his astonishment it had won him a hundred dollars. He looked at Mr Dixon with new respect and, to that gentleman's delight, really began to work hard.

On the Monday morning after Isobel had advised him to accept his publisher's invitation to go to New York, he went to see Mr Dixon.

Mr Dixon could hardly believe his ears as Hank poured into them the story of the book and its apparent success. He immediately insisted that Hank should tell his parents, and warned him of the evils of leaving school without succeeding in obtaining the magical Grade 12, without which there was no hope, he insisted, of leading a normal life. Hank already had the feeling that his life was going to be anything but normal and was adamant about leaving school, but agreed reluctantly to tell his father when next he came home. The clinching argument that Mr Dixon made about informing his father of his literary success was that probably Hank would need help in investing discreetly the earnings of the book, and it was well known that Mr Stych was an astute businessman. Hank was the product of a boom town and knew that money earned money extremely fast; with luck, he could double and treble his capital by investment in Tollemarche.

Mr Dixon heaved a sigh of relief at having gained at least one point, and decided that the question of leaving school could be left to the parents and the Principal. Hank was grateful to him for his promise not to discuss either matter with anybody.

Hank went home to lunch.

His mother was in, seated at her kitchen desk and

gloomily going over the month's bills – her Persian lamb coat made the Hudson's Bay bill look enormous, and, at the rate she was paying it off, it would take until next Easter to clear it.

'Like a bologna sandwich?' he asked her, as he made one for himself.

She grunted assent, and he filled the coffee percolator, set it on the stove and then rooted around in the refrigerator for the ketchup, while he wondered how to approach the subject of his going to New York.

'Ma,' he said in a tentative tone of voice, his face going slowly pink with the strain of trying to communicate with his despondent parent.

'Yeah?' she queried absently. She would wear the Persian lamb to the meeting of the Symphony Orchestra Club tonight, even if it was a bit warm.

He thrust a sandwich on a plate in front of her. 'Ma, I'm going on a trip for a week.'

Mrs Stych swivelled round on her stool and forced herself to attend to her son.

'Y'are?' She sounded puzzled.

'Yeah. I'm going to New York for a week.'

He told himself that it was ridiculous for him to be nearly trembling with fear, wondering what form her explosion would take.

She frowned at him for a moment; then her brow cleared.

'With the United Nations Debating Club?'

Hank accepted the temporary reprieve thankfully. Darn it, why hadn't he thought of that himself? Undermining his mother's social prestige was one thing, having to tell her about the book himself was another.

Her face darkened again.

'Who's payin'?'

'I'm going to pay some. You know I got a bit saved. The rest they're paying.' He hoped she would not ask who 'they' were.

'Well, I guess that's O.K. When you goin'?' It was typical

56

of her that, although she regarded Hank as a child, she did not ask who would be supervising the group she imagined would be travelling to New York.

'Thursday. Be back next Wednesday.'

'O.K. Y' father will be coming by then.'

His legs began to feel weak and he sat down hard on a red plastic and chrome chair, while he held his sandwich suspended half-way to his mouth. He remembered Mr Dixon's persuasive arguments regarding telling his father about *The Cheaper Sex*, but he doubted if Mr Dixon knew what kind of father he had.

'That's good,' he said dully, putting down his half-eaten sandwich.

The book should have been in Tollemarche's only bookstore for several weeks; however, when Hank casually sauntered in and asked for a copy, old Mr Pascall said it had not arrived. It would probably come in the next shipment from Toronto.

Hank had no doubt that, sooner or later, old tabby-cats like the MacDonald woman would get wind of it and would give his mother hell about it. His mother would never get round to reading it and he hoped fervently that his father would not either. Anyway, he consoled himself, nobody in Tollemarche over the age of forty ever really read a book, though they talked about them.

He swallowed the last of his coffee and went to his room to inspect his wardrobe. He decided to put his two drip-dry shirts through the washer that night. His one decent pair of dark pants and his formal suit were too small for him. The rest consisted largely of T-shirts and jeans. Mind made up, he returned to the kitchen, picked up his zipper jacket and departed, officially for school, but in fact for the town to do some shopping. His mother, busy checking the T. Eaton Company's report on the state of her account there, did not bother to reply to his monosyllabic 'Bye.'

Albert Tailors, in the shape of old Mr Albert himself, took one look at him and channelled him to the Teens Room, which was festooned with guitars and pictures of pop singers. But Hank protested firmly that he wanted a dark business suit, three white drip-dry shirts, dark socks and tie, black shoes, a light overcoat and an appropriate hat. The clerk inquired delicately if it would be cash or charge.

'Cash,' snapped Hank irritably, and was hastily rechannelled into the men's ready-tailored department. The clerk stopped for a moment and whispered to Mr Albert, who, realizing that instead of selling a pair of jeans he really had a customer with money to spend, hurried towards Hank.

'I want a good suit. It must look real good. But I gotta have it now.'

Mr Albert humphed and measured.

The first suit was too loud, even Hank knew that.

'No. I want the kind of thing – the kind of thing these big oil executives wear.'

Mr Albert laughed, a trifle scornfully. 'It would cost about a hundred and twenty dollars at least.'

'So what?' replied Hank belligerently. 'That's what I want. I gotta go to New York. I wanna look right.'

Mr Albert's superior smile waned. He sent the clerk hurrying into the back room to get a dark grey suit which had just come in and then said: 'Going to New York? You're a lucky fellow.'

'Yeah,' said Hank noncommittally, as he examined himself critically in Mr Albert's big triple mirror. He was not pleased with what he saw. He tried drawing in his stomach and straightening his shoulders, as instructed by the physical education teacher. The result was better, but not his idea of a distinguished author.

He was soon eased, pinned and patted into the grey suit, the cuffs hastily turned up by the clerk, the back smoothed by Mr Albert. It looked weird over a T-shirt, but it undoubtedly fitted quite well, except for the length of the pants.

He gyrated carefully so that he could see himself at all angles. My, he did look different. The good cut made his shoulders look their proper width and reduced his generally plump look. He grinned at himself. He looked a man at last, not a school student.

Fascinated by this new vision of himself, he continued to stare. He would like Isobel and Dorothy to see him like this.

Mr Albert's voice came from a distance: 'You'll need a good white shirt with it, and a tie . . . ' Mr Albert considered ties. 'One in a quiet red, I think. And plain black shoes.'

Hank did not hear. He was still staring at himself in the mirror, seeing himself for the first time as a man, not a boy. In that moment, his uncertain struggle towards manhood was over. He had always been taught by women, with the exception of Mr Dixon, and ignored by his parents. Unthreatened by war service, he found, like his friends, that the only way to prove to himself that he was grown up was to chase and lie with innumerable young women. Some of his friends had married while still in high school, and all of them, married or single, were agreed that sex was a dissatisfying pastime. None of them had as yet discovered a deep, rewarding love.

Now Mr Albert, with more ability than Hank thought such an old fogey could exhibit, had shown him that he could look quite as dignified as Captain Dawson, not a bent peasant like Grandfather Palichuk or a rugged, outdoor type like his father, but a very respectable townsman called Hank Stych.

Hank was suddenly deeply grateful to old Mr Albert for taking him seriously. He glowed, as he came out of his trance, and said: 'I'll take it. Do you think you could find me a dinner suit as well?'

CHAPTER SEVEN

In the eyes of most Albertans, Tollemarche was a tourist centre second only to Calgary and Edmonton. In order to encourage the winter tourist industry, it had a winter fair featuring exhibitions of interest to farmers, and many winter sport events. Of recent years, the fair had been lengthened into a fortnight-long frolic called Edwardian Days, finishing two weeks before Christmas. The city dressed up in Edwardian clothes, shop windows showed displays of Edwardian families enjoying Christmas, the restaurants served such Edwardian delicacies as Oxford sausages and English beef-and-kidney pie, and the bars offered large glasses of white wine cup. The Tollemarche ladies, in bonnets and cartwheel hats, gave teas at which they coyly sipped at China tea flavoured with lemon and mint. In the evenings, skating parties were held under coloured lights and skates flashed under long skirts to tunes like 'The Blue Danube'. The climax of the fortnight was the Grand Edwardian Ball, which was the most important occasion of the whole winter, and thinking up suitable costumes for this event kept the ladies occupied for weeks beforehand.

The greatest complication about any ball is that one requires menfolk with whom to attend it. Most of the year, the matrons of Tollemarche regarded their husbands as nuisances better out of the house, but the ball was an occasion for which husbands, sweethearts, even brothers, were in great demand. Young women married to salesmen, for once, took an interest in where their husbands would be on the great day; the older men, who ricocheted between various business interests, were lectured steadily, any time they put in an appearance at home, on the necessity of being in Tollemarche at this time; and those males who were doomed to spend their lives in Tollemarche found themselves with intolerable lists of jobs to be done, from laying out backyard skating rinks to pinning up the hems on their female relatives' costumes.

While Mr Stych was canoeing back down a tributary of the Mackenzie, already dangerous with chunks of ice, to an appointment with a helicopter, Mr Frizzell was trying on his last year's brocade waistcoat and finding it too small; Mr MacDonald, Ian's father, was winding up a trying compensation case for his insurance company at Vermilion; and Mr MacDonald (oil) was trying to explain to his superiors in Sarnia, Ontario, why he must be back in a place like Tollemarche by the middle of December. In the ornate new council chamber, Mayor Murphy was trying to convince the city council that to be a real Edwardian Mayor he ought to wear mayoral robes, as they did in England; the newly extended hospital was bracing itself for additional accident cases; and Hank Stych stood in the airport at Calgary waiting for a local plane to take him north to Tollemarche.

Though he had found New York impressive, the people did not seem to him very different from those of Tollemarche. His publishers had been smoothly charming and undoubtedly a little surprised to find their backwoods author a careful, quite business-like man in a town suit, who would not sign anything until he had read the small print several times and understood it thoroughly.

Full marks to Isobel, Hank thought grimly; she had done a lot of homework trying to check what his rights were regarding serialization, filming and translation, and had primed him well. He had met the press at a cocktail party and had stood there answering impertinent questions with disconcerting honesty, a glass of ginger ale in one hand and a canapé in the other; when he could not immediately think of an answer he nibbled the canapé and viewed the questioner with cold button eyes. His childhood exposure to life in the streets of a western town, still so new that most of the people who had founded it were still alive, had left him with no illusions about people or their motives, and it was always for the motive behind the question that he looked.

Now, as he waited for his flight, he felt exhausted, as if he had been playing an enormously difficult game of poker for high stakes. And yet, in spite of the fatigue, he felt good, as if for the first time in his life he had really stretched himself and grown up. He knew that basically he had enjoyed the careful battle of wits.

In his bag was a tiny music box in the shape of a windmill, bought specially from Macy's for Isobel, and a stuffed monkey for Dorothy to sit on her bed. He had also rather reluctantly bought a box of chocolates for his mother and a box of cigars for his father.

On the aircraft the stewardess brought him a copy of the *Tollemarche Advent*. The preparations for Edwardian Days were not yet featured on the front page, but an inner page had a half column on the redecorating of the main hotel's ballroom for the Edwardian Ball. He let the paper fall into his lap.

Up to now, he had always competed in the skating events and had escorted one of his classmates to the Teens' Square Dance, held well away from the elegant ball. Now he had a sudden ambition to go to the ball. Like Cinderella, he told himself with a grin. But there was more to it than that. Attendance at the ball indicated considerable standing in the adult world and he had a sudden savage desire to show his parents, who would be there, that he had made it on his own, without any help from them. The tickets alone were so expensive, not to speak of the need for a good costume, that they would realize that inexplicably he had had some financial success.

He considered taking Dorothy, but she was only seventeen, too young to hold her own in a possibly difficult encounter with the élite of Tollemarche. He wondered if he dared ask Isobel. She had been widowed for five months, very nearly. Did she go out now and, if so, with whom? He felt a pang of jealousy, which was intensified when he remembered the smart army officers who had been at her husband's memorial service. Had any of them made any approaches to her?

He brushed the newspaper angrily off his lap and told himself not to be a fool. She was seven years older than he was. She'd never look at him.

He arrived home at one in the morning. His mother was not yet in; presumably she had gone to a party. He made himself a cup of coffee and then, feeling deflated and not a little depressed, went to bed.

Isobel and Dorothy were battling their way against the wind down to the bus stop, the following morning, when they met Hank hunched up in his old black zipper jacket and a pair of earmuffs, which gave him a quaintly catlike appearance. He had his hands in the pockets of his jeans, which were, as usual, at least two inches too short, and tucked under one arm were one or two schoolbooks. His face was pinched with cold and he looked rather dejected, but he greeted them heartily.

'Hiyer, babe?' he said to Dorothy, and: 'Hi, Isobel.'

'Hello, Hank,' they said in chorus from the depths of the fur collars of their coats.

They were burning to know how he had got on in New York, and Isobel asked him.

'I'm rich, ma'am. I'm rich. Book's doing fine – going into paperbacks next year, and they confirmed about the film.'

'Oh, Hank, how exciting!' exclaimed Isobel, her face going even pinker than the wind had made it. 'Congratulations!' Then she noticed the books. 'Are you going to school?' she asked.

Hank looked guilty.

'No, but I haven't told Ma yet, so I came out as if I were going too school.'

'Hank, you are naughty,' Dorothy chided. 'It's going to be all over town – in fact, I can't think why it isn't already – and your mother will be the last to know.'

He turned up his inadequate collar and executed a dance step or two to keep his circulation going.

'So what?'

Isobel looked at Dorothy reprovingly. 'It's Hank's business, Dorothy.'

'Aw, don't be hard on her, Isobel. She just don't understand. Mind if I work in the garage today?'

'Not at all, Hank. Go ahead.'

'Thanks a lot. Seeya tonight, mebbe.'

He must have worked for a long time in the garage. When Dorothy came home from town, however, he was digging over the vegetable patch, despite its half-frozen state and the gently falling snow.

'You don't have to do that, Hank,' she said, as she came through the back gate. 'Isobel will get a man to do it in the spring.'

'And what do you think I am, honey?' He had stopped digging and was leaning against the spade, waiting, as if the answer was important to him.

Dorothy laughed. 'Oh, Hank, you are an ass.'

'Thanks,' he said dryly, his face taking on the blank expression it usually had when he was annoyed.

Dorothy was puzzled and did not know what to say, so she smiled and then started up the path to the back door, when he called her back.

'Say, Doll, I want to ask you something.'

She walked uneasily back to him, her legs in their tight pants looking like those of a young colt. 'Yes, Hank?'

He weighed her up for a moment, his wide mouth compressed and then asked: 'D'ye think Isobel would come to a ball with me?'

Dorothy decided she had better not laugh this time, though she wanted to, so she said cautiously: 'I don't know, Hank.' She wondered a little resentfully why he did not ask her to go, though she would have been scared if he actually had done so; she lacked a North American youngster's experience with the opposite sex.

'I mean, is she still in mourning? It's over four months now, and it'll be five before the ball comes up.'

Dorothy was thoughtful. 'No,' she said at last. 'She seems to be getting over it pretty well. She goes about a bit

– English women are a bit different from Canadians, you know, Hank.' Then she added in a confiding tone: 'Of course, she was not much with her husband really – and I think that helps – she isn't reminded of him at every turn, like an ordinary widow would be.'

'You're right.' He rubbed the end of his nose with one grubby hand in a puzzled kind of way.

'Why don't you ask one of your girlfriends?' Dorothy inquired, far too intrigued at this unexpected interest in Isobel to remember that she was supposed to be indoors starting to prepare supper.

'Not suitable,' said Hank flatly. Then, feeling that perhaps he was being rather uncomplimentary to Dorothy, he added untruthfully: I'd ask you, honey, only you're too young for this one.'

'Is it the Edwardian Ball?'

'Yeah.'

'Oh, Hank, I'd love to go,' she implored.

'Sorry, babe. You really are too young.'

Dorothy felt crushed, and said bitterly: 'Well, if I'm too young to go with you, I'm sure Isobel is too old.'

This sensitive point made Hank feel as if he had been returned sharply to the schoolroom, but he said unrepentantly: 'Nuts! She's just old enough to have dignity.'

'Well, no doubt she'd feel safe with you,' Dorothy said pointedly. 'You'd better ask her.' And she flounced up to the house, her long black hair swinging rebelliously down her back from under her red woollen cap.

Though rather demoralized by his conversation with Dorothy, he did ask Isobel. He came up to the house that evening, armed with the music box and the monkey. He had changed into a clean white shirt and tie, and his dark pants just fitted him, though Dorothy wondered if they would stand the strain of his sitting down.

Dorothy had already told Isobel of the conversation that afternoon, so she was prepared; but he found it difficult to get round to the real object of the visit. He presented the music box, which was received with every expression of pleasure by Isobel, and the monkey to Dorothy, who could not help laughing when she saw it, because it was so typical of a craze for stuffed animals amongst the girls she had met in Tollemarche.

When finally he did broach the subject of the ball, Isobel refused to take his invitation seriously and said he should take someone his own age. Anyway, Tollemarche would be shocked if she went, she added wistfully.

He caught the hint of wistfulness in her voice and made the most of it quickly.

'For heaven's sakes!' he exclaimed. 'Why should you care what a lot of old tabbies think? Ma and Pop will be going. And for sure you can come – if you feel up to it?'

He wondered suddenly if she had got any fun out of her marriage to Peter Dawson. He remembered him as a kindly man but not a very lively one.

'Perhaps you ought to make up a party with your parents,' Isobel said dutifully.

'Come off it,' he said, grinning suddenly. 'You know I want to shake 'em. And I'd sure see you had a lovely time,' he went on with almost too much intensity in his voice, so that he feared he might have frightened her off.

Dorothy looked at Hank with sudden interest. His eyes were on Isobel, who was staring at her hands, and Dorothy felt a wave of jealousy at Isobel's Dresden china beauty and her look of compliant gentleness. She had taken it for granted that if Isobel accompanied Hank to the ball, it would be a kind of aunt and nephew relationship, but now she wondered.

Isobel looked up and laughed herself, her nose wrinkling up like a child's. She obviously had not noticed anything out of the ordinary, and Dorothy told herself not to be a fool imagining things. Maybe it would do Isobel good to be dragged out by someone she would feel at home with, and a man of her own age would cause much more of a stir in the neighbourhood.

'You should go, Isobel,' she said generously, swallowing her own disappointment at not being asked. 'Dress up in ostrich feathers, or whatever Edwardians wore, and have some fun. It would help Hank out – and probably nobody would recognize you anyway.'

Hank was not slow in taking his cue. 'Sure. You can be disguised,' he said hopefuly. 'Lots of people go as well-known Edwardian characters – everybody wears Edwardian dress.'

It took them an hour to convince her that it would be all right to go, that she would not be disloyal to Peter; but, finally she agreed that she might as well indulge the boy.

Dorothy had an inspiration as to who they could go as, and for the rest of the evening they amused themselves digging through an old encyclopedia to find pictures from which to copy costumes.

CHAPTER EIGHT

The Ladies of Scotland League was holding its fall tea in the auditorium of a large store on Tollemarche Avenue. The decorations committee had spent the morning spreading tables with brown, yellow and green linen cloths and pinning gold-sprayed autumn leaves to each corner of them. Branches of fir, complete with cones also sprayed with gold, had been laboriously pinned to the walls. Brown and white bunting swathed the edges of the small stage.

A small table by the door had been spread with a green cloth embroidered with the insignia of the League, two thistles crossed above the initials L.S.L., and here, armed with white name cards and a bristling collection of pins, sat Mrs MacPhail, a determined young newcomer from Hamilton, Ontario, who had managed to obtain the post of secretary because none of the older members felt like undertaking so much work. Her hat was an aggressively red felt and she peered out from under its big brim like a shrew ready to attack. Beside her sat the treasurer, a formidable figure of some sixty years of age, in a pink gauze turban which did little to soften her high, bald forehead or her arrogant expression. She wore a matching crepe dress, which draped across her large bosom and red neck, and a mink stole was hung negligently over the back of her chair.

Anybody who had hoped to get past these two ladies without paying her dues would have been squelched by a look; and the pile of dollars in front of the treasurer grew as the number of white name cards in front of Mrs MacPhail diminished.

At one end of the hall, a long table, embellished with a lace tablecloth, had been laid with silver coffee-pots at one end and silver teapots at the other, a mass of flowered cups and saucers round each. In the middle of the table was a formal arrangement of chrysanthemums, flanked by white candles in silver holders. Two very old ladies presided over the tea and coffee pots; they were the oldest members of the League, having travelled out to Tollemarche district with their parents in covered wagons before the town itself existed. They therefore received the doubtful honour of pouring out for some two hundred ladies, regardless of the fact that it was a very arduous and tiring task.

Mrs Josephine MacDonald, president of the Noble Order of Lady Queen Bees, was also vice-president of the League and stood with the president in the receiving line, just beyond the treasurer's table. Mrs MacDonald was a Calgarian by birth, and her husband had been moved north by his firm to run the huge refinery that was now the pride of Tollemarche. She regarded the Tollemarche ladies as being outside the pale, and had treated them with such blatant condescension that they had quailed, and had sought her goodwill by voting her hastily into offices in those organizations in which she had deigned to take an interest. Today the president, Mrs Macpherson, in between gracefully shaking hands with each new arrival and presenting her to Mrs MacDonald, decided that she was nothing but a vulgar upstart, and she trembled with suppressed irritation at having to stand in the same receiving line with her. Why, there had been Macphersons grinding flour in the Tollemarche district sixty years ago, and it had taken her years of hard infighting to reach her present exalted rank; now this woman was, after only twelve months of residence, her vice-president. Mrs Macpherson bit her blue lips with her artificial teeth and looked down her beaky nose at the bland, well-powdered face beside her. Hmm! Nothing but paint on a piece of lard.

The piece of lard opened its lipsticked mouth in a thin smile at the next arrival, and Mrs Macpherson hastily recollected her duties, her black, old-fashioned hat bobbing in unison with her white bun, as she spoke to Mrs Frizzell. A nice girl, Donna Frizzell, real nice.

'May I present Mrs Frizzell,' said Mrs Macpherson to Mrs MacDonald.

Mrs Frizzell flashed a dazzling smile at Mrs MacDonald, showing no sign of the resentment against the lady, which she shared with Mrs Macpherson, while Mrs MacDonald inclined her head slightly in acknowledgment.

'We've already met,' they said in chorus, as they shook hands demurely.

'Well, now, isn't that just fine,' said Mrs Macpherson, a note of acerbity in her voice.

No other arrivals were awaiting attention, so Mrs Frizzell paused to speak with Mrs MacDonald, while Mrs Macpherson checked with the treasurer that all was well in the finance department.

'I didn't know you were Scottish,' said Mrs MacDonald, her bright smile looking rather fixed.

'Not me,' said Mrs Frizzell. 'It's Maxie that's Scotch. His mother came from Glasgow.' She enjoyed the opportunity of impressing the president of the Lady Queen Bees. 'He belongs to the Bonnie Scots Men's Association. He did a real funny Address to the Pudding last Robbie Burns Night.'

'Indeed,' said Mrs Mac Donald, delicately checking with one finger that her hat was still on straight. 'He must be a charming person.'

Mrs Frizzell looked a bit doubtful, and then said yes, he was, especially when he got going. She became aware that her beige Sunday suit was looking a trifle out of fashion, compared with Mrs MacDonald's burnt-orange outfit, and this confused her still more. Everybody seemed to have bought a new dress for the occasion, and she had hardly finished paying for her suit.

She searched for a new subject of conversation. 'Will you be going to the Edwardian Ball?' she asked.

'Naturally. Bobby expects to make up a party from the works and we shall come along for an hour or two.'

Mrs Frizzell wished mightily that she could infuse into her own voice just that inflection by which Mrs MacDonald conveyed that she was doing Tollemarche a special favour by coming to the ball. She was dying to ask Mrs MacDonald

70

what she would be wearing, and then thought better of it. Probably the party would come in plain dinner dresses, just to show how far above such things they were.

She shifted the rather heavy, though small, paper bag which she was carrying, and said: 'I guess I'd better get some tea before all the cookies go. See you at the ball, if not before.'

'Right-ho,' said Mrs MacDonald unexpectedly. She had picked the word up from an English film shown on television and thought it charming.

Mrs Frizzell looked a little startled, and retired to the tea table with what she hoped was a stylish bow.

'Afternoon, Donna,' said a small ancient voice behind her. 'Coffee's at the other end o' the table.'

Mrs Frizzell, engrossed in thoughts of buying a new dress, as well as her costume for the ball, which was being made by a dressmaker and was as yet unpaid for, jumped and turned round.

The old tea pourer, Donna's one-time school-teacher, peered up at her through rimless glasses. 'Yer getting nervy, Donna. Should go to bed earlier. Always told yer mother you never went to bed early enough.'

Donna felt again like the girl who had been made to spit her gum into the wastepaper basket. Her depression deepened. Somehow this tea was not turning out to be the delightful social event she had hoped for, full of contented tittle-tattle and scornful criticism of all who were not Scottish and United Church. These Scotch women were tough and sure could make a person feel small.

Mrs Frizzell giggled nervously. 'I'm too busy these days, Miss Angus. Can I have a cup of tea please?'

'Yer can,' said Miss Angus, lifting the heavy silver pot with a shaky hand and slopping some into a cup. 'Sugar and cream's there. Help yerself.'

Mrs Frizzell fumbled with handbag, parcel and gloves, and finally managed to pick up the teacup as well, and to serve herself with sugar.

'Wottya got there?' asked the indomitable old voice.

Donna's face blenched a little under her makeup. She

71

knew Miss Angus had never liked her much; in fact, it was doubtful if Miss Angus liked anyone very much. Donna remembered with sorrow the number of humiliations she had endured from her in school, and the thought of exposing the contents of the parcel she was carrying to such a merciless judge unnerved her.

'Some books,' she finally murmured into her teacup, while she tried quietly to increase the distance between her and the tea pourer.

'Books? Never knew you to read a book yer didna hafta?' Miss Angus sniffed. 'Has Maxie taken to reading? Wottya bought?' Her voice rose commandingly. 'Lemme see.'

Other ladies standing nearby were beginning to take an amused interest in this interchange between the domineering retired school-teacher, who had ruled many of them when they were young, and Donna Frizzell, who could tear a character to pieces in three minutes with her sharp tongue.

'You're busy pouring now,' said Donna desperately. 'I'll show you after and explain about them.'

'Explain?' The old busybody from the back streets of nineteenth-century Glasgow was immediately alert. 'I got time now. Most people have had their first and aren't ready for their second. Come on. Let's have a look.' It was an order.

Mrs Frizzell clung to the paper bag.

'Not now,' she protested. 'I'll explain to you about them later on.'

She would never be allowed by Miss Angus to explain in front of the other women, she felt angrily. Miss Angus would have a field day, happy to emphasize her own high moral principles at the expense of an unloved member of a younger generation. The old devil! No wonder she had never got further than teaching in a one-roomed schoolhouse.

She bent forward to return her teacup to the table. The paper bag slipped, she grabbed it and it tore open at the bottom, spilling its contents onto the empty teacups near Miss Angus and turning some of them over with an attention-drawing rattle.

Several more ladies looked round sharply at the tea table, as Mrs Frizzell tried to snatch her purchases back. But Miss Angus slapped her wrist sharply with a teaspoon, as she picked up a paperback with her other hand and examined it closely. She looked paralyzed for a moment. The female depicted on the cover was stark naked.

'*Butterfield* 8' she read out in a clear, schoolmarm voice. She picked up another, while Donna watched like a terrified rabbit. '*Striptease!*' she exclaimed. '*Love of an Ape Man!*' She clawed for the one hardback in the collection and picked it up. '*The Cheaper Sex* by Ben MacLean.' Her face paled at the sight of the dust jacket on this one. 'Donna Frizzell, I thought better of you!' she thundered.

'But Miss Angus, the Society for . . . '

'I want no explanations. Take this pornography off my tea table!'

'Miss Angus, I . . . ' began Mrs Frizell in anguish.

Miss Angus bellowed like a slightly cracked version of Gabriel's trumpet: 'I said take them away, woman!'

Some of the ladies looked appalled, and others giggled. Mrs Frizzell snatched up her property, tried wildly to wrap the books in the remains of the paper bag, dropped one of them, picked it up and fled to the cloak-room at the back of the hall, followed by the titters and sniggers of not a few ladies who, knowing the reason for her purchase of the books, could well have rescued her from her predicament, but saw no reason to do so. There may be honour among thieves, but there did not appear to be anything similar among social climbers.

In the cloak-room Mrs Frizzell stood in a whirl of used paper towels, like a panting snowshoe hare in a snowdrift. A slow tear ran down her cheek, smudging her green eye shadow. Added to her humiliation was the knowledge that some of her friends, who had seen the incident, could have helped her but did not do so. She put the books down on the vanity table and with trembling fingers opened her handbag to find her face powder. Hastily she dabbed around her eyes, trying to stop the green rivulets running down her face. Her car was parked at the side of the store, and she would have to walk through three or four departments before she could reach the outside door.

She thought she heard someone coming down the passage, so she grabbed two paper towels and wrapped them round the offending literature. The footsteps continued past the cloakroom door, and she relaxed. When all was silent, except for the distant buzz of conversation from the tea, she crept out and almost ran down the back passage, as fast as her high-heeled shoes would permit. Her mind in turmoil, her thoughts entirely on escape, she hardly drew breath until she reached the sanctuary of the tall displays in the bedding and linen department on the ground floor and saw the safety of the store's side door beckoning to her. Thankfully, she allowed the revolving door to take her in its firm embrace and deposit her in the hall.

She stood for a moment, her eyes closed, trying to collect her thoughts, while she struggled to put on her gloves. Those cats and that old tabby, Angus; she could murder them.

The door of a car banged outside. Her eyelids flew up like window blinds wound too tightly.

Swaying gracefully up the steps on heels even higher than Mrs Frizzell's came Mrs Stych. She was dressed entirely in black except for white gloves, and her tall hat, together with the high-heeled shoes, gave her the height she otherwise lacked. Her dress, cunningly draped around her plump figure, made her look almost voluptuous; and over her shoulders was carelessly thrown her Persian lamb coat, which made Mrs Frizzell's eyes glisten with envy. Even her pearls looked real, thought Mrs Frizzell grimly, her thoughts for the moment diverted from her own nightmare frame of mind.

There was no way of escaping Mrs Stych, so Mrs Frizzell

waited while her neighbour pushed through the swing door. ' 'Lo, Olga,' she said mechanically and moved to pass out of the same door; but Mrs Stych wanted to show off her outfit.

'Hello, Donna,' she greeted her with enthusiasm. 'You been to the tea?'

Donna nodded assent.

'Wotcha going so early for?'

Mrs Frizzell made an effort to sound normal. 'Got a meeting of the Committee for the Preservation of Morals tomorrow night,' she said. 'Got to make a report to them – and I haven't prepared it yet.'

'Oh,' said Mrs Stych, moving slightly towards the inner revolving door so that the Persian lamb swung out in all its glory. She paused, however, before going through the door. 'What's that you've got wrapped up in lavatory paper? One o' the clerks'd give you a paper bag.'

Mrs Frizzell was just beginning to feel like someone recovering from near drowning, when this remark sent her under again. She shut her eyes tight for a second behind her spectacles, got a grip on herself, and said firmly: 'Some books for tomorrow.'

'Ah-ha,' responded Mrs Stych, a sly look dawning on her face. 'Betcha have fun reading them before you make a report.'

This was too much for Mrs Frizzell. She had been mortified enough. She could bear no more. She put her hand to her mouth, uttered a mourning cry and ran through the swing door to her car.

There was a parking ticket neatly tucked under the windshield wiper.

CHAPTER NINE

Boyd Stych unlocked the front door and slung his knapsack into the corner reserved for the coats and hats of his wife's visitors, clumped through the lounge in his heavy, laced boots and shouted not very hopefully: 'Hi, Olga, I'm back!' Since Mrs Stych was at the Ladies of Scotland's Tea, there was no reply.

Boyd unzipped his sheepskin jacket and flung it on a kitchen chair, opened the plaid shirt he was wearing and scratched his chest wearily. He was a tall, thin man with knotty muscles and a thin, high-cheek-boned face, his chin at the moment covered with ten weeks' growth of beard. From under fierce black brows a pair of hazel eyes looked out calculatingly at the impersonal kitchen, made spotless by the ministrations of a Dutch cleaning lady.

Although he had hardly expected anything else, he was annoyed that his wife was out. She was always out. He was tired after the long drive home, preceded by an even longer, freezing-cold canoe and helicopter journey. Thank God, that was the last time he would have to do it; after this he would go as an executive, by aircraft and helicopter only. He wondered how Olga would take the news he had for her, and decided grimly that she would not like it.

He wanted to have a shower and to change his clothes, before unloading the car; so he plodded slowly upstairs to his bedroom, leaving a trail of greasy, sweaty garments wherever he went. He remembered, just in time, not to shave – the beard was needed for the Edwardian Ball.

Mrs Stych was singing as she came up the garden path. As far as she was concerned, the tea had been a success. Her Persian lamb coat had overshadowed the treasurer's three-year-old mink, and her hat had caused a sensation. She had heard about Donna Frizzell's frightful taste in literature, and, though she was herself a member of the

Society for the Preservation of Morals and knew why the books had been purchased, she saw no reason to save her neighbour any humiliation, and had expressed suitably shocked surprise. It was gratifying to her to see that woman taken down a peg.

Her song was cut short when she saw the filthy knapsack sitting on the new, pink broadloom and making a smudge against the blush pink wall. Her eyes followed muddy boot tracks across the lounge, through the dining alcove and into the kitchen.

'Boyd,' she shouted. 'Wotcha want to make a mess like that for?' But only the sound of the shower in the distance answered her.

Sniffing crossly, she went upstairs herself and lovingly hung up the Persian lamb in the clothes closet. Then she sat down on the bed, took off her hat and eased her patent leather pumps off her rapidly swelling feet. The relief was great, and she sat massaging her toes for a minute while she looked at the collection of dirty underwear strewn over her genuine-colonial bedroom, and shuddered. Men were horrid, dirty creatures.

The horrid, dirty creature in her life, still bearded, but feeling much better after his shower, came striding into the room, tying a bathrobe as he came.

'Hi, Olga,' he said.

She looked up at him and said sulkily: 'Wotcha wanna make such a mess for?'

'Aw, shut up,' he replied. 'What about a kiss for your long-lost husband?'

She looked mutinous, then lifted a pouting mouth to his and squeaked protestingly as he pushed her backwards onto the bed and on top of her new hat. But Boyd did not care about new hats or new frocks. He had been ten weeks in the bush, a womanless bush, and Olga Stych had to put up with the fact.

She was far too quick-witted to complain and endured silently, but she managed to extract a promise of a new hat and a new dress from him, before getting up an hour later to

77

tidy herself and prepare supper. Neither of them had mentioned Hank.

Hank, school-books under arm, arrived, however, in time for supper. He said 'Hi' slightly nervously to his father, who grunted acknowledgment from behind the *Tollemarche Advent*.

Hank relaxed. Everything seemed as usual. Evidently the school had not communicated with his parents. He was unaware that a harassed Mr Dixon, caught betwen Hank, his parents and the school authorities, had disclaimed any knowledge of Hank's whereabouts, except to say, when asked by the school secretary, that probably Hank had the flu – there was a lot of it about.

As he tackled his cold meat loaf and salad, Hank thought he had better show some interest in his father, so he asked the back page of the newspaper if it had had a good trip.

'Yeah,' Boyd said listlessly, and then, with more animation, as he realized that this might be a good moment to break his news to his family, he added: 'Yeah, I did.'

He dropped the newspaper onto the kitchen floor, looked with distaste at his plate, and began to eat. Mrs Stych brought her plate to the table, picked up her fork and toyed with her food. She had eaten too many cookies at the tea and was feeling nauseated in consequence, but told herself wrathfully that it was Boyd's disgusting ways that had done it. Tomorrow, she promised herself, she would go down to Dawne's Dresse Shoppe – she'd make him pay. Wrapped in her own thoughts, she did not at first hear what her husband was saying and only became aware of his monologue when Hank said: 'Say, Dad, that'll be good.'

'What'll be good?' she asked suspiciously.

'Dad isn't going to have to go away any more – he's been made vice-president – gonna sit in an office all day right here in Tollemarche.'

Mrs Stych went pale as the full implication of this burst upon her. 'Not go away?' she stuttered.

'No,' said her husband cheerfully, 'and am I glad! Had enough of going on trips. Big business – collar and tie – that's me now.'

Mrs Stych's mouth dropped open. A husband always under her feet! A man who came home every night – and slept with her! Why, it was almost indecent – she might even have a kid. She would never be free. This had never happened to her before, and she was dumbfounded that, in the course of a few seconds, her life could change so much.

'Well?' he asked huffily, 'aren't you pleased?'

She said hastily: 'Oh, yeah. Yeah, I'm pleased.' But she looked like a Protestant faced with the Spanish Inquisition. She went slowly to the refrigerator, took out a block of ice cream, cut three slices off it and put them into glass dishes, then plonked the dishes on the table, during which time a new idea came to her.

'What sorta salary?'

'Pretty good,' he said. 'We'll be able to leave here and buy in Vanier Heights.'

She sat down and stared at her ice cream. Vanier Heights – that would be something. That was where Mrs Mac-Donald (oil) lived and she knew two wealthy doctors there already. She looked at her husband with renewed interest. Maybe she would manage after all. Maybe she could manage him, if he was the price of a house in Vanier Heights.

Although Hank was obsessed with his own problems, he was well aware of what was going on in his mother's head. He knew her too well, and he flushed, embarrassed by his own thoughts, and dug into his ice cream. He felt suddenly sorry for his father.

His mother licked her spoon reflectively, and said: 'Vanier Heights would be real good. We could sure entertain up there.'

Hank was just about to say, in order to irritate his mother, that it was in another school district and he would, therefore, have to change schools, when he remembered that he was no longer at school, and shut his mouth. Being out of school gave him a wonderful feeling. For two days now he had sat in Isobel's garage during most of school hours and planned his new book. Twice, when he had run out of ideas, he had driven the little Triumph out of the district to a coffee shop where he was not known, and had sat drinking coffee and talking to the men next to him at the counter, surprised to find himself accepted as a member of the grown-up world. One man had asked him what his job was and he said that he was an author. This had caused such abnormal interest that the next time he was asked he said that he worked in a garage.

One afternoon he had shared a pot of coffee with Dorothy, at her invitation. She was to stay with her sister until Isobel decided definitely whether to remain in Tolle-marche or return to England, and occasionally she became a little bored and was glad of Hank's lively company, though to her annoyance, he treated her as if she were a ten-year-old.

The day before his father's return, he had driven out to a lake some ten miles from the town; it was deserted and half frozen, and he had walked round it, finding that the fresh air cleared his head and that ideas came fast in the silence of the woods. The characters for his book began to emerge as persons and to walk beside him. Now, all he wanted was to get back to his typewriter and put them on paper before they faded. First, however, he had to ask Isobel if he could alter the lighting in the garage, so that he could see better at night.

The meal was finished, his father had returned to the newspaper, rather deflated at his family's lack of appreciation of his vice-presidency, and his mother had finished her ice cream and was rising from the table.

'Hank, now you can just do these dishes for me tonight. There's a meeting of the Queen Bees in an hour, and I've got to get into my robes.'

Hank made a face at her plump back disappearing through the kitchen door and reluctantly began to transfer the dishes to the sink. His father had put down his newspaper and was looking at her, too. He looked old and forlorn, in spite of the ferocious beard, as if he had hoped for something and been disappointed. Hank was so used to being deserted by his mother that he did not think it odd that she should go out on the first evening in ten weeks that his father had been able to spend at home. But he did see that his usually tough, self-sufficient male parent was, for once, looking as if he needed bolstering up.

As he turned on the hot-water tap and got out the dish detergent, Hank abandoned the idea of going back to his garage. 'Looks as if we're going to have a bull session, Dad.'

His father looked almost grateful.

'I guess so,' he said, and then roused himself. 'Here, I'll dry for you.' He took up the dish towel. And when Mrs Stych returned, looking like a fat Christmas fairy and complaining that she could not fix her wings, he was able to pin them onto her dress without rancour and to tell a thoroughly bawdy joke, which made Hank explode with laughter and his wife look outraged. 'Boyd Stych,' she shouted, 'you're disgusting!' He smacked her gold-black-striped bottom, and sent her, fuming, out to her little car.

'Any beer in the house?' asked Boyd, as soon as the car engine had started up and it could be assumed that Mrs Stych was on her way.

'Sure, there's some in the cold room downstairs.'

Boyd's face brightened. 'Say, let's have some. You go down and get it, while I make a fire in the living-room. This place is like a morgue.'

Hank was delighted, though at the same time a little suspicious of his father's prompt response to his friendly overture. The old man had never suggested before that they have a drink together; maybe it was all part of that new world he had entered when he stood in front of Mr Albert's mirror in his new suit. He loped down into the basement, dusted off half a dozen bottles of beer and brought them up, found glasses and an opener and took them into the living-room on a tray.

81

His father, an expert woodsman, had already got a fire going, and the room had lost some of its pristine newness and was looking much more cosy. The wood crackled and hissed, and Boyd drew the brass firescreen across it to stop the sparks from flying out at them. Together, they heaved the oversize coffee table, with its burden of unread art books, out of the way, and pulled up chairs. Mr Stych opened two bottles and handed a glass and a bottle to Hank.

'Ever drunk beer before?' he asked.

Hank did not know how to reply. The Alberta liquor laws laid down that no minors might drink, but it was not difficult to obtain beer or liquor, and he had often drunk himself silly. His silence made his father laugh.

'O.K., O.K.,' he said, 'I won't ask.'

Hank grinned sheepishly. Now, he knew, was the time to tell his father about *The Cheaper Sex*, while he was in such an extraordinarily amiable mood. He would have to be told; any day now it would dawn on Tollemarche that it had spawned its first successful author, and he could guess the kind of jokes his father's colleagues were going to make when they found out what kind of book he had written. He could not, however, think how to start, and the silence deepened.

'How's school?' asked his father, in a sudden valiant attempt to re-establish the frail line of communication.

'I've quit,' said Hank absently, and realized a second too late what he had said.

'You've what?'

He was committed and could only stumble on. 'I've dropped out – I couldn't stand it any more.'

Mr Stych sat up in his chair and glowered at his son. What, he wondered indignantly, had Olga been thinking of to countenance this?

'Are you crazy?' he demanded in horrified tones. 'Where you going to be without Grade 12? You have to go to university.' He looked his offending offspring up and down with angry eyes. 'Just what do you think you're going to do?'

Hank's face went blank. 'I'm gonna write,' he said stubbornly.

His father put down his glass with a bang, so that the beer slopped over on the side table. 'You'll do no such thing,' he shouted. 'You'll go right back to school on Monday morning and finish Grade 12. I'll have no dropouts in my family – we got enough hippie types hanging around. Never heard of such a thing.' He paused to take breath before continuing his tirade, and Hank said hastily: 'Listen, Dad, you don't understand.'

'Understand? I understand all right, and if you think you're going to live off me for the rest of your life you're mistaken. You get your Grade 12, and then you work your own way through university, same as I did.'

With a painful effort, Hank swallowed his own anger. He had either to get his father to listen or otherwise he would have to just walk out. He itched to do the latter, but common sense prevailed; he had seen how uncomfortable were the lives of other guys who had done that, either to marry too young or go it alone. A home was a sensible base for operations. He held up one hand in a conciliatory gesture to try and calm his parent, who by this time was striding up and down the room behind him.

He did his best to infuse good humour into his voice as he said: 'Hold it, Dad. I got fifty or maybe seventy thousand dollars earned, and I need advice about investing it. Believe me, I really need advice.'

Mr Stych stopped in his tracks at the mention of such a sum of money, as Hank had hoped he would, and looked at the boy as if he might have gone dangerously mad.

'Now what are you trying to tell me?' he asked, his mouth twisted in bitterness. He'd always known Hank was no good. Always bottom in phys. ed. and always hated baseball. What could you expect? he asked himself. Just trouble, nothing but trouble. Now the kid was sick in his head. Seventy thousand bucks – that was a good one!

83

'Now listen, Dad, just sit down and listen. I've got a real long story to tell you.'

Mr Stych stopped his perambulation and regarded his son with a puzzled frown. What was the kid getting at? He looked all right; in fact, he had improved. He was definitely tidier, and he had an oddly adult air of authority for a kid still at school. Of course, he was growing up a bit. Mr Stych sat down again and drained his glass.

'All right,' he said with an air of resigned patience. 'What is it?'

He nearly fainted when Hank began: 'You know I rent a garage from a young widow lady.'

Not a young widow at his age, for heaven's sake. Why hadn't he stuck to Grade 12 girls? Hastily, he reached for another bottle of beer and opened it, while Hank droned on: 'So I entered an essay for the No Smoking essay competition . . .'

With agitated fingers, his father felt in his shirt pocket for a cigarette, but he had forgotten to bring them from the kitchen. Hank tossed a packet over to him, and he had lit one before he realized that he had not known that his son smoked.

'. . . Isobel read it and sent me to Professor MacFee – an English Professor – with it, and they both helped me to send it to a publisher in London. I did – and it came back. So I sent it to another in New York, and he took it.'

'Who's Isobel?' asked Mr Stych, trying to catch up with the tale.

'The widow,' replied Hank, with more than a trace of impatience in his voice, and then continued: 'And it's selling so fast that I don't know what to do with the money. We're getting forty thousand dollars for the movie rights, and the serial rights – the first ones – are already sold in the States.'

Mr Stych looked as if someone had struck him. Forty thousand dollars! His no-good slob of a kid was talking of having forty thousand dollars. His heavy black eyebrows made him look fearsome as he glared unbelievingly at

84

Hank. 'You're kidding?' he said finally.

'I'm not, Dad. Ask Mr Hnatiuk at the bank if I haven't got real money. He's been real good. Dealt with me himself, and never told anybody so far as I know.' He took a nervous sip from his glass. 'You can see the letters from New York, if you come over to Isobel's. I been to New York only a short while back.'

Boyd ground out his cigarette. 'Christ!' he said, some of the anger evaporating. For the first time in his life, he really looked at his son, weighing up this product of the first six months of marriage before disillusionment set in.

Hank said earnestly: 'So you see, I sure need advice. I mean, I want to spend some, but I want to invest some, too. And you know about these things, that's for sure.'

His father was looking at him keenly now. Mellowed by two bottles of beer, he was convinced that Hank was telling the truth; his mind was already going to work considering how to double that forty thousand. Money fascinated him. Like a great many others in Tollemarche, he had made it his goal and his God. People who made money demanded respect; people who had none were just trash to be trampled underfoot, no matter what other gifts they had. He licked his lips.

'Sure, Son, you do need advice. You can lose money pretty fast by bad investment.'

Though his face showed nothing of his amusement, Hank laughed inwardly. Money and talk of money got you attention. He sighed with relief.

Boyd was silent for a moment. Then he asked: 'Have you told your mother?'

Hank went cold right down his back and into his feet. 'No,' he said. 'She don't even know I quit school.'

Boyd approved of this, and nodded his head in agreement.

'You're right not to tell her,' he said dryly.

A log in the fire broke and fell, sending out a shower of sparks. Hank silently drank down his beer, and hoped he had made the right move in telling his father. Anyway,

85

Isobel had been keen for him to tell both his parents, and her advice had been sound all through. He knew his father had a fair reputation as an astute businessman as well as an able geologist, and he hoped uneasily that they could deal honestly together over the money.

'If I had that much money and it was the first real money I had ever made,' said the businessman at last, 'I'd put a quarter of it in government savings bonds, and with the rest of it I'd buy as much land or property in and around Tollemarche and Edmonton as I could lay my hands on.' He looked at his son's face illuminated by the firelight. The boy was watching him anxiously. 'Do you expect to make any more like this?'

'Sure,' said Hank, with all the confidence of youth. 'I'm writing another.'

'Well, if you do, you could buy a business, or you could buy growth shares on the stock market. Myself, I'd buy a business.'

'Not me,' said Hank firmly. 'I'm gonna write. And I want to travel a bit. Maybe get a job on a newspaper or a magazine for a while. Feel my way around. Get some experience.'

Boyd leaned back in his chair and lit another cigarette. He had much to think about. In a place like Alberta, with that much capital and a good deal of know-how, which he himself had, the boy could be quite wealthy before he was forty. And amazingly enough, he expected to earn more. For years, he and Hank had exchanged only a few words, but now they began to talk, drawn together by the magic of money; and Hank was surprised and flattered to find that the elder man was entranced by his sudden success.

To Hank's intense relief, at no point did it occur to Boyd to inquire what the book was about. He did not even ask its name.

Mrs Stych came in at half past one, her wings bedraggled from the weight of her coat. She had gone on from the Noble Order of Lady Queen Bees' meeting to a party given

86

by one of the members, and was by now tired, cross and a little tipsy. On the way home, the car had had a tendency to wander from one lane to another on the road. And now Mrs Stych stood rather dazedly inside the front door and wondered if she was in the right house.

The lounge was a mess. The coffee table had taken flight to one side of the room, and two chairs had been drawn up close to the fireplace with their backs to the chesterfield. The fireplace itself was filled with grey ash and cigarette butts. On every side table were empty beer bottles sitting sadly in rings of beer; two empty glasses decorated the mantelpiece, and the piece of petrified driftwood which usually graced it had been shoved to the back, to make way for some empty plates which looked as if they had held meat and cheese.

Mrs Stych's senses reeled. This was what happened when a man was loose in the house. He must have had some friends in. Her nose wrinkled at the smell of beer, and she kicked off her mink-trimmed bootees as if she were kicking Boyd.

She trailed around the room picking up beer bottles, looking oddly like a bee with broken wings. She removed eleven bottles, and then felt sick. The Ladies of Scotland's cookies, followed by meat loaf, succeeded by the Lady Queen Bees' angel cake buried under cheese dips and rye on the rocks at the party, would daunt the strongest stomach. She fled up stairs to the bathroom.

Her Dutch cleaning lady would be coming round in the morning – let her do it, thought an exhausted Olga a few minutes later, as she shakily bathed her face under the cold tap; Boyd could darn well pay her more housekeeping to cover the extra hours of work.

With some difficulty, she unzipped her gold and black dress in the bathroom and then trailed into the bedroom, self-pity and too much to drink tending to make her weep.

Boyd, with most of the bedding rolled tightly round him, was snoring contentedly. Rather than wake him by pulling the clothes off him and having to face the likely consequences, Mrs Stych put her housecoat over her nightgown, got a spare blanket out of her old hope chest, and eased herself down beside the chrysalis which was her husband. She slept immediately.

In his dreams, Boyd Stych made a million for his son out of forty-storey apartment blocks, and was chased by a flying book the name of which he could not see.

CHAPTER TEN

When Mrs Frizzell arrived home from the tea, Maxie
Frizzell was already in, since it was early-closing day. He
was sitting in the breakfast nook, a copy of the *Tollemarche
Advent*, open at a page of advertisements dealing with cars,
spread out in front of him, a cup of instant coffee in his
hand. His overcoat and fur hat were neatly hung up in the
hall and his overboots reposed on the boot tray in the back
sunroom. Maxie was no believer in courting trouble – his
wife nagged enough without adding to it.

He looked up when Donna Frizzell came in through the
back door, and was startled to see that her hat was awry and
her makeup smudged beyond repair. Unbelievable as it
seemed to him, she almost looked as if she had been crying.

He got up as quickly as the tight fit of the table in the
breakfast nook would allow. He'd bet twenty dollars she'd
had a fender bender and that the car looked like a
concertina.

'Had an accident, Donna?'

'No. Only another parking ticket.' She sniffed as she put
down the parcel of books and took off her gloves, and
sniffed again as Maxie sank back on his bench, relieved that
his beautiful black Cadillac was intact. He looked at her
uneasily, however. Something had happened. Donna was
far too tough to cry, he reckoned, and yet it looked
suspiciously as if that was what she was about to do.

He turned the page of the newspaper and then asked
carefully: 'Anything wrong?'

She sat down on the bench opposite to him and looked at
his fat baby face, which was now showing some concern.
Then she put her head down on the table and wept
unrestrainedly, the feathers of her hat dipping unnoticed
into his coffee.

He was bewildered and did not know what to do. 'For

heaven's sakes!' he exclaimed, shocked to find that his wife, usually acidly in command of herself and of anyone else who came near her, could possibly be reduced to tears.

'What happened?' he asked warily.

He was answered by another loud sob and a gesture towards the untidy parcel which she had brought in. He again eased himself out of the narrow space of the breakfast nook and went over to the kitchen counter, looked at the parcel and looked at his wife, who was now almost hysterical. He decided that he must be courageous and investigate, so he unwound the paper towels, picked up the books one by one and read their titles. He guessed they were for the morals group, since neither he nor Mrs Frizzell ever really read a book, and he put them down again, still mystified.

He was fond of his wife in an absent-minded way, especially when she was not nagging at him, so he took a Kleenex out of the kitchen box and went back to her, saying rather hopelessly: 'Here, have a Kleenex.'

The sobs lessened and a hand was extended, into which he pressed the tissue. She sat up with a gasp and blew her nose hard; then, since he was close, she rested her aching head against his ample stomach. He put his arm around her shoulders, as he had not done for many years.

'Oh, Maxie,' she said, 'it was real bad.' For once her voice was faint.

She took off her hat and laid it on the table, and he saw with a sense of shock that her hair was white down the line of the parting where the tinting had grown out. She lifted a lined face to him, and he reached over for another Kleenex and smoothed the wetness away, so that she was almost without makeup. He could not remember how long it was since his wife had leaned on him, and he found it pleasant to be the one in charge of the situation.

In a rallying tone of voice, usually reserved for meetings with his salesmen, he said: 'Here, I'll make you some coffee and you tell me what happened.'

He busied himself with the electric kettle and a jar of

instant coffee, and in a moment or two put the hot drink in front of her. She was grateful to him for his solicitude and the tale came slowly out.

He listened anxiously because, in such an isolated community, any slur on his wife's character could have its effect on his business. The eleventh Commandment, 'Thou shalt not be found out,' was all-important.

When she had finished and was stirring a saccharine tablet into her coffee, he sat silent for a while, his little eyes half closed, his pursed lips showing that he was thinking hard. The refrigerator hummed its usual little tune to break the silence and Donna drank her coffee.

Finally, he said: 'What you need is publicity.'

Donna looked at him, aghast. 'Publicity! My goodness! Publicity! I've had enough of *that!* I've never been so ashamed in my life.' Her voice was hoarse with indignation.

'Yeah, I mean it. Listen, why don't you ring up the social editor of the *Advent*, and tell her about your meeting tomorrow. Complain that the Committee is not getting the coverage it ought to have for the work it's doing. Just tell her the names of those books and I tell you she'll be right over.' He glanced at the offending literature. 'Seems to me you've got a man-sized job on, judging by that lot.'

Mrs Frizzell immediately saw the relevance of his advice and began to look more like her normal self. 'Yeah,' she said thoughtfully, 'we do work hard.'

Maxie went on: 'Y' see, everyone who was at the tea will keep reading the social pages for the next day or two to see that their names are in the report of it; and, with luck, inside that time, on the same pages there'll be a report about your Morals Committee – then they'll know why you had the books, and old Miss Angus will be put in her place.' He, too, had suffered under Miss Angus's overbearing rule when he was at school, and he did not mind trying to make her look foolish.

Mrs Frizzell's face brightened. 'I'll have to ask Margaret first,' she said. 'She's the secretary and does the publicity.'

'Let her ask the *Advent*. It'll sound more official.' He

said this in his firm business voice, not his usually listless home voice, and she accepted his direction as readily as one of his mechanics would have done.

Mrs Frizzell felt a reluctant admiration for her husband swelling up in her. He was not quite such a dumbhead as one would think. Her name would probably appear in the newspaper twice within two days, since she was to deliver the main report to the Morals Committee; and that should really impress both friends and enemies.

The feathers of her hat were again sitting in the dregs of Maxie's coffee, so she hastily retrieved it and looked mournfully at the damaged plumage. 'I sure need a new outfit,' she said absently and without hope.

'Well, go and buy one,' Maxie said expansively. 'We're going to hafta give a big coffee party for the auto buyer from Henderson and Company, so make it a nice one.'

Mrs Frizzell swivelled round to face him. 'How much?' she asked distrustfully.

'What about a hundred dollars?'

Mrs Frizzell was immediately suspicious. To get so much sympathy and then to get a handout as soon as she asked for it, was unnerving. What had he been doing?

She regarded him steadily for a minute with eyes still bloodshot from crying. But he was beaming at her innocently, glad to see that she was feeling better.

'O.K.,' she said, a note of doubt in her voice. 'Is the garage doing all right?'

'Sure. That's why you can have a hundred dollars.'

She breathed a little more easily. He needn't think he was going to be allowed to wander. He had married her and he was going to stay married, and no nonsense about other women and buying her off with unexpected handouts.

She clicked her false teeth together, and announced with something of the normal snap in her voice that she was going to call Margaret right now. Then she would glance through the books she had bought, because she had to make a report on them. And would she ever roast that bookseller, old Mr Pascall!

The telephone call was made, and Margaret, heard amid the distant screams of children quarrelling, gushed that it was a darling idea and she would telephone the *Advent* herself, since she knew the women's editor well. Mrs Frizzell had carefully cultivated her, too, but she let it pass, while Margaret complained that all four children had the measles and that she was going to have to leave them alone if the babysitter did not come soon; she was not going to miss the dance at the Pinetree Club for worlds, and was dear Donna coming?

Dear Donna said virtuously that she had to write her report, and disentangled herself from the conversation before she was asked to babysit.

She disinterred two frozen TV dinners from the big freezer in the basement and put them into the oven to heat. Then she settled down at the dining-room table with her book purchases, which she had picked at random from the shelves of Tollemarche's only book store and from the racks of one of the cigar stores. She had also a sheet of paper and a ball pen, ready for action.

Before looking at the books, she wrote: 'The teenagers of Tollemarche must be protected from obscenity and smut.' That should shake the audience to attention, she thought, as she picked up the first book.

She ran through the first few pages of each of the paperbacks, her mouth falling open as she read. Really, the ideas that some people had! Sex and sin were, to her, synonymous, and she wondered how on earth she was going to convey tastefully to her audience how much sin was in these volumes.

She pushed her glasses back up her nose, clamped her mouth shut firmly, and picked up the hard-backed novel, which had cost six dollars and fifty cents of the Committee's small funds.

On the front of the jacket a naked young girl was spread languidly on her stomach on a seashore, nothing of her anatomy being left to the imagination. Embarrassed, Mrs Frizzell turned hastily to the back, where rave notices from several New York papers greeted her. She opened the back of the book, and found a heading on the fold-in part of the jacket which announced that this section was 'About the Author'. This time her mouth fell open so fast that she nearly lost her top dentures. It was unbelievable, yet there it was, clearly printed: 'The author, aged nineteen, was born in Tollemarche, Alberta, where he still resides . . .' This was followed by four or five lines about the book being a miraculous first novel, etc., most of which Mrs Frizzell failed to take in.

She leaned back in her chair whistling softly under her breath, then remembered that it was vulgar for a woman to whistle. She drummed her fingers on the Canadian maple table instead. It surprised her that Mr Pascall had not used for publicity purposes the fact that the author was from Tollemarche. Then she realized that books were really only a sideline to his stationery business; he sold more birthday cards than books. Even the advent of the university had not done much to increase his sales, she considered shrewdly, since she could not recall seeing a single bookshelf in any of the homes of university staff which she had visited. Probably the old man would announce in his window the book's importance to Tollemarche, next time he changed the display. Or perhaps he wouldn't, she amended, since the exhibition of the jacket itself would be enough to send Tollemarche into an uproar of complaints.

As far as Mrs Frizzell knew, apart from a book on local fish written by an ardent fly fisherman on the university staff, this was the first book to come out of Tollemarche. And it had been written, apparently, by some boy just out of high school, for heaven's sakes.

'Oh, Maxie,' she called. She knew that Maxie was acquainted with the bulk of the male population of Tollemarche, because anyone looking for a car sooner or later strolled through his car lot.

Maxie withdrew himself reluctantly from the excitement of the football game he was watching on televison. 'Yeah?' he queried.

'Do you know anybody in town called Ben MacLean? A boy?'

'Nope. Lotsa MacLeans. Nobody called Ben. Why?'

Mrs Frizzell did not answer. She went to the telephone table, took out the directory and looked up the name MacLean. There were indeed lots of MacLeans – nearly the whole Clan MacLean, as far as she could judge. Irritably, she slammed it down and went to wash and change, while she considered how she could trace this mysterious boy, this disgusting boy, this juvenile delinquent. Her Committee would teach him a lesson, she promised herself venomously, as she powdered her face.

Of course, all the Committee would want to read the book.

Well, they could wait; she must go through it thoroughly first. It was surely part of her duty to find out what finally happened to the seductive female spread out on the front cover.

CHAPTER ELEVEN

The Committee for the Preservation of Morals was to meet at the house of Mrs Murphy, the wife of the Mayor. It was a large split-level home, with unexpected staircases going, it seemed, in all directions, their wrought-iron banisters standing out against the pale-yellow broadloom which covered both stairs and floors throughout the house. The picture windows, thought Mrs Stych, were larger than any other picture windows in Tollemarche, and the huge brick fireplace in the living-room was festooned with real antique brass ornaments, ranging from a warming pan, top left, to a set of horse brasses, bottom right. The two square yards of broadloom devoted to the open hallway were almost blocked by a large bamboo plant, made of plastic, which waved majestically over a little fountain cascading water over two plastic shell-shaped basins which miraculously never overflowed.

Mrs Stych noted carefully all the '*day*core', as she called it, while she removed her coat and gave it to Mrs Murphy to hang up. Soon she would herself be in the market for a new home, and, though she and Boyd could not hope to out-do a contractor like the Mayor building for himself, she could pick up a few ideas and have them incorporated into their new house in Vanier Heights. She knew that in a couple of days' time Boyd's promotion would be announced by his company in the newspaper, underneath a studio portrait of him, and she held her head high as she swayed gracefully into the living-room. Since a few ladies who had been at the tea would also be at the committee meeting, and, anyway, Boyd had messed up her best black afternoon dress, she wore now a pretty gown in green wool which she had picked up in the last sale at Eaton's. As it was after six o'clock, and, according to her much thumbed book of etiquette, a lady might glitter after that hour, she wore long *diamanté* earrings. The result was, in the eyes of the ladies present, very glamorous indeed, and they were nice enough to tell her so. She simpered, and took her place on one of the enormous chesterfields flanking the fireplace, sitting next to Mrs Moore, the dentist's wife, mother of Hank's dead friend Tony. Mr Moore had recently discovered how lucrative preventive dentistry could be, and Mrs Moore was dressed accordingly.

Mrs Murphy had moved a coffee table to the centre of the room and grouped four chairs round it, for the use of the officials of the committee. She was a large woman, flushed with the exertion of constantly having to answer the door, and she still showed in her black hair, grey eyes and lovely skin, traces of her Irish forebears. She found the responsibility of being the Mayor's wife almost too much for her, and was in a constant flutter for fear she forgot something in connection with the entertainment of the steady procession of guests, important to Tollemarche, who filed through her home. She need not have worried, however, for her good nature and naturally hospitable manner covered up any small deficiencies in deportment.

Tonight she was to chair the meeting, so she left the front door unlocked for any late-comers, and, having seated the nervous little reporter from the *Advent* in a position where she could see and hear all the ladies present, giving her at the same time a hastily written list of the names of those expected to attend, she called the meeting to order. As she raised her little hammer to tap on the table, she wondered suddenly why the *Advent* had actually sent a reporter — they usually depended on the publicity secretary to supply them with a report. However, the recording secretary was waiting with the minutes of the last meeting, and Mrs Murphy announced her.

Donna Frizzel, angular in dark brown, sat as secretary of the committee, with the president, chairman and treasurer, while the lesser fry made their reports. She had a thin, satisfied smile on her face, which not even a few smirks and elbow nudgings among those ladies who had been at the tea could banish. She wished that the *Advent* had sent a more experienced reporter. This girl looked as if she was on her first assignment, as she sat with pencil poised over her shorthand notebook. However, she would probably be very careful over names, and that was what Mrs Frizzell wanted.

Mrs Stych's mind wandered as the voices droned on and the current film at the local drive-in cinema was condemned. She was thinking about a telephone call which she had answered just as she was about to leave the house. The call had been for Hank, and had been from one of his classmates, who said that he just wanted to inquire how Hank was. Mrs Stych, in a frantic hurry, had said that he was out but that he was fine, just fine. The caller had sounded a little bewildered, but had said that he was glad to hear it and would telephone again sometime.

Now Mrs Stych was puzzled. Why hadn't the stupid boy said he would see Hank in school in the morning?

The treasurer, in sharp, clipped tones, was listing the committee's various expenditures and was bringing to the attention of the members the fact that there was only twenty dollars in hand. Mrs Stych forced herself to attend, and the little reporter's pencil sped across the page.

Finally, Mrs Frizzell rose to make her report. She hitched her skirt down surreptitiously, cleared her throat, arranged her sample books in a neat pile in front of her, and then, fixing her audience with an angry glare, she began.

'The teenagers of Tollemarche must be protected from obscenity and smut!' she announced dramatically.

There was an immediate murmur of approval, though some of the ladies looked longingly at the lavishly laid tea table just visible in the dining alcove.

'They must be defended, it appears, from their own neighbours!'

It was as if an electric shock had gone through the gathering. Heads snapped round towards Mrs Frizzell. From their neighbours?

Mrs Frizzell's voice sank. 'Yes,' she hissed, 'from their own neighbours.'

She picked up *The Cheaper Sex* with the tips of her bony, scarlet-nailed fingers.

'This!' She paused for effect. 'This shameless piece of pornography was written in Tollemarche by one of our own teenagers. Undoubtedly his parents must have known about it, and that makes it doubly shameful.'

Twenty-four pairs of painted lips let out long-drawn gasps and then broke into speech. Questions poured towards the chair, and Mrs Murphy banged her gavel so hard on the coffee table that it left a mark, which distressed her so much that she forgot for a moment why she was hammering and stared sadly at the dent in the wood.

She recovered herself quickly, however, and cried: 'Order! Order, please! Ladies! One at a time. Mrs Davis.' She gestured with her gavel towards a doctor's wife, whose elaborately casual tweed suit proclaimed her husband's earning power.

Mrs Davis had been a nurse and her cold, crisp voice rose above the clamour. 'We should like to know who wrote the book and who published it.'

The voice had the effect for which Mrs Murphy had hoped. There was immediate silence and eager attention.

Mrs Frizzell surveyed the gathering exultantly. She wished passionately that she knew who Ben MacLean was. But this was her moment, she felt. She would never again have so much rapt attention focused upon her, and she stood silent, until one lady, younger than most of those present, started to rummage in her handbag for a cigarette.

'The name of the author is . . . Ben MacLean, the publisher a firm in New York.'

Conversation immediately broke out again, while each lady tried to recollect all the MacLeans that she knew. Mrs Murphy banged with her gavel, rather more cautiously this time. 'Ladies, please!'

A thin streak of a woman bobbed up at the back. 'What are we going to do about it?'

The voice of the doctor's wife rose above the hubbub. 'Have you read the book?'

Silence again. Everyone looked expectantly at Mrs Frizzell.

Mrs Frizzell went a little pink. She hesitated, and then said: 'Not all of it. I – er – um . . .'

Several ladies turned sharply on Mrs Davis, who was far too efficient in everything she did. 'Be reasonable, Hester. She wouldn't like to read a thing like that.'

'How else would she know it's a thing like that?' retorted Hester, unabashed.

'The first chapter was enough,' snapped Mrs Frizzell indignantly, glad that she did not have to explain that she did not give much time to reading.

Mrs Murphy snatched the opportunity to ask Mrs Frizzell to proceed with her report, which she did, outlining the story as far as she knew it and using as many euphemisms as she could. The name of the author was evidently a pseudonym, but it was hoped that the committee would take steps to find out who he was, would decide what should be done to clean this canker out of Tollemarche, and would take more steps to curb their local bookseller's and cigar stores' choice of books. She omitted to mention that, when they last made representations to the bookseller, Mr Pascall, he had said that he stocked the books he could sell; and if the ladies wanted him to sell better books they should take to buying them and reading them, instead of watching televison all day. Then he might be able to improve the quality of his stock.

Mrs Frizzell, having run out of steps, sat down.

'What are we going to do about it?' asked Hester Davis again, through a haze of cigarette smoke.

Handbags were snapped shut, legs were crossed and uncrossed, ladies leaned forward confidentially to their neighbours, ostensibly to confer, though a number got fits of giggles and had to hide their faces behind their hands. Mrs Frizzell gazed into space and Mrs Murphy smoothed back errant curls from her damp forehead. Almost all the ladies silently decided to go downtown the next morning and buy a copy of *The Cheaper Sex*. Each justified her interest in such a vulgar book by telling herself that in these matters one must be able to judge for oneself.

The little reporter realized suddenly that she had a real story for her editor and went pale with fear as she remembered that lady's ruthless slashing up of her last offering, the report of an insignificant wedding. She shivered and watched Mrs Frizzell apprehensively as the buzz of conversation continued.

Mrs Murphy threw the meeting open for discussion since discussion was already in full flood and refused to be dammed, and wondered if the coffee, left on a low gas in the kitchen, had started to perk yet.

A blonde lady, with bouffant hair above a heavily lined, over-powdered face, addressed the chair. Why, she asked, didn't they form a small subcommittee to inquire into the identity of this young author, and, when they had discovered it, they could report back to the rest of the members, and they could then discuss what action should be taken.

This suggestion met with immediate approval. The ladies were thirsty and wanted something to drink. Agreement on this suggestion would bring the meeting to a close, and most of those present would not have to do anything at all about the wretched book.

The motion was formally put to the meeting and seconded. The blonde lady, Mrs Johnson, whose daughter Hank regarded as little better than a streetwalker, found herself appointed chairman of the subcommittee, and she asked if Mrs Stych and the president, the hawk-faced wife of a real estate man, would serve with her.

Mrs Stych protested coyly that she did not know enough about books to be of any use, while she wondered privately how she was going to fit this new commitment into her already overcrowded schedule of social events. What about Mrs Frizzell? she suggested hopefully. Mrs Davis pointed out tartly that Mrs Stych was not at present serving on any of their other subcommittees, and that she must do something to help. Mrs Stych snapped back that all the ladies present must be well aware of the multitude of offices she held in the charitable organizations of Tollemarche. The ladies murmured reluctant agreement, since most of them had at one time or another tried to oust her from at least one of the appointments which they themselves coveted.

With a delicate sniff in the direction of a slightly cowed Hester Davis, Mrs Stych enrolled herself as a sleuth in search of an author.

The date of the next meeting was agreed upon, as a delicious odour of coffee began to permeate the room, and the ladies rose expectantly and looked towards the dining alcove.

Mrs Murphy had made brownies again, and the faces of some of the ladies fell. Mrs Stych, however, nibbled appreciatively at one of the chocolate morsels, while Mrs Johnson, who had no real idea how to trace an author, outlined a plan of campaign so huge that it would have confused an entire army staff, never mind Mrs Stych.

Did Mrs Johnson spell her name with a *t*? asked the little reporter.

Mrs Johnson said 'No!' indignantly, and Mrs Stych woke up and checked that the girl had her name down correctly, too. She began to take an interest in the Sleuthing Committee. She felt that having her name mentioned more frequently than ever in the social columns was highly desirable for the wife of a company director. She smiled dazzlingly at the little reporter and hoped that she would be referred to as 'charming'.

CHAPTER TWELVE

The women's editor of the *Tollemarche Advent*, having found nothing about Ben MacLean in the office files, decided that the quickest source of information regarding Tollemarche's first author would probably be Mr Pascall, the bookseller. She therefore telephoned him.

Old Mr Pascall saw no reason why he should make life easy for a gossiping female and made her hold on, while he sold two ballpoint pens and a packet of rubber bands.

'It's some high school kid called Henry Stych,' he finally wheezed down the telephone. 'Salesman did tell me sumpin' about a kid from here writing it but I forgot.

'Professor MacFee was in the other day – asked me to order him a copy. Told me the kid's name was Henry Stych. I asked him why the kid didn't use his own name, and he said maybe he thought Ben MacLean sorta sounded better.

'Want me to order you a copy? I sold the two I had.'

The editor ground her teeth. 'No, thanks. Which high school?'

A small girl was messing about with the birthday cards in Mr Pascall's shop. He felt he had wasted enough time on the editor, and replied with asperity: 'How should I know? There're only two high schools, aren't there – public and separate. Ring 'em up, can't you?' He slammed down the receiver and fled to the rescue of his birthday cards.

The editor put the receiver slowly back on to its rest.

Stych! That was interesting. She wondered if the boy was any relation to Mrs Olga Stych. Very thoughtfully, she turned to the telephone directory and looked up the name. Seven Styches were listed. She checked her file again and found that Olga's husband's first name was Boyd. There was no mention of any children.

Olga Stych had a vicious tongue and would not hesitate to use it, if she was mistaken in thinking there was a relationship. It would undoubtedly be wiser to establish the young author's identity and then, if he proved to be Mrs Stych's son, perhaps have a quiet word with the boy first. Since the book seemed to be one that would cause some controversy, she had better proceed with caution.

Her mind made up, she picked up the receiver and dialled the number of the separate school.

The separate school had no Henry Stych on its roll, and the school secretary was left in a state of agonized curiosity at the *Advent*'s interest in such a person.

The principal of the public high school happened to pick up the telephone himself.

Yes, he knew Henry Stych, and, yes, he knew of *The Cheaper Sex*; he had confiscated a copy of it from a Grade 10 child only this morning. Henry Stych had *what*? Written it? Ridiculous!

The editor said she felt sure her information was correct, and could she have Henry's address and telephone number?

The principal was immediately cautious and warned her that the boy was under age. He suggested she should contact the father, Boyd Stych, and he gave the parents' home telephone number, feeling that she would soon trace it anyway.

Deeply concerned, he pressed the intercom buzzer and asked Mr Dixon, Hank's home-room teacher, to report to him without delay.

Mrs Stych had just got up and was still in her dressing-gown when she answered the telephone call from the *Advent*. Hank and Boyd had found their own cornflakes and coffee and had long since departed.

The editor asked for Mr Henry Stych. Mrs Stych faltered for a moment and then realized that she meant Hank.

She said gaily: 'The story isn't about Hank – it's about my husband, Boyd.'

The editor knew nothing of the story of Boyd's promotion, about to be featured in the financial section, and she said firmly that it was Henry she wanted.

Mrs Stych did not want to offend the queen of the social columns by arguing with her, so when that lady went on to inquire when the newspaper could send a photographer, Mrs Stych said in her most gracious tone of voice that the whole family would be at home that evening any time after six.

She rang off, happy that the *Advent* was taking such an interest in Boyd's directorship, finished her coffee and went to take her morning shower. It was only then, with the water trickling down her plump back, that an uncomfortably cold premonition seemed to trickle down, too. Had the Editor really meant Hank, and, if so, what had Hank been up to?

She pulled herself up firmly. If Hank had done something particularly dreadful, either Donna Frizzell or some other nosey parker would have been on her doorstep by now to tell her about it. It *must* be about Boyd.

As requested by Mrs Johnson of the Committee for the Preservation of Morals, she drove out to the library, with the intention of asking the chief librarian for information about Ben MacLean, but when she arrived he had gone out for morning coffee. His languid part-time assistant could not have cared less about books or authors, local or other; she supposed that there was a copy of the book in the new-fiction section.

Mrs Stych sailed majestically to the bookcase indicated, and found the offending volume almost immediately. She had not looked at Mrs Frizzell's copy, so this was her first glimpse of it. Before picking it out, she looked over her shoulder to make sure that no one was looking at her. There was only one person nearby, an elderly gentleman immersed in back copies of the *Edmonton Journal*, so she slipped the book out.

The sultry female depicted on the front shocked her. What a position to lie in – it was indecent! No wonder Donna had been upset. She read the summary of the story and the gushing praise of the New York critics, quoted on the jacket. Finally she turned the book over and read the brief notes about the author; and her deep unease of earlier that morning returned, but she crushed it down.

She read the first two pages and felt a blush rise from her palpitating bosom up her neck to suffuse her face. For heaven's sakes, did girls really do such things? Fancy the library allowing such a book on their shelves! She hastily returned it to its place, and in a state of some agitation went back to her car and sat there until she felt calm again.

She started the car with a jerk and hit the bumper of the car in front. Flustered, she reversed, and the groceries she had bought en route fell off the back seat and flopped to the floor. Damn that book! With painful care she eased the car out of its parking place and into the flow of traffic.

The cover said a high school boy. But what could a kid know about such goings-on as were chronicled in the pages she had read? What *did* a present-day high school boy know?

It came to her as a shock that, although she had an excellent opportunity to be acquainted with high school children through her son, she did not know any of his friends. With a burst of self-pity, she mentally reviled Hank for never talking to her or telling her what he was going to do. He never brought his friends to the house and she had never known where he spent his spare time. What *did* he do, other than ride around in his jalopy and sometimes help out in the supermarket?

As she manoeuvred the car through the traffic, the cold feeling which had menaced her earlier returned to plague her.

She tried to brush aside memories of the eager, tiny child that Hank had been, a child who had adored his ugly, heavy-footed Ukrainian grandfather, a child who had screamed with rage at her when she had thrust him into the arms of an unknown babysitter or had forced him to play alone in the basement, until he became a silent, morose schoolboy. Meanwhile, she had pursued personal aggrandizement at his expense, a whisper of conscience hinted, until he had learned that he was nothing but a nuisance to her.

The memories persisted, until she had worked herself into a peevish bout of self-pity, which was not improved by her discovery when she reached home that Hank had not shovelled the snow off the front walk before leaving for school. The snow would certainly invade the tops of her boots when she stepped out of the car, and she swore softly in Ruthenian as she retrieved the groceries from the floor of the car and turned to carry them into the house.

She had just slammed the car door by hooking it with one foot, when Mrs Frizzell, with a similar brown-paper bag of groceries, came round the nearest corner on foot, having been to the local store.

'Mornin', Olga,' she shouted as she scuttled towards her, a pair of rollers in the front of her hair sticking out like devil's horns from under her woollen hat. 'Where've you been?'

'Library,' said Mrs Stych shortly as she staggered through the snow towards her house.

Mrs Frizzell's face brightened. 'About the book?'

'Yeah,' replied Mrs Stych with an involuntary shudder. She suddenly recollected that she was now the wife of the director of a large company, and drew herself up with what she hoped was some dignity; but she only succeeded in looking more than ever like a pouter pigeon. 'Librarian had gone to coffee.'

'I'd like to know who wrote it,' said Mrs Frizzell wistfully.

Mrs Stych put her nose in the air, and said: 'We shall have the name in a day or two.'

Mrs Frizzell surveyed her neighbour speculatively. Olga seemed to be more patronizing than ever today. She was now looking round at both their houses distastefully, though the houses looked the same as usual, snow on the roofs, snow a foot deep over the yards, snow poised on every twig and leaf, a cloud from the central-heating chimney hovering calmly over each residence.

Mrs Stych had temporarily forgotten about Hank. 'I'll be glad to leave this house,' she said carefully.

Mrs Frizzell's nose quivered as she caught the scent of change.

'Leave it?'

'Yeah. Probably next fall. We're going to build in Vanier Heights.'

The effect of this announcement on Mrs Frizzell was all that Mrs Stych could have desired. The bounce went out of her as if she had burst. Envy sprang into her hard little eyes and gleamed maliciously. She stood rooted to the sidewalk, her mind a whirl of dislike. Vanier Heights? She could have cried. Why hadn't Maxie thought of building a new house there, the old stick in the mud?

She took two or three large breaths over the top of her bag of groceries, while Mrs Stych watched her stupefaction with complacency. She had, however, underestimated Donna Frizzell's powers of recovery. Between gritted teeth, Donna asked innocently: 'Isn't that a bit old-fashioned? We are thinking of buying a small estate outside the city, three or four acres, so that we could have a real nice ranch-type bungalow – and keep some riding horses.' The last was an inspired idea, a riding horse with an acreage to keep it on being quite a status symbol.

Mrs Stych licked her lips. 'Oh, no!' she drawled, determined not to be outdone, as she moved towards her front door. 'We wouldn't like to be far from town – we like culture – and horses smell so.'

Mrs Frizzell reminded herself that murder was not civilized.

Not trusting herself to speak, she right-wheeled and made for her own front door, which now looked hopelessly out of date and shabby. She would get to work on Maxie just as soon as his presence at home should coincide with hers; she had not seen him since returning from the tea, except when crawling wearily into bed.

'Let him just show his face,' she muttered darkly.

CHAPTER THIRTEEN

While his mother and Donna Frizzell sparred in front of their respective homes, Hank laboured in Isobel Dawson's garage. The day was overcast and it was becoming difficult to see what he was typing, so, about noon, when imagination began to fail him, he walked up to the house to inquire from Dorothy whether Isobel would mind if he had better lighting installed in the garage, provided he paid for it. The door was opened unexpectedly by Isobel herself. She was in a housedress and held a duster in her hand. She greeted Hank cheerily.

Hank looked nonplussed, and then asked, rather foolishly: 'Aren't you at work?'

'No. The boss went to Calgary and gave me the day off.' Hospitably, she opened the door wider. 'You'd better come in, it's cold out there.'

He entered gratefully. A strong smell of floor polish pervaded the house and the kitchen was in chaos, its furniture piled in the middle and a vacuum cleaner cord snaking round it to a hidden plug.

She apologized for the muddle and ushered him into the living-room. She gestured towards the chesterfield. 'Sit down. What can I do for you?'

He sat down, feeling somewhat shy in the midst of so much domestic activity, while she knelt and lit the gas fire. 'Canadians are always cold in this house,' she remarked in explanation. 'I don't keep it so hot as they keep theirs.

'Well?' she asked, as she got up off her knees.

Pretty legs, thought Hank, as he explained about the lighting in the garage.

Instead of giving the immediate agreement which he had expected, she said: 'Let's have some coffee. We'd better talk the whole thing over.'

Though he was a little surprised, he smiled and said with

109

alacrity that he could just use a cup of coffee, and he lounged after her as she bustled around the kitchen. She was unlike anybody else he had ever met and secretly he found her intriguing. Today, dressed like a housewife, she looked more human than usual, less distantly dignified. He wondered how he had found sufficient courage to ask her to the Edwardian Ball, and then remembered that it was her air of calm dignity which had made him anxious to take her to impress his parents.

'Where's Dorothy?' he asked.

'She's gone for a skiing lesson – she wants to learn before going home.' She wondered idly if Hank was interested in Dorothy, and the idea made her feel a little forlorn.

She lifted a cup and saucer in each hand, and he took one from her. His fingers touched hers and his heart gave a jolt, but she seemed perfectly in command of herself and had apparently felt nothing, so he told himself not to be a dope, and carried his coffee back to the chesterfield. He stirred it silently, as she settled herself in a rocking-chair opposite to him.

When he looked up at her, he found her regarding him with a troubled frown over the rim of her coffee cup. It seemed to him that in her gentle gaze there was more than a hint of despair, and it grieved him.

'The thing is,' she said, after a moment's hesitation, 'that I am going to sell this house.'

Hank nearly dropped his cup, as his brand-new writing world splintered into pieces around him. 'S-sell?' he stuttered.

'Yes,' she replied, her voice trembling a little. 'I'm going home.'

Hank was thoroughly disquieted. He was still young enough to feel that the present was permanent. Shut up in her garage, his work approved of and praised by her, comforted by Captain Dawson's and her advice, which had in all respects proved reliable, he had felt a safety and confidence unknown to him before. Even now that his father was aware of his activities, it would not be the same;

only she knew the appalling effort he had made, only she had read the manuscript through and appreciated the clarity of his prose and the honesty of his outlook. He had expected that any change in his routine would have been of his own making, not hers.

She was waiting for him to make some reply, and he said slowly: 'I guess you must be homesick, now Captain Dawson isn't here.'

'Well, yes. He wasn't here very much, as you know, but we were looking forward to the end of his army service and then we would have settled here.' She looked sober, and then added: 'I might as well go home – there's nothing to keep me here. My in-laws have other children, and it's always easier in one's own country.'

'I guess your parents will be glad to see you,' he remarked.

'They're dead. They were killed in an accident just before I was married – Peter was my father's friend.'

'Peter must have been a lot older than you?' ventured Hank.

She was not offended at the personal question, but her voice held a trace of surprise in it as she said: 'Yes, he was. He was at school with my father. You see, Father was actually born in Alberta – his parents came here from Wales – but when he was a young man he went back to visit, and fell in love with my mother and with Wales as well, and stayed there.' She smiled and ran her finger around the top of her coffee cup. 'Father always kept in touch with Peter and he planned to come and see us when he got leave from France, where he was stationed. As it turned out, he only came for the funeral.'

Hank was interested. He had heard of girls marrying a father substitute, but he had not met one before. He did not wish to make her unhappy by any further probing after such a flow of confidences, so he just asked her which city in England she came from, this being a question all immigrants were accustomed to.

'I don't come from England – I'm Welsh, from Caer-narvon.'

He failed to realize the difference and his blank expression made her smile. 'Wales and the Welsh are quite different from England and the English,' she said. 'Being Welsh is a bit like – well, like being a French Canadian. I'm going back to my old employers in London, though.'

'I suppose I'd better find another garage,' he said rather hopelessly. Without asking if he could smoke, he quickly took out a cigarette and lit it, and then belatedly offered her one. She was amused at his blunder, but took one from him. He remembered to offer her a light.

He put his coffee cup down on a pile of English magazines, got up and stretched himself. His T-shirt was too small for him and came out of the waist of his pants. The pants themselves were too tight and too short, exhibiting a generous stretch of hairy legs. Isobel stifled a strong desire to laugh.

'I presume you're dressed for school,' she said.

He looked down at himself. 'Yep.'

'Does your mother know about the book yet?'

'No!' he snapped. 'Dad does.'

Isobel asked cautiously: 'Has he read it?'

'Jeepers, no. He don't even know what it's called. Never even asked me.'

He wandered towards the piano and very gently turned the picture of Captain Dawson face down on the top of the instrument. 'Goodbye, fella,' he muttered, but Isobel fortunately did not hear him.

'Do you think he'll mind that it is a rather controversial book?'

Hank sat down on the piano stool and struck a chord. 'It's too late to mind,' he said. 'He should have done a bit of minding years ago.'

'I think you ought to tell your mother.' Isobel's voice was almost imploring. 'She has a right to know, before anybody else tells her.'

Hank broke into the 'Cornish Rhapsody', playing with

such savagery that the little room was flooded with the storm of it. For the first time, Isobel felt a little afraid of him, as all the suppressed fury of a rejected child came pouring out in the music. She sat quietly, however, until the music found its way into calmer waters and then came to an end.

He spun round on the stool so that he could face her. 'Not bad, eh?' he asked, some of the tension gone from his face.

'You are very good,' she said, some of the nervousness receding from her. 'Do you practise much?'

'Most days. Used to practise in the school.' He grinned. 'That left the evenings free to go out, except near exam times.' It dawned on him that he had not had a date for weeks, and his first one would be with her at the Edwardian Ball. Must be going senile, he decided.

'Say,' he said, 'you'd better tell me more precisely about what I am to wear to this ball. We gotta make a hit – let 'em know we've arrived.'

Isobel's face looked suddenly young and animated. 'I'll get the book with the picture in it. I think it'll be fun. I haven't been to a ball since I came to Canada.'

Hank looked at her aghast. 'Honey,' he said, without thinking, 'it's time you started to live it up a bit.'

CHAPTER FOURTEEN

Boyd Stych, looking strangely civilized in a dark business suit and neatly clipped beard, was informed by his wife, when he came home, that the *Advent* was sending a photographer and a reporter to see him this evening and he was not to litter up the lounge – she'd just tidied it.

He grunted guardedly, as he heaved off his overshoes. Though he knew the press would be sending a photographer to take a picture of him for the financial pages of the newspaper, he suspected that their main interest was in Hank. It was not going to be possible to keep from Olga the information that her son had suddenly become quite a well-to-do youngster, though he had warned Hank on no account to tell her how much he had made out of his book. Boyd believed firmly that all women were incurably avaricious and was certain that, once Olga knew about the book, she would try to squeeze most of the proceeds of it out of Hank; and, to his credit, he was determined that this should not happen.

He dropped his briefcase on the chesterfield, and Mrs Stych snatched it up crossly and took it into his den, while he went to the refrigerator in search of ice cubes for a drink. Should he talk to her now, he wondered, or let Hank do it?

'Where's the rye?' he shouted.

'In the bar in the basement – where else?' came the sharp reply.

He went downstairs to the rumpus room and rummaged behind the tiny bar, and, after digging through a seemingly endless collection of empty pop bottles, came up with half a bottle of rye and some ginger ale. He felt he needed a drink – this could be quite a trying evening. Perhaps it was fortunate that he had no inkling of how trying it was going to be.

As he took an eager gulp from his glass, he decided that

114

Hank ought to tell his mother what he had been doing. He rationalized his cowardice by telling himself that, after all, it was Hank's headache, not his.

He wondered idly what sort of tripe Hank had written. Some sort of adventure story, he supposed, which would film well. He must ask him.

Hank drifted silently in through the back door and deposited a pile of school books on the kitchen table and a fair amount of snow on the kitchen floor from his moccasins. He quickly got a corn broom, went out to the back porch again and brushed his footwear clean; then he used the same broom to sweep the snow from the kitchen floor into a safe hiding-place under a scatter rug. No point in drawing fire, he argued, as he put the broom back into the closet.

As he took up his school books again and moved them into his bedroom, he wondered if his father had told his mother about his leaving school. Boyd had not promised to do this, though he had said he would go to see the principal to straighten out the question of his leaving. This promised visit to the school, mused Hank, would be his father's first since he had graduated from it twenty-five years earlier. He had had to ask Hank the name of the principal and what courses he had been taking, since he had never bothered to inquire about these before. So much for parental interest in education, Hank muttered.

He went to the hall table, where the postman usually deposited any mail, in the hope that there might be a letter for him, though most of his mail came via Isobel. He was agreeably surprised to find one from a friend who had joined the Mounties a couple of years previously. It was full of amusing anecdotes about his life as a policeman. For the first time, Hank did not feel a pang of envy at his friend's being already at work; he felt he was doing better than any young policeman could hope to do.

Olga heard him singing in the bathroom and shouted that supper would be ready in a few minutes.

'Put a clean shirt on and comb your hair,' she called.

'Somebody's coming this evening from the *Advent* to see your father.'

Hank stopped singing in mid-bar. Almost certainly, they'd be coming to see him, too. Jeeze, the balloon was about to go up!

'D'yer hear me, Hank?'

'Yeah, Ma.' And he began to hum a funeral march.

The terrible bitterness against his parents that had led to his writing a book meant to shock them had faded into indifference; yet there lingered in him an understandable vindictiveness. He knew he would be happy if, in some way, it taught his mother a salutary lesson, but he could still quail, like a little boy, in anticipation of the violence of her wrath.

At dinner, the hastily prepared steak was tough and Boyd complained about it. Next time Olga bought steak, he said, he would cook it.

Olga Stych was immediately biting about men who dressed up in aprons and fancy hats, and thought they could cook over a smelly barbecue.

'I suppose all the months I was up North you reckoned I had a chef along with me,' snarled Boyd.

Hank hastily finished the store-bought cake which followed the steak, and went to his room. He thought he might as well look over his skiing equipment, instead of listening to his parents snapping at each other. If his mother was already as irritated as she sounded, he decided that the evening would be full of squalls.

He sat down on his bed while he threaded new laces into his boots, and then paused, one lace suspended in his hand, as he wondered suddenly why the wire service had not given the *Advent* any news about him. Then he realized that any such news would be about 'Ben MacLean' and that they would not connect it with him. He chuckled to himself. Probably the paper didn't even have wire service, and if it did, he'd bet a dime that anything which had come in about the book's author had simply been buried in the chaos then reigning in the newspaper office.

The *Advent* had survived for years with a staff of four, plus occasional help from the owner's wife with the reporting of weddings and similar social occasions. Its circulation had grown enormously as immigrants flooded into Tollemarche, and it had expanded into the shops which flanked it on either side. Now, new offices were being built for it on the other side of the road, but they were not quite ready, and meantime, the new publisher from the East and his editors functioned in an atmosphere of such utter confusion that it is doubtful if an efficiency expert could even have fought his way in through the door. Donny O'Brien, the ancient typesetter inherited from the original *Advent*, swore each day that it was only by the grace of God that the paper ever got launched in the taxi which delivered it to the newspaper boys.

Only the queen of the social columns, recruited a couple of years previously from Calgary, sat calmly at her desk, her silver-tipped fingers delicately feeling the pulse of the city's social life. Other editors might make a slip, but let her so much as spell a name wrong and her telephone would blare, and some outraged lady would correct her with withering sarcasm.

She was delighted when the story of Hank fell into her lap; an interview with his mother would fill half a column nicely. Her pleasure was, however, short lived. Like all good stories unearthed by such lady editors, it was snatched away from her, and, barring wars and acts of God, as Donny O'Brien reported to Mr Pascall, the bookseller, it would be a front-page headline on Monday. It was, therefore, no quiet lady columnist to whom Mrs Stych opened the door that evening, but an eager male reporter keen on a front-page story.

He shot through the door almost as soon as it was opened, closely followed by a small, bald-headed individual carrying what looked like a suitcase.

'Hank Stych!' he hailed a startled Boyd, who had half risen from an easy chair, scattering the papers on which he had been working. He wrung Boyd's hand. 'Say, this is

117

great for Tollemarche – really put us on the map.' Then, turning to his companion, he said: 'Pose him against these drapes, Tom.'

Tom hastily opened his case, took out a tripod and set his camera up in the middle of the lounge, while Mrs Stych watched, open-mouthed. Neither visitor had taken the slightest notice of her.

The reporter was saying to Boyd: 'Say, let's have a picture with you reading the manuscript.'

Mrs Stych felt a sudden constriction in her stomach.

The reporter consulted his notes. 'We hafta have a picture of a Mr Boyd Stych as well.'

Tom nodded agreement, and went on rapidly assembling his camera.

Boyd found his voice. 'I'm Boyd Stych.'

The reporter looked up quickly, took in the fact that Boyd's Edwardian Days beard was streaked with grey, and said: 'Say, I am sorry. I sure thought there was a writer hidden behind that beard of yours.'

Boyd hastily bent down to rescue his papers from being trampled. 'The beard is for Edwardian Days,' he said primly.

'Oh, sure, it's a beaut. All ready for tomorrow, eh? You just might win the prize for the best one, at that,' the reporter replied, fingering his own scanty side whiskers.

Mrs Stych listened to this conversation with slowly growing horror. The cold feeling she had experienced that morning crept over her; she remembered the library book, and, with a feeling of panic, recollected Hank's trip to New York. Behind them, she envisaged the faces of the Committee for the Preservation of Morals, as she had last seen them, glistening with almost sadistic anticipation of the crushing of the young author and of giving Mr Pascall and the cigar-store merchants their proper comeuppances.

'I think I'm going to vomit,' she muttered to no one in particular, and sat down with a plop on a new imitation Italian chair, which received her with a reedy groan.

Boyd was calling up the stairs for Hank to come down,

and she watched silently, as if at the movies, while he emerged from his ground-floor bedroom, walked past her without looking at her, and held out his hand to the reporter, who winced as he felt its grip.

'Hi,' said the reporter, wondering if his hand would ever recover.

'Hi,' said Hank. He stared with some scorn at his would-be interviewers, who were some inches shorter than he was. He seemed to fill the room with his contempt for the people present.

'Say, that sure was some book you wrote,' remarked the reporter, to fill the silence. 'Haven't read it myself yet, but I'll get around to it – I sure will.'

Hank's expression was cynical, as he gestured to the man to be seated.

Mrs Stych was thankful for the chair under her, as she felt the colour drain from her face. The lounge rocked in front of her. How could he write such things? she wondered dumbly; how could he know so much about sex, so much about sin? Sin was sex; pride, avarice, gluttony had no place as far as her life was concerned. Only sex was really wrong, only fallen women really burned.

Out of the corner of his eye, Hank could see her stricken face. He felt no pity. When had she ever shown him pity? This was really going to rock her and it would do her good.

'Yes,' he told the reporter, it's called *The Cheaper Sex*.' In response to a further query, he added irritably: 'Sure it's about sex – what else would it be about with a title like that?'

The reporter said soothingly that their reviewer, Professor Shrimp, had given it a lotta praise, and the review would probably be in the arts section, next to the film shows, on Monday.

Mrs Stych whimpered softly and the reporter glanced at her curiously. Queer old bag. What did she think of it?

Mentally, Mrs Stych felt as if she were writhing in her death agonies. The Subcommittee appointed by the Morals girls! How could she face it? And worse, how was she going to face the whole organization when it met? Some of the

119

Morals group were also Queen Bees, some were Daughters of Scotland and strict Presbyterians; the United Church itself – how could she attend it now? It would be all over town that her son wrote pornography. She would never, never, she cried inwardly, as she clutched her handkerchief to her mouth, be able to face the girls again.

Boyd was surprised at the name of his son's book, but, unlike his wife, he had not read any of it, and he supposed that Hank had deliberately chosen a titillating title to help sales. He, therefore, continued a subdued conversation with the photographer, not feeling it in the least necessary to introduce his wife to either visitor.

The reporter snapped a rubber band over his notebook, told Hank he would have rung him about the details of the book but he had not been able to get through. Hank said that was O.K., and the photographer surged forward. The photographs were taken, while Mrs Stych leaned back in her chair, her eyes closed, and chewed her handkerchief savagely; and the camera was quickly returned to its case.

'Must be proud of Hank and Boyd,' said the reporter, pausing on his way to the front door to speak to Mrs Stych for the first time.

Mrs Stych opened her eyes slowly and looked at him as if he had gone mad. Then, with a great effort, she managed to nod her head in vague agreement.

Proud? Mrs Stych wrung her hands behind the reporter's back, and wished passionately she could run home to Mother on the pig farm; she longed suddenly for the smell of hens and milk, for a place where nobody had to keep up appearances or be other than what they were. Why had she ever come to town to get herself an education? Why had she married a dirty type like Boyd, to spawn a boy like Hank, who had never been anything but a damned nuisance to her?

She glared at Hank as he stood by the front door ready to open it for the paper's representatives, and tried not to scream while these gentlemen put on their boots again.

In twenty seconds more they were gone, to the sound of

120

spinning wheels on the ice and grinding gears. And she was left with the shattered remains of all that she had found dear in her life, and two extraordinarily sheepish-looking men.

She suddenly regained the initiative of which shock had left her temporarily bereft, and shot from her chair like a well-punted football. Arms akimbo, her face still white under her heavy makeup, she snarled: 'Will one of you please explain what's been going on behind my back?'

The silence was painful.

She rounded on Hank and screamed: 'You great, dirty slob – wotcha done?'

CHAPTER FIFTEEN

When Boyd was a child of eight, he and his father had had to sit out a tornado while visiting a German friend who had settled in Kansas. Boyd was reminded of the howling noise of that fearful storm by his wife's tantrum.

He and Hank were upbraided, reviled and screamed at, until, without uttering a word in retaliation, Hank took his jacket out of the hall alcove and strode silently out of the front door, followed by a shriek from his mother that he was as disgusting as his father; like father, like son.

Gone to his widow, ruminated Boyd enviously, and wished he had a friendly widow, too.

It had taken him only a few moments to discover, from his wife's tirade, that Hank's book was not quite so innocent as he had imagined; however, any book that made so much money was a good book, in his opinion, and he had defended Hank hotly.

Hank had made no attempt to defend himself. He had stood quietly swaying himself on his heels, an almost derisive expression in the curl of his lips as he smoked a cigarette, his very silence provoking her to further abuse.

He used to do that when he was small, remembered Boyd; it had been unnerving, wondering what he was thinking about while you shouted at him. He had never cried when he was struck, and Boyd felt with a desolate pang that probably the boy was wiser and braver than he was. It was only too apparent, as Olga tore into him about the disgrace she would suffer, that, like a hippie, he cared nothing for the kind of life his parents led; he did not share their values or ambitions. His quiet retreat through the front door had somehow emphasized his scorn.

The crack about his being disgusting like his father, had hurt Boyd. It was apparent from his wife's continuing rampage that much pent-up animosity against her husband was coming out, and the crash of a glass ornament warned him that there was probably more to come.

He knew that she had not enjoyed his homecoming or the renewal of a sexual life; throughout their married life he had been at home for only a few weeks at a time, and she had been free to make her life as she chose. She had chosen, he reflected aggrievedly, to ignore him as far as possible.

The directorship, for which he had struggled for years, represented to her only a house in Vanier Heights. Didn't he or Hank matter to her at all? He stroked his beard and then scratched irritably through it. He knew the answers to his questions very well; all too many men were relegated to the position of drone – and they resented it; they showed their resentment all too often by despising women and taking the attitude that such inept creatures should be allowed to play while men ran the world and did anything in it which was worth doing. He had taken this attitude himself, but was finding it very uncomfortable to maintain, after his long years of quiet in the bush, untroubled by anything worse than wind or weather. He laughed ruefully and his wife whipped round at him.

'You laughing at me?' she demanded belligerently.

He looked up at her, as she swooped towards him like a sparrow hawk. Her face was distorted with rage, a horrible clown's face painted red and white, her body a red tub supported by nyloned legs.

He jumped up and shouted at her sharply: 'Oh, shut up!'

'I won't!' she yelled.

He slapped her soundly across the face twice.

She shrieked at the sting of the blows, which left a red mark down one side of her face. Then she was silent, staring at him with horrified eyes. He had never struck her before. The horror gave way slowly to self-pity, the blue eyes filled with tears and she began to weep, the tears making runnels down her heavy makeup.

'For Pete's sake!' he muttered moodily, and shoved his hands in his pockets and went to stare into the empty fireplace.

'You don't understand,' she sobbed. 'You never did understand anything.' She fumbled feverishly in a fancy box on the table for a paper handkerchief. 'How I am going to face the girls at the ball tomorrow? It's all right for a man; men are used to smutty books and vulgar jokes – women don't go for things like that.'

She collapsed on the chesterfield and tried to bury her face in one of the stony little cushions that decorated it.

Boyd frowned down on her. 'Don't you tell me that! Bet that Pascall sells more of Hank's book to women than he ever will to men.'

He hoped that he was right in this belief. For the first time, he considered seriously his own situation with regard to his son's career, both present and future, and he felt uneasy. He could visualize the sniggers of his subordinates. A new director, responsible for a large section of the company's business for the first time, was not in a particularly enviable position; there were men equally as bright and considerably younger, poised ready to pull the mat from under him as soon as they saw an opportunity; Hank could be their chance. He picked up the piece of ornamental driftwood from the mantelpiece and tried to stand it upside down, while he considered this, and his wife's sobs slowly diminished. He felt miserably lonely.

He became aware that Olga was quiet at last, exhausted beyond words. He turned and looked down at her.

Her face was still turned into the cushion, her dress twisted tightly round her generous curves, the skirt hitched up and exposing her plump, well-shaped legs. He smiled suddenly at her tiny feet encased in shiny, high-heeled pumps. Olga had always loved clothes, and he wondered for whose benefit she dressed; probably for that godforsaken bunch of old hags, the girls. His face clouded again at the thought. This was not the way he had hoped life would be when he had married her. He had believed that a country girl like her would find him wonderful, a college man with great ambitions. Their life was going to be different from those of the married couples around them, he had promised himself.

He wanted badly to creep into her arms and be told he had done marvellously well, that she had put on her red dress and her new pumps specially for him, for his seduction. His loneliness, far worse than anything suffered in the empty north country, overwhelmed him and became intolerable.

He took a hesitant step towards the chesterfield. She did not move, though she must have heard him, so he sat down tentatively beside her. She whimpered and wriggled further into the chesterfield's cushiony depths. If he was to get anywhere, he told himself reluctantly, he would have to do the comforting.

'What are you going to wear tomorrow night?' he asked, with a burst of sheer genius.

She slowly looked round at him, her eyes wide with surprise and doubt, the wretched book forgotten. 'Oh, Boyd,' she breathed, 'just wait till you see it!'

He half turned and put his arm round her recumbent form.

'Is it real pretty?'

'Yeah,' she sighed, still eyeing him distrustfully, 'it's real nice.'

Boyd began to feel better and not a little smug. It was just like the books said – all a man needed was a good technique. He let his hand wander a little, and got it petulantly pushed away as she heaved herself out of the clutches of the chesterfield's upholstery, and sat up on the edge of it. Her face was still sulky and she still sniffed occasionally as she put her feet to the ground.

Patiently, he tried another tack: 'Like a snack?' he asked.

Something of the sulkiness vanished and she wiggled her feet down more firmly into her shoes. There was a suggestion of enthusiasm in her voice when she replied: 'Yeah. I would.'

She rose and tottered, like a child still uncertain of its balance, to the refrigerator and swung open its massive door. Merely viewing its contents made her feel better. A barbecued chicken and a ham, both provided ready to serve by the local supermarket, made her mouth water. She opened the small freezer at the top, and four different types of ice cream, some frozen cream cakes and some ready-to-bake cookie mixes promised further consolation.

Boyd followed her out and, without being told, put some coffee on to percolate. He also got out rye bread and mustard. She always wanted the same things after a fight – ham on rye with mustard, followed by vanilla ice cream with walnut topping, a large slab of cake and coffee. Well topped up with these, thought Boyd as he hunted for the bread knife, she would be in a much more amicable mood, and then he might get somewhere with her.

CHAPTER SIXTEEN

Hank breathed with relief the icy, sweet air outside his parents' house. The night was beautiful, with a clean-swept sky filled with newly polished stars. Low on the skyline, just above the housetops, a red glow marked the reflection of neon signs in the centre of the city and he could hear the steady roar of traffic crossing the old river bridge towards it. The road in which he stood was, however, deserted, its avenue of leafless trees eerily quiet under the high street lamps. His mother's voice came faintly to him through the double doors of the house. He pitied his father, though he knew him to be physically and mentally tough and well able to take care of himself.

He stood shivering on the step, uncertain what to do. He smiled wryly to himself. *The Cheaper Sex* had already done very well what he had originally intended it to do – draw his parents' attention to his existence. It was obvious that during the next few weeks they were going to waste a lot of their valuable time thinking about him. But now he was older he did not care very much whether they were interested or not. He was far more concerned with consolidating his new-born reputation as a writer by producing another book of equal merit as fast as he could. He knew that, like a canoeist, he must ride the current while he could, finding a way through the rapids of life and somehow transforming his experiences into a story that rang with the honesty of his first book. Standing in the cold in front of the house, he realized suddenly that this was his ambition, to mirror life truly, so that people laughed when they saw their own image through his eyes.

His ears were getting numb, warning of frostbite, and he clapped his hands over them. He could not go far without mittens or earmuffs. His first idea on coming out had been to go and see Isobel and Dorothy, and then he had been

127

overcome by unaccustomed shyness. Now he decided he would go and get the car out and possibly call on his old friend, Ian MacDonald, now in his second year at the university; it seemed a long time since they had so light-heartedly rebuilt his jalopy in Isobel's garage.

He stuffed his hands into his pockets and, to keep himself warm, jogged the short distance to the garage.

The curtains had not been drawn over the back windows of Isobel's house, and he stood looking into the lighted rooms for a moment before unlocking the garage door. He chuckled as he saw Dorothy in her bedroom carefully pressing her hair to a fashionable straightness, on the ironing board with the electric iron; her contortions in an effort to reach up as far as possible were as complex as those of a cat trying to reach its middle back. Two students were seated in the kitchen, drinking coffee and laughing over some joke. He waited, hoping to see Isobel, but she must have been in the front of the house. Finally, he unlocked the garage and went in.

The white Triumph, its hood up, awaited his command; the gas stove in the corner roared in its usual muffled fashion. The typewriter on the desk seemed to float like an iceberg in a sea of paper, but he felt too tired to work. He opened the doors of the garage and then got into the car preparatory to backing it out. He sat for a moment, however, slumped in the driver's seat with the ignition key in his hand and no lights switched on, while he went over his mother's bitter words.

His fatigue was overwhelming. He told himself ruefully that too much had happened to him in the previous few weeks. He felt as if he had been blasted, in that time, right out of boyhood into manhood, as if he had been called up for the army and sent to war. And he had not done badly, he felt, especially as he had had to manage in New York without a lawyer or an agent to help him. 'You had nothing to lose but your chains,' he muttered and laughed a little.

What should he do in the immediate future? he asked himself.

Home was becoming untenable, but he dismissed the idea of taking an apartment on his own; living with his mother had been lonely enough. He toyed with the idea of going to stay with Grandmother Palichuk and his uncle, then realized that, once they understood the tenor of his writings, they would try to persuade him not to produce another book. And the new book was growing healthily; soon he would like Isobel to read it, and confirm his opinion that it was as good as his first one, or better.

Isobel! He swung the key ring fretfully round on his finger. Hell! Isobel was going home to that weirdo place in the U.K. from which she came. It struck him suddenly that he did not know how he was going to live without her. He stared blankly through the windshield at his piled-up desk. He knew that even if he had been able to finish his first book, he would never have had the courage to submit it to a publisher; the only other person to whom he might have turned for advice, Mr Dixon, the English teacher, would never have condoned its content. Captain Dawson was gone, and now Isobel was going. He heaved his huge shoulders against the seat back as he considered, rather hopelessly, the emptiness of his life in the near future.

He told himself not to be a fool. He had friends like John MacDonald, Ian's cousin, who was still plodding through high school, and Ian himself, of course; and there was Brett Hill, who had left school to become a flower child and now lived in comfortable squalor in a hut by the river, spending most of his life in a haze of marihuana. The majority of the boys with whom he had gone through school had left last year, and had been either at work or in university for some months past. He had got left behind to do this crazy Grade 12 again, left in a limbo of those really too old for school, too unqualified for work.

God, what a world!

Well, he did not have John's sticking power or Brett's enjoyment of drugs. What he wanted was to work amongst men, strong-minded men who knew where they were going, like his publishers in New York. My, they were tough, but so had he managed to be. All he needed was experience, he decided, and to get out of this goddam town, away from nagging schoolmarms, hysterical mothers and browbeaten fathers. He could try getting a job with a newspaper or magazine in Toronto or, maybe, Montreal – his French could be worse. He could afford to start at the bottom and do anything, just anything to enable him to be an adult.

Tomorrow he would go into action. And tomorrow he was certainly going to attend the ball with Isobel. His first intention had been simply to spite his mother by showing her that he could circulate alone in her world; now he wanted to give Isobel a good time. It would give him, he realized, great satisfaction to show her off in that old cats' paradise. Do her good to have a whirl for once; being Peter Dawson's wife must have been pretty boring and being a widow must be even worse.

As he turned on the car lights, the side door of the garage opened and Isobel entered carrying a table lamp.

He rolled down the car window, and she said, with surprise: 'Hello, I didn't expect to find you here.' Then she lifted the lamp to give him a better view of it. 'Do you think this would give you a better working light?'

'It'll do just fine,' he said. 'Thanks a lot.'

She put the lamp down on the desk, after carefully clearing a space amongst the papers. She wrapped her cardigan closely round her: she was shivering. 'Gosh, it's cold in here.'

Her voice quavered with the chill, and he opened the car door. 'Get in,' he said. 'You'll freeze.'

'It's O.K. Just came with the lamp. I must go back to the house.'

'Aw, come on,' he wheedled, 'stay a minute. I wanna ask you sumpin'.' He looked so like a small boy asking a favour that she complied, easing herself round the car to the opposite side and climbing in, her teeth chattering. He leaned over her and shut the door and rolled up the window. She looked very small and frail beside his huge bulk, and he heaved a rug from the back of the car and cautiously tucked it round her, then turned on the car heater and the headlights.

'That better?' he asked.

Her smile was impish above the plaid blanket as she nodded.

They were very close together in the tiny car, and Hank found himself unexpectedly scared. He was not sure what kind of behaviour she would expect from him, and hastily advised himself to play it cool, even if she was insulted because he made no advances to her. For her part, Isobel had been used, like most English women, to working in close proximity to men, and had crawled in beside him with as much thought as if he were a child of ten. Now, with the warmth of his body slowly penetrating the blanket and his face turned towards her so that he could see her, she was not so sure of herself. His face, in the faint light penetrating the interior of the car from the garage's ceiling light, looked sad, like the faces of Red Indians who hung about the centre of the town; they, too, had a Mongolian cast of feature, and the hardness of their lives gave them an air of grim melancholy. Her eyes moved compassionately over his face; he had their quiet dignity, too, she ruminated, in spite of his hunched-up carriage.

His heart was beating like a tomtom, but he asked her with a grin: 'What you thinking about?'

The golden eyelashes immediately came down to veil her eyes, and when she opened them again, she was her usual quiet, distant self. 'Tomorrow's dinner,' she said flippantly.

'You're having it with me,' he reminded her.

Her eyes twinkled. 'So I am,' she said. 'That will be very nice – though I don't know what my in-laws will think of me, gallivanting round the town.'

'Let 'em rot,' said Hank with heat. 'You can't stay locked up all your life.' Then, to change the subject, he asked: 'What do you think of my beard?' He fingered the wild scrub which, like most Tollemarche men, he had been nursing along for the past ten days.

'It looks ghastly,' said Isobel frankly. 'Perhaps the barber, when he does your hair for the ball, could trim it into some sort of naval shape – show him the picture I gave you of the man you are supposed to be. I think, if you add an artificial moustache, it would help.'

Hank felt deflated. He was proud of the amount of beard he had been able to cultivate in so short a time. Isobel sensed this, and said comfortingly: 'I am sure the barber could make a beautiful job out of it.'

He sighed with mock resignation: 'O.K., I'll go see him. I have to have an English-style haircut anyway.'

Her eager face with its small, pointed chin was turned up towards him. Could a widow be so innocent as to expect him to be unmoved when she was so close to him that he could smell her perfume? he wondered. Sure, he was scared of her, but that was because he did not want to offend her; it did not stop him wanting to kiss her.

His sudden silence bothered Isobel. She asked: 'What did you want to ask me?'

'Waal, I wanted to ask you sumpin' – and, oh yeah, I wanted to tell you sumpin', too.' His Canadian accent sounded to her almost like a Midwest American accent, and yet it had small nuances of sound that made it different. Although Alberta was too young to have acquired an accent of its own, its beginnings could be detected among those born in the province – a certain harshness of voice, a certain slowness of articulation not unpleasant to the ear, which mirrored the calm doggedness of people used to living in a climate which would daunt the bravest at times.

'You did?' Isobel's voice was gently encouraging.

'Yeah, the *Advent* sent a man tonight to see me – and Ma nearly hit the roof.' He chuckled. 'She'd read a bit of my book somewhere, when she didn't know I had written it – and she sure was mad at me!'

He produced two crumpled cigarettes out of the change pocket in the front of his jeans, and handed her one. He leaned over her and lit it with a lighter retrieved from the same pocket. For a moment after the cigarette was alight he

132

held the flaming lighter still before her face, examining her with doubting, narrowed black eyes. She regarded him steadily through the flame, her expression anticipatory, waiting to hear what he had to say. Her calmness irritated him, and he snapped the lighter shut and slumped back into his seat again.

A little sulkily, he went on: 'When we go to the Pre-Edwardian Supper tomorrow, you know it's O.K. to wear your costume? People wander round town all week in bustles and fancy waistcoats – and they will all next week.'

'Thanks, I intended to do so. The town really looked Edwardian when I was down there this morning – all trailing skirts, bonnets and beards.' She stopped and then said shyly: 'Are you quite sure you want to take me? I – I – er – I'm a bit older than you are, you know.'

'Waddya mean? What's age got to do with it? I've asked you, haven't I?' The black brows knitted together, and Isobel was amused to see something of Mrs Stych's well-known hot temper flash out of his eyes. 'I want *you!*' he added passionately.

She was pleased, and said: 'Well, thank you. I would enjoy it very much. My brother-in-law expects to be at the ball – he was a bit shaken when I said I thought I would be going – he wasn't very keen about it.' She hesitated and twirled the wedding ring on her finger. 'You know, this will be the first time I have been anywhere, except to work, since – since Peter was killed.' Her voice failed her.

A twinge of jealousy ripped through him, but he managed to address her very gently while he stared through the windshield, his whole body tensed as he hoped that she would not change her mind.

'Oh, yeah. I forgot that – I guess you haven't. If you feel you shouldn't come, it's O.K. by me.' He turned towards her and said earnestly: 'I can understand about it.' Inside, he was promising himself furiously that if the old biddies at the ball said anything to hurt her, he'd kill them, just kill them.

Her gratitude showed in her face. 'Thank you, Hank, you're a dear. I do want to come.' She stopped, feeling that this was a turning-point in her widowhood, a modest launching into a new life, a point which had to be reached sooner or later. She had not expected that the invitation to the ball would include dinner with Hank, but she told herself firmly that Peter had no need to be jealous, and then added, with sudden insight, that whatever feelings she might have for Hank were immaterial, since she was so much older than he was. That Hank might have any feeling other than gratitude to her did not suggest itself to her.

In the quietness that followed, Hank wondered how she could possibly look so beautiful when she had no makeup on and her hair was scraped back in an unfashionable ponytail. 'You must get pretty lonely,' he said suddenly.

She jumped, and recollected that she should have returned to the house long before. She smiled at him. 'Sometimes I do, though Dorothy has been so good and helpful since she has been here.'

'Well,' he said determinedly, 'we'll have fun tomorrow – it's a promise.'

'Fine,' she replied, as she started to open the door. 'By the way, what time shall I be ready?'

To have his convenience considered by a woman was a shock to him. He managed, however, to say quite casually: 'I'll pick you up about seven. O.K.?'

'Yes, I'll be ready. Bye-bye.' She slipped out of the car, closed the door carefully, and, with a wave of her hand, left him.

Only when she had gone did he remember that she had made no comment about his mother's behaviour, and this seemed to put the occurrences of the early part of the evening into better perspective for him; they were really not worth talking about.

Dreamily, he switched on the ignition and backed out of the garage. An indignant hoot warned him that he had nearly hit another car moving down the back lane, and this brought him back to reality. His fatigue and depression had almost vanished, and he drove off happily in search of a barbershop, outside the town itself, which would probably still be open.

CHAPTER SEVENTEEN

The sky was overcast and the wind moaned softly through the bungalow-lined streets, as Hank brought the Triumph round to Isobel's front door at seven o'clock the following evening. He remembered, from a lesson he had had at school called 'Making the Best of Oneself', that it was bad manners to toot his horn to call a girl from her house, so he squeezed himself carefully out of the driver's seat, giving a sharp yelp when he caught his fingers on a collection of brooches pinned to a wide ribbon strung over one shoulder of his evening suit and tied at his side, and went up the wooden steps to ring the doorbell. He had not bothered to wear an overcoat, despite the cold weather, but he did have overshoes on, and they stuck out quaintly from under his immaculately pressed black trousers. In his hand he held a florist's box, and while he waited for the door to be answered, he pressed more firmly to his upper lip a grey moustache of generous size.

Dorothy came to the door, and did not immediately recognize him. Then she said: 'Good heavens! Come in. Isobel is nearly ready.'

Isobel was in the living-room, having a five-tier imitation pearl necklace clasped round her neck by one of her student boarders, who started to giggle when she saw Hank.

Hank had eyes for no one but Isobel.

'Do I look that bad?' she demanded, as he stared at her.

'No,' his voice was enthusiastic. 'I should say not! You look the real goods.'

Her waist had been firmly laced in to give her a correct Edwardian hourglass figure, and her tiny bosom pushed up. A discreet amount of padding at the rear gave her a Grecian bend of charming proportions.

She laughed, while Dorothy handed her a borrowed fur

135

coat to put over her shoulders. 'I think you look very nice, too,' she said shyly. The barber had cut his beard in British navy fashion, and he looked so English in spite of his Slavonic cast of feature that she felt suddenly as if he were a fellow countryman, and her behaviour became more relaxed in consequence.

Hank handed her the florist's box. It was opened and all three girls admired the Victorian posy of tiny roses which it contained, while Isobel worried privately that he was going to too much expense on her behalf.

Dorothy helped her down to the car, so that she would not spoil her train or silver slippers in the snow, and then stood a little forlornly at the door watching them drive away. She had an uneasy premonition that one or other of the couple was going to be hurt; not even Peter had ever looked at Isobel, as far as she knew, the way Hank had looked at her when he came into the living-room.

The snow had been cleared from the front of the Palace Hotel and a red carpet laid across the sidewalk to the main door. It was a popular place for dining, and cars of every description were drawing up before it to deposit ladies, and then being driven round to the parking lot at the back of the building. Hank did the same for Isobel.

She did not, of course, know any of the ladies standing waiting for the return of their escorts, since she had never moved in Tollemarche's fashionable circles. She let down the train of her dress, however, and, holding her gorgeous nosegay, swept regally through the door of the hotel into the palm-decorated foyer, the commissionaire having opened the doors for her.

Though a few people in the foyer were wearing cocktail dresses or lounge suits and there was a sprinkling of plaid shirts and cowboy hats, most people were clad in elaborate Edwardian evening ensembles. Isobel could not help marvelling at the amount of money and attention to detail lavished on these clothes. But her own costume also caused a stir, and it was apparent from the amused look on the other patrons' faces that the character she had tried to

136

create was recognized. She was pleased, because the dress had been concocted out of three old wedding gowns bought from second-hand clothes shops – or, rather, economy shops, as they were called in Alberta.

Hank arrived quicker than she had hoped, having done a fast sprint round the building. He had shed his overshoes and looked very distinguished. His appearance beside her caused a burst of laughter, and two cowboys, already merrily drunk, clapped and roared appreciation.

When the restaurant's hostess had dealt with Hank's request for a table for this busy evening, she had at first said she did not have one available, implying by her lofty manner that the hotel did not cater to shaggy teenagers. Hank had been determined, however, and she had finally promised one, mentally seating them in an ugly corner by the service door. The old Chinese who owned the hotel, however, had that morning gone through the list of his prospective patrons, as he always did, and had recognized Hank's name. Mr Li probably knew more about the residents of Tollemarche and their visitors than anyone else, and he had seen Hank's real name given in the columns of the *New York Times*. Here, in his opinion, was a local celebrity, and his hostess was surprised when he carefully rearranged the parties she had booked, so that Hank was at a very good table where everyone could see him; Mr Li wanted to make a regular customer of such a successful young man.

Hank was jubilant at being placed where they could see and be seen, and were not deafened by the orchestra. Only three tables away, the Mayor was entertaining a noisy party of out-of-town guests, with a flustered Mrs Murphy trying to keep the horseplay within bounds. Further down the room, the MacDonalds' oil refinery group were ordering a dinner of the more unusual Chinese dishes and casting occasional supercilious glances at their more rowdy fellow townsmen. Several gentlemen ogled Isobel, much to her amusement and Hank's annoyance. Hank was immensely proud of her, and he dredged up for her benefit

137

everything he had ever heard or seen about good manners when escorting a lady – all the half-digested columns of Ann Landers, the dancing lessons of the physical education teacher at school, the behaviour of the New Yorkers whom he had observed with his usual concentration, came to his aid.

Isobel, though pleased, was surprised. Hank's behaviour to her had always been good by Tollemarche standards, but she had not hoped for such courtesy in more sophisticated surroundings. She set out to entertain and amuse him, and readily chose a dinner so that he was spared the agony of coping unaided with a menu, which though written in English, was enormously long; and he was able to say that he would have the same as she did. The problem of wines did not arise, since many restaurants were not then licensed in Alberta, so he did not have to admit that he was under age and could not drink.

While they were waiting for their steaks, she asked: 'Did your parents know you were going to the ball?'

'No.'

She was mystified. 'Why not? How on earth did you conceal the fact?'

He shifted his water glass around uneasily and did not answer her first question. 'Waal,' he said, 'you know I got my haircut real late last night – and I haven't seen them since.'

Her puzzlement deepened and was apparent from her expression. He explained: 'I came out early, before they were up, and didn't go home for lunch. I picked up my suit from the cleaners, and while I was dressing Ma was out – and Dad hadn't got back from the Holyrood Club.'

She was really bewildered now. 'But wouldn't your mother want to know if you had lunch all right, and what you were going to do this evening while she and Mr Stych were at the ball?'

'You nuts?' The tone was incredulous. 'Heck, no! Got my own lunch. They'd think I was going to the Town Square Hop for teens I guess.'

Isobel smiled up at the waiter as he placed her steak before her. 'It doesn't sound very friendly to me,' she said flatly, when the man had gone.

Hank impaled his steak on his fork; it was still sizzling from the charcoal fire on which it had been cooked. While he cut into it he grinned at her from under his false moustache. 'Friendly?' he queried. 'Is anyone friendly with their parents?'

'I was.'

He was sobered, and began to eat. He had actually had no lunch and was miserably hungry. After a couple of mouthfuls, he said reflectively: 'I think things are different in England. Read a lotta English books. The life just isn't the same.'

'I suppose so,' said Isobel circumspectly. She wondered if Peter's young life had been like Hank's. Until that second, she had never considered what his early life might have been like – it had always seemed too far away to be important. He had always been grown up to her, never young – more like her father. And with that thought came such a burst of self-revelation that she found it difficult to go on eating calmly, and only iron determination kept her placidly balancing bits of steak on her fork and eating them.

She remembered the frightful stripping away of all her ordinary life by the sudden accidental death of both her parents, of the terrible feeling of responsibility for Dorothy, so much younger than she was. She remembered the funeral and the tall, capable soldier friend of her father's who had come to attend it and had dealt so well with lawyers and with her fat, harassed uncle, who was one of the executors of her father's will. She had been happy to replace her father with another father figure, who had become her husband. She realized desolately that though he had been immensely kind to her, she had never really known him.

I must have been mad, she thought. But common sense answered her back sharply. Not mad, it said. He was a kindly, decent man and you were not unhappy with him. If sometimes you hankered for a better physical relationship, you loved him well enough to be faithful to him.

'Anything the matter?' asked Hank, who had been watching the play of expressions across her face. Then he leaned over to place his hand over hers, and said softly: 'I guess this outing must be pretty hard on you.'

His effort to understand her situation touched her, and she fought back sudden tears to say: 'Oh, no, Hank. Everything is lovely and I am truly grateful to you for dragging me out. Everyone is so merry – and the dresses are fabulous.'

'Fine,' he said, with a sigh of satisfaction, as he looked round the crowded restaurant. Then he asked: 'Do you like Alberta?'

She grasped at the new subject eagerly: 'Yes, I do.' She paused reflectively. 'It's breathtakingly beautiful. But I don't think I could go on living indefinitely in Tollemarche.'

Hank was watching a sorely inebriated building contractor who was trying to heave the evening shoes off his girl friend's feet. When, with a final flurry of nyloned legs above the table top, he got them off, he proceeded to fill them with rye from a bottle under the table and drink a toast to the assembled company. 'I guess,' said Hank, 'Tollemarche is a bit raw for you.'

Isobel also had watched the incident of the shoes, and admitted that it was so.

'I think you'd like Edmonton better,' said Hank. 'It's really going places now, with orchestras and theatres and stores like we don't have up here.'

'Yes, I've been there,' replied Isobel, now completely in control of herself, 'and it is fun.'

'Sometimes go down myself to see a show.'

'Do you?' asked Isobel, trying not to sound too amazed.

He grinned. 'Sure,' he replied. 'Gotta get an education for myself somehow.'

The waiter brought coffee and dessert and they lingered over them, talking of plays and playwrights. Nobody knew who they were, except Mr Li, and they were left in peace.

'Why do you hafta go back to England?' asked Hank.

'There's nothing to keep me here. And, you know, Hank, I'd like to live a little.'

'Holy cow! You could live here – or down in Edmonton. Waddya mean "live"?'

'I mean to feel alive – to be in the middle of things. Alberta is on the edge of the world and nothing touches it, except the faintest ripples of what goes on elsewhere.'

'Humph, I'd have thought that was something to be thankful for.'

She nodded her head, making her tiara flash like a halo. 'Yes, it is, really. If one is afraid of poverty or war, there's a lot of comfort here. But you see, Hank,' she went on more passionately, 'life isn't just a matter of being comfortable. One wants to try one's strength and see what one can do – and I really long to hear an expert talk about his work, to argue politics, to look at fine pictures, plays, books, and discuss them.' She stopped and clicked her tongue irritably. 'I don't know how to make you understand.'

She looked hopefully at him. He looked very mature in his beard, which, with the hair at his temples, had been rubbed with talcum powder to give it a greying appearance. One day he will really look like this, if he cares to make the effort, she reflected; and I believe he could become a great novelist, too.

He grinned wryly, and said: 'You could teach up North – you'd find it a real struggle up there – and the Eskimos are the world's greatest experts on arctic survival! But there wouldn't be any theatre shows.'

Isobel laughed. 'You're right – but it would be more isolated even than Tollemarche.' After a moment, she added confidingly: 'You know, when I first came here I used to feel sure that if I walked along the highway for any distance, I would drop off the edge of the world – it was so flat and empty.'

'I guess I can understand that.' He thought of the miles of waving wheat, with nothing on the skyline but a couple of grain elevators thrusting their white fingers to a cloudless blue sky, and he thought of the pure, white beauty of the same type of scene in winter – hundreds of miles of snow and the same polished blue sky. To someone used to a crowded, small island perhaps it was frightening. 'It's beautiful,' he said stubbornly.

'Of course it is,' she agreed.

There was silence between them, and then he said: 'Remember you said I should go get some experience somewhere else? Since Ma is so mad and you are going away, mebbe this is the time to do it.'

'I think it would be a good idea, just to have a better idea of what the outside world is like. Do you want to work or just to travel?'

'Jeeze, I dunno. I'd hafta work on my book all the time, anyway.'

'Well what about taking a hiking holiday through Europe first? It wouldn't cost so much, and then – '

His moustache fell off with shock. 'Hike?' he interrupted, horrified. 'You mean walk?' He hastily retrieved the moustache from the saucer of his coffee cup, and clapped it back on again.

She burst into laughter, partly at the moustache and partly at his typical North American aversion to using his legs. 'Yes, I really mean walk. If you walk you will have the chance of talking to all kinds of odd people. You can meet and walk with other young people, from youth hostel to youth hostel.'

He said vigorously: 'I'd drop dead after the first day – you'll have to allow me a car.'

'Oh, come on now, you wouldn't die – you'd lose pounds and really toughen up.'

He looked at her beseechingly: 'I sure would slim – dropping pounds one by one across Europe – don't you feel sorry for me? I couldn't do it – unless you came with me,' he added with sudden inspiration.

'Oh, Hank, don't tease. You know I've got a job waiting for me. I have to earn my living – my pension isn't going to be enough.' She leaned towards him eagerly, her lips parted and her tiny hands gesturing. 'But you go, Hank. You'll be glad you did. Britain, France, Germany, Holland, they are all wonderful in their infinite variety. You haven't seen a single piece of good architecture yet, not a single good painting, never talked to a person whose family has lived in one place for five hundred years. You haven't seen a thoroughgoing slum yet. You can't realize what a war can do to a country and its people. Go, Hank, and see it all – you'll understand a lot of things much better afterwards, and be a better writer in consequence.' She stopped and began to blush, ashamed of her impassioned outburst.

He was impressed by it. 'Say, you do take things seriously, don't you?' he marvelled. 'Even me! Sure, I know I need to see things. And if you think I ought to foot it, I will – but don't expect my feet to enjoy it.' Then he added defiantly: 'I've seen the Empire State Building. Have you?'

She chuckled. 'No, I haven't. No desire to see the States at all – I think Quebec would be much more fun – you might do a bit of exploring there, too. You've got quite a lot of Canada to see yet.'

'O.K. You're the boss. You're the first person I've ever met who cared what I did, anyway.' He sighed. 'Do I have to hike the whole two thousand miles or so to Quebec as well?'

'It wouldn't be a bad idea,' she said with a twinkle in her eyes, and then, as he groaned in mock horror, she added: 'But I think I'll let you off that.'

'Thanks, pal,' he said dryly, and signalled for his bill.

CHAPTER EIGHTEEN

Mrs Stych was far too busy getting ready for the Edwardian Ball to recollect that she had not seen Hank since he had marched out of the house the previous evening. She had spent the afternoon at the hairdressers, and was now standing in front of her Stately Castille dressing table pinning a scarlet flower coquettishly over one ear.

'Boyd,' she called, 'you ready?'

Boyd came into the room, fastening a red and gold brocade waistcoat. 'My, are we ever dressed up!' he said sardonically. Not even two helpings of ice cream with walnut topping had melted Olga's resistance to him the previous evening, and he was feeling irritable.

Despite the appropriateness of her gorgeous costume, Olga was not feeling her usual confident self. Late the previous evening she had announced that she would not attend the ball, just to be sniggered at by the whole town. But Boyd, more for his own sake than for hers, had persuaded her that she ought to attend, notwithstanding the possible reactions of the girls to the publication of Hank's book. Otherwise, he said, it would look as if she was ashamed. Secretly, he felt that it was essential for the promotion of his business that they be seen at all Tollemarche's big social functions. He had, therefore, helped Olga to lace herself into a formidable pair of corsets and then to struggle into a magnificent red satin dress, heavily trimmed with black lace. He had also heated some soup and made sandwiches for their supper, as there was not time, in her opinion, to eat dinner out.

With great care, she now placed on her head a cartwheel hat of black velvet trimmed with dyed ostrich feathers, and examined herself in the mirror. She picked up a long-handled, frilly parasol and a black velvet handbag, and posed with them. The skirt of the dress was caught up at the hem and pinned to the waistline with a flower to match the one in her hair; this left one silk-stockinged leg bare to the hip, in true dancing-girl style, and Mrs Stych felt she looked very daring. She smiled satisfiedly at her reflection.

Behind her, Boyd turned away to hide a smile. The fact that she was so fat made her look much more like the dancing girl she was trying to portray than perhaps Olga would have wished; gold miners had liked their women fat.

Olga felt more content than she had during the whole previous twenty-four hours. With a costume like this, the first prize at the ball would certainly be hers.

'You supposed to be Klondike Kate?' asked Boyd.

Mrs Stych smiled slyly at him out of the corners of her eyes. 'Yeah,' she said, regardless of the reputation of that hardy lady of the Klondike gold rush. ''Cept I couldn't face wearing high laced-up boots – I'm wearing my black pumps instead.'

Boyd allowed that the black pumps looked real nice.

He picked up one of his wife's old gilt necklaces from her open jewel box and draped it across his waistcoat to represent a watch chain. Then he struggled into a high-buttoned black jacket. 'Did you get me a buttonhole?' he asked.

Mrs Stych looked at him in shocked reproach. 'Why, Boyd, I thought you'd surely get flowers for both of us, seeing as you are home all the time now and aren't just coming in at the very last minute.'

Boyd realized the justice of her remark and also that an explosion was imminent. Living at home, he reflected angrily, had its hazards.

'O.K., O.K.,' he said quickly, 'I just asked. I wasn't sure if you would want a corsage with that outfit. If you do want one, we can stop at Bell's Flowers and get one. I can get a button-hole, too.'

The threatening glow of rage in Olga's eyes died; she gave him a sour look, but said only: 'We'll do that.'

Her husband muttered that he would go and start the car, and for the moment she was alone. Her thoughts reverted to Hank and his diabolical book, and she felt sick with fright at the thought of all the slights she might have to face at the ball. Yet she could do nothing about it; Boyd was right that if she stayed at home it would look as if she was ashamed.

She sniffed. She'd show them if she was ashamed or afraid. She opened the fine louvre-board doors to the closet, took out her Persian lamb coat and draped it round her shoulders. Absently she stood stroking its silky lapels; few women in the town had a better coat than this, and it would be paid for by April thank goodness. She lifted her nose in the air, so that her double chin did not show so much, and, with the same bravery with which her parents had faced their first fierce winter, she went out to smite the enemy; in this case, to outdo the girls with the glory of her coat and costume.

In keeping with the period they were trying to reconstruct, many citizens of Tollemarche travelled to the ball at the Donegal Hotel in vintage cars, and many of these were now parked along the side of the street on which the hotel stood. Whether they would ever start again after prolonged exposure to the winter storm which was obviously blowing up, was problematical, but many of the owners felt it was worth paying a fee to Tommy's Towing Company afterwards, just to enjoy the envy of those who did not own such treasures.

The Mayor, who had triumphed over the city council with regard to mayoral robes, had solved the starting problem by sweeping up to the hotel in a well-preserved closed carriage, which had been salvaged from the back of the old Hudson's Bay factor's house and then refinished. The two horses which drew it did not quite match, despite a quick application of boot blacking over the lighter spots of one of them, but the general effect drew cheers from passing carloads of merrymakers.

Mayor Murphy beamed as he handed down his plump wife, who wobbled unhappily in a gown of bright purple velvet, and then helped down two saturnine gentlemen from the Montreal Mortgage and Trust Company, who were visiting the city to buy land on speculation. His coachman, a Cree Indian brought in for the evening from a nearby reserve, was disguised in a black top hat and neat black uniform. As soon as the Mayor was safely inside the lobby, he turned the carriage round and headed for the fire station, where the horses and he would keep warm with the firemen on duty until such time as the Mayor should telephone for him. As the first snowflakes of the storm hit him, he hoped that the firemen had some beer tucked away at the back of the hall.

Olga Stych did her best to control her palpitating heart as she made her way to the cloakroom of the Donegal Hotel, while Boyd went to park the car. She put her hand on the knob of the door marked WOMEN, but was unable to make herself turn it. What would they say? What *would* they say? But it was no good – a new arrival behind her forced her to open the door and walk in.

The place was a mad-house of waving plumes, raucous voices and cigarette smoke.

' 'Lo, Olga', and 'Hiya, Olga,' greeted her on all sides.

Mrs Stein of Dawne's Dresse Shoppe, wearing her grandmother's wedding dress and veil, was squeezed out of the crowd round the mirrors and up against Olga's hefty bulk.

'Say, you look fine,' she said, appraising the scarlet dress with a professional eye through heavy horn-rimmed glasses. 'A real scarlet woman,' she joked. 'Did Mary Leplante make it?'

Mrs Stych felt as if twenty years had been taken off her age. Her enormous bosom swelled to dangerous proportions in such a low-cut gown, as she answered proudly: 'Yeah, Mary made it.'

So the girls were not going to let the book make any difference. They were wonderful! They sure were. She linked her arm into that of Mrs Stein. 'Come on,' she said with gay condenscension, 'let's go find the boys!'

Before leaving home, Olga had glanced quickly at the

front page of the *Tollemarche Advent*, which the paper boy had just flung on to the step as she came out. She had seen on the lower half of the front page, under the heading 'Local Boy Makes Good', an almost unrecognizeable picture of Hank. She was too rushed to read the columns underneath and had left the newspaper lying on the boot tray just inside her front door. Now, she did not pause to consider that, throughout Tollemarche, few of those attending the ball would have stopped to read the newspaper on such a night; it would have been left to languish until Sunday gave time for its perusal. True, the eight o'clock news on the local radio station had also mentioned Hank, between a war and a dock strike, but nobody really listened to the news, anyway. Unconscious of this, however, Olga felt like a reprieved felon, and her relief was so great that she quite dazzled Boyd's fellow directors by her vivacity.

The ballroom was filled with the sharp smell of chrysanthemums, specially flown in from British Columbia for the occasion. Potted palms were grouped round the stage, on which sat a large dance orchestra in full evening dress. Around the sides of the ballroom and in the balcony above were set tables covered with stiff white cloths, for six or eight persons; each table had a vase of roses, also from British Columbia, and a pair of small, shaded electric lamps to light it. Like many of the hotels in Alberta at the time, the Donegal's dining and ballrooms were not licensed, but this did not deter their patrons. Into the iced ginger ales went large measures of rye from bottles kept discreetly under the table and, similarly, gin was being dumped generously into the lime juices of tittering ladies. Some of the parties were already very merry, and it was apparent that some people would have to be carried to their cars before the night was out.

At the door of the ballroom stood one of the members of the Chamber of Commerce, dressed in a white wig, knee breeches and a yellow satin coat. He had volunteered to be the major-domo of the evening; as people arrived, he took their names and announced them in a loud bass. From him, the guests proceeded to an interminably long receiving line, made up of the Mayor and Mrs Murphy, the president of the Chamber of Commerce and his wife, the president of the Edwardian Days' Committee and his daughter, he being a widower, and several very ancient inhabitants, both male and female, whom the committee had agreed it would be easier to include than exclude, most of the ancient inhabitants being both rich and sharp of tongue.

'Mr and Mrs Maxmilian Frizzell, Mrs and Mrs John MacLeod, the Right Honourable Frederick Shaeffer and Mrs Shaeffer, Professor Mah Poy and Mrs Mah, Dr and Mrs Stanilas Paderewski,' roared the major-domo, warming to his job and being careful to keep his voice clear by taking an occasional quick nip from a friend's bottle.

The bustles and fancy waistcoats, the trains and evening suits, flowed slowly past the reception line and down three thickly carpeted steps to the ballroom floor or, if they felt they were past the age of dancing, climbed complainingly to their tables in the balcony.

In a quiet moment, the major-domo took out a pocket handkerchief to wipe his perspiring face, while he remarked to the Mayor that he deserved a city contract as a reward for enduring a wig in this hothouse. The Mayor smiled noncommittally. It would take more than a hint like that to land the office furniture contract for the new city hall; a contract as big as that should be worth something. He fingered his new chain of office, and then, looking past the would-be contractor, he laughed.

Standing waiting to be announced was a dignified woman in a lavender dress embroidered with pearls and sequins. She was made taller by her hair, which had been tightly waved, powdered, and piled on the top of her head. Her big tiara sparkled in the soft light, and a five-tier pearl necklace shimmered delicately over a high neckline of boned lace. She wore across her breast a wide blue ribbon tied in a knot at her hip; a large brooch on the ribbon suggested an order of some kind. In her white-gloved hands she carried a nosegay of roses and a silver fan. She was accompanied by a distinguished-looking man in full evening dress, whose hair was cut English style, whose beard was neatly trimmed in naval fashion. He, too, sported a sash across his chest decorated by a row of medals and two star-like brooches, and below his white tie hung an elaborate enamelled cross; all the medals had been won for skiing or swimming, but nobody noticed the fact. What was noticed was the authoritative air of the pair of them as they advanced unsmilingly towards the major-domo.

The major-domo grinned at them; this was going to be fun. No couple whom he had announced up to now had managed more appropriate costumes. Very quietly, he went over to them and edged them behind a potted palm, whispering hastily into their respective ears. They nodded agreement, and he caught a page-boy and gave him a message for the orchestra. After a moment or two, the conductor raised his head and nodded towards them. The major-domo took up his position again and cleared his throat, while Isobel and Hank advanced slowly towards him, doing their best to maintain their grave dignity, though Hank's moustache was quivering dangerously.

The orchestra brought its current piece of music to an end, and sounded a great chord. Conversation ceased immediately and everyone, including the receiving line, looked round expectantly.

'Their Royal Highnesses, the Prince and Princess of Wales,' roared the major-domo.

The ballgoers looked up in silent astonishment, and then a ripple of laughter went through the crowd, and they began to clap, while Hank and Isobel acknowledged with the faintest of condescending nods the ironic bow of the quick-witted Mayor and the bows and curtsies of the rest of the receiving line, all of whom rose to the occasion admirably, except for a deaf, old lady at the end, who announced crabbily that she did not know what the major-domo was about, talking of 'fences and bales'.

Hank and Isobel moved to the top of the steps and bowed

to the applauding crowd. To some of those present they brought back happy memories, and there was not one person there who did not recall the opening exercises in the little red schoolhouses across the province, when they had stood to attention in front of a picture such as Hank and Isobel now presented, and vowed to be faithful to the flag and to George V and his consort, Queen Mary. Some were nonplussed at the couple being announced as the Prince and Princess of Wales, but their brighter neighbours hastened to remind them that in Edwardian days, the old king, Edward VII, would be reigning.

'Who are they?' was the whisper that ran round the room between the claps. Even the major-domo could not remember having seen them before, and came to the conclusion that they must be some young married couple who had recently come into the town.

Mrs Stych looked cursorily at the Princess, did not know her and turned back to her rye and ginger ale; she barely glanced at the Prince. Boyd thought he knew the turn of the shoulder on the man, but could not place him. He, too, went back to his drink.

The Mayor was not going to betray the fact that he did not know someone in the town who was rich enough to spend forty dollars on tickets for the ball, so, as he and Mrs Murphy moved towards the dance floor to open the ball, he slapped Hank heartily on the back, and bellowed: 'Have a good time.'

The orchestra struck up a waltz, and Hank and Isobel made for her brother-in-law's table, which they had been invited to join; on the way, they passed the table of Isobel's employer, a heavy dark-jowled man, who rose and caught her hand as she went by. 'Happy to see you here, Isobel,' he said.

She smiled and, with a lighter heart, went on to her table. Some people in Tollemarche were evidently going to be pleased that she was in circulation again.

Joanne Dawson, in a tight, low-necked dress of salmon pink, had already consumed two gins, and greeted them effusively while Dave Dawson, a quiet, tired-looking man about thirty-five, pulled out a chair for Isobel.

Isobel introduced Hank to them, and he said politely: 'How d'yer do.' He sat down slowly, eyeing Joanne's rather daring costume with an unblinking stare. She was dressed as a chorus girl, her full skirt hitched up to show tight-clad legs and hips, the low neckline leaving little to the imagination.

'Too much cleavage,' decided Hank. 'No class.'

Dave wore dinner clothes of the period, and Hank knew instinctively that he and Isobel would get on very well together. Hank felt an ill-bred lout beside him, and he wondered how Isobel endured him; he decided he did not like himself very much, and this detracted for a little while from his enjoyment of the masquerade.

'You looked just fine up there on the steps,' Dave said to Hank. 'In the half light, you looked just like old Georgie.'

'Thanks,' said Hank, warming to him. He checked that his moustache was still in place. 'Hope I don't lose this,' he added while Joanne giggled shrilly.

'Say, what are these?' he asked, pointing to some tiny, pink cards with pencils attached to them which were lying on the table.

'Ladies' programmes, stoopid,' said Joanne amiably, leaning on her elbow unsteadily towards him. 'Here, give one to Isobel,' and she pushed one over to Hank.

Hank looked it over, mystified. 'Wottya do with them?' he demanded.

Isobel took it from him. 'See,' she said, 'it contains a list of all the dances. In the old days each girl had one, and the gentlemen came up to her and booked dances with her by writing in their names. It was the job of the M.C. or the host and hostess to see that, as far as possible, all the cards were filled.'

'That's easy,' said Hank, taking the card back from her firmly. He wroted his name across the whole column of dances.

'Say,' protested Dave, 'give us a chance.'

Hank looked at him with mock lordliness. 'I'm the Prince of Wales, remember.' Then, good-humouredly, he passed the card to Dave, who wrote his name against a foxtrot before supper and a waltz later in the evening.

'What about poor little me?' demanded Joanne, with a pout. She regarded Isobel as a drip, and had no intention of spending the evening tied to their table. She was, however placated when Dave wrote his name all over her card, and Hank wrote his name in the spaces of the dances which Isobel would dance with Dave.

She greeted with squeaks of joy the approach of two gentlemen dressed in Edwardian suits and white stetson hats, and made each of them sign his name on her card. Isobel, suddenly nervous of possible censure of their recent hero's widow being at a ball, kicked Dave under the table, and whispered 'Prince and Princess'. He was a quick man and, with exaggerated deference, introduced the visitors to Hank and Isobel, murmuring: 'Their Royal Highnesses, the Prince and Princess of Wales.'

'Let's dance,' said Hank, and dragged her unceremoniously to the edge of the ballroom floor. He stood tapping his foot impatiently in time to the music, while she carefully anchored the train of her dress by a loop hooked over her little finger.

He whirled her out on to the floor at the fast pace demanded by a Viennese Waltz, and was surprised to find her following him effortlessly.

'Say, where did you learn to dance?'

'In England – most English women dance.'

'Ballroom dancing, like this?'

'Yes.'

'I thought they were all swingers.'

Isobel laughed. 'Most of us can dance modern dances as well.'

'Can you?'

'Well, I haven't danced more than a couple of times since I was married, so I'm probably a bit out of date, but I think I could make a fair showing even so.'

He grinned down at her wickedly. 'Mebbe we'll go to a night club sometime and get back into practice. What say?'

'Maybe,' she said cautiously. 'I think more people in England dance than people here.'

He considered this while he negotiated a corner, in which the city editor of the *Advent* appeared to have got stuck with his partner. The partner was saying: 'Now, Joe, one-and-two, one-and-two, one-and-two. Now, turn!'

'Don't you have any fundamentalists?' he asked.

'I don't think there are many. We're mostly heathens.' She added, a little breathlessly: 'When your book is published in England, it won't cause half the stir it is going to cause here.' Then, after being twirled neatly out of the way of the Mayor, she remembered the reporter's visit to Hank the previous evening. 'What does the *Advent* have to say about you today?'

'Haven't had time to look yet. I don't care, anyways.'

He pulled her a little closer, so that she could feel the warmth of him. 'Enjoying yourself?' he asked.

She looked up at him and her face was alight with gaiety. My God, she's really beautiful, he thought. She just needs bringing out. He held her close, and did a dashing double reverse turn with sheer exuberance, much to the discomfort of at least half a dozen other couples who were already finding such a fast waltz rather exhausting and were thrown into confusion by Hank's lively variation.

Dave Dawson was honestly glad to see her flushed face so bright when they returned to the table. She had been the subject of several anxious consultations in the family, who felt responsible for her future and yet found her supercilious English manner very trying. Only Dave's and Peter's father, himself once an immigrant, had understood how profoundly different was her life in Canada compared to her childhood in North Wales and her business life in London. Her mother-in-law was a Canadian who had failed to adapt in Britain and persuaded her husband to emigrate. Had Peter lived, thought Dave, probably Isobel would have settled in, but he had not been surprised at her decision to go home. Now, as he watched her while he drew out Joanne's chair, he wondered if the talented boy who had brought her to the dance might not persuade her to stay in Tollemarche.

Dave was not the only person who watched her with interest. From across the empty floor, Olga Stych, her eyes glazed with horror, had just recognized her son and was saying in a furious voice to her husband: 'Who's that bitch he's with?' She half rose, prepared to sail across the floor to the attack, but Boyd leaned solicitously over her and pressed her back down into her chair with bruising fingers.

'Shut up,' he said in a whisper. 'Remember where you are! The other directors are here.'

She recollected her hostess manner and smiled up at him sweetly; then, turning so that her hat hid her from the curious eyes of their guests, she muttered: 'The impudence of him!' Her bosom heaved as she glared at Boyd from under the safe shadow of her hat: 'You gotta deal with him, Boyd. You really have.'

CHAPTER NINETEEN

Isobel danced the whole evening. Occasionally, Hank had to yield her up to other gentlemen; her employer politely claimed a dance, and one or two friends of the Dawson family visited their table, were introduced and, with varying degrees of good manners, asked for dances. Prompted by Isobel, Hank dutifully asked their ladies for dances, and pulled faces at Isobel over their shoulders whenever they passed on the floor.

By the time the buffet supper in an adjoining room was announced, they were both hungry again. They found themselves the centre of a rowdy party, made up of acquaintances of Joanne and Dave, and as soon as Isobel had collected a plateful of food, Hank found himself conniving with Dave to edge Isobel out of the crowd and back to their table by the dance floor, where they ate quietly together.

Isobel, well aware of the conspiracy, said: 'Thank you, Hank.'

'Think nothing of it,' Hank replied. 'They're not your type. Dave said to tell you he thought he'd better stay with Joanne.'

'I think I'm being spoiled tonight,' Isobel teased gently.

Hank looked bashful. 'I wouldn't know about that, but I sure know the kind of company you should not be in.'

'Well, bless you!' she said, laughing, as they got up to dance.

The city editor of the *Advent*, who had been the original owner of the paper until he had sold out to a syndicate about six months previously, could remember the days when he had helped to set the type himself, and he felt tremendously important when he was asked to judge the costumes at the ball, aided by Mrs Murphy and the wife of the president of the Bonnie Scots Men's Club.

Towards the end of the evening, after a suitable roll of drums from the orchestra, he announced a grand parade of everyone desiring to compete. There was considerable good-natured shoving forward of some competitors by the more shy, and finally almost everyone made the circuit of the dance floor. Twelve were picked out and asked to parade again, among them a simpering Mrs Stych, two Mississippi gamblers tossing a die between them, Hank and Isobel, a prospector whose gold-panning equipment was carried on a donkey which seemed to be slightly inebriated, and an assortment of ladies in fairly genuine-looking Edwardian fashions.

The twelve finally stood in line in front of the judges, who conferred earnestly together, Mrs Murphy being anxious not to accidentally upset one of her husband's political associates by not giving a prize to the Mississippi gamblers. The back legs of the prospector's donkey began to sag, and Isobel was certain they would lose to such a gloriously wobbly donkey.

The judge stood up.

'First prize, a beautiful set of luggage donated by Pottle's Best Brewed Beer, to Their Royal Highnesses, the Prince and Princess of Wales.'

Cheers and claps broke out as Hank and Isobel advanced towards the judge. Behind them, near the orchestra, Mrs Frizzell clapped her hand to her mouth in shock as she recognized Hank. The orchestra behind her made her jump as it suddenly burst forth with a few bars of 'God Bless the Prince of Wales'. 'Bless him!' she sniffed, 'H'mmm!'

'Who are you?' whispered the judge. 'They'd probably like to know.'

Hank looked at Isobel. 'O.K.,' she murmured.

'I'm Hank Stych and this is Mrs Isobel Dawson.'

The judge, with a startled look at them, wrung both their hands and announced who they were, while Mrs Stych went slowly purple with rage.

Just wait till he gets home, she swore to herself. She'd teach him to run around with the widow of Tollemarche's hero, and go to balls meant for adults. Just because he had written an indecent book didn't mean he could invade her world and behave indecently with a woman only widowed six months. She'd teach him!

She turned and glared at that hussy of a Dawson woman.

The hussy did not remember who she was and stared back with queenly coldness, thinking that Canadians did not know how to lose gracefully.

The announcement of Hank's name had little effect on anyone present, except his parents and Mr and Mrs Frizzell. It was doubtful if anyone connected him with his parents. The announcement of Isobel's name, however, gave rise to a fair amount of interested whispering behind hands and fans.

The second prize went to the prospector and his donkey, amid hurrahs from a lively party in a corner. Unfortunately, the back end of the donkey sat down suddenly and had to be undone from the front end and carried off.

Mrs Stych accepted a set of records of Barbershop Singers, courtesy of Mollie's Milk Bar, for the third prize, and was congratulated by the judge, who realized the relationship, on the success of her family in the competition. She was past speech by this time and smiled at the judge glassily, as she withdrew to her table. She hardly heard the congratulations of the Frizzells, who seemed to think she had designed Hank's and Isobel's costumes as well as her own. When her voice returned to her, she said loudly that she needed a drink. Boyd presented her with this, with an alacrity which betrayed his apprehension.

He had spotted Hank during the second dance, and had examined at leisure the pretty girl with him. He had realized that she was not Canadian and that she was probably older than Hank. Was she Hank's widow woman? he wondered. He had watched her tiny, graceful figure as she danced, and had suddenly become nervous for his son's future. She had 'real nice girl' written all over her, he reckoned – the kind of girl one talked only marriage to – and he did not want his son to marry yet.

He looked at Olga, who was downing her drink steadily. He'd got married too young, he reminded himself desperately, and had had almost immediately a mortgage tied round his neck, as if he were a dog with a registration tag on its collar.

He began to consider how to persuade Hank to leave Tollemarche for a while, before Olga nagged him into a state of such perversity that he would marry the girl just to spite his mother.

CHAPTER TWENTY

They were leaving the ballroom after the last waltz and Isobel looked back at Mrs Stych, who, clutching her prize, was talking to a distinguished, grey-haired woman in a black evening gown.

'I didn't realize that lady was your mother, until she won a prize – she looked very pretty,' Isobel remarked kindly.

Hank looked at her sardonically. 'Yeah,' he said. 'And she sure was mad at our getting first prize. Come to think of it, she was mad because I came at all.'

Isobel laughed. 'Wasn't that the idea?'

'Sure.' He looked as pleased as a tiger after a kill. 'She'll have quite a time explaining to the girls how I came to be there – and with you.'

'Really, Hank, you're dreadful.'

'Well, you won't come to any harm from it – you'll be away from here.'

'I suppose so – though I feel very guilty.'

He stopped, while the crowd milled round them towards the exit. 'Listen, honey. I could have gone through all the business of introducing you to her, saying I was taking you and what we would wear, and all I would have got for my pains would have been a real earful.' As he spoke, he shouldered back anyone who pressed too close to her, so that she was not ruffled by the passersby. Then he asked abruptly, 'Would you like to meet Dad? He's over there, by the pillar.'

She moved round so that she did not appear to be straining to look, and saw a tall, thin brown man, very fit looking. In repose, his face appeared hard and a little cunning. He caught her eye and stared back at her; a glimmer of a smile showed, as if they were sharing some secret joke. Then it seemed to her that a shadow of anxiety passed across his face, if such a man could possibly be anxious about anything.

'Waddya think of him?'

'He looks very nice,' she said politely.

'Don't kid me, hon. He's as tough as they make them – and you know it.'

'One can be tough and nice,' she countered, drawing her handbag closer up her arm.

'O.K. Wanna meet him?'

'Perhaps tonight wouldn't be the best night, Hank. Some other time.' This would probably be the last time she would go out with Hank, and she felt there was no point in getting involved with his parents.

'From what you tell me, Mr Stych seems to be taking a lot of trouble on your behalf to see that the money you've made is properly invested,' she remarked to Hank, as he tucked a blanket round her in the car.

Hank was silent while he tried the ignition key in its lock. The engine coughed into life immediately.

'Making some money was the first thing I ever did that pleased him,' he finally replied.

'Hank, Hank,' she said reproachfully, 'what shall I do with you?'

'Well, I could suggest a few things,' he responded promptly, which silenced her.

In the station wagon parked next to them, a childish howl arose. Some child, put to bed in a sleeping-bag in the back of the car, had awakened, presumably cold and hungry. Isobel winced. Had his parents done that to Hank when he was small – or had they just left him in an empty house? she wondered.

The storm was now in full blast, and they crawled carefully through the shadowy mass of vehicles moving round them.

'If this continues till morning, think I'll go up to Banff and ski for a coupla days. Give Ma time to cool off.' He laughed. 'Don't want her to burst a blood vessel.'

'Good idea. You have been shut up too long.'

'So long as I'm not shut up in that factory of a school, I'm fine.'

He stopped at a red light and looked at her with laughter in his eyes.

'Can't imagine you still in school,' said Isobel frankly. 'I can't understand why you didn't just take off years ago.'

'There's a lotta pressure from all quarters here to keep you in school. Education's just become a fashion. They tell you you can't even run an elevator unless you got Grade 12.'

'You can go into the police force if you've got Grade 10 – and the Mounties will take you with Grade 11,' countered Isobel.

Hank chuckled. 'Sure. They don't want their police to be brainy – how'd they get away with what they do, if the police had brains?' His voice was hard and cynical. Then he changed the subject. 'Say, if I come to Europe, can I come and see you?'

'Of course. Both Dorothy and I will love to see you.'

He said practically: 'I'll get your address from you, before you leave.'

The thick snow muffled the sound of the approach of the car to Isobel's house, and when he stopped he did not immediately get out to open the door for her, but sat looking moodily at his hands on the steering wheel.

She gathered up her fan, posy and handbag. 'It's been a wonderful evening, Hank, and I'm really grateful to you for dragging me out.'

He turned eagerly towards her.

'Yeah, it was fun, wasn't it? We'll do something else together soon.' He added baldly: 'I'd expected it to be a dead bore – I just wanted to take a rise out of Ma.' His voice was husky. 'But you're fun – you're lovely.' He put his arm round the back of her seat. 'Isobel,' he said urgently, and then stopped.

She was afraid of what was coming. Remember, he's too young, an inner voice warned her, and she said in her most comradely voice: 'Yes, Hank?'

'Stop being so bloody friendly,' he exclaimed angrily, and leaning half over her, kissed her hard, holding her firmly round the shoulders so that she could not escape it.

For a moment she yielded to him. She had not been kissed by a man since her husband had left for Cyprus, and this strong, healthy youngster aroused feelings in her that no kiss from her husband had ever aroused. Then she began to struggle.

'Hank, please – please, Hank.' She felt desperately unhappy and pushed at his chest, so that he finally let her go, though he did not take his arm from around her shoulders.

'Isobel!' he pleaded.

'Hank – you mustn't, you know.' She laughed unsteadily and thought what a fool she had been to enter into this masquerade. She felt she could not trust herself, and said in a formal tone of voice: 'I must go in.'

His face looked heavy, sulky. He silently climbed out of the car, and paused, the snow whirling round him, letting the icy air cool him, before he walked round the car and opened the door for her. He had not had the slightest intention, when the evening commenced, of making love to her, but now he realized that he wanted her passionately.

She climbed out, and silently he picked the rug up from the seat on which she had been sitting. With a quick flick, he swung it over her head and shoulders.

His voice was trembling, as he said: 'I'm sorry, honey,' and he looked as forlorn as a flag on a windless day, as he held the rug round her with one great fist.

She smiled gently at him, her eyes soft below their golden lashes. 'It's all right, Hank. It was mostly my fault.' The snow was coming through her shoes, and she began to shiver. 'Would you like to come in for a drink? I think Dorothy will still be up.'

'No, thanks. I'd better get home.' He still held the rug close under her chin. 'You'll still be here when I get back from Banff?' he asked.

'Yes – I'm leaving next Sunday. Dorothy will stay a few

days longer to tie up a few ends for me – but I have to start my London job.'

He hardly heard what she said. He stood looking at her as if mesmerized, watching the snowflakes land on her hair and cheeks, to melt into gleaming droplets. She was so different from anyone he had ever met before, and, though he had often talked to her before through the years he had known her, he wanted now to talk to her for ever.

'Like me to carry you up to the house?' he asked mischievously. 'Your feet'll sure be wet otherwise.'

'Oh, Hank! Don't be an ass – I won't melt. And thank you very very much for a lovely evening – all of it,' she added. She was quite steady now.

'Aw, come on – I'll behave – I promise.' And before she could reply he had picked her up like a baby and was carrying her quite carefully, despite her laughing protests, up to the front door. Before he put her down, he put his cheek against hers for a moment and then very gently kissed her again. Then he put her down quickly.

'See you,' he said. 'Thanks a lot for coming. 'Bye.' And he tore down the steps and got his Triumph on the move again, so fast that she had hardly got her key into the lock before the protesting machine was shrieking round the corner on two wheels.

'I'm mad,' he told himself, as he closed the garage door, and opened the trunk in order to put in his typewriter and manuscript to work on in Banff. 'I'm plumb crazy.' He stopped, with the lid half closed. 'I'm in love.' He snapped it shut. 'I've always loved her – ever since I first saw her.'

He put up the collar of his evening jacket and dashed the two blocks to his home, as if trying to get away from more than the storm.

He felt he could not face either parent that night, so he prised open the window of his ground-floor bedroom and hauled himself quietly in through it. Carefully he slid shut both the inner and storm windows. He could hear angry voices, muffled by distance, and was thankful he had not tried to unlock the front door and come in that way.

164

He took off his wet jacket and shook it.

The room was very untidy. He had not made his bed before going out in the morning and it was still in the same muddle in which he had left it. His pyjamas lay on the floor, with yesterday's T-shirt and socks, and a half-read novel, face down, lay on top of them. He was glad he was going to Banff – at least in the motel his bed would be made for him.

From the back of his clothes closet he pulled out a zipper bag, and quickly crammed into it some sweaters and underwear, the novel, and his transistor radio – he'd need the latter on the road, for weather reports. His ski boots were with his skis in the basement, and he decided to get them on his way out in the morning.

Slowly and thoughtfully, he stripped off his clothes and then lay down on the unmade bed. He would sleep for about four hours and start for Banff about six in the morning, before the traffic on the highways got heavy. He told himself he was nuts to set out on a journey of hundreds of miles in the middle of a storm, but he had a great urge to pit himself against the elements, get away from cloying, sickening Tollemarche, and think.

He closed his eyes firmly – better sleep. He hauled a blanket over his nakedness, though the room was warm, but sleep did not come. All he could think of was a tiny queen in a coronet decorated with snowflakes.

'Jeeze!' he moaned miserably.

CHAPTER TWENTY-ONE

While most of his congregation were dancing at the Edwardian Ball, the Reverend Bruce Mackay of Tollemarche United Church was preparing his Sunday sermon. He sat before his desk in his shabby basement den, trying to concentrate on a safe, comfortable theme, while his two sons practised drumming on a tin tray in the kitchen overhead. Above them again, he could hear his wife running the bath water for his younger daughter's nightly scrub. She shouted to the eldest of his children, Mary, aged fourteen, to come and help her put the younger ones to bed.

The noise was excruciating, his bald head throbbed, and the platitudes which usually flowed so easily from him refused to come. He was always very careful, in preparing his sermons, to wrap up well, in fulsome and flattering phrases, any unpleasant home truths which he wished to bring to the attention of his overfed, overdressed congregation. He had an uneasy feeling that a minister who was too unpleasantly honest could find his flock behaving uncommonly like wolves, and it might be difficult to get another pulpit if he wanted to move. It was, therefore, important to find subjects to talk about with which the congregation was in some degree of sympathy; but how one could do this with such a thundering racket overhead, he did not know.

He went to the basement stairs and called to the boys to be a little quieter.

There were moans of protest that they were never allowed to do anything they wanted to do; and this blatant untruth tried his spirits sorely.

'Just for a little while, boys,' he wheedled, holding down his temper with an effort. 'You could do your drumming later on.'

'Aw right,' came the sulky response.

He returned to the neat wooden desk, which he had made himself, and settled down to try again. Within a minute the silence was broken by irregular, sharp thuds in the kitchen, accompanied by excited shrieks. The plumbing groaned and gurgled as the bath water was emptied down the drain, and Mrs Mackay's voice reached a crescendo.

He leaned his head on his bony, capable hands. He could feel his temper rising, and he wished that for once, just once, he could stand up and preach hell and damnation to the filled pews of his fashionable church.

Most of the time he was able to control his inward rage, but he felt now that if there was not some quiet in the house soon, it would explode. All the suppressed bitterness at insufficient money, poor housing and an unruly family would spill out, and it would continue to erupt in ever lessening bursts for several days, until he was left exhausted, abject in his repentance, to pray for forgiveness from both God and tear-stained wife.

The bumps and bangs increased and were accompanied by shouts and screams; a fight had evidently broken out between the boys.

A new sound added itself to the general pandemonium, the sound of hysterical weeping, cries of denial and the outraged voice of his wife. Two sets of heavy feet could be heard clomping down the basement stairs. Mary, pushed by her infuriated mother, stumbled into the room. Her fat face was red, her glasses awry, and her drab, brown hair hung in rats' tails to her shoulders. Her well-formed bosom heaved with her sobs under a pullover which she had long since grown out of.

Mrs Mackay's plain, unpainted face was livid. She still wore a damp apron over her crumpled cotton slacks, and her hands were scarlet from immersion in bath water.

The minister looked up crossly at this sudden invasion; his headache was so bad that he could hardly see who had arrived. 'Whatever is the matter?' he asked.

Mary turned and made a dash for the stairs, only to be

caught by the arm by her mother and be swung back to face her father again. She began to shout defiantly at her mother through her tears.

'You've no right to take it from me. Janice lent it to me – it's her book – and I can read it if I want to.'

'What *is* this all about?' He held his voice down by sheer effort of will, but he still sounded testy. 'I'm trying to write my sermon.'

Mrs Mackay looked at her husband beseechingly. She was obviously in deep distress, though trying to keep calm. With shaking hands, she drew from her apron pocket a battered copy of *The Cheaper Sex*, and flourished it close to his face.

He took it from her and adjusted his glasses on his nose so that he could read the title. Mary stood paralyzed with fright. Upstairs, the boys ceased their fighting and crept down to see what was happening. Their smaller sister was already seated on the middle step, surveying with cold interest the distraught Mary.

'*The Cheaper Sex*,' he read in a deceptively quiet voice. Then, reproachfully, he added: 'Mary, this is not the kind of book you should be reading.'

'Not the kind of book!' cried Mrs Mackay, a note of hysteria in her voice. 'Just look at the picture on the front and then take a look at the first chapter.'

Mary said nothing, but allowed a hopeless sob to escape.

There was silence, while Mr Mackay turned the pages. He went very white.

'Mary!' he exclaimed, and there was such genuine sorrow in that single word that Mary burst into a flood of tears again.

'I want to know about love and things, and Janice lent it to me and she's read it and so have the other girls and why can't I?' The final words came out in a doglike howl.

The Reverend Bruce Mackay felt like Job for a moment. He closed his eyes, remembering Janice, the daughter of the town's leading hardware merchant, brassy and aggressive like her father. She was in Mary's class at school, the class beauty with a diary full of dates. She patronized the plain Mary unmercifully and he was sure she would have got a satanic pleasure out of lending this book to Mary.

His wife's voice intruded upon his thoughts.

'Be quiet, Mary,' she was saying sharply. Then to her husband she said in a tense voice: 'It was actually written by somebody in Tollemarche.'

Mr Mackay's eyes popped open: 'What?' he exclaimed, his mouth open in astonishment.

'That's what it says on the inner flap.'

'Good gracious!'

'Well? Aren't you going to do something about it?'

He shut the book with a sharp plop, and sighed. He was bubbling with anger, but still his voice was calm. 'I will,' he said, 'leave it to me.' He looked up at the open staircase and the three interested spectators seated there. 'Boys, go to bed now. Elsie, kindly take our little Donna and put her to bed, too.' He turned to Mary and she could see the rage dancing in his eyes. 'Mary, you are to stay here.'

Mrs Mackay saw the wisdom of disposing of the younger members of the family, and in brisk tones she repeated her husband's orders to them and herded them before her up the stairs.

Reluctantly and with many backward glances at the weeping but still defiant Mary, who continued to stand in front of her father, they went upstairs to bed. They all knew their father's terrible temper and even Donna, who hated her overbearing sister, felt a sneaking pity for Mary.

Mr Mackay sat down in his chair, closed his eyes and prayed aloud for spiritual guidance and for calmness of spirit. He felt he had, by holding the book, touched something defiling; and he was nauseated at the idea of his innocent Mary reading such a book. Her agonized cry that she wanted to know about love had passed him by. He did not consider how she was supposed to obtain a knowledge of sex in a household where there was no mention of its existence, where there was not even a cat to have kittens and where babies had arrived, neatly bundled up, from the hospital, with a tired and harassed mother, who had gone to fetch them.

Mary's sobs reduced to a sniffle as he prayed, and she looked apprehensively at him over a soaked paper handkerchief.

'Amen,' said her father, and after a pause, added: 'You may sit down, Mary.'

She sat down uneasily on the only other chair in the room.

'I will take charge of this book. I shall return it to Janice's father.'

Mary was terrified. 'Oh, no!' she exclaimed, 'he'll kill her!'

'I doubt it,' replied her father dryly, 'but she will get what she deserves.'

Mary began to worry about what she herself might be thought to deserve.

It began as a quiet talk on maintaining the decencies of life, and that included reading only good books.

'What about television?' asked Mary, now sufficiently recovered to consider laying a few red herrings.

The daily injection of murder, sadism and sex administered by his television set to his children had bothered the Reverend Bruce Mackay for years. He had discovered, however, that if he turned the set off, the children merely wandered off to the homes of their friends, and watched it there; a number of sermons on the subject had failed to produce any parents capable of turning their sets off, too. He therefore endured the presence of this servant of Mammon in his house, where occasionally he managed to insist on censoring the programmes his younger children wanted to view; he had given up battling with Mary.

Mary had picked the wrong red herring. It reminded him of all his frustration at arguments lost with his ugly, rebellious daughter. He lost control of his temper, forgot he was a priest, and flew into a passion.

Mary quailed. She often baited her parents, driving them to the limits of their endurance and then retreating. But this time there seemed to be no retreat, no placating her father in any way. Her courage, already badly sapped, left her, and she sat on the wooden chair unable to move for sheer terror of her raging parent.

She had set out to read the book because she had hoped to learn the secrets of that dreadful sin, Sex, which everyone verbally disapproved of and in practice tolerated comfortably wherever it was exploited, be it in advertisements or on the street. She wanted facts about it and found herself denied them at every turn. Apparently gluttony, sloth, pride, envy and avarice were not nearly so serious, and, judging by her father's present mental state, neither was anger. She now realized, as she quivered in her chair, that sex must be truly deadly; otherwise, there would never have been such a fuss.

The Reverend Bruce Mackay had now reached a stage where he could not trust himself not to strike her, so he pointed to the staircase and told her to get out and stay out. No television, he roared, no pocket money, no desserts, no treats of any kind for a month. One chapter more of the Bible was to be read every morning, and Psalm 37 was to be committed to memory and recited to him on the last day of the month.

She forced her trembling legs into action and fled up to her bedroom which she shared with her little sister. She wept fiercely and silently until at last, still in her clothes, she slept.

Mrs Mackay heard her husband's voice raised in anger and later heard Mary go up to bed. She knew better, however, than to intrude upon her husband at such a time or to interfere between him and Mary by going to see the girl when she came upstairs. She argued, as she crawled into bed herself, exhausted from her long day's work, that she must show a united front with her husband in their disapproval of Mary; she could not own, even to herself, that she was just too tired to care what Mary's punishment was to be.

The book lay on top of Mr Mackay's sermon notes.

Distastefully, with the tips of his fingers, he flicked it open. Despite his best intentions, he began to read.

Hours later, he closed the book and read the notes about the author. It was unbelievable that Tollemarche could give birth to such a book. Its brutally truthful description of life amongst young people in the town went unappreciated; it dealt with a boy's sex life, and that was enough.

Inwardly burning, he went up to the kitchen to make himself a cup of coffee to calm his nerves, before he attempted to finish writing his sermon. On the kitchen counter lay the evening newspaper and he scanned the headlines while he waited for the water to boil.

The story of Hank leaped out at him. He felt as if he were being crucified. The son of members of his own congregation! Only then did he realize how deeply he had hoped that the author would prove to be some atheist from the university or, perhaps, a Roman Catholic. Dumbly he turned to page twelve, where, page one informed him, there was a review of the book.

The reviewer praised the book's honesty, clarity, tight plot and use of regional background. He hoped the author would continue to speak for the younger generations.

The minister was dumbfounded.

He slammed the newspaper to the floor, snatched up his cup of coffee and marched downstairs again to his desk. Breathing deeply and with most unchristian hatred in his heart, he tore up his sermon notes, took fresh paper and began to write.

CHAPTER TWENTY-TWO

Boyd Stych refused to be roused in time for Sunday morning church. When Olga shook him by the shoulder and told him crossly that he should show himself sometimes at church, he snapped at her and pulled the bedclothes over his head.

She put on a mutlticoloured striped duster and, closing her eyes as she passed her mirror so that she could not see her bleary-eyed morning appearance, she tottered into the kitchen to have breakfast alone. The moment Hank showed his face, she muttered, he would get his comeuppance from her, even if his father didn't care enough to give it to him.

She made herself some coffee, heated and buttered two large iced buns, and settled down to read Saturday's newspaper as she ate.

As she spread out the newspaper, she thought about the ball the previous night. She had enjoyed it until Hank came along and spoiled it. She had felt honoured to meet again Dr and Mrs LeClair. Dr LeClair was the president of Boyd's firm and normally did not stir far from his office in Montreal. He had decided, however, to venture into the wild and distant West because of the sudden upsurge in business in Tollemarche, and had extended his stay over a couple of months except for an occasional journey by jet back to Montreal to check on his vice-presidents' efforts to keep that end of the business going.

Mrs Stych sighed. Mrs LeClair sure was ladylike, so slim and elegant, with a lovely, snarly French-Canadian accent in which she had discussed her main interest in life, the care of exceptional children. Mrs Stych was painfully aware that her Ukrainian accent sounded heavy beside it. She had done her best, however, to express her admiration for anyone who could work with such unprepossessing children. She had not, thank goodness, had to introduce Hank to her. At least he had had enough sense to stay away from their party.

Hank's photograph stared up at her from the newspaper's front page. She thought it made him look older than he was. Under it was a fairly accurate history of his life and the news that he had written a daring and forward-looking book, reviewed on page twelve, which was proving a best seller and would be filmed shortly. The movie rights had been sold for – Mrs Stych gasped unbelievingly. It must be a misprint – Hank's lousy book could not be worth that much! Even if you took a zero off the sum mentioned, it was still a lot of money – more than a down payment on a house in Vanier Heights. No wonder Hank had been acting up, she sniffed to herself. Still, money or no money, she'd soon take him down a peg.

Five minutes later, when getting up to refill her cup, she saw a note scrawled on her kitchen blackboard. It said: 'Gone to Banff – back Saturday. Hank.'

Mrs Stych nearly screamed aloud. That was the way he had always been. He could duck out of bad situations quicker than a boxer in the ring. But he need not think he could escape this time, she promised herself. She'd teach him.

She sat down again and turned to the review on page twelve. This had been written by a young professor at the university and was full of praise. Everything that Hank had written was perfect.

This was too much for Olga Stych. It was a dirty book and she felt like sitting down right then and writing a letter of protest to the editor. Then she remembered how nice the girls had been the previous evening; they had proved themselves very kind by not mentioning it. Perhaps it was better not to draw more attention to the matter.

While she drank her coffee and perused the professorial effusion, fifty other ladies in fifty other kitchens were also catching up on the local news by reading Saturday's paper over their morning coffee. Many of them had attended the meeting of the Society for the Preservation of Morals, or had heard, from someone who had attended, about the terrible book which had been written by a Tollemarche student still in high school. Now, as it dawned on them that the author was Olga Stych's son, they chuckled and smirked almost fiendishly. A few of them positively purred like cats full of mice, as they realized that at last they could get their own back on Olga Stych, the woman who had cut so many of them out from senior offices in the many social groups, charitable and otherwise, in the town. Now, at last, they could challenge her unrivalled leadership of the aspiring coterie of Tollemarche matrons. Mrs Frizzell after the first shock of discovery, felt nearly ecstatic.

Into the ears of those husbands sufficiently awake to understand, they poured the shocking news, but in general all that penetrated to their alchohol-dulled brains was the fact that Olga and Boyd Stych's boy had made a pack of money out of a dirty book.

What, the ladies inquired rhetorically of these gentlemen, had Olga and Boyd Stych been doing to allow the publication of such a book? They must be out of their minds!

A few husbands, between groans about headaches, muttered that a man who allowed his son to accept a sum that big from a film company could not be out of his mind. They just wished their boys could make money like that.

The ladies were united in expressing their horror at such sentiments. Men, they said, had no culture, they were all sex mad and all they read were girlie magazines in the cigar store.

These were old bones of contention being dug up again, and, as the men all *did* read girlie magazines in the cigar store, they all clapped their mouths shut like well-sprung screen doors.

Mrs Stych was a few minutes late for church, owing to her detailed perusal of the newspaper, and she slipped into her usual pew near the front of the church, under cover of the first hymn. The florid female with two children, who

175

usually shared it with the Stych family, was already seated, and she turned to stare at Olga with her mouth open as she braced herself for a top note. Mrs Stych hastily found her place in the hymn-book and joined in the final verse.

There was a rustle of closing books, and Mrs Stych smiled brightly at Margaret Tyrrell, the secretary of the Committee for the Preservation of Morals, who, with her husband and mother-in-law, was in the pew across the aisle. Margaret looked embarrassed and gave close attention to the arrangement of her skirt as she sat down. She did not seem to see Mrs Stych.

Puzzled, Mrs Stych turned her gaze upon the Reverend Bruce Mackay, who, strangely, proved to be looking straight at her. Did she imagine it or did he really mean to look so malevolent? She wondered if he disapproved of her hat, which was an expensive creation of Persian lamb and violets, to match her coat.

There was an abrupt quietness amongst the congregation and Mrs Stych felt as if every eye was upon her. Then, to her relief, the Reverend Bruce Mackay cleared his throat preparatory to addressing the Lord, and Mrs Stych relaxed.

She was totally unprepared for the blow when it came some three-quarters of an hour later. The minister mounted to the pulpit and put down his notes before him. He paused dramatically and then brought his fist down on the edge of the pulpit with a thwack which gave him the immediate attention of his audience. The published title of his address that morning had been 'Work in the Mission Field', so they were unprepared for such an assault on their nervous systems.

Mrs Stych was jolted, too. This tirade had nothing to do with foreign missions, but at first she did not connect what he had to say with herself. Then his outraged comments began to penetrate. She and Boyd were being preached at in a fashion which had gone out fifty years before. They were being held responsible for the work of their son – as if anyone could be responsible for what one's children did!

They were being held up as people who had allowed their son such licence that he was now in a position to damage minds younger than his and create a society of loose-living reprobates. Parents who filled their lives with empty social events to the detriment of their children's training were more of a menace to society than the delinquent child himself. The angry minister did not name the particular parents he had in mind for, indeed, he was saying to a whole group what he had been longing to say for years. However, not a single worshipper was in doubt about whom he spoke, and all eyes were turned again upon Olga Stych, and it seemed as if even the artificial violets on her hat were beginning to wilt under the collective glare.

Some of the eyes gleamed with satisfaction. Olga could be insufferable, and she was getting a good old-fashioned talking-to. Mrs Frizzell, her face inscrutable, was inwardly rejoicing, and promised herself the satisfaction of cutting Olga dead as soon as they got out of church. That two of the Stych family had won prizes at the ball rankled like a festering wound.

Mrs Stych had patronized the Reverend Bruce Mackay casually for a number of years, and had thought him a dumb, acquiescent mouse. Now it was as if the mouse had clawed her like a cougar. She could feel the colour go from her face, while the two children in the pew sucked their sweets noisily and regarded her with cold eyes; their mother's eyes, a quick glance told her, were equally icy.

She was too shocked to feel anger at Hank – she had for the moment forgotten that he was the instrument of her destruction. She knew only that her life was collapsing around her; the carefully built façade of importance and prestige, of money and influence, came tumbling down. All that she had striven for – to improve herself, to get away as far as she could from her father's pig farm, to become a leader of Tollemarche society – was swept away as if by an avalanche. She could feel the animosity which flowed around her like a cold fog. The silence, except for the accusing voice from the pulpit, was profound; not a handbag clicked, not a shoe shuffled.

At the end of twenty minutes he had finished. With firm fingers he folded his notes and put them back into his pocket. As he stared out over the congregation, he knew that they were with him, and he was thankful for it. A bitter lesson had had to be taught and he felt himself to be God's instrument to teach it. He hoped sincerely that many of the women facing him would realize that his sermon had applied to their vapid lives, too.

He announced the final hymn, and dumbly Mrs Stych stood up. She did not sing, however; her throat was too dry. For the first time in years, she wished passionately that Boyd had been with her to sustain her with his masculine strength. She had no hope that he would sympathize or understand what she was going through, but he might at least have felt some indignation at the clerical condemnation of his lack of parental responsibility; it would have put him on her side.

The service was soon over. Mrs Stych sat down suddenly, fearing she was going to faint, and the florid woman and her two sticky children pushed past her to get out, without even her usual smile and 'Hiya?' The minister raced round to the front door in order to be in time to shake hands with each member of his flock, and only when the great building was practically empty did Mrs Stych rise and go out by the side door. Being a late arrival, she had had to park her car down a side street, and now she was glad of it. She crept home through snowy streets under skies as leaden as her spirits.

Not one woman, she realized with a pang, had slipped into her pew to sit with her and comfort her. Presumably this was going to be the time for paying off old scores, and Olga quailed as she realized how many old scores there were.

178

CHAPTER TWENTY-THREE

Olga arrived home from church earlier than she usually did because she had not stopped to talk on the church steps, and she could hear Boyd in the basement, chatting with a neighbour as they played pool. Boyd had installed the table on an earlier visit home, mostly as a status symbol, and had then discovered that he enjoyed the game.

It was symptomatic of Olga's distressed state of mind that the Persian lamb coat was dumped with hat, gloves and handbag on the living-room chesterfield, and not immediately hung up in her clothes closet.

The telephone rang just as she was patting her hair back into place in front of the hall mirror. She could clearly hear Boyd swearing in the basement, and she called that she would answer it.

An excited Ruthenian babble greeted her. Grandma and Uncle were pleased Hank had written a book. Had she seen the paper? Was she coming out to visit them today? Please bring a copy of the book, so one of Joe's kids could read it to her and translate it for her. The newspaper picture was nice; could she have another copy of it? Who had been on their phone all morning? She had not been able to get through until now.

Olga forced herself to think. Of course, the grandmothers would want to read the book, and she felt she had reached the end of her stamina when she realized this. She determined to make Hank face his grandparents – she had enough battles of her own to fight.

'We haven't got any copies yet, Ma,' she stalled. 'Hank will have some soon, and he'll give you a copy.'

'Where's Hank?' demanded the cracked voice in the telephone receiver. 'Put him on. I want to tell him I'm proud of him.'

'He's gone to Banff,' said Olga thankfully.

The babble at the other end dwindled in disappointment.

Olga made a valiant effort to sound normal. 'I'll come and see you next week, Ma.'

'Well, bring Hank and bring his book.'

Mrs Stych made her farewells and leaned her head against the wall, as she dropped the receiver on its cradle. The telephone immediately rang again.

'Mrs Stych?'

'Yeah?'

An eager young feminine voice said: 'I just wanna tell Hank I think his book is real sharp, Mrs Stych. Is he home?'

'No,' said Olga shortly. With a voice like that, the girl could not be more than fifteen.

'Oh,' the voice was deflated, forlorn. 'When he comes in, just tell him Betsy called.'

'I will.' Olga put down the receiver quickly. The Reverend Bruce Mackay's remarks about influencing a whole generation began to have some meaning for her. 'But it's not fair to blame us,' she thought defiantly. 'We didn't write it.'

The telephone rang again. This time the voice was male and belonged to Tom in Grade 12, but the tenor of the conversation was similar. Mrs Stych began to feel sick.

She could hear Boyd showing his visitor out of the back door and promising that they would have another game next Sunday. He came slowly back in, looking pleased with himself, and saw her with her hand still on the telephone.

'That damned thing has rung all morning,' he said irritably. 'Hank this and Hank that – I couldn't sleep – I took the receiver off for a while – the kid must know the whole darn town. And where is Hank, anyway? He must have got up real early.'

'Gone to Banff,' said Olga briefly. 'Musta gone for skiing.'

'Better get some dinner,' said Boyd, opening the refrigerator. 'Suppose you'll be going to see Mother this afternoon?'

Olga was reviewing this engagement with Grandma

Stych with trepidation; she was not sure how much the old lady would know about Hank's book. She attended a different church, but she would have read the *Tollemarche Advent* – everybody did.

She said dully to her husband, 'I suppose I'd better go – she'll be expecting me. Get out that cold roast beef and some tomatoes.'

Silently they prepared and ate their meal, interrupted only once by another telephone call, this time from the local radio station's morning commentator, who said she would telephone again when Hank returned.

'Might as well come with you to see Ma,' said Boyd, wiping his mouth on his paper table napkin. 'Have to look through some papers tonight – might as well get out this afternoon.'

Normally Mrs Stych would have disliked this intrusion into a feminine visit, but today she was so dismal that she was grateful for any human interest.

'O.K.,' she muttered. 'We'll go right away.'

The visit was uneventful. The old lady was interested that Hank had published a book, but why, she asked, had he chosen such a vulgar name for it?

Olga's heart sank. This was it. This would be where Grandma would blow up.

Boyd was lighting a cigarette. Without a flicker of an eyelid, he said calmly: 'You have to have names like that nowadays for books, otherwise they don't sell.'

Olga looked at him in silent admiration.

Mrs Stych Senior tut-tutted and said she didn't know what the world was coming to. Olga hastily agreed, and equally hastily asked if Grandma had planted any tulip bulbs this year.

Grandma Stych was launched safely on a new subject, and Olga leaned back to listen, too wrapped in depression to talk much more. The old lady's English was almost perfect, her grammar painstakingly correct. She had a slightly Scottish burr to her accent, learned from the Scottish woman recruited to teach her by her father when they had first landed in Tollemarche; and Olga, remembering the hours when Hank had sat at her feet playing with toy cars, wondered if this was where he had learned English well enough to enable him to write.

Olga watched her husband as he talked about getting their lot fenced. He, too, had tried to get away from the Old World ties of his parents – he was more agressively Canadian than a Nova Scotian – and she could see that some of his mannerisms still offended his mother.

They had trouble getting the car to move when they were ready to go home; the back wheels spun and dug hollows in the packed snow of the driveway. A fuming Boyd had to push, while Olga turned the ignition key and accelerated. A friendly passerby lent his shoulder to that of Boyd and between the two of them they got it rolling down the slope to the road. Since Olga was in the driver's seat, she continued in it and drove them home. Boyd put down her unusual silence to the need to concentrate on driving over such treacherously ice-covered streets.

After supper, he retired to his den to look at the work he had brought home from the office. He assumed that, as usual, Olga would go to practise with her Sacred Song Chorus Group, but, later on, he was surprised to notice that she was still moving about overhead.

Mrs Stych had intended to go to her practice, but, as the time for it drew near, her courage began to ebb. Most of the members would have been in church and would have heard the Reverend Bruce Mackay deliver his harangue, and Olga wanted to find out first what position the girls would take, after they had had time to talk the scandal over amongst themselves, before she laid herself open to snubs.

She stood in the middle of her sitting-room, which looked just like a picture in Eaton's catalogue, and wondered how to occupy herself. She was shocked to find herself chewing at her long scarlet fingernails, and hastily decided to tidy up the cupboards and drawers in Hank's room. She had not done this for years and was motivated by a sneaking curiosity to know what he had in them.

The girls made their decision sooner than she had expected. Soon after the chorus could reasonably have been expected to finish its practice, the telephone rang. Olga extricated herself with difficulty from the back of Hank's clothes closet, which she had found cluttered with several different sizes of ice hockey armour, indicating the different ages at which he had attempted to play the game. Provoked by yet another telephone call, she clicked her tongue irritably as she trotted down the passage and lifted the receiver.

It was Mrs Jones, the secretary of the chorus, a lady whom Mrs Stych did not know intimately. She was a pompous, narrow-minded woman, whose children were left to run wild and unattended in the streets as soon as they could stand, a lawless rabble dreaded by small children and cursed by shopkeepers. She did not ask Mrs Stych to resign; she ordered her to do so.

The chorus, she said, was united in feeling that Mrs Stych could not be considered a suitable person to assist in singing sacred songs, since she must have assented to her son's writing that dreadful, obscene book. And, if Mrs Jones might say so, it showed a shocking state of affairs in the Stych home.

Mrs Stych was stung into retort by the gross injustice of Mrs Jones's remarks.

'I suppose,' she said, her face aflame and her voice icy, 'you will also be asking Mrs Braun to resign, because her son stole a car recently, and Mrs Donohue, because of that bond scandal her husband was involved in?'

Mrs Jones gasped, and Olga slammed down the receiver in the hope that it would hurt her ears.

She stamped back to Hank's room and continued her rummaging. She had a morbid desire to see if she could exhume anything of his writings from it, but there was nothing – not a slip of paper, not even a book with a sexy looking cover; just his usual collection of classics in sober bindings. Two of them were *A Thousand and One Nights* and *The Decameron*, but Mrs Stych had never read these

183

and knew only that they were very old books, so she dusted them and put them back unopened. The dust was thick on a few of the volumes, because she had always left this room to the mercies of her cleaning lady, who had not been very thorough.

Hank was expected to make his bed and keep the place tidy himself; this he had failed to do, and his shelves and drawers were in a chaotic mess. Mrs Stych decided that this was something else to take up sharply with Hank on his return.

Finally she shook out her duster and dropped it down the laundry chute. Because she could not think of anything else to do, she went to bed.

This, she reflected, as she lay in the dark, had been one of the most miserable days of her life. None of the girls, she recollected dismally, had telephoned, and she wondered if they all felt as Mrs Jones did. She also wondered bleakly what she was going to do in the future, if they all did take the same attitude.

CHAPTER TWENTY-FOUR

The next week was a frantic and unhappy one for Mrs Stych.

Mr Dixon, the English teacher, telephoned on Monday morning and asked if he could speak to Hank.

'He's up at Banff, skiing,' said Mrs Stych shortly, for the twenty-second time. She was tired of Hank, sick of the disturbance he had caused her. In a moment of startled self-revelation, she was aware that she had regarded him as nothing but a trial and impediment to her since the day he had been conceived; she had made every effort not to have any more children, so that she could give all her attention to her own ambitions. Her sudden sense of guilt increased her irritation.

Mr Dixon's faded voice became a trifle more enthusiastic.

'I wanted to congratulate him, Mrs Stych. His choice of subject was unfortunate, but it is not every young man who can write so well. I feel that I have had some success with him, if I may venture to say so.'

'Mr Dixon!' exclaimed Olga, her voice quivering. 'Wotcha sayin'? You shoulda stopped him. You musta known what he was doin'. Why didn't you stop him?' She snorted. 'The school should do sumpin' about boys like him.'

Mr Dixon's resentment of lazy parents flared up. He remembered that when he had advised Hank to tell his parents what he was writing about, the boy had refused. Mr Dixon had been aware for some time that Hank was writing a book of which his elders might not approve. He had got wind of it through stray remarks of Hank and his friends' and it had worried him very much. No amount of kindly counselling had been able to break through Hank's pigheaded hatred of his parents, thought Mr Dixon, or make

185

him try harder to study his other school subjects. Now this woman was trying to tell him he was responsible for her son's behaviour.

He spoke coldly. 'Parents do not seem to realize, Mrs Stych, that schools have little hope of curbing young people if their teaching is not reinforced by the home.' He paused, and then added: 'A novel is an effort to show some order in life and find meaning in it. Judging by Hank's novel, his experience of life cannot have been very happy, Mrs Stych. We should perhaps remind ourselves that the whole of Hank's young life has been spent in his home at Tollemarche.'

'Mr Dixon!' cried Olga indignantly. 'Are you suggesting that he learned those things at home?'

She was still speaking when Mr Dixon said: 'Good-bye, Mrs Stych. I will speak to Hank another time.' The receiver went dead.

Mr Dixon was not without courage, and he grieved for many of his pupils, some of whom got into far deeper trouble than Hank would ever do. He sat for a while after his conversation with Olga Stych, his hands folded on his desk, wondering what one unimportant bachelor schoolteacher could do to help. Even some of the women teachers on the staff, he knew, had children who were not adequately cared for – apparently two pay cheques were more important than caring for one's children.

There was a small knock on his door, so he closed the books he was using to prepare a lesson, and said resignedly: 'Come in.'

A tall, lank-haired girl entered. Her eyes were black-rimmed in her white face. She clutched her books for her next class to her stomach, and looked at him entreatingly.

'Mr Dixon, could I talk to you about something? I don't think my counsellor, Miss Simpson, will understand – a man might understand better.'

'Oh, good grief,' he thought to himself, 'not another pregnancy!' And even as he said: 'Sure, come in,' he was thinking that the tart-tongued Miss Simpson would think

186

he was trespassing on her ground if he dealt with this girl and would demand an explanation. Miss Simpson could be very trying.

Still, he could lend an ear. He could give a little time to these youngsters, time that nobody else seemed able to spare.

Mrs Stych, that redoubtable socialite, that ardent hostess to the socially prominent, had time to spare. It began to hang very heavy on her hands, and every day seemed to make matters worse.

The secretary of the Committee for the Preservation of Morals telephoned to say, in her girlish, gushing voice: 'Olga, you must understand. It just won't do to have you on the committee. I mean to say . . .'

Mrs Stych resigned; and Margaret Tyrrell got rid of a dangerous competitor for the post of vice-president next year.

The Lady Queen Bees were even more crushing. The chairman wrote and demanded her precious Queen Bee medal back within three days. The Queen Bees could not tolerate even the merest breath of scandal, she stated peremptorily.

Boiling with rage, yet feeling that she had no alternative, Mrs Stych dropped the medal into an envelope and got Boyd to post it for her.

She had been president of the Community Centre; and two members of the executive committee, both suave real-estate salesmen who found the Community Centre a convenient source of information about houses likely to come up for sale, called upon her and smoothly explained that many members were uneasy at her continuing in the presidency; there was a general feeling that she and Boyd must have condoned the publication of Hank's book. Neither man had seen a copy of the book, but they both assured her that neither of them had any special feelings about it; they were just unfortunate that they had been given the unenviable task of explaining the Community Centre's quandary to her. They hoped that she would not take it amiss, and that she would not hesitate to call upon them to sell her home when she moved to Vanier Heights.

Mrs Stych ventured to argue that the responsibility was not hers, but she was no match for two salesmen, so eventually she agreed to resign.

Mrs Frizzell, who was the vice-president, rejoiced, as she was immediately installed as president.

The Ladies of Scotland did not communicate with her, and, remembering Miss Angus's denunciation of Donna Frizzell's taste in literature at the last tea, Mrs Stych kept out of their way, feeling that her fate would be much the same there.

Usually the Stychs gave an at-home at Christmas. They announced the date and time of it on the Christmas cards they sent out, and could usually expect about a hundred guests to flow through their living-room in the course of the evening. This year, Mrs Stych decided, they would not hold it. She also decided that she and Boyd would not attend two coffee parties to which they had earlier been invited. Boyd received this information with relief, as he was very busy at work.

Despite the cold-shouldering from which she was suffering, all those ladies connected with charities in the city sent special appeals to her, to Boyd and to Hank. Money was money, after all, they told each other.

Boyd remained untouched by the general disapprobation. His long absences from the city meant that he could not conveniently hold any office in service club or other community endeavours, and his friends were old ones who had gone to school with him.

None of his colleagues had read a book since they left university, and, though they had heard of Hank's book through their wives, the only thing they remembered about it was the mighty sum paid for the film rights, and this was enough to reconcile them to anything.

Only in the emerging world of polite society in Tollemarche, a world ruled by women, a tooth-and-claw world, was its impact felt, just as Hank had originally planned that it should be. Mrs Stych's rivals found it a priceless opportunity to displace a woman who had been rapidly becoming a very influential lady in the city.

During her fortnightly visit to the supermarket, the shoppers she knew seemed suddenly blind and had a tendency to vanish down the other end of the aisle just as she entered it. Even Mrs Stein of Dawne's Dresse Shoppe, where her charge account was one of the largest, left her to a young, careless girl who did not understand the needs of a forty bust.

Feverishly she checked her engagement diary. The church tea and bake sale was to be held on the following Saturday and she had promised to contribute two cakes to it. With her finger on the entry, she considered whether she should prepare the cakes. The Reverend Bruce Mackay loomed before her, shaking a menacing forefinger, and she cringed. A report of his attack on obscene literature had been featured in Monday's *Tollemarche Advent*, and Mrs Stych's double chin quivered with horror at the thought of facing him again. The Lord would have to do without cake.

The diary showed that she was due to go curling the following day with some of the girls; it was a good team and they had done well the previous winter.

Mrs Stych loved curling and felt she could not forgo this pleasure without putting up a fight. She dialled the captain of the team.

The telephone was answered by the captain's six-year-old daughter, who said her mother was out and she did not know when she would be back.

Mrs Stych inquired where Chrissie and Donald, her elder brother and sister, were.

'Gone skating,' said the small voice laconically.

Mrs Stych asked the child to request her mother to telephone back about curling the following day.

'Oh, Mother doesn't want you on the team any more,' said the child with devastating honesty. 'She's asked Mrs Simpkins to play instead.' There was a sound of munching, and then the child continued. 'She says Mrs Simpkins doesn't play so well, but she has to 'tain the moral character of the team. What's moral character, Mrs Stych?'

Mrs Stych was rocking unsteadily on her high heels. Her face was pale. She swallowed and said quite kindly: 'I'm not sure, honey. I guess . . . ' She sought for words. 'I guess it means being truthful like you are?'

'Am I truthful? Say, thank you for saying so, Mrs Stych.'

'Is your baby-sitter with you?'

'I don't need a sitter. I just come in from school. I'm big enough to manage now.' She sighed. 'I gotta a door key hanging round my neck. And I'm eating a cookie – listen!' And there was a crunch as small teeth went through a cookie.

Mrs Stych, never very good with children, felt out of her depth, so she said: 'It's been nice talking to you, honey. See you.' She rang off.

She went and sat down by her picture window and thought about the little girl to whom she had been speaking. She had left Hank like that, with a key hung round his neck, as she tore from one social event to another, assuring herself that she was the busiest woman alive and that one must keep up one's interests; otherwise, what would one do when one was widowed?

Now look where she was! She wondered what the little six-year-old would be doing in the empty hours after school ten years hence – and she shuddered. Hank had written in uncomprising terms about what they did.

She watched idly as a taxi drew up outside Mrs Frizzell's house. Betty from Vancouver had evidently come on a visit with the new baby. Her eldest boy, a three-year-old, stood in the wind, waiting for his mother to pay the cabbie. His parka was unzipped and his hood thrown back, despite the cold. He turned and clumped up the path to his grandmother's front door, and Mrs Stych nearly passed out. It could not be – it couldn't! A tiny, wooden-faced replica of Hank! She opened her eyes and looked again. A second look only confirmed her horrid suspicions.

Olga Stych closed her eyes and prayed fervently that Donna Frizzell would not see the likeness. A feeling of consternation swept through her. What else had Hank embroiled himself in?

CHAPTER TWENTY-FIVE

Hank fought his way back from Banff in a near blizzard, spending fifteen hours on the road in a determined effort to return before Isobel left. He arrived about midnight, having telephoned from Edmonton to say that he was on his way.

Sandwiches, cake and a warm welcome from both Isobel and Dorothy awaited him. In the privacy of the porch he kissed Isobel good-bye, leaving her pale and shaken, and promised himself privately that his tour of Europe would be short, so that he could spend a lot of time in London or Llan-whatever-it-was with Isobel. Without her, he knew after stern self-examination in the silence of the Rockies, he might as well be dead.

He had no desire to meet his parents that night, so he ploughed through the snow round the side of the house to the window of his room, which his experienced fingers quickly forced open. He pushed his bag in first, then clambered in himself, bringing enough snow with him to ruin the wall-to-wall broadloom.

His parents upstairs did not hear him, but Mrs Frizzell saw him through her bathroom window and, with a smug smile, promised herself the pleasure of spreading the news around Tollemarche in the morning that Hank Stych had been out so late that he had had to climb through his bedroom window to avoid his father.

She saw herself telling the story to Mrs MacDonald, with appropriately significant pauses, to suggest with whom she thought Hank had spent the evening. That young Mrs Dawson, thought Mrs Frizzell sourly, might queen it at the ball, but she was no better than the rest of them in leading Hank astray. The widow of Tollemarche's hero had no right to go out with any other man, never mind a boy. How Mrs Dawson Senior could endure her as a daughter-in-law was beyond Mrs Frizzell's comprehension.

Her malevolent contemplation of the probable relationship between Hank and Isobel was broken by the return of Mr Frizzell, aggressively drunk, from the Bonnie Scots Men's Association. He had just missed hitting another car, on turning into their street and was raging about careless young drivers.

Mrs Frizzell agreed that teenagers were plain crazy.

A cry from one of the bedrooms made it necessary for her to break the news to Maxie that Betty had brought the three children for a visit.

He cursed, and she was glad she had not told him how a nearly hysterical Betty had dumped them on her, with the news that her patient, law-abiding husband had left her and had gone to the United States to join the army. He had expressed the hope that he would be killed in Vietnam, and Betty had now returned to Vancouver, ostensibly to consult a lawyer friend. Mrs Frizzell had a horrid sinking feeling that the lawyer might be more than a friend and that the children might be with her for some time.

She shut the door so that she would not hear the baby's howls and went to bed. Tomorrow she would get a baby-sitter. No child was going to stand between her and the gratifying number of offices opened up to her by the fall of Olga Stych.

Unaware of the gaze of the witchlike female next door, Hank divested himself of his wet clothes and went to bed, still throbbing with the strength of feeling roused in him by Isobel. She was perfect; and he smiled as he remembered his farewell to her – he hoped she would remember it until he could see her again.

The scratched recording of bells, which served to call the faithful to the Tollemarche United Church, woke Hank on Sunday morning.

He lay in bed listening to it, while he recollected painfully that Isobel would be on the plane going eastward, having been seen off by her in-laws. He was back where he had started years ago – alone.

He told himself scornfully that he had a host of girl friends – and realized emptily that he had not called any of them for weeks. He knew every fellow in the neighbourhood, too, but mentally dismissed the lot of them as a pack of immature nincompoops; he had been through so much in the past few months that he felt old beside them.

He turned on his transistor radio and flicked hopelessly from station to station; every one had a preacher on it, busy saying how fast the world was travelling to either extinction or eternal damnation.

The Bible Belt, my God! It was time he got out of it.

He went through his mail, which had been delivered to Isobel's house. From an epistle from his publisher, he realized that he would need to go to Europe via New York.

He trailed off to the bathroom, turned on the shower to cold and stepped under it. The water was icy and he yelped and hastily turned on the hot tap as well.

Through the roar of the water, he heard his mother's sharp voice call: 'That you, Hank?'

He stopped scrubbing. He had imagined that she would be at church.

'Yeah, Ma,' he shouted.

She realized the impossibility of carrying on a conversation over the noise of the shower, which sounded like a miniature Niagara, so she went back to her breakfast coffee and buns, fuming silently.

On realizing that his mother was at home, Hank's first instinct had been to take refuge in bed again. But he was very hungry, so he put on a pair of jeans and a battered T-shirt, and, still drying his head with a towel, proceeded to the kitchen, from whence came the welcome odour of coffee.

'Don't dry your hair in the kitchen,' snapped Olga promptly. It was easier to squash people if you started by catching them in a genuine wrongdoing. She shifted her chair round to get a better view of him and glared at him distastefully.

'Why don't you get a better haircut – you look real foreign like that.'

He hastily plastered down his George V haircut with his hands, and looked at her speculatively. She had not yet dressed or made up, and she looked untidy and haggard, her face hard and unfriendly.

Silently he returned to the bathroom and replaced the offending towel. He stood for a moment, his hand on the towel rail, considering how to deal with his mother.

He thought of taking an apartment. An apartment home, based on seventy thousand dollars carefully invested, was a different proposition from a single room maintained by a schoolboy out of his earnings as a part-time grocery market clerk. If ever he came back from Europe – and he was beginning to wonder if he ever would – he would take one of the new apartments being built in the city, and, if his second book was a success, he would find a Japanese servant to look after him. He decided that he would pack up all his personal possessions before he went away, and store them in a corner of the basement.

Cheered up, he returned to the kitchen, opened the refrigerator door and was just taking out two eggs, when his mother put down the Saturday's *Advent*, which she had been reading, and addressed him.

'And just how long do you think you're going to live here for free?'

He was paralyzed with shock, the two eggs in his hand, and the refrigerator starting to hum because he still held its door open. The unexpectedness of this angle of attack had caught him unawares, and he did not know how to deal with it. He had been ready for upbraidings, but not this.

He had always taken the same attitude as his fellow students, that if his father insisted upon his staying in high school he could not earn much, and his parents must, therefore, be prepared to maintain him in food and lodging. He had managed to provide his own pocket money and clothes by doing odd jobs after school and, more recently, by his writing, since his fifteenth birthday. Now his mother was challenging this basic assumption.

He swallowed and carefully closed the refrigerator, after replacing the eggs. He turned guiltily towards her. The fact that the situation had changed on his leaving school and having money in plenty had honestly escaped him.

She saw that she had hit him on a tender spot and she was glad. She would teach him that if he thought he was adult enough to attend the ball, he was adult enough to maintain himself entirely. She would wear him ragged, she vowed.

Her smile was thin and sneering as she waited for his reply.

Hank sought for words. He was dreadfully hurt. The merest reminder would have been sufficient to make him produce his pocket book. This was tit-for-tat with a vengeance.

Finally, he stuttered: 'Of course I'll shell out for keep. I just forgot, that's all.'

'I should think so,' she said sourly.

He hadn't finished speaking to her. He drew himself up straight, till his six feet of height towered over her, and she flinched at the totally disillusioned, sad eyes he turned upon her. Mr Dixon's remark that his life could not have been a very happy one flashed through her mind.

'Look here,' he said in a dangerously quiet voice, 'you and Father wanted me to make Grade 12, not for my own sake, but because it would be a disgrace to you both if I didn't. I had no choice but to take my board from you.' He took a long breath, and years of pent-up resentment poured out. 'Neither of you cared what happened to me. You were so busy with your stupid teas and bake sales, and Dad with his trips to the North to get away from you. The cars got more care than I ever did! I'm sorry I didn't go years ago – I would have gone if it hadn't been for Grandma Palichuk, I think.'

He paused to gather up his self-control, which was slipping fast. 'Well, I don't want to be a drag on you any more,' he nearly shouted. 'I'm going to New York and then to Europe and I doubt if I'll ever come back.'

He felt for his wallet in his hip pocket, drew it out, sought through it for twenty-dollar bills. He flung the six that he had on to the table in front of her.

'I left school about a month ago. Here's my rent. I'll pay again before I go, and I'll eat out.'

The sum was more than double that which she could have expected from a lodger in similar circumstances, and she sat staring at it, trying to be happy that she had crushed him, while he turned on his heel and went back to his room.

He flung himself onto his rumpled bed. The pain inside him was so intense, he did not know how to bear it. In his calmer moments, he had long since realized that children in Tollemarche were more endured than loved, now that they were no longer needed as unskilled labour on the farms; and he had often said bitterly to his fellow sufferers in Grade 12 that rats nurtured their young better than Tollemarche mothers did.

He had, as a small boy, made excuses to himself for his mother's neglect, and he had endowed her with feelings of affection which, he told himself, she had no time to express because she had a lot of work to do. As he matured, he realized that most of her activity was busywork, and to think that she loved anyone was just a dream on his part. He had become desperate to finish school, so that he might acquire financial independence, yet such was society's indoctrination, he was convinced he could not function at all without that magical Grade 12.

Now he had disproved this fallacy and was financially well launched. He had, too, a degree of emotional emancipation. And he hoped he had Isobel.

The knifelike pain eased and he became calmer. He told himself to stop being a fool. He had hit his mother with the aid of his book and she had merely done the natural thing and hit him back. Fair enough. What he needed was a good breakfast – and tomorrow, a travel agent.

He found a faded car coat and some earmuffs, rescued his boots from the corner into which they had been tossed

197

the previous night to drip mournfully on the rug, and carrying them in his hand, tiptoed to the front door.

A pile of letters addressed to him had been flung carelessly on the top of the boot shelves, and he gathered them up as he went out. He sifted through them in the privacy of his car. They were mostly congratulatory letters from his fellow students, but one was from his Ukrainian grandmother in her own language, with a scrawl from his uncle at the bottom of it. He said that he and Grandma and his young cousins all wanted to see his book, but most of all they wanted to see him, to tell him how proud they were of him. He was to come down to the farm as soon as he returned from Banff.

He decided that at this moment the smell of pigs and hens would be nicer than even the best breakfast, and he swung the car out of the garage and headed for the highway, hoping that the snowploughs would have cleared as far as the farm.

He wished wistfully that he had been born to Uncle Joe's wife. She had died, of course, but his grandmother had a wonderful, primitive motherliness which permeated the whole contented existence of his cousins.

Grandma, he thought, had done her best to spare her daughter the intolerable work load which had turned her own hands into revolting claws. She and her silent peasant husband had decided the girl was smart, had sent her to Tollemarche to high school and then to college.

He smiled grimly to himself. Tollemarche must have seemed wonderfully sophisticated, with its college, schools and churches, its homes with bathrooms and its many small stores; a handsome Ukrainian girl would feel she could better herself there. And Boyd Stych, just graduated from the University of Toronto and about to join an enterprising firm of consulting geologists, would have looked like a film star to a girl from a Ukrainian pig farm.

He drove fast along the road, set high above the surrounding country. He could see for miles across the bleak, snowy land, unbrokenly smooth except for an

198

occasional windbreak of trees sheltering a cowering farm-house.

Where a letterbox nailed to a post marked the entrance, he turned into a cart track leading to the farm. He wished he had Isobel with him; he felt she and Grandma would get along together very well; they were both of them honest and practical – and, yes, gentle.

As he drew up between the barn and the back door, he suddenly remembered that he had not seen his father that morning. He would never have gone to church without being dragged there by his mother, and yet he was sure he had not been in the house.

He dismissed the question from his mind, as the door opened and his cousins came tumbling out to greet him and to admire the Triumph, which they had not seen before.

CHAPTER TWENTY-SIX

Olga Stych heard the front door close after Hank and her triumph at his humiliation slowly evaporated. Boyd had gone out early to see Mayor Murphy immediately upon his return from Mass, about purchasing a lot in Vanier Heights. He expected that these negotiations would be protracted, since the demand for serviced land was heavy and Mayor Murphy could name his own price. Without the presence of either man, the house was so quiet that even the creaking of its wooden frame seemed unnaturally loud. The snow outside and the double windows muffled all sound from the road, and Mrs Stych shivered and pulled her robe around her. Perhaps she should have gone to church and faced the supercilious stares of her erstwhile friends, rather than endure the emptiness of the house. The memory of the dislike in Hank's eyes as he left her battled in her mind with earlier memories of him as a frightened child left uncomforted.

She told herself she must be getting old to feel sorry for a great hulking brute like him. Next week she would give a dinner party for Boyd's more senior colleagues – that would keep her busy.

Making herself move briskly, she took a shower and made up her face. She tried on her new artificial eyelashes, sold to her by Monsieur de la Rue in his new Lady Fayre Beauty Boutique. He had sworn that they were just as becoming to mature beauties as to their daughters, and now, as she fluttered them cautiously in front of the mirror, she felt sure he was right. She added a further touch of blue eyeshadow and then put on her black dress, so that she would be ready to visit Grandma Stych in the afternoon.

Garbed in full visiting regalia, she felt much better, and began to consider that perhaps she had accepted her social eclipse too readily. Boyd had pointed out that they ought to cultivate some of the senior university staff, who were increasing rapidly in number and importance in the city. There were also one or two Canadian Broadcasting Company staff now resident in Tollemarche, not to speak of several new businesses being established with their concommitant executives. Perhaps, she pondered, it would be possible to drop the old Tollemarche residents almost as fast as they had tried to drop her.

Boyd had said: 'Those girls of yours don't really care a hang about Hank's book – or maybe the Reverend does – but nobody else. They are getting at us.'

Mrs Stych had been incredulous. 'Us?' She had squeaked.

'Yeah. Us. Y'know, the new pecking order in this town isn't yet quite clear – and we have been doing a bit too well. Hank's book is a good chance to put us back where we belong – way down.'

'Wotcha mean – pecking order?'

'Well, every town has a pecking order – like the hens in your Ma's back yard. Ours was fixed for years – Scottish Presbyterians at the top, Métis Roman Catholics at the bottom, the Indians nowhere, and everybody else in strictly acceptable order in between.

'Now, since the oil wells were discovered, so many new people have come in that it's all upset. Ukrainians and Germans, like us, have more money than some of the old Scots who've been here two generations. You can see I'm right – we have an Irish Roman Catholic for Mayor, with money in his wallet. Where was he fifteen years ago? Or even five?'

'We been here two generations,' Olga had said stubbornly.

'It doesn't mean the same thing. As far as the big people were concerned, we didn't exist until the past ten years. I tell you – now, I own more real estate in this town than the chemical plant does – more'n Tyrrell or Murphy even.' Then he added in a rueful tone, 'Except I don't have a lot in Vanier Heights.'

Mrs Stych ruminated over this conversation as she carved a store-cooked ham for Boyd's and her lunch. Apart from any entertaining they might manage to do to re-establish themselves, there were a number of public functions which they could attend, where it might be productive to show themselves; there was the Amateur Ballet Show, a full-evening-dress affair, and public lectures at the university – quite big people went to those.

She had just poured a commercial dressing over a quartered lettuce to go with the ham, when there was a heavy banging at the back door as if someone were kicking it.

She put the bottle of dressing down slowly, and considered what the new yellow paint on the back door must be looking like after such treatment. Indignantly, she marched to the door, yanked it open and peered through the glass of the outer screen door.

A small head in a snow suit hood was leaning against it at the level of the lower ledge, and a small foot in a rubber overboot was systematically kicking it. She pushed the door open, nearly toppling the owner of the head and foot.

'Just waddya think you're doing?'

She glared down at the peaceful face of a three-year-old boy, who, finger in mouth, stared unafraidly back at her.

He pointed a finger towards the house next door. 'Mummy says please come.'

'And who is Mummy?'

'She's my Mummy,' said the low-pitched voice patiently.

'Well, who are you?'

A note of irritation was noticeable in the child's voice, as he replied: 'I'm Michael.'

The cold wind was penetrating Mrs Stych's dress.

'Well, what do you want?'

Exasperation at adult stupidity brought a sharp answer: 'Mummy wants you!'

In an effort to stop the conversational circle being repeated, she asked him where he lived.

'Next door.' And he again pointed to the house of her immigrant neighbours, whose acquaintance, of course, she had never sought.

'And Mummy wants me?'

'Yeah, she burned herself and she can't feed Henny and she wants you to come.'

'Oh!' Mrs Stych was immediately attentive. 'Is anything on fire?'

'Only Mummy,' was the tranquil response.

'For Heaven's sakes!'

Mrs Stych snatched from its hook on the back of the door the coat which she usually wore when emptying the garbage, and whipped it over her shoulders. Without waiting for the child, she ran across the back of the unfenced lots, her golden house-slippers filling with snow as she went. She flew up the steps of the next house, struggled with the springs of the screen door, and then burst into the kitchen.

There was nothing on fire in the spotless kitchen, but a woman with one hand and arm wrapped in a tea towel and clutched to her chest ceased her agonized walking up and down and turned to her thankfully. Her round, flat young face was tear-stained, and it was clear that she was in great pain.

'Dank you, dank you for coming so quick,' she exclaimed gratefully, her guttural pronunciation of the words not helped by her laboured breathing. 'I haf burnt me.'

'Show me,' said Mrs Stych abruptly, as Michael pushed slowly in through the back door. He carefully took off his boots and placed them in the boot tray.

'It was the kettle – I somehow drop it and try to catch and the boiling water spill.'

She slowly unwound the towel to reveal a badly scalded right forearm and hand, on which big blisters were already forming.

Mrs Stych said tersely: 'Better get a doctor.'

'We haf no doctor, and if they don't know you doctors say go to the hospital.'

Mrs Stych nodded agreement. Doctors were in such short supply that it was unlikely that even her own doctor would come to a new patient; he would just direct them to the emergency department of the nearest hospital.

'I'll get out the car and take you up to the hospital.'

'Dank you – but I know not what to do with the children – I cannot leave them – my husband is in Toronto at a conference.' Despite her efforts at controlling them, she was nearly in tears again as she wrapped her arm once more in the tea towel.

'Lock 'em in a bedroom,' said Olga. 'They'll be all right.'

She looked quickly round the kitchen. Michael, his snowsuit half off, was watching his mother fearfully, and in a high-chair sat a slightly older child at which Mrs Stych stared in astonishment. It must have been about four years old, but its head wobbled and rolled erratically and its eyes stared emptily at her. Its tongue protruded from its mouth and it slavered slightly.

The mother saw her look, and said defensively: 'She is retarded. She cannot feed herself. She hungers.' She gave a faltering sigh. 'How could I lock them in a bedroom – alone?'

Mrs Stych felt physically sick at the sight of the retarded child. Since this immigrant woman seemed to think it was made of china, she would have to get more help from somewhere.

'Have you got a friend I could call?'

'Nobody close here – we are very new, you understand. In Toronto we know many people.' She moaned, and Michael ran to her with a whimper. She put her good arm round him lovingly and soothed him in a foreign tongue.

Mrs Stych felt cornered.

'O.K.' she said. 'Got any baking soda?'

'Ja,' and she indicated a cupboard.

Mrs Stych was not sure that she was doing the right thing, but she made a solution of baking soda and cool water, soaked a soft cotton pillow-case in it and wrapped this round the injured arm.

The mother gave a sigh of relief.

'Better,' she said thankfully.

'Now,' said Mrs Stych, with the firmness of desperation, 'I'm going to call Mr Frizzell, who lives over the other side of me, and ask him to take you to the hospital. I'll stay with the kids.'

'Their dinner?'

Mrs Stych looked at the little monster in the high-chair. 'What do they eat?'

'Stew is in the oven. Will you feed my Henny?' The voice was imploring.

Mr Stych licked her lips. 'Yeah, I guess I can.' Her voice was full of reluctance.

She went to the telephone and called the Frizzells' well-remembered number. Mrs Frizzell answered.

In a lofty tone, Olga asked for Mr Frizzell.

'That you, Olga?'

'It is.' Mrs Stych sounded frigid, and Mrs Frizzell was daunted as well as mystified. She called Maxie.

Mr Frizzell might be fat, but in a crisis he proved a wonderful help. He was also thankful to escape from three wailing grandchildren. He had his car at the front door inside three minutes.

The harassed mother cuddled Michael to her, and told him in her own language to stay with Auntie from next door and she would return before the big hand of the clock had gone round once. She kissed Henny, told Mrs Stych she was very kind, and, still in her pinafore, departed with Mr Frizzell.

A perplexed Mrs Stych was left with the slobbering little girl in the high-chair and with Michael, whose lips were trembling as he tried not to cry.

She found a casserole, ready for eating, in the gas oven. Aided by Michael, she found the necessary utensils and poured out glasses of milk for the children. Her repulsion for Henny was so great that she decided that she would give

Michael his meal first, in the hope that the mother would have returned by the time she was ready to feed Henny. Michael announced, however, that he could feed himself while she fed Henny.

He showed Mrs Stych a small baby spoon with which he said his mother fed the child, so Mrs Stych mashed up a small plateful of food, stuck a paper serviette under the child's chin, and tried to stuff a spoonful of dinner onto the protruding tongue. It dribbled down Henny's chin and she began to cry.

'She doesn't like anyone to feed her, except Mummy and her lady at school,' announced Michael. He was managing to tuck his own dinner into himself, though a fair quantity was getting plastered down his front and on his hands.

Mrs Stych did not answer. She was too busy holding down Henny's wavering hands, while she tried to get another spoonful in. Henny continued to dribble and blubber at the same time, while Michael climbed down from his chair and came to stare at her.

He put his sticky hands on Mrs Stych's elegant black lap. 'I'll show,' he announced, and climbed up on her knee, completely ruining her dress. 'Mummy showed me.'

He did manage to demonstrate roughly how to insert the spoon, and, without a word, Mrs Stych made another attempt.

Henny swallowed.

As pleased as if she had won a lottery, she followed it with another spoonful, and said to Henny: 'That's good'.

Henny stopped crying, and slowly and wearily Mrs Stych shovelled down most of the helping. At the end of half an hour, Henny refused to take any more, and Mrs Stych assumed thankfully that she was full.

She was a little pleased at her success. She wiped Henny and Michael clean and did the best she could, with the aid of the dishcloth, to the front of her dress. Michael called her Auntie and began to chatter to her. He got out his toy box and showed her each tiny car and teddy that he owned, while she washed the dishes and put the casserole back into the oven, to keep warm for the mother.

'What's your full name?' she asked Michael.

'Michael.'

'And what else?'

'Michael van der Schelden,' he said.

'Where does your father work?'

'University, 'course.' He ran a small truck round himself.

Mrs Stych wiped her hands dry and looked around the kitchen.

Michael glanced up at his sister. 'Henny wants a new diaper,' he said shrewdly, and Mrs Stych nerved herself for another ordeal.

She felt very squeamish and thought at first she would wait until Mrs van der Schelden returned. It wouldn't hurt the kid to stay wet for a while, she reckoned.

Then Michael said: 'She'll get in an awful mess if you don't hurry.'

With a sigh, she decided that probably Mrs van der Schelden would not be able to do the job when she did come back, as she would be bandaged up, so she asked Michael to explain to her how his mother did it.

Michael took her into a bedroom, bare except for a chest of drawers and a double bed. The wooden floor had been polished to a high gloss, and, when she opened the chest of drawers, neat piles of children's clothing and of diapers were revealed.

At Michael's direction, she spread a plastic crib pad on the bed, took the child out of the high-chair and laid it down on it. Henny dribbled down the back of her dress during this operation, but Mrs Stych was so absorbed in her efforts to get the child on the bed without dropping it that she did not notice this further spoiling of her new dress.

She took a large breath to steel herself against vomiting, and cleaned and changed the little girl, who watched her with what seemed to be a faint gleam of intelligence. She did not cry.

'Henny naps after lunch,' announced Michael suddenly, omitting to say that he was supposed to nap, too.

207

It occurred to Mrs Stych that Henny might be able to walk, so she put her carefully down on her feet, holding one hand firmly in case she collapsed. Held like that, she could balance herself and did walk in a shambling fashion. She looked up at Mrs Stych and gave a chuckle. Mrs Stych managed a thin smile in return.

She led her, on Michael's instructions, to a large cot in another room, lifted her over the rail and gently laid her down. The child was acquiescent, so Mrs Stych covered her, pulled down the window blinds and left her.

She suddenly remembered that Boyd would be home for lunch, so she telephoned him.

He had just come in and was in a very bad temper as a result of Mayor Murphy's refusal to sell him a lot in Vanier Heights. He wanted to know where the hell she was.

She told him what had happened, and he listened dumbfounded as she described what she had done with Henny, only interjecting an occasional 'You did?' as if he hardly believed her. Finally, he told her to stay where she was until Mrs van der Schelden came home.

Mrs Stych then rang Grandma Stych, to say that she did not think she would be able to come that day. Once again she described her morning's adventure, and Grandma Stych quavered her approval. Olga had done just what she would have done herself and had been most neighbourly.

Mrs Stych began to feel that she had been very noble. Then, as she walked slowly back to the kitchen, she began to think what coping with Henny twenty-four hours a day might be like.

'Why doesn't she put her in a home?' she wondered.

At half past two, Mr Frizzell returned with the accident victim. Mrs van der Schelden was feeling much more comfortable after some sedation. She clutched a small bottle of pills in her good hand.

The kitchen seemed suddenly to be full of pleasant, cheerful people. Mrs Stych felt better than she had for some time.

'You sit down quiet,' she said to Mrs van der Schelden,

'and I'll make some coffee. I've kept the dinner hot, and you should eat a bit if you can. You like a cup, Maxie?'

Maxie said he could just use a good cuppa cawfee – he was kind enough not to mention that he had had no lunch – and Mrs Stych busied herself with the coffee percolator. 'After you have this, you just go lie down a bit and rest yourself. I'll watch Michael.'

Tears filled Mrs van der Schelden's wide blue eyes. 'You are both so kind,' she said with feeling. 'Here we have felt so alone. Now I know I have good neighbours. How can I thank you?'

Mr Frizzell leaned over and patted her shoulder and said it had been real nice meeting her.

He turned to Olga. 'The intern said we should send for her husband. He says she mustn't put her hand in water for a while yet.'

Olga nodded agreement, and said to Mrs van der Schelden: 'We could phone him.'

'Ach,' said the young wife, 'that would be good. Then I say not to fear, just to come.'

'Have your lunch first,' said Mrs Stych in quite a motherly tone.

Michael had been chattering non-stop to his mother in Dutch while this exchange had been going on, and she suddenly grasped what he was saying. She looked up admiringly at Mrs Stych. 'How clever to feed and change Henny and get her to sleep. She not like anyone to touch her except her teacher or me.'

'Yeah?' Mrs Stych queried. 'I didn't have no trouble with her.' She put a small dish of casserole in front of the mother, with a plate of hot buttered toast. She then poured coffee for all of them. 'What kinda school does she go to?' she inquired, and then added baldly: 'Why don't you put her in a home?'

'Oh, we could not put her in a home!' the mother exclaimed passionately. 'We all love her.'

Mrs Stych, remembering the slobbering child, looked at Mrs van der Schelden in blatant disbelief.

209

The Dutch woman continued, as she fed herself awkwardly with her unhurt hand: 'We haf started on our own, a school for children like her, just some mothers together. We read how to help the children and we try everything to teach them. We teach Henny to hold a spoon. One day we will teach her to put it in her mouth. She walk better now – in the university comes a physiotherapist. He has much interest and try lots of new ideas. Soon we raise funds, have a real school like in Edmonton.'

Maxie, who had been quietly sipping his coffee during this exchange, now asked: 'How do you staff the school? What kinda people teach?'

'All volunteers,' replied Mrs van der Schelden, flourishing her fork. 'They gives days and days of work for little Henny and the others.'

Mrs Stych, hearing this, felt a little less noble than she had done earlier; it was evident to her that, for some unknown reason, Maxie was interested in this school.

The call to Toronto was put through, to Dr van der Schelden, and he promised to take the first flight home. Mrs van der Schelden was persuaded to go and lie down, a small boy called for Michael and they went out to play; on his mother's instructions, Mrs Stych made sure his hood was firmly tied and his mittens pinned to his sleeves, so that he could not lose them. Mrs Stych thought this was fussing unnecessarily – Hank had got by without any such attention – but she attended to the child's clothing without demur, anxious to appear gracious before Maxie.

Maxie said goodbye and departed. Mrs Stych was feeling rather weary herself and thought she might now go home. Then it struck her that someone would have to prepare the evening meal and feed the revolting Henny again. She pondered for a moment, and then put her head through the bedroom door to say she was going home but would return at five o'clock to help with the evening meal.

Mrs van der Schelden protested that she could manage, but this only served to strengthen Mrs Stych's resolve to return, so she just said: 'See you 'bout five,' and paddled back through the snow to her own house.

'God! You must have had quite a time!' exclaimed Boyd, emerging from behind a pile of graph paper on the living-room chesterfield.

Olga's black dress was a sticky mess, her makeup was hopelessly smeared and she had lost the eyelashes from her left eye. Her new gilt slippers were soggy with snow.

'Not too bad,' replied Olga abstractedly. 'Going back round five.' She turned her back to him. 'Unzip me,' she ordered.

Boyd obliged, glad that she had not asked him about his interview with Mayor Murphy.

She went upstairs, took off the dress, looked at it without a pang, and put it ready for the dry cleaners.

She was still thinking about the glimpse she had had of a different outlook on life, when she lay down on her bed and closed her eyes. She had not rested for more than a few minutes, when she realized abruptly that she was very hungry – she had forgotten to have lunch.

As soon as she felt rested, she got up and washed her face, found an old cotton housedress and put it on. From the back of the closet she retrieved a pair of flat-heeled summer shoes and slipped her feet into them. The gilt slippers lay in a dismal pool of melted snow. She picked them up and dropped them into the metal wastepaper container.

She found that Boyd had kindly put a plate of ham and lettuce ready in the refrigerator for her, and she sat down at the kitchen table and ate it absently.

CHAPTER TWENTY-SEVEN

'Tomorrow I think Henny cannot go to school,' remarked Mrs van der Schelden to Mrs Stych, as that lady patiently pushed Henny's evening dish of Pablum into her. 'It is a pity. She make good progress. Nobody else go from this part of Tollemarche – and me, I cannot drive at present.'

Mrs Stych thought of the appallingly empty Monday hovering over her, with only the throb of the washing machine for company.

'If you can help me dress her, I'll take her, and I could bring her back, too,' she offered on impulse.

Mrs van der Schelden protested that she could not allow Mrs Stych to do so much. Mrs Stych had already been so kind.

Olga was moved unaccountably by the near-affection apparent in Mrs van der Schelden's expression as she said this. Nobody had looked at her like that for years.

'Sure, I can do it,' she said firmly. 'I'll go to the stores in between.'

Monday morning was grey and icy. Mrs Stych had forgotten all about Hank and did not see him. He did, however, sleep in the house, eating breakfast at a coffee shop in the town before going to see a travel agent. The only sign that Boyd had left of his presence was an empty cereal dish and coffee cup in the kitchen sink.

Remembering the fate of her black dress on the previous day, Mrs Stych put on a pair of slacks and a car coat.

Henny was accustomed to her special seat in the van der Schelden's ancient Chevrolet, so it was decided that Mrs Stych would use their car instead of her own. The car was cold and Mrs Stych's fingers were clumsy on snowsuit zippers and seat buckles. Henny made protesting noises, and her arms and legs flapped wildly as she struggled to return to her mother. Mrs Stych did finally get away, however, with Henny slumped angrily down in her seat, slobbering and howling alternately.

Mrs Stych had been given the address of a church hall which had been lent to the embattled group of mothers, and she was thankful when, after crossing the river in a heavy flood of construction trucks serving the contractors building a new bridge, she found the shabby hall tucked behind an ugly red-brick church.

Henny, by this time, had given up her complaining, and Mrs Stych unbuckled her and lifted her out onto the sidewalk. It had been finally agreed that she would deliver Henny to the supervising mother, with Mrs van der Schelden's apologies for her own absence and the promise that Henny's father would collect her later in the day.

Henny staggered uncertainly around on the sidewalk, like a puppy searching for its mother's milk, while Mrs Stych locked the car. Feeling uncomfortably responsible for the child's safety, she ran to her and caught her hand. She guided her up the pathway to the open door of the hall, and, when Henny teetered uncertainly at the top of the basement steps that led down into the building, Mrs Stych picked her up and carried her down.

She pushed open the inner door and found that school was already in session. There seemed to be seven or eight ladies present in the gloomy basement room, with about double that number of children. Mrs Stych stood uncertainly in the doorway, holding Henny in her arms, and a grey-haired lady in a smock hastened towards her.

'Mrs Stych!' she exclaimed, her husky voice and her accent unmistakably French-Canadian. She grasped Mrs Stych's elbow and propelled her in a friendly fashion into the middle of the room.

At first Mrs Stych did not recognize her, her wispy, unset hair and bedraggled smock acting as a disguise. Then she was shocked to realize that she was faced with the wife of the president of Boyd's firm, whom they had entertained both at the Edwardian Ball and at the West Enders Club, to which Boyd belonged. Then she had been exquisite in black, hand-woven silk and real pearls; now she looked as if she had been on her knees cleaning a house for hours past.

'Good morning, Mrs LeClair,' Olga finally managed to stutter, as, still in her high-heeled snow boots, she found herself the centre of attention. She was still clutching Henny to her ample bosom and was finding her extremely heavy.

She put the child down, and another lady promptly came forward and greeted Henny in soft, clear tones, as she knelt down to help her off with her snowsuit. Mrs Stych, despite her confusion, was interested to see how the lady took one of Henny's hands and guided it to the pendant of the zipper, pinching the tiny fingers firmly over it. Henny made no real effort to help in the unzipping, but allowed her hands to be guided. The lady did the same with the little boots, and here for a second Henny did show some interest before her bobbing head turned away.

'Ladies,' announced Mrs LeClair, the French rasp of her voice carrying to the rafters, 'may I introduce a new helper, Mrs Stych – perhaps I should say Olga – the wife of one of my husband's colleagues.'

The mothers murmured a greeting, and Mrs LeClair turned to Olga. 'Let me show you where to put your coat. I presume Mrs van der Schelden was unable to come?'

'She couldn't,' confirmed Olga, and then began to add: 'I'm not supposed to stay – ' But Mrs LeClair had already started off towards a door marked WOMEN and did not hear, so Olga trailed after her rather helplessly, anxious not to offend the wife of the company's president.

Mrs LeClair led the way into the cloakroom.

'I did not know zat you are interested in exceptional children,' she remarked, turning her intelligent brown eyes upon Olga, who automatically had begun to take her boots off.

'Well,' said the floundering Olga, 'I – I don't know anything about them – I didn't know there were so many.'

Mrs LeClair clasped her hands together in a gesture passionate enough for a prima donna about to strike high

214

C. 'It does not matter. We none of us know much. I have worked with them in Montreal, and when Father Devereux here mentioned this group to me, I came to see if I could help during the little time my husband and I are staying in Tollemarche.' She smiled. 'We pooled our experience, and, by taking turns in caring for the children, we give the mothers a small respite.'

Mrs Stych gathered her wits together and opened her mouth to say that she would not be staying to help, having promised only to deliver Henny, but she did not stand a chance of getting a word in, now that Mrs LeClair was securely mounted on her hobby horse.

'Of course, we all read everything we can. One husband is a doctor and he is going to bring a new physiotherapist from the hospital, and they will try to think of new ways in which we can teach these poor children as much as they can absorb. We have also written to other groups to ask about their experiences.'

Tears came to her eyes as she went on: 'If you only knew, my dear! So many children are kept indoors, because their parents are ashamed of them, and some, which we have not been able yet to gather in, we are sure are thoroughly ill-treated. I dream – I dream . . . ' she raised her clasped hands towards the ceiling, 'of building a beautiful school in every major city, designed especially for them.'

Mrs Stych came to the conclusion that if she was not to offend such a dedicated and important lady she had better stay, so, with a sigh, she removed her coat and hung it up.

'Why don't they put them in homes?' she asked.

Mrs LeClair's eyes flashed.

'And leave them like vegetables to rot?' she asked. 'No! Not as long as I have strength to fight for them. They are all capable of love and they respond to love. I encourage these mothers! I say to them to work on! They can accomplish much if they try.'

She opened the swing door with a flourish, and passed through it so fast that Mrs Stych was nearly brained by its backward swing, as she followed her.

Mrs Stych looked around her cautiously.

Some of the children looked quite normal, and were sitting on the floor playing simple games with bricks and marbles. Henny was on a mattress, having her legs exercised and obviously enjoying it. Two youngsters lay in Karrycots and their attendant mothers were laying out mattresses on which to put them. One child sat on a mother's knee and was looking quite intelligently at a picture book. The mother was pronouncing very clearly the names of the objects depicted in the book and then trying to persuade the child to say them after her.

Mrs Stych was acutely aware that she was wearing slacks, her makeup was not good and altogether she was not looking her best, but she soon realized that she did not know any of the women present, except Mrs LeClair. She wondered where they came from. Four of them, in cheap slacks and blouses, worn without foundation garments, were obviously not of her social circle, but some of the others looked as if they might have money. They all had in common a look of intense fatigue.

She did not have long to ponder about the status of her fellow workers. With firm, bony fingers Mrs LeClair clasped her elbow once more and shot her into the kitchen attached to the hall.

'Sixteen small glasses of milk, and a biscuit for each child. Eight – no, nine coffees, please.'

Despite a subdued resentment at having been caught up so ruthlessly to help, Mrs Stych managed her best receiving-line smile for the benefit of Mrs LeClair, and said: 'Sure, I'll soon fix that.'

As she waited for the water to boil for the coffee, she thought about the pile of washing waiting to be put into the machine at home. She remembered that, had she stayed at home to do it, all she would have heard throughout the day would have been the slosh of the water in the washer and the hum of the dryer, interspersed with commercials if she had turned on the radio. Any telephone calls would almost certainly have been for Hank or for Boyd. The front door

216

bell would have been unlikely to herald anyone but a collector for charity.

If she had been less tough, she would have wept with self-pity. As it was, she felt that she might just as well stick around to please Mrs LeClair, as face such a dull and empty day alone.

To get all the children to drink their milk proved a slow task, and Mrs Stych's coffee was left to get cold on the kitchen counter, as she struggled to get small fingers to grasp their glasses. All the mothers were anxious that the children should learn to feed themselves. They were not sure how to go about this, but they repeated the same movements every time they tried, and they had succeeded in getting some of the children to grasp their cookies or sandwiches, and two boys could drink from a glass.

A ripple of rejoicing went through the patient helpers when it was whispered that Henny had picked up her cookie and had, moreover, aimed it for her mouth. She had had to have help to actually eat it, but this tiny effort on the part of a single child gave new impetus to the day's work.

Mrs Stych was bewildered that such a small movement could be construed as a victory, but she managed to murmur politely that it was just wonderful.

The mothers, after discovering that she herself did not have a subnormal child, received her assistance with every demonstration of gratitude, and several of them expressed wonderment that she should be so good as to interest herself in their problems.

She helped fairly willingly to prepare a simple lunch from ingredients brought by the mothers, after which some chidren were taken home, and three other mothers arrived with a total of five or more children among them. All the time, Mrs LeClair, drawing on her experience in Montreal, trotted up and down the hall, encouraging, organizing, instructing. Her hair grew wilder, her hands became grubbier, as the dust from the floor rose, and she looked like some demented female from skid row, rather than the wife of a man making enough money each year to buy the whole church hall. One mother said wistfully she wished Mrs LeClair could stay in Tollemarche long enough to get the school on its feet.

In the afternoon Mrs LeClair asked Olga to learn from another mother the principles of patterning. Mrs Stych was informed that when the brain had been damaged so that the child could not control its limbs properly, it was sometimes possible to teach another part of the brain to take over, if the limbs were exercised several times a day in the pattern of behaviour normal to them. The task, even to help one child, was a stupendous one, more than a mother alone could hope to achieve; sometimes in large families, it was possible to recruit enough people to take turns at exercising the child, but in most cases outside help had to be found.

'Twenty-four girls from Tollemarche Composite High School take turns coming to our home,' explained the mother who was teaching Mrs Stych, 'to put Beth through her exercises.'

Mrs Stych was astonished. 'High school kids!' she exclaimed.

'Sure,' the mother confirmed, as she smiled down at the golden-haired Beth, and then said to the child: 'You've got lots of friends, haven't you, honey?' She bent and kissed the smiling face, as she continued: 'When we started, she lay on her back and propelled herself along with wriggles. Now she can crawl on her tummy.'

The mother looked down with such obvious adoration at Beth that Mrs Stych felt embarrassed. She had never felt like that about Hank.

Mrs Stych was invited to try doing the exercising. The child at first whimpered at her touch, but Mrs Stych was very careful and she soon submitted more cheerfully to the manipulation of her legs, arms and back.

Many years before, Olga Stych had been a bright Ukrainian country girl doing her first year in college, the only Ukrainian in her class. Her teachers had told her that she had brains and should use them, so Olga had had a dreamy ambition of becoming a doctor or a lawyer, a Portia or at least a Florence Nightingale. Then she had, from many acid remarks and much cold-shouldering, learned that a Ukrainian was an ignorant, peasantlike clod. She became ashamed of her Ukrainian surname, and it seemed her Greek Orthodox Church connections were fit only for the illiterate. To struggle towards a profession with the two strikes against her that she was both a woman and a Ukrainian would be too hard, she decided. She therefore concentrated on finding a husband who was not a Ukrainian.

No Scottish boy would look at her: they could look much higher for a wife – theirs was the kingdom, thought Olga bitterly – and when Boyd Stych had offered himself, it had seemed a good compromise. And he had really loved her, thought Olga wistfully, as she bent Beth's small legs in the direction they should go.

Now, as Olga warmed to the work, she began to think, as she had not thought for years, about Boyd, about the children round her, even, rather painfully, about Hank, and she forgot about that very important personage, Mrs Olga Stych.

By half past three Mrs Stych was ready to drop dead with fatigue. Her blouse was stuck to her back with sweat and she guessed that there was not a scrap of makeup left on her face. The mothers were dressing the children, and a graceful, expensive-looking blonde had dressed both Henny and her own child in their heavy winter clothes. Mrs Stych thankfully rescued her car coat and boots from the cloakroom.

She took Henny by the hand to try to get her to climb the steps to the front door.

'Ah, you have the idea, Mrs Stych,' exclaimed Mrs Le-Clair, pouncing upon her as she waited for Henny, who, hampered by her snowsuit, was making a not very successful try at climbing the steps. 'Always make the child do as much as it can.' She patted Mrs Stych's arm. 'You will come tomorrow, of course. We need all the help we can get.'

'Well . . . .' began Mrs Stych, trying to make a determined stand.

Mrs LeClair clapped her on the shoulder. 'Ah, I knew you would! You will feel so rewarded.'

Mrs Stych opened her mouth again and managed to commence: 'But . . . ' when Henny, stranded on the second step up, began to howl, her head winding to and fro like that of a serpent.

Mrs Stych bent and set the child's hands firmly on the third step, and laboriously she climbed another. By the time she had got the rhythm of climbing, Mrs LeClair had darted to the other end of the hall, to assist a mother with a Karrykot.

Mrs Stych's lips narrowed to a thin line. She was not accustomed to people rushing off when she wished to speak to them. If Mrs LeClair had no time for her, she had no time for Mrs LeClair; she would not come tomorrow – nobody was going to make her work like a slave for a pack of crazy kids.

Henny allowed herself to be buckled into her car seat without demur. Mrs Stych climbed in beside her and glanced down at her in disgust.

Quite unexpectedly, Henny looked up at her and laughed like a young baby. The empty face with its slightly protruding tongue looked for a moment no different from that of any other tiny girl, and Mrs Stych hastily looked back at the road.

Dr and Mrs van der Schelden greeted Mrs Stych and Henny, on their return, like long-lost kissing cousins. Dr van der Schelden was a huge, fair-haired man and he nearly wrung Mrs Stych's hand off as he thanked her for all she had done. Mrs Stych felt so guilty about her dislike of Henny that she blushed and said hastily that she had done nothing at all.

She took gratefully the chair offered to her – she had not felt so tired for months – and accepted the hot coffee pressed upon her by Dr van der Schelden. It was very pleasant to be made a fuss of, and her face gradually resumed its normal colour.

'Mr Frizzell took me to the hospital again,' reported Mrs

van der Schelden, 'and sat with Michael in the waiting-room while the doctor look at my hand. He also is so good.'

'Yes,' said Dr van der Schelden. 'He has also suggested that he gets together a committee of interested businessmen, to raise funds for a proper school for Henny and the other children. Do you think he could do it?'

Mrs Stych assured him sourly that Maxie could do anything he set his mind to.

'Would it not be wonderful, Mrs Stych?' asked Mrs van der Schelden, patting Mrs Stych's hand gently.

Mrs Stych agreed that it would be, and wondered privately what the hell Maxie had in his head to suggest such a thing. Anything Maxie did always benefited Maxie in the end.

On the doorstep, her conscience pricked her and she said: 'I'll take Henny again tomorrow – your husband will have a lot to do for you and Michael.' Maxie Frizzell was not going to be allowed to outdo her.

Mrs van der Schelden's wide blue eyes moistened. 'Would you do so? That would be so kind,' and before Mrs Stych could stop her, she had put her arms round the elder woman's shoulders and kissed her.

Mrs Stych could not remember when another woman had last kissed her; they had toadied to her, deferred to her, tried to squash her, fought to keep her down, all with the sweetest of smiles over their teacups, but nobody had kissed her with warmth and gratitude before. Her face was still pink as she walked slowly through the snow across the adjoining lawns to her own front door and let herself in.

On the Frizzells' front lawn, a baby-sitter and two of the Frizzell grandchildren were making angels in the snow, and Mrs Stych was reminded uneasily of Hank.

221

Mrs Stych felt better after she had taken a shower, put on a loose red housecoat and a pair of red mules, and combed her hair. She felt too tired to paint her face. She did, however, go down to the basement and set the washing machine going with its first load of sheets; then she prepared a supper for Boyd and herself. Brown-and-serve meat chops were soon slapped into a frying pan and frozen chips put into the oven to defrost.

She laid the table in the breakfast nook for two people, and wondered where Hank would eat. A pang of conscience struck her – perhaps she should not have bawled him out quite so hard. Fancy if he had been like one of those kids she had been working with! What would she have done?

She squirmed inwardly as she answered her own question. She knew she would have repudiated him and put him in a home. As she worked, she uneasily compared the care given to Mrs LeClair's exceptional children with that given to the children in her own circle.

'It's ridiculous,' she told herself defiantly. 'So much fuss spoils kids – it isn't good for them – they gotta learn to be independent.'

Absorbed in her own reflections, she did not bother to greet Boyd when he came into the kitchen, grey and tired. He went straight to the refrigerator to get himself a glass of rye.

He eyed her tentatively over his glass, surprised to see her arrayed in her best housecoat. He reminded himself that he had yet to tell her that Mayor Murphy would not part with one of his lots in Vanier Heights, because he was waiting for the price to rocket even higher. He slumped down in a chair and finished his drink quickly, after which he felt strong enough to say 'Hi' to his wife.

'Hi,' she said back.

'Where's Hank?'

'Dunno.'

'Didn't see him this morning. Mebbe he'll be in for supper.'

She looked at him, and her lips curled. 'I doubt it,' she said.

'Why not?'

She took the potato chips out of the oven before she replied. Then she said carefully: 'Said he'd eat out.'

Boyd sensed that something was wrong. He spun the ice cube round and round in his empty glass. The rye was warming him, and he felt better.

'Something happen?' he asked, pouring a little more rye onto the ice cube. He guessed that Hank was doing one of his usual fast retreats from an unpleasant situation. Presumably Olga was still mad about the book. He watched his wife out of the corner of his eye as he drained his glass again. Her face had hardened, and he felt an unexpected pity for his son.

'I just told him he must pay his board now he's working.'

Boyd ran his tongue round the tips of his teeth. It was not an unreasonable request for a mother to make. He wondered, however, how she had approached the subject.

'What did he say?'

She put a plate of chops and chips in front of him, following it with a knife and fork and a bottle of ketchup. He put down his glass and picked up his fork, still watching her.

She filled the coffeepot and put it on the stove to percolate.

'Said he'd pay rent and eat out,' she said as laconically as she could, under his distrustful gaze.

Boyd slowly laid down his first forkful of chop and said in a shocked voice: 'Now, Olga, he's not some student boarding with us. That won't do.'

Mrs Stych brought her plate to the table and sat down. 'That's what he wanted, that's what he got.'

223

Boyd stared at her. He had never taken much interest in Hank. He had been away from home so much that he had, in fact, frequently forgotten the boy's existence for months at a time. But this upset his sense of propriety. It savoured of his grudging his son food from his table, which he did not. It offended his sense of western hospitality, a hospitality which demanded that even strangers be fed like fighting kings and his bulging refrigerator kept full for the use of the family.

His wife was looking mutinous, so he said heavily: 'I'll talk to him when he comes in.'

'You'll have to be quick,' she snapped. 'Says he's goin' to Europe soon.'

He knew that the smallest spark would light the fires of temper and she would start a tantrum, so he tried to eat his dinner.

The long evening he and Hank had spent together, when Hank had first told him about his literary success, had established a friendliness between them, quite separate from any fatherly feeling which Boyd might reasonably be expected to harbour for the boy. Boyd had first been amazed, and then had felt a sneaking admiration for a youngster who could defy a whole town and its heavily paternal school board, and make a small fortune out of it. He knew that Olga had lost some friends through Hank's choice of subject, but he had no desire to see the boy bullied out of the house because of it.

Olga ate her dinner and then retired to the basement, to sulk over the washing, leaving Boyd to wash the dishes.

A stony-faced Hank came home about nine, to find his mother had gone to bed. His father was, however, sitting smoking in his den, with the door open. He got up as Hank came through the living-room, and stood at the door of his room.

'Hi, Son,' he said tentatively; and, in spite of his own preoccupation, Hank noticed the weary droop of the elder man's shoulders and his general air of anxiety.

'Hiya, Dad.'

224

'Come in here. I want to talk to you.'

Hank was immediately on guard, but went in and took the chair indicated by Boyd.

'What happened between you and your Ma this morning about board money?'

Hank relaxed, and told his father what had occurred. Finally, he said: 'Honest, Dad, I just forgot. I'm not mean. Only she didn't ask so nice.' He grinned sheepishly. 'Guess I'm not altogether used to being independent.'

Boyd laughed. 'It's O.K. I'll fix it with your mother. You had better pay something – you have to get used to standing on your own feet – and one day you'll be having to make your wife an allowance.' He changed the subject. 'Your mother said you're going to Europe?'

'Yeah, thought I'd travel around for a while. I got a book coming along just fine. Feel I oughta see sumpin' before I settle down?'

Boyd sat silent. He had gone away from home to university at eighteen, so he supposed Hank would be all right. He remembered he had promised to help Hank invest his earnings, and thought he had better mention this.

'Do you want me to do anything about the money you've got, while you're away?' he inquired.

'Sure, Dad. Not all of it's in yet, of course.'

'Do you like to give me power of attorney?'

Hank had been considering this for some time, but his distrust of both parents was so great that he had not been able to convince himself that this would be a wise move. Boyd could see that his question was causing some confusion to Hank, though he fortunately did not realize why.

The boy stirred uneasily. 'Think I'd sorta like to sign everything myself. I'll be in London, and stuff don't take so long by air mail.' He hastened to add: 'I think your advice was great – and I wanna do just what you suggested – but I'd have a better picture of how I stood if I signed everything myself.'

'O.K.' said Boyd. 'I'll fix it – you give me an address.

225

Would London be where Mrs Dawson has gone?'

Hank flushed crimson and Boyd had to laugh, despite his anxiety that the boy might marry too young.

'O.K., O.K.,' he smiled, 'I won't ask. Just be careful what you do. She's a real nice girl and you have to give a girl like that a square deal. She's no Betty Frizzell.'

The colour which had suffused Hank's face drained as rapidly as it had come. Boyd's idle remark had hit a raw nerve; Mrs Stych was not the only member of the family who had noted the appearance of Betty's eldest boy. Hank had seen him and had felt thoroughly sick; he wondered how he could have gone near such a girl, and he wondered, too, how he could ever approach Isobel after the kind of life he had led up to now. He felt like crawling on his knees to her; he could understand how men could humble and humiliate themselves before women to gain their forgiveness.

'You don't have anything to worry about, Dad,' he said, his expression so desolate that Boyd began to worry about him as he never had before.

CHAPTER TWENTY-NINE

Two days later Hank left for New York, on his way to London. He hardly spoke to his mother and did not bid her goodbye. She was surprised to find after he had gone that he had cleared his room and packed all his possessions into cardboard boxes, which he had transported into the basement storeroom, stacking them neatly in a corner, so that she could hardly complain that they took up too much space. His bedroom looked like a hotel room, without a personality.

She told herself she did not care; he was nothing but a quarrelsome interruption in the mainstream of her life. Then she rememered that her life's mainstream had dried up. No amount of attendance at public functions or entertaining new people could put her back into the exalted position she had previously enjoyed. The real residents of Tollemarche had rejected her out of hand – and all because of Hank. Suddenly, in the horrifying vacuum her life had become, she was thankful for Henny.

When, after his conversation with Hank, Boyd had climbed the stairs to their bedroom, he had found Olga lying awake in the middle of the three-quarter bed they shared, staring at the gilt stars on the ceiling. The bed had a hollow in the middle where she had for years slept by herself, and she had absent-mindedly crawled into it.

While he was getting undressed, he thought he might as well tell her about his interview with Mayor Murphy.

'About that lot in Vanier Heights,' he commenced, his voice muffled as he removed his undershirt. 'Murphy won't sell.' His stomach felt constricted and he wondered if he was starting an ulcer.

His wife's voice was listless when she replied: 'Well, we gotta home, so we don't have to worry. Mebbe a riverside lot, one of those you got down by the creek, would be nicer.'

At first he could not believe his ears. 'You don't mind?'

'Why should I?' She sounded as if she was not really attending to his words.

He was stunned. He had expected a tirade lasting most of the night, and she was not even really interested; he wondered if she were well.

Thankful for small mercies, he got into bed and she reluctantly moved over to make room for him.

He usually smoked a last cigarette before turning over to go to sleep, and Olga watched with disgust the cloud of smoke that soon obliterated the gilt stars.

'What did you do today?' he asked.

Olga was immediately more alert. 'I worked with Mrs LeClair,' she announced smugly.

'Our LeClair's wife?'

'Yeah,' she said, half turning towards him, and she went on to tell him about her day with Henny.

'You should go again,' he said, quick to see the advantage of a closer association with his company's president. LeClair had holdings in a dozen first-class mines in Canada. With tips from LeClair, Boyd saw himself rising into the tight inner circle of businessmen who, working closely with their American associates, had made themselves millionaires.

He lifted himself on one elbow, so that he could see her face to face. 'See here, Olga,' he said confidentially, 'you've seen how difficult the LeClairs are to get to know personally. They've always kept themselves to themselves. They're mighty hard to really get to know – you get to know her real well and we're made.'

Olga, who had just been about to say that nothing would induce her to spend another day with those horrible kids, changed her mind. Anything that was in her self-interest was to be considered carefully. She stared thoughtfully at her husband, and then said: 'I suppose I could go again – they sure need help.'

'Sure you could, honey,' he wheedled, and bent and kissed her.

So Henny found herself again escorted by Mrs Stych, a Mrs Stych who seemed a bit easier to get along with than she had been on the previous day.

CHAPTER THIRTY

Olga Stych was, at best, no child lover, and the pupils of the School for Exceptional Children at first sickened her, with their grotesque movements and occasionally repulsive looks. Without encouragement from Boyd and bullying by Mrs LeClair, she would never have returned to help in the school; but once having got a little accustomed to the idea, she found that it at least filled her empty days and made her forget the many snubs she received. The children's mothers were very impressed that a lady whose name had appeared so often in the pages of the *Tollemarche Advent* should be prepared to spend so much time with them, and they did not seem to associate Hank with her at all.

Perhaps because Olga was able to look more coldly at the children than their closely involved mothers, she was able to see each child as a living problem which had to be solved. For years she had not used her brains or her organizing ability for anything more intelligent than arranging teas, spring 'fayres' or the affairs of the Community Centre. But now, faced with the quiet despair of the mothers at the school, she began to consider seriously what long-term plans could be made to help both parents and children.

She had long conversations with Mrs LeClair regarding similar schools which she had seen elsewhere, and Mrs LeClair introduced her to the Baptist minister in whose hall the school met.

Olga was thankful to help the minister organize some Christmas celebrations for the children and their parents, while Mr and Mrs LeClair went home to Montreal to spend the holiday with their family. In spite of having Christmas dinner with Grandma Palichuk, the festival without the children would have been so bleak and lonely that Olga shuddered at the very thought of it and pressed a not unwilling Boyd into helping her decorate the church basement with tinsel and balloons. It was, however, a visit of Mr Frizzell to the school early in the new year which really galvanized her into action.

Mr Frizzell, who wished to stand at the next election for alderman on the City Council, had for some time been looking for an organization with which he could not only identify himself but be identified by. The Bonnie Scots and other service organizations to which he belonged were all very well, but he did not get much personal publicity out of them. He wanted to start something new, so that when he tried for a seat on the City Council, people would say: 'Yes, he's Maxie Frizzell, that wonderful man who started thingumabob'. All he needed was a thingumabob, and he felt that in the School for Exceptional Children he had found it. One Tuesday morning, therefore, when business was at its quietest, he rolled gently into the church hall, with the same friendly unobtrusiveness which made him such a superb salesman.

The noise level lowered considerably as he entered, and startled mothers looked up. Mrs LeClair, whose time in Tollemarche was nearly ended, flew forward, and Olga Stych exclaimed: 'Why, Maxie, what you doin' here?'

With a look of disarming candour on his round face, he told Mrs LeClair that he had become interested in the school through the improvement in the behaviour of Henny van der Schelden, and he had come to see how it had been achieved. Mrs LeClair, fluttering like a hummingbird, showed him around and introduced him.

When they had got as far as Olga, who was composing an appeal for funds, while supervising two children playing with bricks, she left her appeal and the children for a few minutes and circulated with them, eyeing Maxie suspiciously as he expressed interest in all he saw. This was her new domain, she thought savagely, and no supercilious Donna Frizzell was going to be allowed to muscle in on it.

Maxie Frizzell, to his credit, was genuinely touched by the mothers' efforts to help their children and each other, with only makeshift equipment and inadequate, unsuitable accommodation. Surely, he thought, these kids, ignored by the school board and every other government department, deserved a better break than they were getting. He had thought of the school as just another stepping-stone towards a seat on the City Council, but as he began to realize the suffering of parents and children and was informed that there were many more children in the city in an even worse state, the quick, shrewd mind that had won him a small fortune in the rapid growth of Tollemarche was put to work to consider the basic needs of better accommodation, paid help, and an organization that would involve the doctors of the city.

Mrs LeClair was explaining her impending return to Montreal and her worry that the school might disintegrate when she left, since the mothers involved could not be expected to undertake the full organization and running of the school.

'I'm not tied down with kids,' said Olga firmly, her black eyes narrowed while she tried to get under the fence before Maxie. 'I can give time to it.'

'Wait a minute, wait,' cautioned Maxie, seeing his fine new project slipping out of his hands before he had even got started on it. 'Suppose we try and get a committee together, maybe with some of the kids' fathers. We might be able to sponsor a fund drive – rent a house, pay some skilled help or somethin'.'

'Don't try and start too big,' warned Mrs LeClair, as she accepted a cup of coffee from one of her helpers and offered it to Maxie.

When the three of them were holding wobbly paper cups of coffee, she said: 'Let's sit down with some of the mothers and talk about it.'

From that talk in the dusty church basement grew the Tollemarche Exceptional Children's School, with Mr Maxmilian Frizzell as president and Mrs Olga Stych as director of the school. As the months went by, it began to endear itself to the citizens of Tollemarche. Every car that went out of Maxie's booming car lots had a pamphlet in its glove compartment describing the work being done. Physicians of every kind were pestered for advice. A group went down to Edmonton to see the work being done there. Mrs Stych imbued the mothers with enough courage to get them to hold a tea in the school, so that interested persons could see the children at work. Parents who had been ashamed to show their subnormal children in public gained enough confidence to bring their offspring out of hiding and ferry them rapidly to the school, where they discovered that they had plenty of company and were given a degree of hope that their children might be more trainable than they had imagined.

Olga worked as she had never worked since her college days. She forgot to nibble, and over the year lost fifty pounds in weight. She was so busy that, at one point, three months went by without her adding anything to her Hudson's Bay charge account; she had no time to spend money on clothes. She was happier, too, when she had time to think about it, and this was reflected in her relations with Boyd. At last she had something worthwhile to talk to him about, and he became interested enough himself to volunteer to drive some of the children to picnics and other small outings. Olga spent little time at home, but her Dutch cleaning lady continued to keep the house spick and span, and in the evenings the couple frequently shared the chore of cooking the evening meal. It could not be said that they fell in love again, but a warm friendliness grew up between them, now that the house was no longer cluttered by a mass of bridge-playing, tea-drinking women. Olga's hot temper tended more and more to be directed towards people who thought her exceptional children were only fit for a kind of human junk yard, or towards officials in Edmonton and Ottawa who had never given them any thought before.

Of course, all this activity did not go unnoticed by the girls. Mrs Stych, in the course of her new occupation, never ran into any of her old cronies, but Mrs MacDonald told Miss Angus that she had seen Olga Stych running – actually running – down Tollemarche Avenue. Olga was wearing dreadful, flat-heeled shoes and her petticoat was showing below her skirt.

Miss Angus replied tartly that Olga Stych always was a fool, and poured another cup of tea – Miss Angus without a silver teapot in front of her would have had no reason for existence.

Margaret Tyrrell, when she went to be fitted for a new frock at Dawne's Dresse Shoppe, was told by Mrs Stein that Mrs Stych's clothes were hanging off her because she had become so thin, and it was Mrs Stein's opinion that only someone with cancer could slim so fast. A rumour, therefore, went round that Olga Stych was dying of cancer, and some of the girls' consciences smote them at the way they had treated her. Olga, however, continued to live and to feel extraordinarily well.

Donna Frizzell finally got wind of what Maxie was doing, and she held forth shrilly on the way he was wasting his time – time was money, and he should be on his car lot, not playing around with a lot of idiot kids. And that Olga Stych should not have anything to do with kids – look how her son had turned out.

Maxie was diplomatic enough not to point out that his three grandchildren still occupied the spare room, and nobody knew where either of their parents were. Betty was not much credit to her parents. Donna did not let her grandchildren interfere with her life much – she left them with a baby-sitter most of the time, and this worried Maxie more than he liked to admit. However, to stop the uproar, he suggested that she needed some more clothes and doubled the amount she could have on her Dawne's Dresse Shoppe account. Donna's complaints dwindled to a grumble.

Mrs Murphy, the Mayor's wife, her three chins trembling gently as she tried to keep track of the city's pecking order and at the same time see that her husband ate three meals a day, asked her priest about the new school and, particularly, about Mrs Stych's work there.

The priest was very old and it is not too certain that he

234

fully understood what she was talking about, but he answered that, for sure, 'twas the work of God that was being done there and it should be supported by all good Catholics.

'But,' quavered Mrs Murphy, 'it was Olga Stych's son that wrote that terrible book – and she must have known about it, Father.'

' 'Tis perhaps a penance that she is doing,' said the old man, his wizened face peering up from between hunched shoulders.

Mrs Murphy nodded agreement and immediately took out from the sideboard drawer a tattered notebook and added Mrs Stych's name to the list headed 'Do-gooders,' so that she got asked to the right Murphy dinners.

The person most astonished by Olga's new interest was Hank. His father wrote to him from time to time regarding his business affairs, and told him what his mother was doing; and, though Hank never wrote to Olga, a large box arrived one day at the school from London, England. It contained a number of very helpful books on mental retardation. It did not contain a copy of Hank's second book; this he sent privately to his father, and, after reading it, Boyd decided not to mention its existence to Olga; the distilled bitterness of the story might have really hurt her.

CHAPTER THIRTY-ONE

In the late fall, nearly two years after Hank had left for England, the great bridge across the treacherous North Saskatchewan River was to be completed, and the City Council was hopeful that a royal princess, on a tour across Canada, would condescend to stop at Tollemarche and open it.

'She can't just stop here and cut a ribbon,' expostulated one lady alderman, who was worried because she did not know how to address a princess. 'She'd have to stay overnight – it's too far for her to travel onwards the same day – unless she went back to Edmonton – and that bunch down there will surely monopolize her, if they get the chance.'

The other aldermen looked at her scornfully. One of them said firmly: 'We'll keep her out of Edmonton – there must be some way of filling up a day here.'

His eyes wandered round the council chamber, and alighted on the sole member of the Edwardian Days Committee who happened to be present. 'I know – she can drive through the city, have a civic luncheon, open the bridge and drive over it, and in the evening the Edwardian Days Committee can organize a dinner and ball for her.'

The Edwardian Days Committee man was nearly stunned at having a princess thrust at him, but recovered sufficiently to bat the ball back firmly to the Council: 'Who's going to pay?' he asked darkly.

Amid the flurry of discussion, a voice said: 'There'll be the Lieutenant-Governor and his wife, maybe the Duke, and ladies-in-waiting and equerries.'

The Edwardian Days Committee representative reeled with horror – he could not imagine what an equerry was.

Alderman Maxie Frizzell saw his opportunity and seized it. 'That leaves her with most of her afternoon unaccounted for – '

236

'She could rest,' interposed the lady alderman.

Maxie froze her with a look. 'I think she should spend the afternoon at the Exceptional Children's School – we really got somethin' to show her.'

The Council received the suggestion with relief. It was agreed upon immediately, and Maxie grinned to himself. He had never, in earlier times, dreamed that he would consider a child being taught to go to the bathroom by itself a great victory to be boasted about, but he knew it was. He wanted more money for the school, and nobody could give it publicity like a princess could – publicity meant money.

The Princess, with her usual kindliness, had the request added to her already overloaded schedule.

On a golden fall day, therefore, an astonished Olga Stych, accompanied by a triumphant Maxie Frizzell, found herself, in a plain black dress covered with a white apron, curtseying to a princess. When she took the royal hand, she was acutely aware that not even two layers of cream the previous night had lessened the roughness of her own hands, which had been long neglected. She knew she looked dowdy in comparison with Donna Frizzell, who stood forgotten in the background amid a bevy of minor officials, but she had not had time to buy a new dress for the occasion and had fallen back on an old black one which did not hang too loosely on her. Donna was looking gorgeous in raspberry pink wool worn with a pink georgette turban and hair dyed shocking red; her hard, thin face, however, was frozen into such an expression of envy that it was obvious that she should have been dressed in green.

The Princess did not seem to notice the shabby dress, and, indeed, all she saw was a very tired, capable-looking woman, whose long black hair was dressed in neat braids round her head, helping a blank-faced little girl to present her with a bouquet. The Princess had inspected many charitable institutions during her long life, but she felt very moved by the quiet patience of these Prairie women, who, she was told by the Lieutenant-Governor, had begun the school knowing nothing of the care or training of subnormal children. Perhaps it was because they were so isolated that they were evolving methods which were beginning to attract attention from all over the continent.

The Princess spent over an hour going quietly from child to child, escorted by a group of nervous officials, helpers and, of course, Maxie Frizzell.

The children had been lovingly dressed for the occasion, and nobody cried or wet his pants during the visit. It must be admitted that some of the mothers standing quietly in the background, holding those children unable to walk, let the tears course down their faces as they watched. They knew that the Princess's visit would benefit the school immensely, and they appreciated what Olga and Maxie had done for their children. They had often said to each other that Olga need not have come to their rescue. She didn't have a retarded child – her own boy was so brilliant that the whole world had heard about Tollemarche, just because it was his home town; yet she never spoke about him, never rubbed it in.

After all the cars were gone, the children dismissed for the day, an exhausted Olga sat on the veranda steps to rest for a minute in the mild sunshine, while she waited for Boyd to come and collect her. She would go home and lie on her bed for a while, after which she and Boyd would attend the ball given for the Princess.

She leaned her head against the balustrade and closed her eyes, remembering the last ball she had attended, the Edwardian Ball to which Hank had taken Isobel. She could bear to think of Hank now.

For a long time, she had felt so furious with him that it was as well he was separated from her. She had blamed him for all her woes, hated him for not saying goodbye, for never writing to her. Then, as she became more involved in Henny's school and had seen that there was another Tollemarche, one of·suffering, of always having to face doctor's bills, of tenacious love of children, of love for marriage partners, a Tollemarche that did not care a hang for social success – it was too busy trying to stay alive – she had begun to see herself for what she was, a grasping, selfish woman. This had made her angrier still, and she had plunged still deeper into the work she had undertaken, working off her self-hatred in her fight for recognition of the needs of the very helpless.

Boyd came silently up the path and stopped half-way to view the picture that his wife made as she dozed in the sun, her hands folded in her lap, her face tranquil.

'My! She looks more like her mother every day,' he thought; and he was happy – he liked his mother-in-law. Here, waiting for him on the steps, there seemed to be again the country girl he had married, a girl who seemed to have made a very special niche for herself in the hearts of the people of Tollemarche.

'Hiya, Olga,' he called cheerfully, 'got news for you.'

Olga's eyes popped open.

He was waving a letter, and he came up the veranda steps and sat down beside her. 'It's from Hank.'

The letter was addressed to both of them and invited them in friendly terms to attend his wedding to Isobel Dawson in a month's time. A formal invitation from Isobel's aunt was enclosed.

Olga put the letter carefully down in her lap. She remembered the tiny, fair-haired girl at the Edwardian Ball, and asked Boyd cautiously: 'Wotcha think of it?'

'I think it's great,' replied Boyd firmly, having spent half the morning, while trying to deal with his work, in thinking out what attitude he should take. 'She is older than he is, but she's got something he needs. She must have, seeing it's lasted this long.'

Olga fingered the letter uneasily. She said in a low voice: 'Y'know, Boyd, I know now I never gave that kid a square deal' – she hesitated, as though she found it difficult to drag out of herself what she had to say – 'and, y'know, I often feel sorry about it. I coulda done a lot better.' She picked up the engraved wedding invitation and turned it over. 'I guess he turned to her just because she showed an interest in him – like I never did.' Her voice, her weary, drooping eyelids, indicated a quiet, bitter sadness. 'Mebbe she's just kinda kind. Wotcha think?'

Boyd patted her hand uneasily. 'Well, he hasn't done so badly,' he comforted her. 'And, y' know, it's my belief she's not doing so badly regarding a mother-in-law.'

'Waal, I wish Hank would feel like that,' she replied with a small sigh, 'but I guess he never will.'

'Aw, I don't know,' said her husband, as he hunted through his pockets for a cigarette in a manner very reminiscent of his son. 'You be real patient with this Isobel of his – like Grandma Stych was with you – and, you'll see, he'll come round.'

A slow smile spread over Olga's face. 'Yeah, I never thoughta that – she was always patient with me. I never thought of it before. You're so right – I'll try.'

A new idea occurred to her, and she said: 'It was sure funny this morning, watching Donna Frizzell as I was talking to the Princess. It made me realize that I'd sorta arrived socially – that Princess didn't make no point about me being Ukrainian or anything like that – she was just kinda nice to me, and so was everyone else.'

Boyd put his arm round her. 'You've done really well, honey, and I'm proud of you – and what about a mink coat for the wedding?'

'Oo, my!' she exclaimed. 'That would sure be nice.' She paused, and then said: 'Provided there's enough in the bank to buy Isobel and Hank something real handsome as well.'

'There is,' said Boyd dryly. 'Believe me, there is.'